A VERY BADD

Christmas

Jasinda Wilder

A VERY BADD

Christmas

ONE

Emerson

MY PHONE BUZZED ON THE COUNTER AS I BRAIDED MY wet hair. Beside me, McKenna was doing the same thing, and all around the locker room, my teammates were in various stages of stripping out of practice kit, showering, and getting dressed after a particularly brutal practice. We'd kept biffing the play Coach Anderson wanted us to have down by the game this Friday, and he was getting pissed, so we ended up running laps around the practice pitch more than we did running the damn play. The real bitch of the thing was that I, as the goalie, couldn't do a thing to get the girls to run the play right, but I still had to run laps with them.

"You gonna answer that?" McKenna asked, glancing down at my phone, which was still buzzing.

I finished plaiting the last of my thick, curly, red hair, tied it off, and tossed it back. "It's Delia, I'll call her back."

McKenna finished her hair at the same time, tilting and twisting her head this way and that to make sure there weren't any flyways or bumps. Since my hair was wacky on the best of days, I tended to braid it and forget it since it would be wisping and frizzing out of the braid in an hour anyway.

"I can't believe Lexie on that play," McKenna groused, fishing lip liner out of her makeup bag. "She should have that shit down. It's a simple play. Pass, pass, shoot. What's her issue?"

I shrugged. "She's been off all week. She bombed a test in math, and math is her whole thing. She does pages of calculus to calm down when she's stressed."

"Did Jake break up with her or something?" McKenna asked, leaning toward the mirror with her eyes wide, now applying mascara.

I swiped on some lip gloss. "I don't think so? I saw them sitting together in the cafeteria yesterday and they seemed fine. I don't know what's bugging her."

"Well, she needs to figure her shit out because if we have to run any more fucking laps this week, I'm gonna have some sort of episode. I swear to god, we've run a marathon this week alone just in fucking laps."

"No kidding," I mumbled, applying mascara

myself now, doing the weird-mouth-eye-makeup thing. "I don't mind running, but this week has been a lot."

"You should talk to her," McKenna says, capping her mascara and rifling through her makeup bag for something else.

I pull the wand away and turn to look at her. "*Me*? Why me? Lexie hates me."

"She does not *hate* you." She couldn't say that with a straight face because Lexie did, in fact, hate me.

Or, at least, she didn't like me. The feeling was mutual.

"She wouldn't piss on me if I was on fire and you know it, Mac."

"Okay, fine, she doesn't like you, but just because you're the star even though she's the captain. But she scares me, and no one scares you. So…just ask if she's okay."

Behind us, Lacey, Tonya, Keisha, and Maria were gathering their stuff, half listening to our conversation.

"She may not like you," Maria said, "but she listens to you."

"Fuck," I groaned, capping my mascara. "*Fine*! I'll talk to her. But you bitches owe me."

"Better catch her then," Keisha said, tying her box braids back. "She got out of here real fast."

"You're all a bunch of pussies," I said, tossing my stuff into my duffel, pocketing my phone, and heading for the locker room exit, ignoring the good-natured return jabs from the other girls.

I spotted Lexie already halfway to her car—a baby blue BMW M4 convertible that she drove as if she were Lewis Hamilton. She was from Seattle, so she didn't live on the UW campus but rather in an apartment that her loaded parents paid for.

"Lex!" I called, jogging toward her. "Hold up!"

She stopped, blond hair still held back by the plain black headband she wore for practice. She hadn't even changed out of her kit, only having removed her shin guards, socks, and cleats and put on a pair of black Adidas slides.

She didn't reply, but she did wait. When I caught up, she resumed walking toward her car, bleeping the locks as we approached it.

She paused at the driver's side door, giving me annoyed side-eye. "What?"

Just out with it, I guess. "Um. Are you okay? We're all a little worried about you. You haven't been yourself lately."

"I'm fine." She yanked open her door and tossed her bag on the passenger seat.

"Lex—"

"I said I'm fucking *fine!*" she snapped.

Okay, well, that cleared things up. "Lex. Look. We're not friends. Cool, whatever. But you're *not* fine. Our captain has been playing like shit for two weeks, and we have regionals coming up. I'm not asking you to, like, bare your soul to me. But something *is* up. If you don't wanna talk to me, great. But we need you to figure your shit out."

She closed her door and leaned back against it. "You wouldn't understand."

"Oh? Well, maybe try me."

A sigh and an eye roll. "You really wanna know? Okay. My dad got caught cheating on my mom with his assistant, which is like, whatever—she's not even a year older than me. And my mom is *not* taking it well, even though this isn't the first or even the second time. They're talking about divorce. And I mean, I'm out of the house and whatever, but it still sucks. And they have to sell the house, and they want to sell my apartment and have me move into the dorms. I'm a senior! I have literally never lived on campus. It's like, what the fuck?"

That's the big issue? For real? She was right about one thing: I didn't understand how that was something to have a meltdown about. But I didn't say that, and I hoped it didn't show on my face.

"God, Lex, that sucks. Why would they want to sell your apartment?"

A shrug. "I don't know. I heard Dad arguing with someone on the phone on Monday and it sounded bad, like it was about money. Maybe they're in trouble. I don't know. They don't tell me anything."

My phone went off again—Delia, I'm guessing. If she was calling me twice, it wasn't just to chat. I silenced it again. "I'm sorry you're going through that, Lex. We're all here for you."

She wriggled her nose, blinked hard a few times. "Thanks. I…" a hard swallow. "I just…it seems so random. They've always made it work, even though Dad is a cheating horndog and Mom likes her pills and champagne a little too much. I just don't want to have to pick sides, you know? Remember when Kelly's parents split up, how ugly it got and how she got pulled into the middle of it?"

Kelly was the captain last year, a talented midfielder who graduated with honors and moved east to pursue her master's at Harvard despite what she went through last year.

"I remember. That shit was messy." I didn't really know what else to say. "I guess I just…if there's anything we can do, you know we've got your back, girl."

She shrugged, rolled her eyes. "Yeah, thanks." A sarcastic grin. "How'd you get tapped to do this? Pull the short straw, so you have to go comfort big bad Lexie?"

I grinned. "Pretty much. But we *are* worried, for real. You're our captain, and we need you on your A-game for regionals. We have a real shot at the title this year, but not if you're distracted."

"So it's about soccer, not me."

I sighed. "Lex—" I cut myself off. "You know what? Yeah. Pretty much. But it seems to all of us like you're not talking to *anyone* about it. Plus, you bombed that math test, which is when I knew you were going through something."

She huffed. "For real. That was the day Mom first dropped the D-word."

"I *am* sorry. And I *am* here for you if you ever need to talk."

She frowned at me. "Why, though, Emerson? Like you said, we're not friends."

"Doesn't mean I don't give a shit."

"Why would you give a shit about me? I've always been a bitch to you."

"Because I've been through a lot, and I know how it feels and what it looks like. And it looks like you're going through it alone." I grabbed my phone as it buzzed a third time. "We don't have to be friends for me to think no one, even a bitch like you, should have to go through something hard alone. Not when you've got a whole team behind you."

She sniffed. "Thank you, Emerson. Really." She glanced at my phone. "Looks like someone wants to get ahold of you."

"Yeah, it's Delia. She hates it when I ignore her. But three times means she's serious. I better call her. But we're all here for you, Lex. You're not alone."

"I'll get my shit together, I promise. We're gonna take regionals, states, *and* nationals. Just you watch."

She got in her car, and the engine coughed to life with a snarl. I hiked my bag higher on my shoulder and dialed Delia back.

It rang once. "Emerson Grace Day! You are *not* allowed to *ignore* your best friend."

I cackled. "Oooh, the full name from Delia Emmaline Badd."

"I called you *three whole times*, you whore." She sounded grumpy.

"What's got your panties in a twist?"

A sigh. "I think Garrison is either cheating on me or he's gonna propose, and I don't know which is worse."

"I thought we liked Garrison?" I asked, heading for the cafeteria.

"We *like* him. He's cute, funny, and decent in bed. But I don't *love* him. It's not like that between us and I thought he knew it. It's not, like, casual, but it's not serious either. But he's acting weird."

"Weird how?" I asked.

"Hiding his phone when I'm around, gone a lot, not answering texts." She groaned. "God, I don't want to deal with this. I wanted to have a boyfriend for Christmas."

I laughed. "Just *a* boyfriend? Any old dude with a dick and a job?"

"I mean, yeah, basically. My relationships always end before the holidays. I just want a guy to do Christmas with."

I cackled louder than ever. "Good luck with that. You *do* know *why* your guys always break up with you before Christmas, right?"

Silence. "No?"

I sighed. "Delia, babe. Come on. Your family is

fucking *nuts*. I grew up with them so it's whatever for me, but to an outsider, they're pretty intimidating. I mean, for one, there's, like, a thousand of you people. For another, they're all fucking hot as hell, half of 'em are famous, and the men are all huge and scary. Doing Christmas with the Badd Clan is not for the faint of heart, honey-bunny."

"But they're all nice once you get to know them."

"Well yeah, but it can be overwhelming, Dee. I love them, you know that. Big Daddy Bast and Mama Dru are more my parents than my parents. But for the uninitiated, it can be a lot."

"I hate it when you call him that," she huffed, "and I can't help how my family is. We're close, we're loud, and there's a metric shit-ton of us. Is it so much to ask to find a guy who's not scared shitless of Daddy and my uncles?"

"I mean, normally I'd say no, but when your dad is your dad and you have seven uncles, each bigger, scarier, and hotter than the last, no matter which order you put them in, yeah, it can be a bit of a big ask."

"Why are you always talking about how hot my family is?"

I laughed. "Um, because they're Zaddies, baby. Zaddies."

She faked a gag. "No, no, no. They're *not* zaddies, and if my dad heard you call him a zaddy, he'd have words for you."

"Promise?"

"*Stop!*" She shouted. "*DON'T BE GROSS ABOUT MY FATHER!*"

I couldn't help but laugh because we both knew I considered Sebastian Badd my real father. "Sorry, sorry, sorry. I'm done now, for real." I paused outside the cafeteria building. "So, you're blowing up my phone about Garrison why?"

"I just needed to vent."

"Well, based on what you told me, I'm gonna say he's cheating. He wouldn't need to suddenly turn his phone off whenever you entered the room if he was planning a proposal. That's cheater one-oh-one."

"Ugh. You're right. I guess I just needed outside confirmation of my feelings."

"Well, validated, then."

"So, are you coming home for Thanksgiving?"

I sighed. "Probably not. Christmas I will, though. But we have practices up to regionals. Assuming we make it, nationals are the first week of December."

"Meanie."

I laughed. "Babe, I can't do anything about the tournament schedule."

"I know. But you better be home for Christmas. If I can't have a boyfriend, I at least have to have you."

"I'll be there," I said. "You know I never miss a Badd Clan Christmas."

"Jax asks about you every other week."

I groan. "Still? That boy needs to get over the

crush. Your cousins are like my cousins, which means I will never, *ever* date a Badd. I told him that."

"He says hope springs eternal."

"Well, his hope spring needs to dry up. I played dolls with that boy. He's like a brother to me."

"He's committing to Caltech for the fall, so we're all hoping he'll find a new girl to be infatuated with down there." She sighed. "He's held this flame for you for like ten years."

I groaned. "Everyone knows, huh?" I winced. "They don't hate me for shooting him down, do they?"

"God, no. You're family. Everyone agrees it would be weird if you *did* date one of the cousins."

"Whew," I say, pretending to wipe sweat off my forehead, even though she couldn't see me. "That's a relief."

"You know, you could bring a boyfriend with you for Christmas," Delia says, the shit-eating grin evident in her voice.

"As *if*," I say, in my best valley girl accent. "For real, what boyfriend?"

"You literally never date anyone, Sunni. You're gonna die alone."

"I'm twenty-two, ding-dong. I have time. I'm focused on my degree and soccer. And besides, there *are* boys; they're just single-serving boyfriends."

"You and your single-serving boyfriends."

"Hey, I'll have you know I hooked up with Trace four whole times. A new record."

"Ooooh, really turning a new page, there, sweet cheeks."

"I'm not your sweet cheeks, bimbo."

"I'm not a bimbo, skank."

"I'm not a skank, slut."

She laughed. "Enough, enough. I have to go meet Garrison. I'll probably break up with him just to get it over with. Maybe I can still find a boyfriend for Christmas."

"You should be more like me. Until my life is in order, boys are for fun. I don't have the time or interest in a serious relationship." I pulled my lanyard with my swipe card out of my bag and twirled it around my finger.

She huffed. "I couldn't do that. I'm not built that way, you know that."

"Yeah, because everyone in your family has been married for a billion years and still look at each other with gaga eyes," I said, snark ripe in my voice.

"You saw that too, Sunni."

"Yeah, but..." I sighed, shaking my head. "I'll find a guy someday. I just don't even know what I want in a guy, you know? Like, my boytoys are all so different. I don't even have a type."

She laughed. "Maybe when you come up for Christmas, the Badd Family Love Charm will strike, and you'll meet a guy and have a super sexy rom-com Christmas."

"Do *not* get me started on the Badd Family Love Charm bullshit, Delia Badd. *Do—not*. It's not real."

"You know the stories as well as I do, girlie. You know it's true."

"Then why has the love charm not struck anyone in twenty years?"

"Because everyone got married. Now it's just waiting for us kids to be old enough."

"You talk like it's a sentient thing. Which is fucking weird." I accidentally hit myself in the nose with the swipe card, looking around to make sure no one saw. "Also, I'm not even an actual member of the Badd family, so the Badd Family Love Charm cannot work on me."

She blew a raspberry. "Do not underestimate the power of the Badd Family love charm, Sunnie-girl."

"I won't hold my breath, how about that?"

"Well, now you've gone and done it. According to family lore, when you deny it and insist it won't happen, that's when it does."

"Then why don't *you* get the love charm to strike you?"

"Because I'm not ready. I want a boyfriend for Christmas, not a husband by the New Year."

I laughed. "And according to the lore, that's how it works."

"Exactly." She makes kissing noises. "Okay, gotta go. Love you bye!" Click.

I pulled the phone away from my ear and looked at it. "Okay, bye to you too, weirdo."

Laughing and shaking my head at my lifelong best friend's antics, I pocketed my phone and headed in to eat.

TWO

Hayden

"MOM—WILL YOU LISTEN A SECOND—YEAH, I KNOW it's a big deal for you guys, but *I'm* not going on the cruise, you are…so? So it doesn't matter which excursions *I* think you should do, Mom. Because it's not my cruise!" I clapped my hand over my face and did some deep breathing in an attempt to keep from tossing the phone across the room. "Yes, Mother. I'm sorry for raising my voice. But you've called me six times in the last four hours about my preferences for a cruise I'm not going on. I have to get this work done—my boss is all over my ass about it."

She yammered at me about work-life balance for another ten minutes, during which I put it on speaker and tuned her out.

When she sounded like she was running out of steam, I picked it up. "Mom, listen, okay? You and Dad have been saving for this cruise for years. It's your fiftieth anniversary. You should do whatever *you* want to do. Not me—you and Dad. If there are too many to choose from, which seems to be the case, then pick the ones you *know* you want to do and leave some room for spontaneity. Yes, I know, Dad likes to have things planned out down to the minute. But it'd be good for him to try to loosen up and bit and let fate pick a couple of excursions. Yes, I think seeing a moose would be amazing. Yes, I know they're much bigger than you expect. Ride one? Mom, good *lord* no—no one is riding moose in Alaska." Before she can start in on her next subject, whatever that may be, I cut her off. "Mom, I love you. I love you like crazy. But I *have* to work. You have to stop calling me and just make the decisions with Dad. Okay, awesome. Yes, I'll come over for dinner one day this week, I promise."

It took another fifteen minutes to get off the phone. But, true to her word, Mom didn't call back for another two hours. Which, for her, was a record.

I did manage to finish the latest batch of analyses my boss had been hounding me for, so there was that. But he also wanted the firewall buffed, in his words. And he wanted me to look at the latest data breaches from, like, everywhere, to see if we're susceptible... you'd think he'd have a little more trust in my abilities, seeing as he hired me for this job.

I knew I shouldn't think this way, but I just wanted Mom and Dad to go on the cruise already. They'd been planning and saving and talking about it for literally a decade, and now that it was right around the corner, Mom in particular was going a little batty with excitement. I mean, I got it, as much as I could—it's not every day you get to go on a fiftieth-anniversary Christmas cruise to Alaska.

By the end of the day, I got through most of the work Mr. Cox sent, so I shut down my home office and got changed for the gym.

That's the nice thing about my job: I'm a cybersecurity engineer for a Silicon Valley tech startup, which meant I worked from home in good old West Lafayette, Indiana. I could finish work and be at the gym in five minutes because my apartment was just down the road from the gym.

On the way home from the gym, my phone rang. I expected Mom's name on the screen, but it was Dad.

"Hey, Dad, what's up? You good?"

Dad rarely called. Mom? Every day, several times a day at minimum. Dad? Once a month, maybe. He figured since I live ten minutes from them and see them multiple times a week, calling was redundant. I agreed, but try telling that to Mom.

"Hey, kiddo." His voice was slow and tired.

"Dad? You all right?"

"Yeah, yeah, just under the weather."

"So what's up? You need something?"

"Oh, well, I know your mother has been going a little crazy about the cruise."

I laughed. "Yeah, well, she's excited. She should be. Are you?"

"God, yes. We haven't had a real vacation since you were in high school." A pause. "I just wanted to make sure she wasn't driving you nuts. I know she can...um...suffocate you sometimes."

I chuckled. "Dad, I wouldn't know what to do without her suffocation. I just tell her to stop calling for a bit, and she does. She knows I'm not mad. We have a whole thing."

He sniffed a few times, his version of a laugh—they're opposites, my parents. Mom was loud and a chatterbox and made friends with every clerk, teller, and person behind her in line, whereas Dad was reserved, quiet, and careful.

"Well, that was it, kiddo. Just checking on you. We'll see you for dinner this week, yeah?"

"Yeah, of course. I'm thinking Friday." I hesitated. "You're sure you're okay? You sound different."

"Ehh, haven't been sleeping too well. Get to my age and sleep gets tricky. I'm alright, son."

A twinge of worry settled in my gut. The last time Dad said not to worry, his appendix burst and he almost died.

"Dad." I hunted for the right words—get on his case too much about his health, and he'd clam up. "No bullshit. You're sure you're good? This isn't another appendix thing, is it?"

A gruff sigh. "No, Hayden, it's not. I'm okay. Swear."

"All right, just, you know, don't be a hero. I'm a phone call away if you need anything."

"I know, I know. I just hate to worry you. I just need to get some rest and I'll be right as rain. You'll see."

We agreed to see each other Friday and hung up as I reached my door. After a shake and salmon-quinoa bowl, I headed for my office, thinking I'd get a head start on the work for tomorrow.

But Mom's advice earlier about taking time for me that's not working out or sleeping rang in my skull, so I left the door closed, plopped on the couch, and put on Diablo. I was close to level seventy with my barbarian, and I knew my online raiding party would be getting on soon.

So, fuck it. Work could wait.

Friday evening found me at my parents' house, the house I grew up in, at the counter chopping cucumbers for the salad. See, weekly dinner with the folks wasn't just a "show up for dinner" thing. It was a whole day affair for the three of us. I'd come over after lunch and we'd plan the meal, go shopping, and spend the afternoon hanging out, talking, doing a puzzle, or playing Scrabble, and then we'd cook together. Dad did the meat, I did the salad, and Mom handled the sides. Every once in a while, we'd switch things up, mainly because Mom insisted I know how to cook more than hot dogs, Mac 'n cheese, and ramen.

"So, Hayden." Mom's voice had that tone.

My shoulders hunched, and I suppressed a sigh as I used the knife to scrape the cucumbers off the cutting board into the bowl and then started on the red onions.

"So, Mom." I didn't turn around. I knew what was coming.

"Meet any pretty girls lately?"

Dad, coming in from the deck where he was grilling the steaks, gave me a sympathetic look and a head shake.

"Yes, Mother, actually, I'm engaged. Her name is Candi with an I, and she's a stripper with a heart of gold. You'll just have to give her a chance." I couldn't stop the sarcasm—I tried.

Wait for it…

Wait for it…

"Oh, you." She slapped me across the arm with a towel. "So saucy, Hayden. Not nice."

Nope, not yet.

I traded glances with Dad.

He held up three fingers…

Two…

One…

He pointed at Mom exactly as her mouth opened and the expected diatribe emerged.

"It's just that I'm not getting any younger. You know we had you late, and I'd love to have some grand-kids before I go to be with Jesus."

There it was.

Mom was at the stove, peeking under the lid at the broccoli, poking it with a fork. I set my knife down and slid up behind her, holding her delicate little shoulders.

Mom was a tiny woman, barely over five feet and slender—despite the classic chin-length gray bob, she was the farthest you could get from a Karen. I have her eyes—bright green, the color of pine needles and holly leaves.

"Mom." I turned her around. "I'm twenty-six."

"I know, Hayden," she says, reaching up to pat my cheek. "But I'm almost seventy. Time is running out for me." She even had the shimmery eyes going, damn her.

"Mom… The tears, Jesus." I palmed my forehead.

"Language, Hayden Reginald McCaffery."

"You know, I'll never forgive you for saddling me with that middle name," I said.

"It was your great-grandfather's name. It's a regal name."

"Regal for the nineteenth century, maybe."

She just rolled her eyes at me. "You're changing the subject, Hayden."

"Yes, yes, I am." I cupped her face. "No one is

going anywhere, Mom. I will give you grandbabies, I promise. I'm just…"

"You spend all day in front of those computers. How can you expect to meet a nice, pretty girl to marry if you're always in front of a computer?" She turned away from me. "This is almost done, so get a move on with that salad. You'd think you'd be faster at chopping after all these years of making salads."

I pinched the bridge of my nose; when I looked at Dad for help, he studiously avoided looking at me as he pulled the chicken for Mom out of the marinade. "You know, Mom, sixty percent of couples meet online now. So, I actually *could* meet a girl while sitting in front of a computer. Also, my job is computers."

"*Sixty* percent?" She stopped what she was doing and turned to look at me. "You made that statistic up."

I laughed. "No, Mother, I did not. I can show you the report. Sixty percent of all couples now meet online."

"Through those apps, right? Bimble and Kindle? No, Kindle is the e-reader. What's that other one?"

I spluttered a laugh. "Bumble and Tinder."

"Yes, those. Are you using those apps?"

I just barely resisted the urge to decapitate myself with the knife. "No, I'm not. I'm focused on work. The cybersecurity field is viciously competitive. I can't get distracted."

"Your career is supposed to *support* your life, Hayden, not *be* your life."

"Kaye." Dad moved up behind her and kissed her cheek. "Enough, sweetheart. He'll meet a girl. You'll get grandbabies. You just have to be patient."

I spluttered in an attempt to cover a laugh, and Mom whirled to glare at me. "What is that laugh about, young man?"

"Nothing. Nothing." I went back to slicing onions.

"I teach kindergarteners all day," she said, poking me between the shoulder blades with each word. "I am a *very* patient woman."

"Different kinds of patient," I muttered.

"When we were young, twenty-six was old to be unmarried, let alone without kids. We didn't have you till I was forty-two, which was positively ancient. It's still old to have kids these days, but back then? I may as well have had one foot in the grave." She waved her hands in a wild gesture. "Nowadays, you kids aren't even getting married till thirty! It's ridiculous."

"It was a fertility issue, Mom, not a choice. And who cares what other people think?"

"I do! All my friends at my book club spend the whole meeting talking about their grandbabies walking and talking and all these funny stories, and I've got nothing. Oh hey, guess what? My son debugged another line of code! Or…something."

I looked at Dad for help, but he vanished out the door with Mom's piece of chicken. Nice.

"Mom, please. I know it's important to you— it's important to me, too. I want to have a family, I promise. But I'm not gonna rush into it. Things are different now. I can't just snag some random girl off the street, drag her to the nearest church, marry her, and knock her up just so you can have something to talk about at book club!"

Oops—that may have been too far.

I turned just in time to see her shoulders lift and her head duck. "I'm sorry, Hayden. I know I shouldn't push you. I just...I'm feeling my age and starting to think about things."

I set the knife down and pulled her into a hug. "That was rude, and I'm sorry. The truth is, I..." I huff into her hair. "Meeting girls is hard. I'm not...it's just not that easy. Even online."

She frowned up at me. "Why? You're handsome, successful, and funny. What's not to love?"

"Extreme social awkwardness?"

"So what if you're not the typical swaggering alpha male jock? You have plenty to offer!"

I choked on a laugh. "Jes—" I caught myself and course-corrected. "Geez, Mom, backhanded compliment, much?"

"What?"

"Never mind."

"What? What did I say?"

I shook my head. "Nothing."

"Hayden."

I sighed. "It's just that not being the typical alpha male swaggering jock is something I've been self-conscious about my whole life. It's what women want. Not computer nerds."

She snorted. "Hogwash. Not *all* women want that, Hayden. I didn't. When I met your father, he was the poster boy for extreme social awkwardness. He had an actual pocket protector, always wore a tie and penny loafers, and could barely say two words to me without blushing."

"Nice."

She chuckled. "I loved it about him. It was endearing. And once he got comfortable with me, he opened up and I saw a whole new side of him. And once he opened up, he couldn't keep his hands off me."

"Mom! Jesus crickets!"

"LANGUAGE!"

"Would you two stop yelling at each other?" Dad said, coming through the door with the meat.

I almost missed it. And even though I saw it, it didn't register, even though it should have.

As he set down the platter with our steaks and Mom's chicken on it, he rubbed his left bicep.

But Dad was a lefty, and he played tennis with a few of the other professors every Friday morning before classes, so I just figured he had a sore arm.

He flexed his arm, shook his hand, rolled his shoulders, and started setting the table.

And I didn't think about it again.

Not until two weeks later.

THREE

Emerson

I SHIFTED MY LUGGAGE AROUND FOR THE FOURTH TIME AS the ferry approached Ketchikan from the airport. I had too much shit for a simple Christmas vacation, but one whole suitcase was just gifts. When your unofficially adopted family has something like seventy-some people, gift-giving is a whole thing. Mama Livvie and Mama Dru especially are truly incredible gift givers, and I'm closest to them of all the adults, so I have to get them great presents. Obviously, I have to get Delia something. Daddy Bast (or, as I like to call him, Big Daddy Bast). Papa Lucas. Liv. Duncan and Dane, my adopted brothers. I can't afford to get everyone something, and no one expects that of anyone. Generally, you buy for the people in your immediate family, and then when the whole clan gathers, you do a white elephant for under a hundred dollars.

I suppose a quick historical context explainer is in order.

Delia Badd is my best friend. We met in kindergarten. The first day, we were at the same table together. She was loud and confident and sassy and had a killer pink backpack and cool light-up shoes, and her lunch had all this amazing food in it—a big sandwich with lots of salami, cheese sticks that you peel apart, Oreos, goldfish, an apple, *and* a banana.

I only later found out that she had packed her own lunch (sandwich excepted), and her parents had just rolled with it.

I, meanwhile, had a single piece of bread folded in half with the skinniest spread of peanut butter and jelly you'd ever seen. That was it. Because that's all there was. Mom had been to the casino that weekend and gambled our food and rent money away (I knew this already, even then). Delia, being herself, had looked at my lunch, and then hers, and then mine again, and had loudly and firmly announced, "That *simply* won't do."

She gave me half her lunch.

The next day, she brought extra again and gave it to me. I was embarrassed, and part of me didn't want to accept it, but I was too hungry. Beggars—in this case, literally—couldn't be choosers.

That's how it started. She played with me on the playground and helped me with my reading (I have mild dyslexia). She insisted on coming over to play with me after school one day, and nothing I said could dissuade her, so she came over. The girl was game, that's for damn sure. She never batted an eye at our dirty, cluttered little trailer with the crumbling cinderblock steps, sagging, leaking roof, and peeling Formica counters. She didn't ask for a snack because she knew better. She played with my shitty, one-arm, one-leg, frizzy-haired Barbie—the only one I had. She ignored the mouse droppings and the roaches in the corners.

She also never came back. But instead, she brought me over to her house. God, what a wonderland *that* was. They have a huge house on the Inside Passage with floor-to-ceiling windows, a leather sectional bigger than my whole trailer, big shiny appliances, and a pantry. Good lord, the pantry…it's a whole room.

Let me repeat—*a whole room* full of food.

I stood there for probably a full minute, staring, jaw dropped.

After that, I went to Delia's house after school every day. I didn't want to go home.

Bast and Dru never asked me if I needed to call my mom to stay the night. They never made a big deal about anything. They just took me in, fed me, clothed me, talked to me like a person. They bought me school supplies. They put a whole bureau in Delia's room for me and filled it with brand-new clothing.

God, I'm gonna get all weepy just thinking about it.

I went home once a week at most for the first year. Mom didn't usually notice, and if she did, she was fine with it. I told her I was at Delia's, and her only response was to remind me not to break anything expensive.

Mom wasn't a drug addict or even really an alcoholic—she drank a lot, sure, but that wasn't her problem. Her problem was gambling. Dad, too, but Dad only showed up a few times a year—he worked on oil rigs…and was a professional gambler. Just not a good one.

By middle school, I'd all but stopped going to Mom's house and referred to Delia's as "home."

I still remember my first Christmas with the Badds.

I had no clue what I was in for.

Around noon Christmas Eve day, Mama Livvie and Papa Lucas—as they insisted I call them that very day—came over. Mama Livvie is Olivia Badd, and Papa Lucas is Lucas Badd.

I should draw a chart or something because it's a big, complicated family.

Delia's parents are Sebastian and Dru Badd; Sebastian goes by Bast, and he's the oldest of the Badds. He has seven brothers and three cousins—identical triplets. They're all married with a billion kids.

The Badd Clan, then, is: Bast and Dru, Zane and Mara, Brock and Claire, Baxter and Eva, Canaan and Corin—identical twins—and their wives, identical twins Aerie and Tate; Lucian and Joss, Xavier and

Harlow Grace (yes, *that* Harlow Grace); the triplets are Roman, Remington, and Ramsey with their wives Kitty, Juneau, and Izzy, respectively. And then the triplets' father, Lucas, the uncle of the eight brothers, met a woman named Olivia Goode, she moved to Alaska, and they got married. Olivia, Mama Livvie to one and all, has five daughters who all got married and ended up in Ketchikan—mostly. The Goode girls—although they all legally took their various husbands' names, everyone refers to them collectively as the Goode Girls—are: Cassie and Ink, Charlie and Crow, Lexie and Myles (as in North, and yes, *that* Myles North), Torie and Rhys, and Poppy and Errol.

They all have bajillion kids, like thirty-six between them, which are known as collective as "The Cousins." I know all of them, having grown up with them. But with there being literally thirty-six of them, no one ever bothers trying to introduce them all to anyone at once. You just have to jump in and figure it out.

Anyway, my first Badd Christmas.

Mama Livvie and Papa Lucas came over around noon, apparently because Bast and Dru's house was the default place to gather when the whole clan was expected. They only had three kids—Bax and Eva had five, and Rome and Kitty had six—but their house is huge and designed for entertaining, with a huge open-concept living room, kitchen and dining room, a large den/TV room, and a mammoth basement, so there was plenty of space for the whole family to gather.

My prior experience with Christmas, for context, was me and Mom, and sometimes Dad. Both of my parents were estranged from their families and were before I ever came along, so I never had any extended family. If I got a present at all, it was probably from Dollar General.

Mama Livvie and Dru started baking cookies and pies while Bast and Papa Lucas split firewood, and Delia, Duncan, Dane, and I watched *The Grinch* in the den and had hot chocolate and as many snacks as we could stuff into our bellies—pretzels, cheese puffs, potato chips and dip, corn chips and salsa, a meat tray, a cheese tray, a cracker tray…I couldn't believe the amount of food I was seeing. When I asked Delia why there was so much food, she just laughed as if she didn't understand the question. I guess, looking back, she didn't.

Before the first tray of cookies and the pies were done baking, people were streaming in—Bax and Eva and Claire and Brock and their kids. And suddenly there were four more kids in the house.

Bax and Eva only had three at that point—Anya, Ella, and Kieran; Brock and Claire had just adopted a two-year-old girl named Nina. I'd never been around so many kids outside school before. I didn't know how to play with them, but that didn't seem to matter. They just dragged me around with them and included me like I'd always been part of the gang.

We played tag in the basement, and then air hockey, and then we rolled the billiard balls around the table—Kieran got his fingers bashed a dozen times because he couldn't stop trying to grab them while they were flying around, even though Anya, the oldest, kept trying to get him to stop.

And then Rome and Kitty showed up with their brood—also three at that point: Donovan, Dillon, and Riley. So then there were eleven kids. And then more, and then more.

There was always a handful of adults down in the basement with us, playing pool or just sitting at the bar sipping and chatting and watching. When a kid fell and got hurt, they got picked up and hugged and kissed, regardless of whose kid it was, and if it was serious, the appropriate parent was summoned. Squabbles over toys were squashed with firm fairness. No one got yelled at. I watched, played, and marveled at the spectacle of twenty-some kids all playing together, getting along, and having fun.

I wandered upstairs and just watched the adults. For a while, I was so quiet and unobtrusive that no one noticed me sitting alone at the kitchen island, wide-eyed, watching the thirty-some adults all being cool with each other.

And then Bast noticed me and swaggered over.

Leaned on the counter opposite me. "Loud in here, huh, munchkin?"

I nodded.

"Wanna get some air?"

I just stared at him, not understanding and too shy to say so.

"Go outside. Sit on the dock. Look at the stars."

I nodded.

He grabbed a huge, thick, brown-and-white cow-print fur blanket and came over to me. "Can I pick you up?"

No one ever picked me up, so I wasn't sure how to feel about it, but I liked that he asked, so I nodded. He had scooped me up in the blanket, wrapped it around me in a tight, warm little bundle, and carried me out into the frigid Alaskan winter night. It was a clear one, the kind of bitter clarity that you only get once in a while. The stars were…well, if you've ever been to Alaska on a clear winter night, you know. If not, I can't describe it.

He carried me out to the dock and sat down, put me on his lap, and wrapped the blanket around us. Leaned back and looked up.

Scared and confused at first, I had sat stiff and still. He didn't say or do anything. Just waited until I relaxed.

And then he spoke. "I know things at your house ain't good, Emerson. You don't have to tell me. I asked around, so I know. And I just want you to hear this from me, okay? You're a good kid. Even with how things are for you, you're polite and all that. Delia thinks the world of you."

Under the blanket, he was in nothing but a T-shirt, and his massive body radiated heat. I remember his tattoos and being fascinated by them. By his sheer size. How deep and rough his voice was, but how gentle his words were.

"So, Emerson. We are your family now. This is your home. You come and go as you please. You eat food when you're hungry. You ask for things you want. You can call me whatever you want—Bast is fine. I ain't your dad, but if you ever want to, you can call me that. We adopt people in this crew—it's just what we do. And we've decided you're ours for as long as you wanna belong to us." He had touched my chin with a big, callused, gentle finger, so I looked at him. "You understand what I'm tellin' you, darlin'?"

I nodded. Paused and thought. Then shook my head no.

"Okay. What don't you understand?"

"Why?"

"Because we can. We've been blessed. We got so much of everything, you don't even know. Especially love."

I'd thought about it and then looked up at him. "What if I'm bad?"

He'd chuckled. "I don't believe there's such a thing as a bad kid, only bad parents. What it means for you is we know you ain't gonna be perfect. Something happens, we deal with it. No one gets hit or screamed at or any of that bullshit. We talk about it and work on making better choices next time."

My eyes had burned and my stomach felt funny. "So…" It was the hardest thing, then, to speak my deepest fear. "Will you ever make me go away? Back to…where Mom is? I don't like it there. There's no food. She leaves me alone and I get scared. I know she wants to be better, but she just can't. And I…I don't wanna go back."

He'd cleared his throat and tipped his head back. "*Fuck.*" This had been under his breath; I had very little understanding of adults in general and men in particular at that stage of my life, so it didn't occur to me until many years later that he'd been on the verge of tears at what I'd said. "No, Emerson. You don't ever have to go back if you don't want to. Your home is with us, now. You're safe."

You're safe.

To this day, those words are seared into my soul.

Every day after that, Bast and Dru proved to be as good as their word. They took care of me in every way and loved me as if I were one of their own children. Mom never really…did anything. She was content to let me be taken care of by someone else, I guess. Looking back, it's odd, if nothing else, that she never even made sure I was telling the truth, or that the Badds were good people, or established any kind of legal custody.

I usually saw her whenever I was back home, a

quick visit full of awkward pleasantries; she was more like a distant relative or vague acquaintance.

Now, standing with my luggage as the ferry docks with all this going through my head, I thought about the gift I have for my adopted parents, and I got choked up. It's long past time. I talked to Delia about it before I pulled the trigger to make sure she felt they'd be okay with it.

The dock workers tied the ferry off and got the gangway in place, and I hiked my backpack higher and my duffel onto my shoulder and picked up my two roller suitcases. I hadn't been sure when I'd arrive, so I didn't tell anyone when I was coming, which meant I wasn't expecting anyone to meet me at the dock.

I was surprised, therefore, to find Jax waiting for me in the parking lot, leaning back against his truck—it was his baby, a vintage Chevy Li'l Red Express. He'd bought it himself and restored it with help from his dad, Zane, and some of his many uncles.

I suppressed a groan—Jax was great. Aside from being tall and ripped, he was just a good dude, cool, funny, and always the first to volunteer to help. He had his mom's blond hair and his dad's big brown eyes. Objectively speaking, Jax Badd was hot as fuck. Uncle Zane's and Aunt Mara's oldest son, he was a carbon copy of his father, but with his mother's fair hair. Sharp, angular features, muscular and athletic and funny and effortlessly cool, he was, in every sense, the perfect catch…but he's my best friend's cousin, and the cousins are all as close as siblings, which makes him my sibling; as has been covered previously, he's nursed a major crush on me since we were little kids. I've shot him down literally hundreds of times—nicely, sweetly, sadly, brutally, bitchily, publicly, privately.

"Hey, Sunni." He pushed off his truck and grabbed my suitcases, tossed them in the bed of his truck, and then took my duffel and tossed it in as well. I kept my purse and backpack.

"How'd you know I was coming in? I didn't even tell Dee."

He shrugged. "I have my ways."

I snorted. "Meaning you hacked something."

He's his uncle Xavier's protege. A wizard with computers and electronics, he grew up idolizing his uncle Xavier—the world's foremost expert in robotics and electronics. Xavier's inventions have been used by NASA and are currently roaming Mars, and another is on the way to Venus, on top of being in just about every home in one form or another, be it appliances, toys, or gadgets.

He grinned. "Caught me."

"Well, I wasn't looking forward to carrying all this to the house, so I guess I'm grateful, even if it is a bit stalkerish."

Jax just laughed. "I'm not a stalker, I'm just…" he trailed off and looked at me. "Wait, *are* you actually creeped out?"

"Honestly, no. But I know you. I grew up with

you. I was there when you hacked into whatever it was and got in all that trouble. But when you go to Caltech, don't try that shit, okay? Girls who don't know you *will* be creeped out."

"Emmy…"

God, the look. The big brown eyes.

"Jax." I made my voice firm. "No. Nothing has changed. Nothing ever *will* change. I think of you like a brother, okay? I love you, truly—as a *brother*. So just… don't, okay? *Please*?"

He sighed. "Actually, I met a girl when I did my tour and commitment at Caltech. Jessie. A physics major. She's won a whole bunch of awards."

I grinned at him. "She hot?"

His eyes went wide. "So hot she left me tongue-tied." He turned onto the narrow dirt road that led to Bast and Dru's house. "What I was gonna say was thank you."

I frowned at him. "Thank you? For what?"

"Being so cool about my stupid crush for all these years." He winced as if embarrassed. "You never made me feel bad about it."

I patted his forearm where his hand rested on the gear shifter between us. "Jax, honestly, if I hadn't grown up with you, it would have been different. But all of you cousins are family to me. And I just…I couldn't go there. I *can't* go there."

"Not sure if that makes me feel better or worse," he said, chuckling. "So you guys won nationals, huh?"

I grinned. "Fuck yeah, we did."

"How's it feel?"

"Amazing. I mean, it was my last shot. Regionals were a little dicey because our captain was dealing with some shit, but she got her act together for states, and we kicked ass at nationals. So yeah, it feels good. Especially after last year. God, that was rough."

Last year, we were heavily favored to win, only to lose in a shootout. I made some good saves, but McKenna missed her shot, the game-winner. She went into a deep depression after that and only recently started pulling out of it after therapy and medication and, honestly, just some good old-fashioned winning games.

"So now what?" Jax asked.

"Not sure. Finish my degree. They're sending out invitations to the US Women's National Team tryouts early next year, and I'm hoping I get one. I still want my degree, but I'm really hoping to make the national team. It's a long shot because it's competitive as fuck, but I figure I have a decent chance."

"You've got it in the bag, Em. You're, like, one of the best goalies in the country."

"Yeah, *one of.* And everyone else who's just as good as me will be there, too." I shrugged. "All I can do is put in the work and see what happens."

We pulled up to the house then, and my heart lifted as I saw what will always be home. It didn't look as big as it was from the driveway. It looked like a decent-sized ranch until you went in and saw how far back it went and how expansive and open it was.

Featuring a wide, deep front porch framed by thick square wooden pillars soaring ten feet overhead, with a pair of heavy French doors with thick-paned glass, it extended to the left in a four-car garage and to the right in a private owner's suite, with the other bedrooms facing the Inside Passage along the rear of the house off the open-concept kitchen, dining room, and living room. The house's eaves, ridgelines, and peaks were lined with warm white Christmas lights, and a huge, handmade wreath bedecked with holly, mistletoe, and twinkling white lights adorned the front door.

Jax already had my luggage and was pushing inside, so I grabbed my bag and purse and followed him. I heard him greet Dru and Bast, and then he gave me a quick side hug. "Gotta get home—Dad wants me to split wood for tonight. See you round, Emmy!"

I called my goodbye to him, waving as he drove off.

Inside, Christmas had exploded. A twelve-foot-tall natural tree stood in the corner of the living room by the floor-to-ceiling windows, wreathed in white twinkle lights and strung with faux cranberry garland and hung with ornaments ranging from expensive crystal figurines to laminated drawings made by Delia, Duncan, Dane, and me. A six-foot tall nutcracker guarded the foyer, one hand holding a spear and the other a bowl full of freshly baked sugar cookies. I grabbed a cookie as I set my duffel by the front door, marveling at Dru's decorative magic. The huge mantel over the fireplace—a live-edge log a foot thick and six feet wide, squared off on top, was draped with more white twinkle lights and faux-fir garland, and heavy iron sculptures in the shape of reindeer pranced along the mantel, each one holding a stocking with our names on them.

Mine said "Sunni," which is what most of the Badd clan call me, thanks to Delia. It's sort of an inside joke: my name is Emerson Day, and most people shorten my name, naturally enough, to Em or Emmy. But Delia loves to be different, so she decided she needed her own private nickname for me; she tried Mercy, as in Eh-MERS-son, Mercy, but that didn't stick. Then she tried Sun, as in Emer-SON. Sunni. And also, Sunni Day? Haha. But it stuck, and now the whole Badd clan calls me Sunni as much as they do Emerson or Em—they're interchangeable.

The stockings were handmade by Mama Livvie out of flannel material with leather bottoms, and each person's name was hand-stitched across the top. She spent an entire year making them for *everyone* in the family. When she gave me mine that Christmas, I sobbed like a baby. Being accepted as part of the family is one thing, but having my own stocking with my name on it?

It's not something I ever, ever take for granted.

Even the kitchen was decorated. Elves and gnomes

and reindeer pranced along the tops of the upper cabinets, and the salt and pepper shakers were Mr. and Mrs. Claus. The white tea towel hanging from the oven handle said "Merry & Bright" in red stitching. The artwork on the walls was Christmas-themed. Coasters had snowmen on them. Throw pillows featured snowflakes. Throw blankets were buffalo plaid.

A fire roared in the fireplace, crackling and spitting occasionally, and I heard an axe thunking steadily outside, punctuated by the raucous laughter of Dunc and Dane—who probably spent as much time goofing off as they did splitting wood.

Mama Dru was in the kitchen, dressed in dark jeans and a white V-neck sweater, a buffalo plaid apron around her neck and waist, Ugg slippers on her feet, her hair—a few shades darker red than mine, leading most people who see us together to assume I'm naturally hers—tied up in a loose chignon. A glass of white wine was on the counter nearby, red lipstick staining the rim. Big Daddy Bast had her up against the counter, his huge body framing hers, and he was kissing her so intensely that I had to look away.

"Bast, honey," Dru murmured against his mouth, gently pushing him backward. "Look who's here."

He turned his head, saw me, and lit up as bright as the Christmas tree. "Sunni!"

I did what I always do when I come home for holidays: drop my purse and take a running leap. He caught me as easily as ever, spinning me around. He smelled like woodsmoke, whiskey, and cologne. His beard, now as much gray as brown, was scratchy as he kissed my cheek.

"Here's the national champ herself," he said in his growly voice. "Saw the game, sweetheart. Some kick-ass saves. Sorry we couldn't make it out in person."

I just hugged him tighter. "All good. I knew you were watching—I could feel it."

"We put the game on all the TVs in every bar. Anyone rooting for the other team got kicked out." He set me down and tugged on my braid. "Missed you, Sunni-girl."

"Missed you too."

He wasn't kidding, either—when Nina, Brock's and Claire's daughter, made the state finals in basketball, they did the same thing. Put the game on all the TVs in every Badd's Bar establishment in Alaska, and if you got caught rooting for the other team, you were booted. The Badds do *not* fuck around.

Dru glided over to me and enveloped me in her soft, warm presence. "Do we get you through New Year this year?"

"Yeah. I'll have to hit the gym and get some drills in, but I don't have to go back to Seattle until the semester starts. My college soccer career is officially over."

She hugged me again. "So, *so* good to have you home, honey."

Maybe it was my gift to them making me emotional, but I was feeling all weepy at the welcome. I mean, it's how they always welcomed me—with hugs and kisses and warmth and so much love it almost hurt.

"Where's Dee?" I asked, looking around.

Bast answered, pouring me a glass of wine. "At the Kitty, wrapping up some paperwork. Should be here any minute."

"Anyone else coming today?" I took my glass into the kitchen and hopped up on the island.

Dru shook her head. "No, just us today. There's a thing at Bax and Eva's tomorrow night, something at Mama Livvie and Papa Lucas's the next night." She whirled her hand vaguely. "I've got a schedule written down somewhere—we spent a week planning all the parties so none interfered with the others."

I just laughed because that's how it was this time of year around here—there was a party at someone's house every night between the first of December and New Year's Eve. If you were smart, you spent the weeks between Thanksgiving and Christmas break cutting calories and saving your liver because Christmas break with the Badds meant eating until you could hork and drinking all day.

The volume in the house suddenly went from zero to a million as Dunc and Dane entered, each of them coated in the snow falling outside, carrying armloads of firewood.

"Oh fuck off, Fortnite is *not* the best game ever," Duncan said, stomping his feet.

"It's the *most played* game in history. It's not even close." Dane came in next, stomping his feet too.

Their argument continued as the boys—Irish twins a little under a year apart—brought the wood inside and stacked it in the rack by the fireplace.

"You boys better wipe that snowmelt off my floor," Dru yelled from the kitchen. "I just cleaned up in here."

"We will," they yelled back in unison.

Duncan was the older, three years Delia's junior. Dane was the youngest, a little less than four and a half years her junior, making them nineteen and almost eighteen to Delia's twenty-two.

They didn't even notice me until after they'd cleaned up and discarded their coats.

Dunc saw me first and came over for a hug, shaking his snow-wet hair at me.

Both boys strongly resembled their dad—towering and muscular with brown hair blessed with a touch of red from Dru and the family-characteristic brown eyes. Dunc was taller and leaner, while Dane was a few inches shorter but more solidly built. They were both firecrackers like their mom: loud, boisterous, hysterical, and often in trouble. Never bad or violent trouble, just the kind of trouble that half-wild boys with more energy than sense tend to get into.

Dane joined the hug, and suddenly the two boys were carrying me around the house on their shoulders, singing "We Will Rock You" at the top of their lungs until I had to kick and shout to get them to put me down, laughing so hard I was almost crying.

By the time I collected myself, Delia was walking in, juggling four big paper sacks full of carryout from Badd Kitty while kicking the door closed with her foot.

The bags covered her face, so when I went to take them from her, she didn't know it was me at first.

"Thanks, bro," she murmured, kicking her boots off.

"No problem, bro," I said, waiting for the shriek.

"*SUNNI!*" Yep. There it was—the Delia special, an ear-piercing shriek of absolute joy, whether she saw me the day before or two months before. She leaned in and hugged me, crumpling the paper bags between us. "When did you get in?"

"Just a minute ago," I said, carrying the sacks to the kitchen. "What's all this? Smells good."

"Lunch," she answered. "There was a bachelorette party and they barely touched the food, so I brought it home."

Delia—the spitting image of her mother, with the same dark red hair, blue eyes, and killer curves—is Bast's protege. The only career she ever wanted was to run the Badd's Bar empire after Bast retired. She started as a hostess at fourteen—officially, that is, having spent her whole life up until then filling in on the weekends and after school in the kitchen and office. Bast made her earn it every step of the way, putting her advancement in the hands of the managers. She started waitressing at sixteen, bartending at eighteen, and was an assistant manager of the original Badd's Bar and Grille at twenty. Now twenty-two, she was the general manager of Badd Kitty. The next step was upper management, helping Bast oversee the running of the rest of the franchises. The whole operation included the original Badd's Bar and Grille, as well as Badd Kitty, Badd Night—a music venue—and Badd's Bar Anchorage. They've talked about expanding into Juneau, but so far, nothing has come of it. I'm proud of her, even though not everyone gets it. She's gotten a lot of shit from a lot of people for skipping college to work at her family's business, but she's always known what she wanted, and what she wanted was to be CEO of the Badd's Bar company. And she was well on her way to that goal.

We unboxed all the food together—chicken fingers, fries, mozzarella sticks, potato skins, deep-fried pickles, Bavarian pretzels…deep-fried carb-heavy goodness I forgo most of the year.

As we were unloading, she leaned close. "Did you do the thing?"

"The thing?"

"For Christmas. For Mom and Dad?"

"Oh! Yeah. I did." I glanced at her, worried. "Why? Should I not have? I thought you said they'd be happy about it."

She just grinned at me, her Aegean-blue eyes, so

much like her mother's, twinkling. "This is gonna be the best Christmas ever."

"Why?"

She put her lips to my cheek as if to kiss me but gave me a raspberry instead. "Oh, no reason. It just will be."

The mischievous look in her eyes told me she knew something more, but I knew better than to pry. Mainly because I love surprises, and no one does big gestures like this family.

The boys came swooping in with paper plates, long arms doing their best Hungry Hungry Hippo impressions as they reached over us for food while Dru and Bast watched, grinning, happy to have all their kids under one roof again.

Delia's enthusiasm was infectious, or maybe it was my excitement for another holiday season with this crazy crew, but happiness and joy bubbled up in my heart as I took my place at the long table next to Delia.

It felt like maybe it *was* going to be the best Christmas ever.

FOUR

Hayden

I SAT AT MY COMPUTER FOR THREE DAYS STRAIGHT, CRANKING away at a giant project my boss dumped on me. Fueled by energy drinks, coffee, and microwaveable mini pizzas, I barely left my desk for seventy-two hours, only grabbing a handful of power naps in that time.

I was so hyperfocused—my superpower as well as my greatest flaw—that I never looked at my phone.

Once I finished the project, I crashed for twelve hours, sleeping like the dead. I woke up at eight the next morning and sat bolt upright, on the verge of a blind panic for what felt like no reason at all.

I checked my phone—the usual missed calls from Mom, but no voicemails; if she needed something important, she left a message. She never texts, nor does

Dad. I tried showing them how, but even using the voice-to-text, they just didn't want to do it.

I tried to go back to sleep, but once I was up, I was up. So I had some coffee, changed, hit the gym for a quick burnout session, and came home. No calls, no messages; I still had the churning in my gut, the sense of something wrong, a feeling of impending doom.

I tried to work, but the feeling was so bad I couldn't shake it. I picked up my phone to call Mom but opted to just swing by.

On the way, my phone rang. I answered it half-way through the first ring. "Mom? Is everything alright? I've had—"

"Hayden." Her voice was…broken. Barely a whisper, shaking, tiny.

"Mom? What—what's wrong?" I put it on speaker and set it on my thigh as I made the turn onto their street. "I'm about to pull in."

"Hayden, your father…" she trailed off, shattering into sobs, unable to finish.

I floored it, the tires of my vintage Wagoneer squealing. "I'm here, Mom. I'm pulling in."

"I'm…I'm at the hospital." I could barely hear her.

"What happened?" I asked, hauling ass past our house and making a right to head back to the main road.

"His heart." Not even a whisper—a breath. "He had a heart attack."

My throat was tight and hot. My eyes burned. "He's…Dad, he's not—"

"He's gone, baby."

I remember screaming, but I don't remember driving to the hospital. I remember parking illegally and not caring. I remember running up the steps to the cardiac floor, too much in a hurry to wait for the elevator, as if I could do something to change the facts if I got there sooner.

I remember stumbling to a halt in the doorway, gasping for breath. Mom was a tiny, motionless lump on the bed beside Dad. A nurse was quietly and unobtrusively disconnecting leads and unhooking machines, and another was tidying up the crash cart. The monitor was off—no flatline tone.

The room was silent.

I stood there for a very long time, staring almost without seeing. Eventually, I made my feet propel me forward to the bed. Dad was…smaller, somehow as if the lack of his animating spirit had somehow shrunk his physical form. His eyes were closed. Had I ever noticed how his veins stood out so prominently on his forearms? That scar on his temple?

Mom was barely breathing. Snuggled up against him, her hand on his chest, over his hand.

"Mom."

She just shook her head.

I didn't know what to say. What to do. I was too shocked, too stunned to feel anything.

A doctor came in and pulled me out, explaining that he'd suffered a massive cardiac arrest while grading papers in his office. A student had found him slumped over, gasping, and had called 911, performing CPR until they got there. He had been kept alive for almost half an hour, but in the end, there just wasn't anything to be done.

I handled the necessary arrangements. Eventually, it was time for the hospital to take him. Which meant I had to get Mom to let him go.

I went around the bed to where Mom was. Touched her shoulder—she was shivering. "Mom. It's time to say goodbye." My voice cracked on the last word.

"I can't."

I tucked her hair away from her eyes and behind her ear. "I know. But we gotta."

"It hurts, Hayden. What do I do without him?"

I scooped her up, and she put her face into my chest and shook. My eyes burned, but I knew I couldn't let go. I had to be strong for Mom.

She peeked up over my shoulder. "Wait, wait. Put me down. I have to say goodbye. I have to—I have to say goodbye."

I set her on her feet, holding her shoulders. She pulled away, leaned over the bed, cradled Dad's cheeks in her hands, and kissed his lips. Whispered something that was none of my business.

She straightened, inhaled deeply, held it, and let

it out slowly. Squared her shoulders. Turned to me. "Your turn." Her voice was shockingly firm.

I didn't know what to do, what to say. I moved beside Mom and touched Dad's hand—it was cold, dry, papery. Wrong. Empty.

"Dad, I…" my voice gave out. The burn in my eyes turned to a hazy blur that I blinked away frantically. I bent over his body and held an image in my mind of him alive, grinning at me after telling a horrible dad joke. "I love you. I'll miss you."

It seemed so inadequate, so paltry. Pathetic. But what words could capture my feelings in this moment?

There weren't any. Especially because I was still in shock, not fully comprehending the reality of what had happened.

Mom's hand rested on my back. Rubbed in circles.

I straightened, blinked away tears. How did you just…walk away? How were you supposed to do that?

In the end, it was Mom who pulled me away. She tucked her hand around my bicep and gently guided me out of the room. Down the hall. Down the elevator. To the parking lot. She'd driven here but rode home with me.

When we got there, she walked in and set her purse on the narrow table by the front door, laden with mail and decorated with a little pumpkin and a cross-stitched "Give Thanks" sign. Just stood there for a moment.

"Mom, can I…what can I do?" I jingled my keys in my pocket.

She shook her head. "I just…I need to be alone, sweetheart. But will you…will you stay here tonight?"

"Yeah, Mom, of course."

"You don't need to work?"

"That doesn't matter. I'll call my boss later."

She just nodded without looking at me. Shuffled for the stairs. I followed her up. Halfway from the stairs to their room, her legs gave out, and I caught her. She pushed to her feet, one hand on the wall.

I helped her to her room, where she crawled onto her side of the bed. "I'll be downstairs."

She nodded.

"Is there anything I can do?"

A shake of her head. "I just need to be alone."

"Mom, I…" Words failed me.

"I know, Hayden."

Thanksgiving was weird.

For the first time in my entire life, there was no turkey or stuffing or any of that. Mom and I went to a local Chinese restaurant and shared Kung Pao and Sweet and Sour Chicken.

Midway through the meal, Mom looked at me. "I don't know what to do about the…trip."

She couldn't even say the word "cruise," associating it with Dad.

"You already paid for it, didn't you?" I asked.

She nodded, scooping up a peapod with her chopsticks. "Yes, it's all paid for."

"I guess you probably don't want to just…go anyway."

Her laugh was bitter. "No, Hayden, I do not want to go on my fiftieth-anniversary cruise by myself."

"But you can't get a refund."

"No."

"I'll go with you. We can get the room switched to two adjoining rooms."

I hate boats. I get seasick. But for Mom? No question.

She looked at me for a long time. "I don't know, Hayden. I know how you feel about being on the water. I hate to waste that much money, but…it just seems so stupid to go by myself. What would I do?"

I reached across the table and took her hands in mine. "Mom, I *want* to go with you. I need to get away, too. Our first Christmas together without…" I had to stop and clear my throat. "Without him…I don't know if I can do it here in that house. You know? And a cruise ship is barely like being on a boat at all, from what I hear. They have all sorts of stabilizers, so unless the weather is awful, you barely feel it roll."

She just rolled a shoulder. "You don't have to do that for me, Hayden. It's okay. I'll just gift it to one of the ladies in my book club. I know Barbara Reynolds and her husband have a big anniversary coming up."

I squeezed her hand. "I'm not doing it for you, Mom. We *both* need it, now more than ever. It'll be fun. We can go on all the excursions you want."

She blinked hard. "You hate boats, Hayden."

"But I love *you*."

"You're sure?" The hope in her eyes was physically painful to see—she needed a getaway more than anything.

She was just existing right now. Dragging herself out of bed, drifting to work.

"I…I know it won't be the same. But…yeah, I'm absolutely sure. I may have to hang by the pool and do some work now and then, but I'll get as much time off as I can. I've got a lot coming since I work so much. I'd love to go with you, if you'll have me."

She laughed. "Oh, you're diabolical, you are. Turning it around like I'm doing you a favor."

It was good to see her laugh. "You are! I don't think I've ever taken a vacation."

She frowned thoughtfully. "You haven't, have you? You do work too much, I've always said that. You don't have any friends, let alone—"

I laughed and cut her off. "Okay, okay. Let's not go down that road. Yes, I might meet a girl on the boat. We'll see. But I'm doing it to spend time with you, not meet women."

She rolled her eyes. "You can do both, you know."

I sighed a laugh. "Yes, Mother." I ate a piece of chicken and a peanut slathered in Kung Pao sauce, with one of those tiny corn things. "When do we leave?"

Good god, that's a big damn boat.

I stood next to Mom as we waited in line to board. The thing was a floating skyscraper. I'd done plenty of research in the weeks between agreeing to go and now. I knew about the morgue they have for the inevitable deaths, the statistics on safety, how the stabilizers worked, how many crewmembers there were, the captain's credentials, the itinerary, which excursions Mom wanted to do, and which ones sounded interesting to me…I'm a nerd, okay? Facts and stats make me feel more comfortable.

I'm not gonna say I was excited, but I wasn't dreading it, either. I *was* ready to get out of West Lafayette, Indiana for the first time in my life—other than that one family vacation to Disney World when I was in fourth grade, courtesy of a raffle Dad won at work. I grew up in Indiana, went to Purdue because Dad got a killer discount on tuition and I lived at home, did a virtual interview, and got hired by a startup without ever setting foot in California, where the company I work for is located.

So yeah, I was a little excited, I guess. Not about the actual cruise, per se, so much as getting out of

Indiana and seeing new places. New people? Not as much. I was socially awkward around people, and was about to be stuck on a boat with a few thousand new people.

But in the end, this is about Mom.

Turns out it was actually pretty fun. Lounging by the pool with Mom, sipping a drink, swimming, and yes, working. The days were long and filled with things to do together, and I never got sick as long as I didn't stand by the railing and look at the water. I made that mistake once and nearly chunked over the railing. Mom just laughed and told me not to look down and then went back to reading her Agatha Christie novel.

Ketchikan itself was amazing. It was easily the most beautiful place I've ever seen—not that the list is hard to beat. West Lafayette is nice and all, and Disney World is cool, but Ketchikan, Alaska?

Mind. Blown.

Mom and I did a flightseeing and kayaking tour of the Misty Fjords, and I've never enjoyed anything more in my life. I didn't think about work or my laptop once. Mom was so happy she kept saying, "This is so much fun I could cry." I think she did cry, actually. That alone made the whole trip worth it.

The day after the kayaking trip, Mom decided to stay by the pool and read again, claiming to be wiped out from the day before, and encouraged me to go do something on my own.

I hugged her, locked my laptop in the room,

grabbed my wallet and phone, and headed for shore. For a while, I just wandered around town on foot, popped into touristy places, and bought a hat for myself and a sweatshirt for Mom. By then, I was hungry. Wasn't much around except bars, so I figured fuck it, why not?

I picked one at random and wandered into a place called Badd Kitty.

It was a pub sort of place, dimly lit with a lot of dark, aged wood and metal, with TVs in the corners playing sports replays and Atmosphere streams, loud rock music blaring from hidden speakers, and deep booths with red velvet cushions along the wall. Opposite the booths was the bar, which was the *pièce de résistance* of the whole place. Hewn from what had to be a single gigantic tree, the facing live edge wove in a long sine wave, the top polished and lacquered, the whole thing extending a good hundred feet from end to end. The service bar occupied the far end by the entrance to the kitchen, and a Keno machine sat at the end by the door. The high-backed stools were solid and had cushions of the same red velvet as the booths, with a railing running around the bottom of the bar for the feet and a high back on the stools. Despite being midday, it was pretty busy, which wasn't entirely surprising considering the number of cruise ships in port.

I found a spot at the bar near the service station and waited for the bartender to come by. She was a gorgeous girl with dark red hair, stunning blue eyes, and a figure I had trouble keeping my eyes off of.

She shot me a friendly grin. "Hey, welcome in. I'm Delia. What can I get you?"

"An amber. Something local?" I said, grinning back.

"Sure thing. Want a menu?" She tossed a napkin in front of me and pulled the beer.

"Yeah. Well, no, actually—what's good?"

"Everything. But if you like a burger, ours has been voted best in Ketchikan six years running."

"Sign me up. Thanks."

She winked at me and went to punch in my order. My beer was fantastic, malty and smooth. I nursed my beer and watched sports replays, even though I didn't know the first thing about sports.

When the replay program ended, a re-run of the women's national finals for college soccer came on. I never watch sports of any kind, but I found myself enjoying it. The U-W goalie was the hero of the game, stopping everything that came at her with incredible feats of athletic prowess, not to mention some serious panache.

My food came, and I dug in. Halfway through, I felt a tap on my shoulder. "Mind if I sit?"

I answered without looking, not wanting to miss the play that was happening—an excellent drive by the other team since I was rooting for UW based on the goalie alone. "Sure, all yours."

"Oh god, really?" The voice was a little raspy, not like a sore throat—it seemed natural, maybe from yelling a lot; why didn't matter, it was hot, so I looked.

Fuck me.

Bright, curly red hair—true ginger—loose around a heart-shaped face and shocking, mesmerizing green eyes. Her skin was...shit, I don't know. Ice cream? Butter pecan ice cream, with freckles scattered across her nose and cheeks.

She was the most heart-stoppingly beautiful human being I'd ever seen. I couldn't speak.

I cleared my throat and forced words out. "Oh god, really what?"

She was dressed in dark gray leggings, fuzzy, fluffy, calf-height boots, and an ivory V-neck sweater that hugged her ample bust like a second skin. She set a worn leather purse on the bar and then grabbed a cocktail napkin from the bar, wadded it up, and tossed it at the bartender.

"Hey, wench, gimme a beer!" She shouted.

The bartender didn't turn away from the point-of-sale computer as she flipped the bird.

"You know her, I take it?" I asked.

The siren beside me just cackled. "She's basically my sister." She pointed at the game I was watching. "The game. That's what I said 'oh god really' about."

I glanced at her as I dragged a fry through ranch dressing. "Not a soccer fan?"

She stared at me, blinked twice. "Are you?"

I shrugged. "Never watched a game in my life." I pointed at the TV. "This is a hell of a game, though. The U-W goalie is a rockstar."

She cackled at this, for some reason. "You don't say?" She leaned forward. "Delia! This guy here says the U-W goalie is a rock star."

Delia threw he head back and laughed uproariously. "Dude, are you for real?"

I frowned, looking from one gorgeous girl to the other. "Um, yes? Did I say something stupid?"

The bombshell beside me leaned close. She smelled like lavender, which, for reasons I could not begin to explain, had the effect of making me hard as a rock.

"Look closer at the keeper," she said. "And then look at me."

Gulp.

At that precise moment, the cameraman zoomed in on the goalie. Curly ginger hair pulled back in a tight braid with a headband to keep the flyaways out of her face. Same heart-shaped face. Same eyes.

Yup.

It was her—the girl next to me.

I turned to her and grinned sheepishly. "Uh, hi. Nice to meet you—I'm Hayden McCaffery." I held out my hand.

She slid her hand into mine and squeezed—firm, but not trying to prove anything. Her hands were soft and small. "Nice to meet you, Hayden McCaffery.

I'm Emerson Day, goalkeeper for the University of Washington women's soccer team." She still had my hand in hers, and her eyes twinkled. For real, they glittered in the low light, and my breath caught in my throat. "Spoiler alert—U-W wins."

"No kidding? So you're a national champion." I didn't want to look away, didn't want to let go of her hand.

I wanted to lean close and inhale her scent. I wanted to see if the rest of her creamy, milky skin was as soft as her hands.

She pulled her hand from mine and huffed on her fingernails, then buffed them on her shirtfront. "What can I say, I'm a rockstar." She grinned at me. "I have it on excellent authority, you know."

Her smile set fire to my nerve endings. I groped the recesses of my suddenly vacant mind for something intelligent to say.

"So, um. Come here often?" As soon as the words exited my big dumb mouth, I groaned and slapped my forehead. "Can you maybe forget I said that?"

She snickered. "Sure. Try again, hotshot."

Okay, brain: smart time. You were valedictorian of your class at Purdue. You can do better than that.

I took a breath. "Are you from the area or just visiting?" Okay, that wasn't too bad.

She eyed Delia, who was at the service bar with a ticket and a cocktail shaker, then leaned up and over the bar and reached way down the other side—incidentally providing me a long look at her butt, which was, in a word, glorious: generous, firm, and heart-shaped. I swallowed hard. She came back down to her seat with a bottle of whiskey; another quick reach brought a pair of rocks glasses.

I watched with a raised eyebrow as she poured a finger of whiskey into each glass and replaced the bottle. Sliding one glass to me, she lifted hers in a toast.

"To rockstar goalies and no dumb questions." She said this with a wry, teasing smirk.

I clinked my glass against hers. "I'll drink to the first part, but I'm pretty sure I proved there are in fact *some* dumb questions."

We tossed back the shots—I hissed and winced as the whiskey burned its way down my throat. "Jesus. What is that? Turpentine?"

"The bottomest of bottom-shelf," Delia said, collecting our glasses and setting them in the wash sink. "I only keep that bottle in stock for giving out free shots. Why do you think I let her do that?"

Emerson rapped her knuckles on the bar. "Delia, bestest bestie, may I please have a beer and something horribly unhealthy to eat?"

Delia pulled a beer—Something yellowish-orange with a thick cap of white foam and then punched something in the POS. "Food's on me, beer's on you."

Emerson took a sip, coming away with a foam mustache. "Thanks, sweet tits. You're the best." She didn't seem to notice the mustache as she looked at me.

"To answer your second question first, I am proudly Ketchikan born and raised. To answer your first question second, yes, I do come here often. Mainly because *she*—" she gestured at Delia, "manages the place and happens to be a workaholic, so it's the only place I can get quality time with her." Another sip, adding to the foam-stache. "And by manages, I mean her family owns it—and all the other Badd's Bar establishments."

Come to think of it, Badd's was listed on a brochure I'd leafed through when we arrived in port as a local favorite hang-out spot, along with two other spots bearing the Badd name.

I grabbed a napkin from the stack and reached toward her, stopping short of making contact. "You have, um…" I gestured at my upper lip with my other hand. "May I?"

She lifted her chin and pushed her face toward me. "Please do."

I swiped the napkin across her lip, folded it, and swiped again. There was still a bit of foam, so I brushed my thumb over her lip.

My heart pounded, and an electric shock sizzled through me at the skin-to-skin contact.

She looked at me from a few inches away, eyes searching mine, looking for something. "Thanks." Her voice was soft. Intimate.

"Uh, yeah. Yeah." More conversational brilliance from the one and only Hayden McCaffrey, everyone. Thank you, thank you, I'll be here all week.

"So." She leaned back in her chair and took another swig, this time wiping her lip with the back of her hand. "Cruise?"

I laughed. "Yeah. Is it that obvious?"

"I mean, yeah, but when you grow up around here, tourists are easy to spot. Mainly because the rest of the year, Ketchikan is actually a pretty small town, so we mostly know everyone."

"Gotcha. You have a beautiful place, here. It's incredible." I'd forgotten my food and went back to it.

"There's nowhere like it," she said. "Seattle is cool and all, but there's nowhere like Ketchikan."

Delia brought her the same thing she'd brought me, and Emerson and I spent a few minutes eating in silence.

"What'd you think of the cruise? Fun?"

I shrugged. "I wasn't sure if I'd like it, to be honest. I don't like boats much. But I've had fun. More so being here than the actual cruise part, though."

She gave me a puzzled frown, laughing. "If you don't like boats and weren't sure you'd like it, why go?"

I sighed. "Long story."

She snorted. "You know, I've noticed people tend to say that when it's not actually all that *long*, just personal or hard to explain."

"More the former," I said.

"Well then, forget I asked."

I shook my head. "Nah, it's okay." I took a long drink for fortification. "So, my parents had been saving for a Christmas cruise to Alaska for their fiftieth anniversary. They'd been planning it for at least a decade."

Emerson's eyes widened as she abruptly pulled her pint glass away from her mouth mid-sip. "*Fifty* years? Holy shit. That's amazing."

I nodded. "Yeah, they…yeah. But, um, anyway. My dad…" I trailed off, throat going hot and tight, eyes burning. I worked like hell to push past the emotion. "He, uh, died. Heart attack. A few weeks before Thanksgiving. My mom didn't want to go alone, but the whole thing was already paid for, no refunds. So I went with her." I swallowed hard. "She's had a lot of fun. It's been really great to see her smiling again."

Emerson didn't answer, didn't look at me for a moment. "Shit, Hayden. I'm sorry. I didn't mean to… stir anything up." Her eyes went to mine, full of sympathy and sorrow. "I'm so sorry for your loss."

I had to look away and shove the emotions back down. This girl was incredible and I wasn't about to start bawling in front of her. That would be super cool and amazing and attractive.

When I felt less on the edge of a meltdown, I shrugged and shook my head. "Thanks. I…except for telling my boss why I needed last-minute vacation time, I haven't talked about it."

"I mean, it's only been, what, a couple months? Not even? It's gotta still be fresh."

I nodded. "Yeah, it is, I guess."

She glanced at me after a moment. "You know, I

think it's really amazing, you going on the cruise with your mom. Especially if you don't like boats."

"I get seasick. But the thing is more like a floating hotel than a boat. So as long as I stay away from the railing, I'm fine." I pushed my empty plate away.

"You and your mom are close then?"

I nodded. "Oh yeah. Maybe a little too close, some people would say." I laughed. "Nah, I'm just kidding. But yeah, we're close."

The look in her eyes, then, is...shuttered, unreadable. "I don't think you can be too close to someone you love. Especially a mom. One who cares, anyway."

I searched her face. "I stepped in something, didn't I?"

A shake of her head, red curls bouncing to and fro. "No, it's fine."

"You know, the only woman I'm close to is Mom, but it seems to me when a woman says something is fine, it's usually not."

She rolled her eyes at me. "Oh shut up." Her smile took the sting out of the words. "But you're right. I have a...let's just say a *difficult* relationship with my mother. My actual mother, at least." She pointed at Delia with a fry. "Her mom is more my mom, and Mama Dru is the best."

Delia, half-listening as she worked, thrust a credit card in the air overhead. "Hear, hear!"

"Well, I'm glad you have her, then," I said.

"Me too," she answered. "More than I can say." A

beat. "So, if it's a Christmas cruise, what are you and your mom doing about actual Christmas, like on the day?"

I shrugged. "I think there's a whole thing happening on the boat. It's our first one without Dad so we're skipping all the usual traditions. We'll probably just exchange presents in one of the cabins and spend time in the saloon or whatever they call it."

Emerson frowned. "That doesn't sound..." she hesitated. "Very Christmassy. I mean, I get avoiding the traditions, but..." she sighed and shrugged.

"Yeah, I know what you mean," I said. "Thanksgiving was weird. We went to a Chinese place. Didn't feel like a holiday. But how can it, you know?"

Emerson gave me a long, speculative look and then glanced at Delia. "Yeah, I get that," was all she said.

My phone buzzed, face down on the bar beside my beer.

Mom: *There's a formal dinner and dancing tonight. Did you remember to bring a suit?*

My eyes widened as I realized I had not, in fact, remembered to bring formalwear. I meant to, and I'd had a niggling I'd forgotten something the whole cruise.

"Shit." I scraped my hand through my hair, glancing at Emerson. "I don't suppose you know where I can get a suit...like right now?"

She grinned. "Actually, I do."

FIVE

Emerson

HAYDEN STOOD AT THE FOOT OF THE PORCH, LOOKING uncomfortable. "Are you sure about this?" he asked. "I meant, like, buy one. At a store."

I went back down the steps, grabbed his hand, and pulled him up. "I'm sure. Duncan and Dane are both around your same height and build. They both have, like, a dozen good suits. They're both in sports, and their coaches make them wear suits on game days. I promise you, they won't notice one missing. And you can bring it back when you're done. It's really no big deal."

"When I was in high school, the athletes just had to wear slacks and button-downs with a tie on game days." He went up the steps with me but still seemed very hesitant.

"Yeah, well, their coaches are extra. And Dunc and Dane are captains, so they have to step up." I snorted and rolled my eyes. "But really, they just like wearing suits. They're divas like that. They spend an hour preening in front of the mirror, asking each other if they look dapper in horrible British accents."

Hayden spluttered a laugh. "They sound like real characters."

"You have no idea." I pushed open the door and dragged him in behind me; as the door opened, a wall of noise hit. I may have forgotten to warn Hayden that an informal get-together was happening.

See, on top of the planned and scheduled parties, throughout the holiday season, people would just sort of collect at someone's house, and then a scouting party would be sent to grab a keg from one of the bars and a tower of pizzas would be ordered, and word would get out and suddenly the impromptu party would bleed into the planned one.

This was an impromptu one.

Hayden halted just inside the threshold, jolting me to a stop. "Holy shit. People."

I laughed. "Yeah, there's a lot of Badds."

"You didn't mention it would be a family reunion." I turned and looked at him—he was wide-eyed and a little green around the gills.

"Hey, are you okay? It's not a reunion, they all live around here. It's just a hangout."

"A hangout? Like there's like fifty people!"

I scanned the group, doing a quick count. "Looks like about half the clan."

"*Half?* Jesus crickets."

I snorted so hard I choked on my spit. "Jesus crickets?"

He closed his eyes slowly, embarrassed. "Mom says Jiminy Cricket instead of Jesus Christ. To tease her, I started saying Jesus crickets, and now I can't stop."

"Sounds like you need a support group." I tugged him toward the kitchen where the crew was gathered, playing some sort of rowdy drinking card game that involved a lot of shouting, taking shots, and throwing cards across the island at each other. "Come on."

"Emerson…" he started.

By then, we were in the kitchen, and Uncle Bax had spotted us.

"Emmy-Lou, my sweet Sunni-girl!" he barged around the island, arms wide, scooping me up in a bear hug, damn near crushing me against his anvil-hard chest with his pythonic arms. "Been a minute, darlin'. Saw the game. You kicked ass!"

"Thanks, Uncle Bax," I wheezed, my feet dangling half a foot off the ground. "Crushing, crushing!"

"Oops." He set me down and popped a kiss on the top of my head. "Who's he?" His gaze went to a wide-eyed, slack-jawed Hayden. "Who are you?"

I grabbed Hayden and pulled him forward. "Uncle Baxter, this is my friend Hayden. We just met, what, an hour ago?"

Bax's eyebrows went up. "Very interesting move, Sunni. I approve."

I shoved his chest—it was like pushing an aircraft carrier. "Oh shut up, you big lunk. It's not like that."

He just cackled. "Just teasin', just teasin'. So, what brings you to Chez Badd, Hayden?"

"Um. Emerson?"

God, he was awkward. It was fucking adorable—hot, even. Well, *he* was hot. The awkwardness was adorable. Therefore, hot awkwardness. Hawkward? Hot-kward?

Hayden was taller than Uncle Bax, standing at least six-two, and was lean with corded forearms and big hands. His hair was jet black, glossy as a raven's wing, longish and messy in an absent-minded way, curling around his ears and temples and the back of his neck. His eyes were holly-leaf green, a few shades darker than my own. He wore a cranberry button-down tucked into fitted black jeans and newer black Nike sneakers. A black leather bomber jacket with a fur collar completed the look. The arm of a pair of glasses hung outside the pocket of his shirt, and I had a mental image of him wearing the glasses, looking like Clark Kent. I swooned a little on the inside.

Bax laughed. "Literal one, ain'tcha? Want a beer?"

"Oh, um?" He looked at me, then at Uncle Bax.

"I…we were just…I need a suit, and this was where Emerson brought me."

Bax blinked. "Cool. So…yes beer, or no beer?"

"Yes beer?" Hayden scrubbed a hand through his hair and shrugged his shoulders. "Please. Thank you."

"Comin' right up. I hope you like IPAs because my dipshit brother decided to bring a keg of pine sap instead of real beer." He went around the island, flipped a Solo cup off a stack, tossed it in the air, bounced it off the back of his hand and caught it, and then squirted in beer from a keg.

I leaned in close to Hayden. "You good? You seem…I dunno."

He swallowed hard. "I um…I have the world's worst case of social anxiety. I'm fine in a crowd, like at a bar or concert where I don't know anyone and don't have to interact, but at parties where I have to talk to people, I turn into a tongue-tied caveman."

Come to think of it, he did look like he was about to puke.

I rubbed his shoulder. "Hey, breathe. It's cool. They're my family. Unofficially, but for real."

"That guy looks like he could rip my arm off and beat me with it," he said.

"Oh, he could. He used to be an MMA fighter, and now he's a trainer. Well…he trains the top-tier fighters these days and owns a chain of gyms all over the Pacific Northwest." Bax brought over two beers and handed them to us, and I leaned against him. "But despite his intimidating appearance, Uncle Bax is a teddy bear. Right, Uncle Bax?"

He grinned, tugging on one of my ringlets. "Oh yeah, I'm harmless. Long as you take good care of my Sunni-girl. She's real special, hear me? I wouldn't wanna have to pull your kidney out through your dick-hole because you upset her, know what I mean?"

I reared back and smacked his shoulder, hard. "Bax! He's not used to this many people. Don't be a dick."

Bax chortled, clapping Hayden on the shoulder. "I'm kidding, I'm kidding."

Hayden faked a laugh, looking unsure whether Bax was joking.

"Yo, Badds! C'mere. Our girl brought a dude. Come say hi." Bax wrapped an arm around Hayden's shoulders and guided him into the fray.

Within seconds, Hayden was surrounded by Badd men, as Bast, Brock, Lucian, and Xavier heard and answered the call. There were handshakes and an overlapping slew of personal questions—what do you do? Cybersecurity. Where'd you go to school? Purdue. Got any tattoos? No. What kind of car do you drive? An Eighty-seven Grand Wagoneer. Play any sports? No.

He handled it like a champ despite the barrage of questions, and soon, he was being taught the card game, which was a Badd family original wherein the rules changed every time you played and largely didn't matter in the first place since it was mainly an excuse to drink and be loud and insult each other.

Before long, Hayden was laughing and getting the hang of it, although he avoided the insults part of the game, which was too bad because that's the whole point of the game, which we call Howlers.

I got into it, too, of course, and was hurling insults and throwing back shots and whipping cards at cousins, aunts, and uncles. Hayden and I kept finding excuses to bump into each other, and I grabbed his arm a couple of times as I ducked behind him to dodge a thrown card. And let me tell you, for a computers guy, he's got some *guns*.

About an hour in, he grabbed his phone from his pocket, glanced at it, winced, and whipped off a text message.

He leaned close to me. "I really gotta go, Emerson. The dinner starts in an hour and I still don't have anything to wear."

"Shit!" I shouted, throwing down my hand of cards. "I forgot! Come on." On the way past Duncan, I smacked him on the back of the head. "I'm loaning Hayden one of your suits, Dunc. Cool?"

Dunc snagged one of my curls with a sharp yank. "Yeah, for sure." He glanced at Hayden with an assessing look. "The slate one would look good on him."

"Thanks, bub!" I sang, hauling Hayden by the hand down the long hallway off the kitchen along the back of the house.

My room was first, then Dane's, and then Duncan's on the end; Bast's and Dru's suite was on the opposite side of the house by itself.

Dunc's room was open and as neat as always, unlike mine and Dane's rooms. I went to his closet, flipping through until I found the slate suit, and held it up to Hayden.

"Yup, he's right. This'll look hot on you." I hadn't meant to say that out loud. Me and my mouth.

I pushed his jacket off and tossed it on the bed, then went back to the closet for a white button-down and a sapphire tie.

I'm a doer, okay? I fixate on something and get it done. And I was fixated on getting Hayden ready to go to the fancy dinner with his mom.

Which is why I started unbuttoning his shirt. I wasn't thinking.

"Uhhh…" he very gently grabbed my wrists. "I can, you know, dress myself."

I looked up at him and saw humor in his eyes… along with something a whole hell of a lot more potent. As if he'd had to make himself stop me from stripping him down in my adopted brother's room, with my entire family a few feet away.

"Yeah, um…of course." I stepped back, my cheeks flaming. "Sorry. I, um…" For once, words utterly failed me. "Sorry?"

He smiled, and it was soft, and kind, and intriguing, and sexy as hell. "Your family is incredible. I'm a total stranger and they just…" he shook his head. "Pulled me right in."

"That's the Badd way," I said. "It's just what they do. It's why I'm here."

"You'll have to tell me that story, sometime. I'd love to hear it."

His shirt was hanging half-open, revealing well-formed pecs and a hint of washboard abs. His glasses were still in his shirt pocket, and I, unable to control my impulses apparently, took them out and slid them onto his face.

"Hi, Clark, I'm Lois," I said, grinning like a dork.

He even had a little curl of hair on his forehead. My lady bits were suggesting some very inappropriate ideas to the rest of me.

"I'm no Superman," he said.

I shrugged, ignoring the fact that my fingers, the traitors, had decided to unbutton his shirt the rest of the way. Because abs. "You could be. You've got the look down."

He blinked at me, and I could see his processors working overtime. "You're fucking gorgeous, and I feel like a bumbling idiot around you," he blurted.

A blast of laughter spurted out of me. "You're anything but a bumbling idiot. I should have warned you there'd be people here."

"I'm an only child, and I've never had a big social circle. It was just a lot. But they're amazing. Loud, but amazing." He swallowed hard, looking down at me without blinking.

His hand lifted, and a single index fingertip ghosted across my cheeks and nose, tracing my freckles. "How can you be cute and sexy at the same time?" He asked, sounding like he wasn't sure if he meant to say it out loud.

I shrugged. "Same way you can be awkward and sexy."

He laughed. "I have awkward down to a science."

My fingers found a groove in his abs—warm skin, hard muscle. "What are we doing?"

"I don't know," he whispered. "I like it, but we can't—we shouldn't. Not here, not now." He pinched a curl between his fingers, pulled it straight, let it go. "I just can't seem to stop."

"Get dressed. I'll bring you to the marina." I stepped back, even though everything inside me wanted to push forward.

He stood motionless, abs and chest peeking out in the gap of his open shirt. I felt his eyes on me, lingering on my face, flicking down to my chest and then back up immediately.

"Stop looking at me like that," I whispered.

"Then stop looking like that."

"Like what?"

"Perfect."

Oh. Jesus crickets. What a line. The naughty ideas

being put forth by my lady bits became positively sinful. The things I wanted to do to this boy, good lord.

Boy?

He may be awkward and socially anxious, but he was all man, hard and lean and sculpted and fucking gorgeous. And he loved his mama. That was a major plus in my book.

I took another step backward, now mostly in the hallway. "You're dangerous, Hayden McCaffrey."

He shook his head, smirking and snorting. "Far from it."

"That's what makes you so dangerous—you don't realize it."

I pulled the bedroom door shut before my lady bits took the reins.

The moment I hit the kitchen, I was swarmed by aunts and cousins.

Claire grabbed my shoulders. "Who was *that*?"

"His name's Hayden. I met him at Badd Kitty. He's on a cruise with his mom."

Confused silence.

"His *mom*?" This was from Mara, her fine blonde hair shot through with gray at the temples, wrinkles at the corners of her eyes, her usual minimal makeup accentuating her beautiful features.

"Explanations are in order," Mama Dru said.

"His father just died right before Thanksgiving. The cruise was already paid for, so he went with his mom, so she didn't have to go alone or give up the tickets. So she would be able to have fun again." I paused for effect. "He gets seasick."

"Well, a cruise ship is barely a boat when it comes to seasickness, but still." This is Aunt Joss, Uncle Lucian's wife, a stunning woman with light brown skin and dreadlocks pulled back with a thick length of braided leather ending in dozens of small brightly colored beads.

"That's the sweetest thing I've ever heard," Dru said. "But why did you bring him here if you just met him? I mean, it's fine, but it's not like you."

I didn't bring boys home. I never have. Mainly because the only boys I spent time with were at school, and they weren't boyfriends, they were hookups. Hayden is the only guy I've ever brought here.

And I didn't have an answer. Or, not a good one. "I, um…he has a fancy formal dinner and a dance with his mom and forgot to pack a suit. He'd never find anything good around here, not in time, and he's the same height and build as Dunc. I figured he could borrow one. It's not a big deal."

Dru pinched my cheek. "Then why are you all glowy?" She smirked at me knowingly.

"I'm not glowy. It's just warm in here." I batted her hand away.

Lena, one of Uncle Canaan's and Aunt Aerie's four kids, poked me on the top of the nose. "You're catching feelings."

She was the spitting image of her mother, with

platinum blonde hair and amber eyes with green streaks around the edges. And, like her mother and aunt before her, she was a model, carefully managed by her mother. I doubted she'd do it much longer, though—I'd heard her complain about it a bunch; she talked about getting behind the camera instead of in front of it.

"I am not." I said this to the ceiling over her left shoulder because I was fairly certain I was lying through my teeth.

Bast pushed into the circle and slung a heavy arm over my shoulder. "You good to drive, Sunni? Brock has a flight later, so he's sober."

My unofficially adoptive father had grown a thick beard since I last saw him—it had more silver than his hair and was neatly trimmed. It smelled like pine and tickled my ear and cheek as he squeezed me against himself in an affectionate side-hug.

I assessed myself and came up with an honest answer. "Actually, that might be a good idea."

"Brock!" Bast yelled. "You're flying Sunni's new boyfriend to the marina."

Brock held his hand up over his head, thumb extended, from where he sat on the couch with his sons Liam and Lennox, watching them play some shoot-'em-up video game.

"He's not my boyfriend!" I said, shoving at Bast's arm. "I just met him."

Bast just laughed. "Okay, honey. Keep telling

yourself that. The Badd Family Love Charm has struck again."

"It has not!"

Dru bumped me with her hip. "It has, honey. Better to just accept it and go with it."

Claire, one hand in front of her mouth, which was full of Doritos, shook her head, chewed and swallowed. "No! That's terrible advice! Fighting it and losing is where all the fun is."

Everyone went quiet all of a sudden, and I turned to see why.

My mouth went dry and my lady bits resumed their sinful suggestions.

Hayden in a suit. Oh dear Jesus crickets—that was a heck of an addictive phrase.

It fit him perfectly, the sleeves hugging his arms and shoulders, the trousers clinging to his thighs. He'd wet his hair and slicked it back. He was still wearing his glasses.

Fuck.

Fuck me.

I was speechless. He was so beautiful it was…well, it just wasn't okay. No one should be allowed to be that hot.

"Well that's fucking annoying," Duncan said, breaking the silence. "It looks better on him than it does me."

"Cuz you're ugly," Dane said. "And also, you're right, it does."

Duncan threw a peanut at his brother, nailing him in the forehead. "Shut up, loser."

I jolted myself out of my stupor and circled the island, stopping in front of him. I reached up and adjusted his tie, straightening and tightening it.

"You look…" I shook my head. "Like James Bond."

"I'm not British."

I laughed. "No? Really? I must have missed that."

He tugged at the sleeves of the jacket. "Also, James Bond wears tuxedos."

I smoothed his tie. "Okay, Mr. Literal. We should go. Uncle Brock is taking us because I've had enough to drink that I don't want to drive."

Brock pushed up off the couch, grabbed a thick sheepskin jacket from the back of the couch, and shrugged it on. "Come on, kids. I'll fly you over."

Hayden frowned. "Fly?"

I jerked a thumb at the windows overlooking the water, where Brock's twin-engine seaplane was tied up at the dock. "He's a pilot."

Hayden nodded. "Okay, then. I've never been on a seaplane before." A blink. "Well, I did the other day with Mom. This would be my second flight."

"Oh, you did the Misty Fjords tour?" Brock asked, preceding us out the back door and onto the deck.

"Yeah, it was amazing. So beautiful around here." He shoved his hands into his trouser pockets against the cold. "The kayaking was fun."

Brock barked a laugh. "Kayaking? In this weather?"

"Right?" Hayden laughed. "There were only a few people interested, and the guy wanted to cancel, but Mom talked him into it. It was a hell of a time, though, despite being cold. She wants to do a whale-watching tour tomorrow."

"I didn't think those excursions ran in the winter," he said. "Just the skiing and snowshoeing and all that shit."

"It was only offered by this one guy, I guess. The indoor ones were all sold out, so we picked one that wasn't, for obvious reasons." Hayden held my hand and helped me up into the airplane and then climbed in after me while Brock slid behind the controls.

Hayden fidgeted as we pulled away from the dock, taxied out to open water, and took off. It was a quick hop by air, and Uncle Brock touched down as close to the cruise ship docking area as he could get.

"I left my clothes there," Hayden said, apropos of nothing. "But I'll need to return the suit anyway."

For some reason, that made me feel better because it meant I was guaranteed to see him again.

"Yep," I said. "You'll just have to come by. And maybe bring your mom."

He laughed. "My mom and your family would be…interesting. I don't think she'd know what to make of you all."

For a moment, neither of us said anything; Brock was typing something on his phone and pretending not to hear us.

"I'd better go," Hayden said. "I can't thank you enough for this." He leaned forward, extending his hand toward Uncle Brock. "Mr. Badd, thank you so much for the ride. I appreciate it."

Brock snorted. "Mr. Badd? Jesus, dude. Call me Brock. And you're welcome."

They shook hands, and Hayden turned to me, seeming unsure how to handle the goodbye. Shake my hand? Hug me? Wave?

"I'll see you soon, Emerson. Thank you again for everything. And thank your brother for me. I forgot to and feel kind of like an ass about it."

Then, abruptly, he leaned forward and pulled me into a hug. "I feel like I've known you longer than a couple hours," he murmured in my ear, pulling away slowly.

"Me too," I whispered back. "Go dance with your mom, James Bond."

He shot me a grin that made my stomach do somersaults and my thong melt away. And then he was gone, jogging across the marina.

He was still wearing his sneakers, which should have looked weird with the suit but somehow didn't.

Brock arched an eyebrow at me as I crawled forward into the seat beside him. "For someone who never brings home strays, you sure picked an interesting one for your first time."

I rolled my eyes at him. "Shut up, Uncle B. He's

not a stray. It was an impulse thing. I couldn't let him let his mother down."

Brock just laughed. "Keep telling yourself that, Sunni-girl."

It was attraction, nothing more. Pure, unadulterated lust. He was hot and sexy and absolutely *nothing* like the guys I usually hooked up with in pretty much every way there was. I wanted to do bad things to him before he went back to Indiana with his mom.

That's all there was to it.

Seriously.

He had a life, I had a life, and they were nowhere near each other.

And besides, I'm not officially a Badd, so the Badd Family Love Charm didn't apply to me.

I put Hayden firmly out of my mind as we returned to the house, and I got back into the fun and games. I tuned out my heart, told my perpetually horny lady bits to shut up and take a nap, and focused on spending quality time with my family.

I didn't think about Hayden McCaffrey even once the rest of the night.

I won't go into the dream I had, but that's a different story.

SIX

Hayden

MOM WAS STANDING OUTSIDE THE MAIN BALLROOM OR whatever it was called, dressed to the nines in a black, sequined, floor-length gown that hugged her trim figure. She wore black ballet flats on her feet, and her hair was done up off of her neck. Her diamond earrings and necklace—a gift from Dad for her 65th birthday—shone at her ears and neck.

I swept up beside her, startling her. "Hey, Mom, sorry to keep you waiting."

She put her hand to her throat. "Hayden, you scared me!" She stepped back and assessed me. "Why, you look so handsome, Hayden! Is that a new suit?"

I grinned sheepishly. "It's borrowed. I did forget to pack formalwear."

Her eyebrows furrowed. "Borrowed? From whom?"

Oh boy. Here we go.

"Um...I made a friend when I was out, and her brothers are the same size as me."

Her eyebrows went the other direction, now, shooting up toward her hairline. "*Her* brothers? Who is she?" She peeked behind me. "Is she here?"

I chuckled. "No, Mom, she's not here." When Mom looked positively disappointed, I side-hugged her to myself. "But, they did invite us back. I forgot my clothes there, so I have to go back anyway, and they want me to bring you."

"They? Your new friend and her brothers?" She looked up at me with such hope that my stomach flipped.

"Something like that." I let go, took a half step away, and offered her my arm. "Shall we, my lady?"

"Why, yes, my good sir, we shall." Her eyes shone with her usual effusive spirit for the first time in months.

I knew her sorrow was still there and always would be, but for now, she was happy and having fun, and that was enough.

We danced, sipped champagne, and chatted with the captain and his first mate for a few minutes, ate a spectacular five-course meal and then danced some more.

By the time the evening was wearing down, Mom was visibly flagging.

"You about ready to call it, Mom?" I asked her.

She smiled, tired but happy. "I think I am. It's been

so much fun I don't want to stop, but the days when I could dance all night long are far behind me, I'm afraid."

"You? Dance all night?" I said, laughing.

She frowned up at me. "Why yes, Hayden, *me*. I used to cut quite a rug back in my younger days. Your father and I went dancing every weekend for years before you were born." Her eyebrows went up. "What, you think we sat around playing Scrabble and watching Jeopardy before you came along?"

I shrugged. "Yeah, sort of."

A sarcastic laugh. "Oh, son. You have *no* idea. Children don't tend to see their parents as people until they're much older."

"I think I'm starting to understand what you mean," I said as we exited the ballroom and headed for the elevator.

I walked her to her door—we'd changed the single berth to adjoining rooms.

Wait for it…

Wait for it…

She fidgeted with the sequins at her stomach, not looking at me. "I promised myself I wouldn't pry or push, but…"

I just laughed. "Her name is Emerson Day. She's a goalie for the University of Washington women's soccer team, which just won the national title. She's been unofficially adopted by a family that owns a few bars around here, but I don't know too much about it. She's beautiful and funny and way out of my league, but she seems to like me, I guess. Don't get too excited, though—she's going back to school, and we're going back to Indiana."

Mom sighed. "A mother can hope, right? Just let me dream, my sweet boy." She patted my cheek and then lifted on her toes to kiss my cheek. "Love you, Hayden. Thank you for a wonderful evening."

I kissed her forehead. "Love you, Mom. And thank *you* for letting me come with you on this cruise. I've had way more fun than I thought I would."

"Does a certain young lady factor into that at all, I wonder?" She smirked at me, humor glinting in her eyes.

I decided to go for honesty. "You know, it actually does. She's really cool, incredibly beautiful, and very funny. I don't see how it can go anywhere, though."

The humor in her eyes transitioned to motherly wisdom. "Hayden, my advice to you is to keep an open mind. Life is a funny old thing, and you never know what will happen. I know I've been a bit of a harpy about you getting married and all that, but I just want you to be happy."

"I'm not gonna lie and say it doesn't drive me a little bananas sometimes, but I know it comes from a place of love. I just…." I shrugged. "I really like Emerson. Her family is crazy, so just be forewarned. They're the most welcoming bunch I've ever met, but they're…a lot. I just…I don't know what can happen. I'm not into a vacation hookup. I want a real relationship. After Darcy, though, I'm just a little gun-shy, I suppose."

Mom's expression darkened. "That girl didn't deserve a single minute of your time and attention, Hayden. She never cared about you, only what she could get out of you."

I sighed and shook my head. "I know it, now. You and Dad tried to tell me, but I…" I rolled my eyes, hissing in disgust. "I saw what I wanted to see—a hot girl who wanted me."

Mom cupped my jaw. "The right woman is out there, Hayden. She's waiting for you. She's living her life and dreaming of you, too. So just keep an open mind when you spend time with this Emerson girl. And your eyes."

I leaned down and kissed the top of her head. "I'll do my best. Night, Mom."

"Night, son."

I let myself into my room and took off the suit, hung it on the hangar, and set it out with a request for housekeeping to have it dry-cleaned. I was too amped up to sleep, so I set up shop with my laptop in the bed and got some work done.

I was starting to fade after a few hours, so I closed the laptop and flicked on the TV, mindlessly scrolling through the channels to find something boring to put me to sleep. I settled on a nature documentary.

Thirty minutes in, my phone dinged. Confused as to who would be texting me—at all, let alone at 1:30 am—I grabbed it and slipped my glasses on.

> UNKNOWN: Please don't be creeped out, but this is Emerson. We never exchanged numbers. My cousin Jax is good with computers and found your phone number for me. I just wanted to see if you wanted to make plans for tomorrow.

> ME: You're a creep, you're a weirdo, what the hell are you doing here...

I saved her number and waited for her to text back. The gray dots danced, and then her message came through in a gray bubble.

> EMERSON: Good one, Thom Yorke. Seriously, I hope you're not weirded out.

> ME: No, not at all. Now, if you start referencing my credit score and my bank account number...

> EMERSON: Oh, he has the skills. Xavier Badd is my uncle, after all.

My brain exploded.

> ME: Wait, what? *That* Xavier Badd is your uncle? The guy I met earlier is THE Xavier Badd?

> EMERSON: I mean, how many people in the world do you think there are with that name?

ME: I suppose that's obvious but still mind-blowing. For someone in the tech field, Xavier Badd is, like, a god.

EMERSON: I'm literally LOLing rn. He and Aunt Low will be there tomorrow, too. Assuming you and your mom still want to come hang out with us crazies.

ME: Of course we do.

ME: So, real talk. Does it ever get weird that Harlow Grace is your aunt? Or is it old hat?

EMERSON: I mean, both. She's very down to earth, very real. I was just a little kid when I first met her, so in a sense, she's just always been Aunt Low to me, not really HARLOW GRACE, A-List movie star. But then, she's arranged private screenings of her movies for the whole family before they hit theaters. We got to see an unreleased director's cut of *By Dawn's Early Light*.

ME: No shit? That's crazy. I loved that movie. Mom, Dad, and I saw it in the theaters. Dad was a history nut and said it was amazingly accurate.

EMERSON: I suppose you should be prepared, though. Canary, the band, is my Uncle Canaan and Aunt Aerie. Eva Badd, Uncle Bax's wife, is a pretty famous artist. Myles and Lexie North are family, too.

ME: Thanks for the heads-up. Mom'll probably freak out a little when she meets Harlow. Or should that be Miss Grace?

EMERSON: If you call her Miss Grace, she'll just look at you like you have two heads. And then hug you and tell you to call her Low like everyone else does.

ME: I might just not tell Mom about any of the famous people until we get there. Might be safest.

I hesitated and then went for broke.

ME: Also, you should probably know that my mother is…well, she's been obsessed with me meeting someone, so she may get a little…forward, shall we say.

I deleted the message, rubbing my forehead. I didn't want to presume that Emerson felt the way I did. Or put pressure on her or make things weird.

EMERSON: Wanna know a pet peeve of mine?

ME: Yes.

EMERSON: When someone starts texting and the bubbles jump around for a long time like they're texting something long, and then…nothing. It drives me nuts. My curiosity goes haywire.

ME: Meaning, what did I type and erase?

EMERSON: Yes.

ME: I erased it because I didn't want to make anything weird.

EMERSON: It'll be weird if you don't tell me. I can be very persistent.

ME: It was just about my mom. When I told her I'd made a friend and the whole thing about borrowing a suit, she started seeing hearts everywhere, if you know what I mean. She's been on my case for years about meeting someone, so she sees things in everything.

EMERSON: That's adorable. She loves you and wants you to be happy.

ME: She does. But she can be very persistent as well. And she may be a little forward when she meets you.

EMERSON: What would have been weird?

ME: I'm not sure. Maybe I was overthinking things.

EMERSON: Maybe. Maybe not. We did have…a moment.

ME: I didn't mention the moment. But when I used the pronoun "she" about my new friend who helped me procure a suit…

EMERSON: I get it. My family gave me shit, too. Probably for similar reasons.

Seconds later, another gray bubble popped up, and the contents made my breath come short.

EMERSON: I can't stop thinking about our moment.

ME: Same.

EMERSON: I've never brought anyone to the house before.

ME: No? No one? Ever?

EMERSON: Nope. I didn't date much in high school. I was too focused on soccer. I still am, TBH. HBU?

ME: Um, well…similar, but also different. I didn't date much (meaning, at all) in high school, but that was more of an involuntary thing, lol. Pretty sure if you looked up INCEL during my high school years, you'd have found a pic of me.

EMERSON: I find that hard to believe.

ME: Thanks, but for real. I was in the computer club, the chess club, the D&D club, and ran sound for the drama department. The cool kid I was not. Big glasses, terrible taste in clothes, braces until I was a junior, and hadn't discovered weightlifting yet, so weighed about a hundred pounds soaking wet and fully clothed.

EMERSON: So when was the glow up?

ME: Yesterday, when I put on the suit and you looked at me like you did.

EMERSON: You're making me blush.

ME: You want the real story?

EMERSON: Duh. Of course.

ME: Freshman year at Purdue. Homecoming. There was a girl in several of my classes that I had a crush on. Sienna Daughtry. I spent a month and a half working up the courage to ask her out. She told me, and I quote: "I may be a nerd, but I don't date nerds. Get some contacts and lift weights. Maybe someone will actually want you."

EMERSON: She said that? To your face? Out loud?

ME: Yup.

EMERSON: What a colossal cunt.

ME: Um.

EMERSON: I can use that word. You can't. Just so we're clear.

ME: I would never.

EMERSON: So let me guess...you got contacts and lifted weights?

ME: I did. I went to an expensive salon and got a fancy haircut, got contacts, and joined a gym. Hired a personal trainer and told him to denerdify me. Spent a year killing myself in the gym, put on muscle, and gained confidence.

EMERSON: And Sienna?

ME: Funny thing is gaining confidence made me realize I didn't have a crush on her, I just thought she was hot.

EMERSON: An important distinction, to be sure. So, then. Did your hard work pay off?

ME: Lol, yes. I dated another girl from my physics class for a few months.

I'm probably embarrassing myself by admitting this, but she was my first girlfriend. As a sophomore in college.

EMERSON: Not embarrassing at all. But in the interest of quid pro quo, I'll tell you something embarrassing. I've never had a boyfriend.

ME: Never?

EMERSON: I don't date. I've been hyper focused on soccer and my degree. That's not to say I don't talk to guys, but I just don't get into relationships.

ME: Think you ever will?

EMERSON: Yeah, I will. When I meet the right person at the right time.

EMERSON: Was she your only serious relationship?

ME: No. I dated a girl named Darcy for a year and a half. This was after college.

EMERSON: Why'd it end? You don't have to tell me. You can tell me I'm being nosy.

ME: It's fine. It's hard to admit because I feel like an idiot, but she was never with me for me. I'd just started at the company I work for now. I was making good money, really good. I'd just bought my car and a condo. Met Darcy at the gym, and we hit it off. Things progressed. I had money, a lot of it, and for the first time in my life, a beautiful girl to spend it on.

EMERSON: Oh boy. I think I see where this is going.

ME: Probably, yeah. I took her on expensive dates. Bought her jewelry. I even paid off her car loan for her birthday. I did it because I wanted to. I liked doing it. But then for Christmas that year, I got her tickets to a show she'd been talking about. A band she loved. They were in Indianapolis just after Christmas so I got the tickets and a hotel room.

EMERSON: That's a great gift.

ME: I mean, I thought so.

EMERSON: But she didn't I take it?

ME: Not exactly. She was like, Indianapolis? What about somewhere cool? Like LA, or New York, or Paris. Also, a concert is not an appropriate Christmas gift for our first Christmas together.

EMERSON: How ungrateful. What did she want?

ME: Bling. Bigger earrings. A tennis bracelet. That kind of shit. I tried to see past it, but I just couldn't. So I ran an experiment.

EMERSON: Do tell.

ME: I stopped the extravagant gifts and fancy dates to high-end see and be seen restaurants and just sort of dated her. Normal stuff. Not, like, Applebee's, but not the caliber she was used to. Just to see what she'd do.

EMERSON: Hey now, don't knock Applebee's. I go there all the time.

Mozzarella sticks are my cheat day special.

EMERSON: So what did she do?

ME: Cheated on me, dumped me, and told me a man is only as good as his dick and his wallet, and she was only with me for my wallet.

EMERSON: No.

ME: Yes.

EMERSON: She didn't say that.

ME: She absolutely did.

EMERSON: That is fucking WILD. What a shallow, horrible, cunty piece of shit.

ME: It made me question my taste in women. Like, if the two women I've dated have turned out to be absolutely horrible, then what does that say about me?

EMERSON: Have you dated anyone since?

ME: Nope.

EMERSON: I promise I'm not a vain, shallow, greedy cunt.

ME: Please stop using that word. LOL it makes me VERY uncomfortable.

EMERSON: I do not use that word lightly, Hayden. And those two women deserve it for the way they treated you. That's not okay.

ME: Thanks. It didn't feel great. Also, I know you're not like that.

EMERSON: I mean, I hope that comes across.

ME: Loud and clear, Emerson. Truly.

ME: Especially about money. I came from…well, nothing very good. Delia's family took me in and provided for me. Gave me a home. A family. They'd have paid for my college if I let them—I got scholarships and grants because I wasn't going to allow that, not after all they've done. The Badds have done very, very well for themselves, but they worked their asses off for all of it, and I have never taken them for granted. To me, that girl saying a man is only as good as his dick and his wallet is just disgusting and unforgivable.

ME: If I'm being honest, it made me insecure for a long time. About money, and about my…self. She didn't say anything outright negative about my body, but the implication was clear.

EMERSON: Again, not okay. That's not something a man can change. And it shouldn't matter. It DOESN'T matter.

EMERSON: I'm gonna be straight with you, Hayden, and you may not respect me as much after this, but the truth is that when I say I don't date, I mean I just hook up. I'm not talking a different guy every night or anything. I guess my point is that I've been with a variety of different kinds of men, and not once have I ever been like, that dick isn't good enough for me. There IS good sex and not good sex, but for me, that's NEVER been about size.

EMERSON: Who made it weird now?

EMERSON: I'm freaking out. I shouldn't have said any of that.

ME: Why would I respect you less, Emerson? That would make me as shallow and shitty as Sienna and Darcy.

EMERSON: You're different than anyone I've talked to before. IDK why. I guess I just...I want you to like who I am. It's scary being this honest, and if you want the 100% truth, I'm not sure why I'm saying any of it.

ME: I do like who you are. You handled my social anxiety freak out and didn't make me feel stupid for it. You're so far out of my league it's not even funny, and yet here you are being vulnerable with me. It means a lot.

EMERSON: Out of your league? That's the dumbest thing I ever heard. You're smart, successful, stupid hot, funny, and you love your mama. Who's out of whose league?

ME: Maybe we just agree there are no leagues?

EMERSON: I like the sound of that. Just two people...

EMERSON: Who like each other?

ME: I know I do.

EMERSON: Are we crazy? I go back to Seattle, and you go back to Indiana.

ME: I said that to mom. She told me to just keep an open mind because life is a funny old thing and you never know what will happen.

EMERSON: I like her already.

ME: I think she's amazing, but I'm biased. I mean, she's a little nuts, but who isn't?

EMERSON: I mean, you met my family. Well, some of them.

EMERSON: How was the dance?

ME: Great. Mom had a great time, and so did I. I can't thank you enough.

EMERSON: You already have. It wasn't a big deal.

ME: It was to me, and even more so to Mom. So, thank you.

EMERSON: You're welcome.

EMERSON: So, if you and your mom are up for it, Uncle Brock can pick you guys up tomorrow around five.

ME: We'll be there. Should we bring anything? Dress code?

EMERSON: Dress code? Don't make me laugh. It's a family get together. Just show up. Please don't bring anything except yourselves.

ME: Ok. Showing up empty handed goes against Mom's religion, so I make no promises on her behalf.

> **EMERSON: I'm excited to see you again.**
>
> **ME: Same. I really want to see more of you.**

After I sent it, I realized how it may have sounded and my finger hovered over the unsend button. I left it, though. It felt risky, more forward than I was typically comfortable with.

But then, maybe it was time to take risks. Maybe it would be safe to take risks with her. It certainly felt like it.

Didn't mean I wasn't squirming with anxiety, though.

> **EMERSON: You want to see more of me?**
>
> **ME: Yes. A LOT more.**

I gulped, feeling my heart pound and my palms sweat.

A very long pause ensued, during which I thought about typing a million different take-backs and excuses and stopped myself.

A photo popped up in the thread.

Emerson, bathed in a dim light. Laying down in bed, lush red hair splayed out on the pillow around her face. She was topless, with one arm barred across her breasts, hiding her nipples with her forearm, the rest of her lush, pale, soft breasts spilling above and below her forearm.

My mouth went dry and my cock turned hard as a rock.

ME: Holy shit, Emerson.

EMERSON: call me Em.

EMERSON: And for the record, I'd like to see more of you, too.

ME: Not much of a selfie taker, but...

I was already in bed in just my boxer briefs, so, before I could talk myself out of it, I held the phone at arm's length and snapped a shot of me. I flexed my abs, propping one knee up, the other leg stretched out.

What the fuck am I doing?

It wasn't until after I sent it to her, heart pounding a mile a minute, that I realized one minor issue. The... um...evidence of my reaction to her hot-as-fuck selfie was on full display. No zoom needed.

Mortification blazed through me, along with a massive and bitter dose of insecurity.

EMERSON: Hayden...

ME: Emerson?

EMERSON: You played fast and loose with the truth, hotshot.

ME: How so?

EMERSON: You said Darcy alluded to you lacking in the packing department.

ME: She did.

EMERSON: Is she blind? Asking for a friend.

ME: No...

EMERSON: You're sexy AF, Hayden. I'm sweating over here.

ME: Your own fault.

EMERSON: How so?

ME: The pic you sent. That's what you do to me.

EMERSON: I've never done this before. Sent pix to a guy.

ME: Me neither. To girls, obv.

ME: You're beautiful, Em. Words aren't my strong suit. But you're literally the most beautiful woman I've ever seen.

EMERSON: You're doing pretty well from where I'm sitting. Also, you ain't so bad yourself.

EMERSON: That was lame. Let me try again.

EMERSON: I've never been attracted to a guy the way I am to you. On all levels.

ME: Had to one up me, didn't you?

EMERSON: I'm a competitive athlete. Sorry not sorry.

EMERSON: This convo has my heart racing.

ME: My heart is pounding. It has been. I didn't realize how visible… things…were when I sent that. I almost had a heart attack.

ME: Mainly because when I said that what Darcy said left me insecure for a while, I meant I still am.

EMERSON: You absolutely should not be. At fucking all.

ME: Not sure how to react to that, but… thanks?

EMERSON: I could text you all night. But we probably shouldn't.

ME: Probably not.

ME: I want to see you. I want to take you out.

EMERSON: I'd like that. A lot.

ME: We probably can't go on a date now, huh?

EMERSON: Lol no prob not. But I'll see you tomorrow.

ME: I guess that'll have to do.

ME: At least I have your picture. BRB, spending the rest of the night staring at it. And wishing I had the real thing here with me.

EMERSON: Thought you weren't good with words.

ME: So did I. I'm just being honest. I don't want to presume or be too forward.

EMERSON: It's not. I like honesty. Good or bad, always be honest.

ME: I will be. And same.

EMERSON: The truth is, right now, I'm flustered and turned on. But things start early around here, so I should go.

ME: I don't want to keep you up.

> EMESON: Funny, I DO want to keep you
> UP.
>
> ME: Not helping. Because you do.
>
> EMERSON: Pics or it didn't happen.

Nervous, hands shaking, I took another selfie, this time intentionally putting the evidence of my arousal center frame.

I sent it.

Instead of a text, she sent another shot of herself.

This time, she had the sheet pulled up to just barely cover her nipples, showing a healthy expanse of pale pink-brown areolae, and she had her leg pulled up out of the sheet so it pooled between her thighs, covering her core, revealing the fullness of her thick, smooth, powerful thigh.

> ME: How far are we taking this, Em?
>
> EMERSON: No idea.
>
> ME: How about I give you my hot take.
>
> EMERSON: Please do.
>
> ME: As much as I want this to keep going, as much as part of me selfishly wants to see all of you, I also really want to see you in person. I want to, I don't know, save it, I guess? Does that make sense?
>
> EMERSON: It makes SO much sense and matches what I was thinking.
>
> ME: So, as much as I don't want to, how about we say goodnight?

> EMERSON: I agree. Good night, Hayden. See you tomorrow.
>
> ME: Goodnight, Em. I'm glad Jax hacked my number for you.
>
> EMERSON: Me too.

I hearted the message so there would be a response but left the conversation temporarily ended.

It took a very long time to fall asleep, and when I did, I dreamed of Emerson. In my dream, she was naked beneath a white sheet, and I couldn't quite make out her features, only getting teasing glimpses of her curves.

I woke up late, hard as a rock, aching.

I took a cold shower and forced my mind to think about work instead of Emerson's naked body.

I only partially succeeded.

SEVEN

Emerson

I HAD COCK ON THE BRAIN.

Shut up—I have a high libido, alright? I like sex. I enjoy it. I pursue it. I always want more of it. Unlike a lot of other women I know, I'm pretty good at keeping emotions out of it—I'm sure there's a psychological reason for that—probably something to do with my father abandoning me.

My usual M.O. for hooking up was pretty simple. I'm a confident, attractive girl—the boys come to me. I'd study at the library or a coffee shop, and inevitably some cute or hot guy would sidle along and chat me up, and I'd let them think they were charming me into bed. It's not manipulative or deceitful or anything…it's just lazy. Let them do the work. Play up their ego and in the process they play up yours. They'll suggest going somewhere else, and you coyly agree. Before any shenanigans ensue, you set the expectation—you're not looking for anything, we don't need to exchange numbers or socials. I won't be there in the morning. Yada yada yada. Get what you need and get out.

It's worked throughout college. I've never felt guilty about it, I've never apologized for it, and I will not. A dude acts the same way and his bros slap his back and dap him up or whatever they call it, *yeah, champ, ugha-ugha-ugha*. Women do it, and we're sluts. Fuck that. I reject that double standard and fuck anyone who thinks otherwise.

I've never wanted an emotional connection. And before you go crying double standards about my conversation with Hayden, let me explain something. I don't expect anyone to pay for me. I don't accept gifts. I make it crystal clear we're just hooking up, so don't get cozy and don't get any ideas. I recognize the worth of the men I spend my time with—they're human beings with faults and qualities, dreams and fears, all of that, just like me. I'm just not interested in getting to know them on that level. I'm interested in some quick, consensual physical fun.

All that said, I've been on a hiatus for the last several months. It started involuntarily—midterms kicked my ass, and then the soccer season started ramping up to finals and I had to focus on my grades and my game, no time for boys. And then, after a few weeks of involuntary celibacy, I started noticing some acute changes occurring.

The thought of meeting some rando and getting naked with him for a few hours of sex interspersed with desultory, surface conversation didn't sound fun anymore. I was still swamped with school and soccer, so there also wasn't time. And the free time I did have, chasing a hookup was not very high on my priority list for the first time since I began exploring my sexuality at sixteen with Nicholas Moriarty in the back of his shit-brown Volvo.

And now, back home for the first time since summer break, it's been almost six months since I last had sex. I jilled off plenty, of course, because my sex drive didn't suddenly dry up.

And then I met Hayden McCaffrey.

He wasn't a hookup. He didn't have to spell it out for me to understand it. It's written between the lines in the things he's told me. As far as I can tell, he's had two girlfriends, both of whom fucked him over royally, epically, and spectacularly, doing a hell of a number on his self-esteem in the process. Yet despite that, he put himself out there with me and took some risks that I know damn well had to be scary as fuck. He showed me himself. In this context, I mean that in the personal, emotional sense.

And then…he showed me himself physically.

And now I have cock on the brain.

Specifically, his.

Lying in bed with the sunrise spraying orange and scarlet rays across the Passage and into my room, I had my phone in one hand, his selfie on the screen, and my hand on my belly, my fingers tucked under the elastic of my panties.

I was trying to talk myself out of masturbating to him. It wasn't working.

He was sinfully hot. I mean, I'd had an inkling he was ripped—I got a pretty good glimpse yesterday. But shirtless, in nothing but a pair of tight gray boxer briefs, hard as fucking rock? I didn't stand a chance. He wasn't a beefcake like Bax, Bast, and Zane. Honestly, he reminded me of Uncle Xavier. He had that same unawareness of his attractiveness that wasn't humble, merely simply unaware. Couple that with how easy it was to talk to him, how intelligent he was, and how forthcoming he was with someone he just met about deep vulnerabilities? Sinfully hot.

The hard, flat, sculpted pecs, rippling six-pack carved out of marble, the thin dusting of dark hair leading down beneath his boxers, the powerful legs, and those deep, expressive green eyes? I was a goner.

But then…there was his penis. Bulging against the boxers, straining against the elastic waistband, it was on display in a way that left very little to the imagination, and I have a hell of a visual imagination. Long, thick, and straight, in the photo it was angled to the left a bit, hugged by the fabric. The tip of it was *this close* to protruding from his underwear.

And suddenly, I was feeling each individual second of the last six months of celibacy.

I'd nearly sent him a fully topless photo. Last second, I chickened out. I still have the pic on my phone because, honestly, I looked really damn good, if I do say so myself.

And do you have any idea how much of an ego boost it is, seeing that kind of a monster erection on a guy and knowing *you* put it there?

I flipped my phone face down on my belly and clapped my hands over my face, muffling my squeal of frustration.

He wanted to "save" taking things further. If he'd even hinted, I'd have sent him the topless shot. Shit, I'd have gotten on FaceTime and gone way beyond that.

But he wanted to save it.

He didn't want the first time he saw me naked to be digital. Impersonal. He wanted to savor the full experience of getting to know me.

That told me everything I needed to know about how he viewed sex. It was personal to him. It meant something. It wasn't something he shared easily or with just anyone.

And for the first time in my life, I felt…weird, shall we say, about my sexual history. Not tawdry, exactly, or guilty, or ashamed. I just…I guess because he's so different from anyone I've ever met and my attraction to him goes way beyond the mere physical, I want it to be different with him. I know he'd never hook up with me and then be cool with me being gone when he woke up.

For the first time in my life, I was faced with a terrifying fact: I had real feelings for a man, and I wanted our physical relationship to match that, to mean something.

And I was scared that, despite what he said, he did think less of me because, so far, I've never treated sex as anything super important, just a natural, normal part of life.

It was a hell of a quandary to be in.

I closed my eyes, hands covering my face. I was desperately horny, wildly aroused. I needed to get off in the worst way, and with that picture of Hayden, I could take care of myself in two seconds flat.

But it didn't feel right. He would never know. But I would.

And somehow, I just knew he was probably experiencing something similar. Maybe he was lying in his bed on the cruise ship, looking at the pics I sent him and trying not to jerk off to them because he didn't want to use me that way. He wanted to save it.

"Fuck," I grumbled, scrubbing my face. "Be different, Emerson. Try something new. Take a risk."

Talking to myself out loud was an embarrassing habit of mine—I had to talk myself into things quite a lot. When I jogged out onto the pitch and took my place between the posts, I'd give myself a pep talk out loud. Tell myself I was the best keeper there was and that I could stop anything that came my way, this was *my* net and nothing got past me. I'd do it before big exams or whenever I had a big decision to make or faced something scary.

I picked up my phone, fully intending to swipe away the photo, get up, and do something productive to get my mind off of Hayden McCaffrey, incubus extraordinaire.

Instead, my traitorous fingers swiped to the second pic he sent. The one that had his big, lovely cock center frame. Barely hidden by his underwear. If anything, the thin layer of fabric only made me hornier.

I saw myself in bed with him, both of us half-dressed. I'd touch him over his underwear first. Just trace the length of him, watching him react—maybe he'd hiss, or groan, eyes half-lidded, stomach flexed. And then I'd hook my fingers into the waistband and tug the material away, and it would straighten, unfurling, and I'd see it in all its bare, rigid glory.

Wrap my hand around it. It would be warm and soft, yet hard and thick. I'd slide my hand down, and he'd buck upward. Precum would bead at the tip. Maybe I'd lick it away. Keep him wondering…would I give him my mouth? Or keep toying with him with my hands?

My fingers slipped inside my underwear. I was soaked, positively dripping with need. My fingers touched my clit, and I jolted, gasping, as arousal seized me. I stared at the picture and imagined him arching his back off the bed as I caressed his length.

Fingers pressing and circling, my hips began to

buck as I neared the edge, imagining Hayden reaching that cusp with me…

Literal seconds before I came, my phone suddenly warbled, and Hayden's name popped up on the screen.

He was Facetiming me.

Fuck it—risk it for the biscuit, right?

Crazy, maybe, but I answered it. All I had on were my panties, the sheets and blankets kicked away in my sleep and then in my arousal. I was panting, flushed, and so close to orgasm it wasn't even funny.

Yet, I swiped to answer. Like a fucking lunatic.

"Em, hi." He was in bed, the sunrise making his skin glow and his muscles stand out in sharp relief.

"Uh, h-hey?" I gasped, trying not to sound out of breath. "What's…what's up? It's early."

He swallowed hard. "Yeah, sorry. I'm an early riser. Did I wake you up?"

I shook my head, carefully keeping the camera trained on my face. "No, I'm an early riser, too."

He scrubbed at his hair, frowning. "I woke up thinking about you. About talking to you last night." He passed a hand down his face. "About the pictures you sent me."

"Yeah?" I reached down and tugged the flat sheet up over my chest and let the angle widen a bit. "Honestly, same."

He seemed surprised. "You too?"

I smiled at him. "Yeah, Hayden, me too."

He swallowed hard. "I…" he sighed, hunting for

either words or courage or both. "I dreamed about you. Woke up, um, all…uhh, hot and bothered." He paused, shifting in the bed. "This is difficult. I, um. I'm calling you because I just…I'm going a little crazy. I don't know what I'm doing or why I'm telling you this. Fuck. I almost…you know, um, took care of things. Thinking about you. Looking at the photos you sent. But I didn't. Because it just…it didn't feel right. And I thought you should know. Maybe I'm an idiot. God, I'm really an idiot, aren't I?" He closed his eyes and covered them with a hand, groaning. "This was stupid."

"Hayden." I cut in, my voice pitched low.

He moved his hand and opened his eyes. "Yeah?"

"You're not an idiot. Not at all. Far from it."

"Who calls a girl he's interested in and tells her that?"

"Hayden." I swallowed hard. "You wanna know what I was doing when you called?"

He rubbed his face again and then let out a long sigh and met my eyes through the screen. "Yes. I would like to know."

"What you *almost* did, I w*as* doing." Cheeks flaming, it was my turn to hide behind my hand, embarrassed and terrified. "I was masturbating and thinking of you, Hayden. In fact, I was literally about to come."

His silence was stunned. "Em…" He frowned, blinked, shook his head. "For real?"

"Yeah, for real. Can't you tell? Flushed cheeks, out of breath, and in bed?"

"I'm sorry I interrupted."

I laughed. "Hayden, god. I answered, didn't I?"

"You were thinking about me?"

"Looking at your photo and thinking about you and touching myself."

"I thought maybe if I called you, talking to you would...I don't know. I just wanted to talk to you. See you. See more of you. Be alone with you."

"I'm glad you called." It came out in a whisper.

Nerves jangling, I pulled the phone up and away, showing him myself covered in the sheet. The sun was high enough now to bathe my room in bright light, turning the thin white flat sheet almost see-through. My erect nipples pressed against the sheet, and it pooled between my thighs, draping over my body. I may as well have been naked, but wasn't. Turned on all the more, I held his eyes. Deliberately, I let him see my hand steal under the sheet, moving beneath the fabric. Awkwardly, one-handed, trying not to let the sheet slip, I wriggled out of my underwear, pulled them out from beneath the sheet, and showed them to him. Red lace, visibly soaked at the crotch. I tossed them aside and slipped my hand beneath the sheet again.

"Em, god. Holy shit."

"Don't leave me hanging, Hayden."

He mirrored my action, removing his boxers while carefully not revealing anything. Like me, the sun bathed his room in light and turned the sheet almost see-through, and when the sheet settled back down, it draped over his cock. The sheet being thinner than underwear material, it left even less to the imagination, showing me all but the veins.

I swallowed hard. "God, Hayden. I want you."

"Em, I've…I've never felt like this. I want you so fucking bad." He covered himself with his hand, not quite grasping, more just cupping.

"It's okay, Hayden. Do it. I want you to."

"I've never done this before. On the phone or whatever, I mean."

"Neither have I." I slid my hand down my belly and settled it between my thighs. Crooked my finger inside myself—there was an audible squelch, and I gasped. "Hayden…"

He slipped his hand under the sheet and grasped himself; I wanted to see. No sheet in the way.

He groaned. My pussy spasmed, and I touched my clit with my middle finger, whimpering, my eyes fixed firmly on Hayden on the screen.

He was doing the same—watching me, rapt and agonized. His fist moved faster, sliding up and down and up and down beneath the sheet. My finger pressed and circled faster as well, matching his pace.

He let out a long, low groan, shoulders pushing into the mattress as his hips lifted. I arched off the bed, heedless of the fact that the sheet was sliding inexorably downward. Cool air bathed my breasts and my nipples, already hard, turned to diamonds. I felt his gaze on my chest, and I loved it. I wished it was his hands, his mouth.

"Hayden. I'm gonna come," I murmured.

"Ahhh, god, me too. Fuck, you're beautiful." His voice was low and rough and ragged.

"Let me see you. Please, Hayden. I need to see all of you."

He kicked away the sheet, and now he was naked, bared to me, and holy fuck and Jesus crickets. His cock was perfect. If only it was my hands on it instead of his, or my mouth. My pussy wrapped around it. I settled for watching him stroke himself with rough, quick jerks. His shredded abs were tensed into hard blocks, pulsing and shifting as he arched into his fist.

My sheet slipped away as I spasmed, legs kicking as my orgasm ramped up, reaching the crest. "Hayden!"

"Fuck—oh god. Em...Emerson. I'm—I can't—"

"Let me see. I want to watch you come."

"Now—I'm—I'm coming, Em." His eyes squeezed shut and he threw his head back and his hand blurred on his cock, and then slowed to short hard jerks.

Oh, fuck. The fat, round head of his cock was almost purple from the force of his grip, and then he came, spurting up onto his belly in a thick white stripe of come. He came again and again, his groans ragged and hoarse.

"Hayden, fuck, that's hot. Watch me, now."

I cried out, then, jackknifing forward and then spasming backward as my orgasm claimed me, ripping through me. I almost dropped the phone but caught it and held it back up, wanting him to see, to not miss a moment of how he was making me feel.

"Wish I was there," Hayden said, panting. "Wish that was me making you come."

"You are. It *is* you. It's all for you."

"Hottest, sexiest thing I've ever seen. Ever done. You, like this. Us, sharing this." He paused to catch his breath. "You're so fucking gorgeous, Emerson. You take my breath away."

For some reason, my eyes burned. Stupid. I don't cry. "Hayden, god."

"Hey, Emerson…what? I…I'm sorry, I didn't mean to make you cry. Jesus." His voice was so concerned that my eyes flew open, and tears slid down.

"No, no. It's—it's…you didn't. Well, you did, but good tears. You just…you make me feel…" I swiped at my face and then winced. "My fingers smell like pussy, now," I said, laughing.

"You say that like it's a bad thing." He huffed a laugh. "I'm a mess, too. I've got come all over myself and nothing to clean up with."

I brought the phone closer to my face. Held his eyes. "I'm really, *really* glad you called, Hayden. This was *so* hot."

"I am too." A pause. "Em, you didn't finish. How do I make you feel? Why were you crying?"

"Seen," I whispered. "Beautiful. You make me feel seen and beautiful and desired in a way I…I've never felt before." I laughed, wiped at my face again. "Not all tears are bad. And I promise, I don't usually cry after sex. This has never happened before."

"It's okay, as long as I didn't say anything to upset you."

"God no. Just the opposite."

Hayden barked a laugh. "I just had phone sex. Or video sex. Whatever you wanna call it."

I laughed, and the laugh made me snort, which is my most embarrassing secret. I clapped my hand over my mouth and nose, blushing. "That's so fucking embarrassing."

He laughed, a true belly laugh. "It's not—it's fucking adorable. And I'm going to make it my mission to make you laugh-snort as much as possible."

"It's not adorable, it's horrible and embarrassing."

"Random question, but are you ticklish?" His deep green eyes sparkled with humor, mischief.

Have I ever felt this comfortable with anyone? This fast, or ever?

"Not telling," I said.

"I'll find out." The humor faded. "When can we be alone together?"

I shook my head. "It's gonna be tricky with all the parties going on. I'm not, like, expected at all of them, but I haven't been back since summer so I want to see everyone as much as I can."

"We have a few excursions lined up, still, too. We have one this morning, after breakfast." He passed his hand through his hair and then stopped, rolling his eyes with a wince. "Oh god, gross. Wrong hand."

I spluttered a laugh, which turned to a snort, and then I clapped my hand over my face again, still laughing and now snort-laughing and unable to stop. It was contagious because now he was laughing too.

When we recovered, both of us panting and gasping, I sat up in bed a little. "I really like you a lot, Hayden McCaffrey. And I promise we'll get time alone. Where and when I don't know. But we will."

"I'm not leaving Ketchikan till we do," he said, serious now. "I should go, though. I really have to shower now, and I'm meeting Mom downstairs for breakfast in an hour."

"I should go, too. Wish I could shower with you."

"Same." He frowned. "Is this crazy, Em? You and me? Like, it just sort of went zero to a hundred."

I shrugged. "If it is crazy, then I'm crazy, and I'm okay with that."

On a whim, I posed, bringing my arms together tight against my sides, pushing my boobs together, lifting my chest high, making what I hoped was a sultry expression, and took a still from the FaceTime. Swiped and tapped into messages and sent it to him, along with the one from last night I never sent.

"You want me to have to go again, Em?" he asked, his voice husky and low. "Because holy shit, woman. I watched you take that, and it was still magical."

"I almost sent that other one last night, but I chickened out."

"I can't believe this is happening to me," he murmured as if to himself. "Someone as beautiful and talented and amazing as you...fuck, how'd I get so lucky?"

"Funny thing is," I said, "I feel the same way about you."

He laughed. "That's crazy, but okay."

I frowned at him. "Hey, no. It's not crazy. You're sexy, smart as fuck, successful, and dedicated to your mother, which, in case you've missed it, is a huge thing for me. You're amazing, Hayden. I got lucky, too. So don't let me hear that self-deprecating shit, okay?"

He blinked at the camera. "Wow. I..." a sigh. "Okay, I hear you. I do."

"I should hunt those bitches down and beat them up," I muttered. "They messed with your head."

"Yeah, they did." He went to mess with his hair again and stopped. "I'm working through it, but it's not a fast process, you know?"

"I'll just have to undo what they did," I said. "And in that vein...Hayden McCaffrey, I want you to know that you have an absolutely exquisite cock. Truly. Why do you think I was masturbating when you called?"

He covered his face with the crook of his arm, hiding his vivid blush. "I have no idea how to respond to that, Em."

"You don't have to. I just wanted you to know. It's

beautiful and perfectly proportioned. And I cannot *wait* to get my hands on it. And my mouth. And my pussy."

He moved his arm to look at the camera. "Fuck, Emerson. Holy shit." He bit his lip. "Your tits make me so hard." A pause, his voice dropping to a whisper. "I want to taste you. I want to eat your pussy till you can't breathe." He laughed, not out of humor but more in disbelief. "I can't believe I just said that."

"Hayden, fucking hell. We have to stop, or we'll just keep doing this. We both have things to do."

"I know. But I don't want to. I have the most gorgeous, sexiest woman in the fucking world naked on FaceTime with me. Where else would I want to be?"

"In my bed with me, fucking me six ways to Sunday?" I suggested.

He laughed. "Well, yeah, that, obviously, would be…I don't know. I don't have the words. That would be heaven."

"For me too."

He groaned. "But you are right. We have to go."

"Bye, Hayden McCaffrey. See you on the docks at five."

"See you, Emerson Day."

I hung up first. Tossed the phone aside, palmed my face, rolled to put my face in the pillow, and screamed, kicking my feet.

That boy is fucking dangerous.

And I'm in trouble.

EIGHT

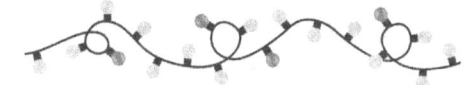

Hayden

S NOWFLAKES SWIRLED IN THE AIR, STIRRED BY A RESTLESS wind coming off the passage. The sky was gray and leaden, the color of pewter. Beside me, Mom held the black rope handles of the gift bag she insisted on—inside was not a bottle of wine or whiskey, but a humungous three-wick holiday scented candle and a kit for mulling spiced wine.

"I'm not showing up to a holiday party empty-handed, Hayden McCaffrey," she'd said, as expected.

I had told her it was just a get-together over the holidays, but that didn't matter to Mom. I hadn't told her anyone famous would be there because Mom would most likely freak out. Better to just blindside her with it.

A buzzing became audible, and then after another few moments, the buzzing became a twin-engine seaplane, bright yellow with a black stripe on the trailing edge of each wing and the vertical stabilizer. The aircraft settled gently onto the water down the middle of the Passage and then taxied toward us, coming to a gentle halt at the end of the dock just a few feet away. Spotting Brock behind the controls, I waved and pressed my fingers against the small of Mom's back.

"This is us," I said, hiking the bag containing the dry-cleaned suit on my shoulder.

Brock waved as we approached. I opened the door and helped Mom in and then slid in after her, putting Mom in the seat beside Brock and taking the rear bench for myself. Brock handed us both headsets and then helped Mom get buckled in while I handled my seatbelt. Moments later, we were airborne and banking around.

Once he had the seaplane on the correct trajectory, he grinned at Mom. "Evening, Mrs. McCaffrey. How are you this fine evening?"

Mom held the gift bag on her lap and returned the smile. "I'm doing just wonderful, thank you. But you must call me Kaye."

"My name is Brock Badd." He indicated the bag on her lap. "I hope that's not a gift."

Mom lifted her chin. "It most certainly is. I have never once shown up to the home of a stranger without a gift, and I don't plan to start now, young man."

Brock snickered. "Yes ma'am. Understood."

Mom nodded.

"That's what I told Em," I said. "Showing up empty-handed goes against her religion."

"We aren't imposing, are we?" Mom asked. "I wouldn't want to feel like I'm crashing a family affair."

Brock just laughed. "Not even remotely, Kaye. It's just a big ol' shindig, and we're always happy to have new faces around. Makes a good time even better."

I reached up and squeezed Mom's shoulder. "Told you, Mom. It'll be fun." To Brock, I said, "So, is this the whole crew, or what?"

He nodded. "Just about, I think. Poppy and Errol won't be showing up till later on; their flight gets in at…eight, I think? They're coming from New Zealand. One of the cousins is picking them up from the docks since by then all the adults will be in no shape to drive."

It was a short flight, and we were touching down and tying up at the private dock less than ten minutes from taking our seats. Brock helped my mother down and then offered her his arm, charming her and making her laugh as they ascended the long, shallow steps leading up to the house.

The house was lit up, glowing a soft, inviting yellow, and the murmur of voices and peals of laughter echoed off the water. As we approached the back deck, Christmas music floated to us—Bing Crosby crooning about a white Christmas. On the deck, low rectangular tables featured flickering gas fires set within beds of glass beads and blocks, and tall propane space heaters stood guard by the accordion sliding doors, which were open a few feet, letting out the noise and heat and letting in cold air. A handful of men were clustered around one of the fireplace tables, sipping whiskey and puffing on cigars, barking laughter overlapping with chatter. A swarm of kids ranging from perhaps ten or eleven to young teenagers were gathered at the top of the hill on the far of the house, bundled up in snow gear, each one clutching a saucer sled. The hill was magnificent for sledding, a long, steep slope. The hill had been groomed for sledding, too, the snow packed down and sprayed with water to make it extra slick, steps dug into the snow beside the run with a thick rope as a guide rail. At the bottom of the run, the snow had been piled up into a high snowbank to arrest momentum safely. Kids were screaming as they hurtled down the run at what had to be dangerous speeds, only to slide up the end of the hill and back down. One figure stood at the bottom and another at the top, and as soon as the run was clear, the figure at the bottom would raise his or her hand and drop it, and the next person in line would take their turn down the hill.

Mom's hand fluttered at her throat. "Oh my, that looks… dangerous."

Brock just laughed. "Nah. Bast has been making that run for years. The worst that's ever happened was a bloody nose. That was…god, who was that? Liam? It was Liam, I think, and he decided he wanted to throw himself off the sled halfway down just to see what would happen. No one has ever broken anything. The older cousins take turns making sure only one sled goes down at a time." He grinned. "The adults have been known to make a few runs once the booze has been flowing. You want to take a run at it, Kaye?"

Mom just stared at him. "My hip might break just watching, but thank you. I'll leave that to you youngsters."

Brock cackled. "I'm over fifty. Hardly a youngster. And you can't be, what, a day over sixty?"

Mom rolled her eyes, playful swatting his shoulder as we reached the deck. "Oh, you. You're a real charmer, aren't you?"

The group of men gathered on the deck were all new to me, but they all waved at me with either a tumbler or a cigar as if it was normal for random strangers to show up.

I followed Brock and Mom inside. Mom froze just inside. I stepped in and rested my hands on her shoulders, murmuring in her ear. "Breathe, Ma. I felt the same my first time."

She sucked in a sharp breath, and her shoulders sank back down, and then she squared them, let out the breath, and marched forward.

Dru was at the stove, stirring something in a huge pot, wearing a bright red apron with Rudolph on the front, his nose a red-blinking Christmas light. Around the island—which was laden with a mind-boggling array of food—people were clustered and crowded, having roughly ten different conversations, some of which were being shouted across the room. In the living room, the massive sectional was stuffed with more people, as was the ottoman; a few people were even sitting on the back of the couch with their knees wedged around the shoulders of the person in front of them. The door to the basement was open, and more laughter and chatter and music floated up from the stairwell. The TV was on in the den, playing *Elf*, and several of the oldest cousins were in there, half-watching the movie and mostly trading playful insults and good-natured arguments about who-knew-what.

Bast saw us, grabbed a hand-made wooden box from a counter, and came toward us with it. He leaned toward me and clapped me on the back in a half-hug. "Hayden, good to see you again. This your mom?"

I wrapped an arm around Mom's shoulders. "Bast, this is my mom, Kaye McCaffrey. Mom, this is Sebastian Badd, and this is his home."

"Sebastian," Mom said, offering her hand. "Thank you so much for having us. Did you invite half the city?"

Bast threw back his head and laughed. "First, call me Bast, B-A-S-T, been my nickname my whole life. And believe it or not, this is just my immediate family—brothers, sisters-in-law, nieces and nephews, cousins, and whatever a cousin's wife or husband would be.

Cousin-in-law? I don't know. It's all family. And we're glad to have you."

Mom shook her head. "This all just family?"

Bast nodded. "Yup. I'm the oldest of eight brothers, and we have three cousins, identical triplets. Their father, my uncle, married a woman with five daughters who all got married and we brought their husbands into the fold. And we're all one big, wild, crazy family."

Mom just shook her head again with a disbelieving laugh. "My husband and I are both only children, and my son is our only child."

Bast hesitated. "I, um...I heard about why you and Hayden are doing a Christmas cruise. So sorry to hear of your husband's passing."

Mom's smile dimmed for a moment, and then she rallied. "Thank you very much. It was unexpected and painful, to be sure. We're adjusting." She looked around, her smile regaining its brilliance. "My husband would have loved a party like this. You all seem so close."

Bast grinned and threw out an arm, gesturing at the party at large. "We are, very much so. Most of us live in the area, and even those who don't live here full time are here whenever life allows." He lifted the box he had tucked under one arm and opened the lid; inside were dozens of cell phones. "We only have two rules at our parties. One, if you're drinking, your keys go in that box over there by the front door. Two, no cell phones—they go in here. We always take a few group shots at some point before the kids are asleep and the adults are sloppy. So, if you don't mind, toss it in."

There was another identical box by the front door, the lid propped open; as Bast mentioned it, Brock tossed the keys to the airplane into the box and then came back this way and tossed his phone in as well.

Mom and I put our phones with the rest, and then Mom touched Bast's huge arm. "May I please be introduced to the lady of the home?" She lifted the gift bag. "I have something for her."

Bast hooked a burly arm around her shoulders. "Right this way—she's fixing the stew." He glanced at me over his shoulder. "She's downstairs."

I watched Mom for a minute as she met Dru, who hugged her, exclaiming over the gift and pulling her into the circle of women huddled together on that side of the island. Within seconds, she had a glass of wine in hand and was laughing.

I wasn't worried about her—the initial reaction was merely shock. She was the most outgoing and social person I'd ever met, and I had no doubt she'd be fast friends with everyone by the end of the evening.

I made my way downstairs. Pentatonix sang "Hallelujah" in the background, mostly drowned out by the chaos down here. This was clearly the younger adult space. The pool table had been turned into a beer pong table, where a dozen or so cousins were playing. Others played darts and foosball, and more yet sat on couches talking over each other.

Emerson was at the beer pong table, and the moment I saw her, my heart lifted. She was wearing skintight black jeans with low, wedge-heeled black boots and a green sweater adorned with a festoon of flashing, multi-colored twinkle lights; two lights larger than the rest were strategically and suggestively placed over her boobs, pointing straight outward. Her hair was loose and down, teased into a wild profusion of tight ringlets. She had a red Solo cup in her hand and her other arm was around Delia's waist as the bartender from Kitty's prepared to take her shot.

"JAMES BOND!" Someone shouted. "You're back!"

I lifted the suit at the shouter—Duncan. "I am back, and I have your suit."

Duncan snagged a solo cup from a stack, pulled a beer, and wove through the crowd toward me. "It looks like that suit has been dry-cleaned," he remarked.

"That's because it has," I said. "Thanks again, Duncan. I appreciate you lending it to me."

Duncan took the suit by the metal hook of the hangar. "Glad to be of service. You didn't have to dry-clean the damn thing, though."

I shrugged. "I was raised to do the right thing. And in my house, we always returned an item we borrowed in better shape than we received it."

"Well, it's appreciated." He shoved the cup of beer into my hand. "Come play beer pong with us.

Girls against boys, and we boys are getting our asses handed to us."

Em sunk her shot after Delia missed hers, and then Em's eyes found me. She whispered something to Delia and headed over to me.

Delia's eyes widened and she hurriedly took her shot for missing and then scurried after Em.

"Hey, you," Emerson said, not stopping as she reached me, instead closing in for a hug. Her arms slid around my neck and her hands buried in the hair at my nape.

I let my arms wrap around her waist, her hair tickling my nose, smelling of lavender. "Hi."

She pulled her face away from my chest and looked up at me from inches away, eyes searching mine. Her gaze spoke of our secret, shining with amusement and joy and arousal. "You look handsome." She plucked at my sleeve. "I love the ugly sweater."

I had on dark-wash blue jeans and a red sweater which was adorned with an embroidered 8-bit scene across the front: reindeer, a sleigh, and Santa flying above a rooftop and chimney. It was gloriously garish and had won me more than one ugly sweater competition.

I wanted to kiss her so bad it hurt, and it took all my willpower not to. "You look amazing, Em."

She stepped back and cupped her boobs. "Like my headlights?"

I laughed. "I love 'em. I'll be trying not to stare at them all night."

She leaned in against me, lips to my ear. "Or... don't try. Go ahead and stare all you want—you have my permission."

I groaned. "You want me to have a semi all night?"

"Maybe I do," she said. "You should be glad this a kid-friendly party, or I'd be wearing my special reindeer sweater."

I frowned. "Your special reindeer sweater?"

She laughed. "I cut a hole on one side and my bare boob hangs out, and I put a reindeer pasty with a flashing light over my nipple. It's hot. Delia and I have matching ones—my right boob is out, and her left."

"I'll need pictures," I said. "Of you, at least."

She laughed again. "I'll send it to you later; my phone is in the box." She tangled my fingers in hers. "Come on, you can help the boys lose at beer pong."

And so I found myself across the table from her, surrounded by her male cousins—I did not attempt to remember all the names, although I caught a few: Lennox, Riley, Dillon, Kieran, and Dakota. I couldn't say which name went with which face, however.

Dunc, as everyone seemed to call him, was beside me, keeping up a running monologue about the various cousins, imparting tidbits of information and wild stories that were increasingly unbelievable.

I only half-listened, and he didn't seem to care—I was more focused on Emerson. Watching her move was a turn-on. She was graceful, easy and comfortable in her body and comfortable with everyone around her. She and Delia were attached at the hip, always leaning in to whisper something to the other, which inevitably had them cracking up.

The game of beer pong seemed pretty loose as far as rules and points went, rather than a serious competition.

After a while, Emerson whispered something to Delia and then left her place opposite me at the table, taking me by the hand.

"You have to introduce me to your mom," she said.

"Sounds good." I followed her up the stairs. "Who won beer pong, by the way? I couldn't tell."

She gave a broad, hands-flapping shrug. "Who the hell knows? We just play to play. I'm not sure we've ever actually kept score."

"I thought you were a competitive athlete? I figured you'd be playing to win."

She just cackled. "We learned a *long* time ago to set our competitive natures aside. We're all like that, so if we start actually competing, shit gets *really* wild."

"Oh, I suppose that makes sense."

"We save that for the annual boys versus girls softball tournament. Now *that* gets fiercely competitive."

"With all the monster dudes in your family, I wouldn't think that would be very fair."

She snorted. "You'd think, and yeah, the bigger

uncles always blast a few clear out of the park, but pretty much all the women, especially us older cousins, played softball in school, so we have some killer fast-pitchers. The big scary men turn into babies when Anya launches a seventy-mile-per-hour rocket at them. Sort of evens the field a bit."

"I suppose it would."

We reached the kitchen and found Mom firmly ensconced within a circle of women, leaning against a counter, nibbling from a plate and sipping wine while deep in a conversation with an older woman about her age, maybe a few years younger.

"Oh, she found Mama Livvie—awesome," Emerson said, dragging me over to the group.

Emerson and I reached the circle of women, and they all stopped their conversations as we approached.

"Hayden, these are my aunts and Mama Livvie." She pointed to each woman in turn as she named them. "Eva, Joss, Kitty, Charlie, Lexie, Mara, and Tate. That's Mama Livvie your mom is talking to, obviously. Aunties, this is Hayden."

I reached for an outstretched hand to shake it and found myself pulled into a warm, maternal hug by a beautiful woman with brown skin, dreadlocks, and a killer smile. The next woman in line hugged me, too, and so it went, landing me with Olivia Goode last, also known as Mama Livvie, the matriarch of the Badd-Goode Clan.

It turned out that Charlie and Lexie were two of her daughters.

It was my turn. "Mom, this is Emerson. Emerson, this is my mom, Kaye McCaffrey."

Mom embraced Emerson as warmly and effusively as the women had me. "Call me Kaye, my dear. Wonderful to meet you—my Hayden has had amazing things to say about you."

"And he about you," Emerson said, returning the hug with an equal amount of enthusiasm.

"So, Hayden." Mama Livvie focused her attention on me, and so did everyone else's. "Your mother tells me you're a computer scientist."

I laughed. "Almost. I'm a cybersecurity analyst."

Mom flapped her hand, waving a cracker-and-cheese sandwich. "I can never remember. I don't know even what he does, really, just that it involves a lot of sitting in front of a computer."

The front door opened, then.

"XAVIER! LOW!" Someone shouted. "ABOUT FUCKIN' TIME!"

Mom flinched at the curse word, and I laughed, leaning close to her. "You want to say 'language' so bad, don't you?"

She covered her mouth as she laughed. "You have *no* idea. I think I've heard the F-word more tonight than ever before in my life combined." She waved her hand. "But you were absolutely right. This is the warmest, kindest, most welcoming group of people I've ever met in my life." She stage-whispered to me. "If a little rough around the edges."

Mama Livvie overheard and burst into laughter. When she recovered, she leaned back and yelled, "Lucas!"

"WHAT?" A booming male voice shouted from across the room.

"Did you know you're a little rough around the edges, my love?"

Heavy footsteps came this way, and an absolute bear of a man appeared, roughly six feet tall and massively heavy with muscle as well as a little bit of padding; he was older, with blond hair and a goatee, both gone mostly gray. Tattoos covered his biceps and forearms.

"Me?" he boomed. "Rough around the edges? I resemble that remark."

Mom's mouth flapped open and closed a few times. "I...I..."

Lucas guffawed, gently patting her shoulder; even gently, she almost collapsed under the weight of his hand. "Darlin', I'm so rough around the edges you could use me as a pumice stone." Another even larger human lumbered past, and Lucas snagged his colossal arm. 'What about you, Ink, m'boy? You rough around the edges?"

The man was...there aren't words for how huge he was. About seven feet tall and nearly as broad, he had jet-black hair with a touch of gray at the temples and traditional native-style tattoos all over his visible skin.

"More rough edges than smooth, Uncle Luke," the giant said in a voice that came from the bottom of a well.

Mom, barely over five feet tall, boggled at the gargantuan man. "Good grief, what did they feed you?"

The man just laughed, the corners of his eyes crinkling in a way that spoke of a lifetime of easy laughter. "Giant pills, I was told." he extended a hand that could have engulfed Mom's entire head. "Ink Isaac, ma'am."

"Kaye McCaffrey. Call me Kaye, please."

Ink glanced at me. "You must be Hayden. Rumor mill is buzzing about you."

I frowned. "Rumor mill?"

He just shrugged. "Our girl Sunni has never brought anyone to one of these. Must make you somethin' special."

"Sunni?" Mom asked. "Who's Sunni?"

Emerson raised her hand. "Me. It's my nickname. My last name is Day, so Delia has always called me Sunni...as in Sunni Day."

Mom chuckled. "Oh, well, that's just adorable. Can I call you that?"

Emerson rested her head sideways on Mom's shoulder as if they were age-old besties. "I'd love it if you did."

Something about seeing Mom and Emerson so cozy made my heart do funny things.

That's when a strong pair of hands grabbed my shoulders and pulled me backward, and then I was airborne, held aloft six feet in the air by multiple people.

I found Emerson, looking for help, but she just covered her mouth to hide her laugh.

"Just go with it, Hayden. It's a rite of passage around here," She said. She reached for me. "Give me your wallet."

I fished it out and tossed it to her. "What's happening?

"You're going for a swim." I found the speaker—Bax.

"A swim? In the Passage? In December?" My voice went higher with each word until I was almost squeaking by the end.

"Someone gets tossed in every year," he answered as the many hands carried me outside and across the deck. "This year it's you, since you're new."

"I'm not new, I'm temporary," I argued.

He just laughed. "Horseshit, son. The Badd Clan Love Charm has claimed you and Emmy. Y'all can fight it all you want, kid—all of us did. Won't do a lick of good."

"You can swim, yeah?" This was Bast.

"Yeah, but—"

"Then just fuckin' relax, bro," someone else said—a familiar voice.

I twisted around looking for the speaker—Myles North, country music superstar and an absolute legend.

Feet clomped on wood, and water chucked against pylons. Snow swirled—small, sharp shards of ice tossed by the restless wind.

Hands shifted grip on me, from merely supporting my shoulders, hips, and legs to gripping wrists and ankles. My stomach lurched upward as they swung me down and began rocking me back and forth like medieval besiegers with a battering ram.

"On three, boys," Bax said. "One…two…*three!*"

In case you were wondering, four mammoth and powerful men can throw a fully-grown human male a *very* long distance. I was airborne for what felt like a full minute—it was a fraction of that, obviously, but it felt like much longer.

My arms and legs windmilled and icy air stung my eyes and snowflakes bit into my cheeks, and then water so frigid it shocked the air out of my lungs smashed through me like a sledgehammer through plate glass. I gasped a lungful of air at the last second, right before the water swallowed me. I was surrounded by pitch blackness, the harsh currents of the inside Passage pulling at me, my clothes water-logged and heavy. I kicked upward as hard as I could and pulled at the water with my arms, surfacing with a spluttering gasp.

Something smacked into the water near my face.

"Grab the ring!" A voice shouted—Bast, I thought.

I reached out and grabbed blindly—a life preserver attached to a rope. I clung to it and frog-kicked as the men on the dock hauled me toward them. I blinked away water and spluttered and gasped, teeth chattering a mile a minute, every muscle quivering and quaking.

And then hard strong hands were lifting me with laughable ease.

"F-f-f-f-fuck—m-m-m-me," I chattered. "C-c-c-cold."

"Strip, kid." This was Myles again.

I didn't hesitate or question—I needed my icy, soaking wet clothes off ASAP, so I struggled out of my wet jeans, sweater, and everything else until I was stark naked under the Alaskan winter sky. Someone wrapped a hot blanket around me, and hands guided me along the dock away from the water. I was dazed, disoriented, shivering, and chattering, and I allowed myself to be moved.

We didn't go back up to the house. Instead, we angled perpendicular to the house, around the side of the hill the house perched on. The hillside cut away dramatically, held in place by a thick timber retaining wall that funneled inward to a stout wooden door with a small window through which infrared light bloomed.

Around me, clothes rustled. I looked around to see the other men peeling out of their clothes and tossing them into a waiting wicker basket.

And then Bast, naked, yanked open the door and hustled me through.

A wall of heat slammed into me. A sauna?

"Fuck, it's cold," someone muttered as he entered.

"N-n-no sh-sh-shit, Sh-Sh-Sherl-l-lock," I stammered. "Try being w-w-wet."

The speaker laughed. "I got dunked last year." I found him—someone I hadn't been introduced to yet.

He was one of Emerson's Badd uncles; he had the look, being around six feet and built like a brick shithouse, with brown hair and brown eyes and the same nose and mouth as the other Badd men I'd met. He had a tattoo that I recognized as the Navy SEAL logo on his bicep, and his bare, muscular torso bore a myriad of scars.

He indicated the benches running the perimeter of the room in a U-shape, one low, one high. "Have a seat, kid."

I shuffled to the nearest section of the bench and sat down, letting the blanket pool around my lap. The other men, nine of them, all had white towels around their waists.

Bast, his many colorful tattoos made otherworldly by the infrared light, sat beside me. "You met everyone here?"

I shook my head. "No." I scanned the faces. "Bax, Brock, and you. The rest I haven't been introduced to."

Bast gestured as he named them. "Myles North you probably recognize, he's made some music. Next to him is Crow, Myles's best friend and brother-in-law. Over there is my brother Zane. And then you've got the Terrible Triplets, my cousins, Rome, Rem, and Ram."

Myles, obviously, I did recognize—he's been in

commercials, he's won six Grammies, several CMAs, an Emmy for best original soundtrack, and has dabbled in acting. Everyone knows who Myles North is and what he looks like.

Crow was Native American, with long black hair plaited behind his head and sharp, angular features. His eyes were black, glittering with intelligence and wisdom, giving nothing away as to what he was thinking or feeling. He lifted his chin at me as I met his gaze.

The SEAL was Zane, making my original assessment correct. The triplets had similar Badd features, but with blond hair instead of brown, and were every bit as massive, muscular, and intimidating.

I scanned the room again. "So. I'm assuming this is where you guys tell me that if I hurt Emerson, you'll hurt me?"

Zane laughed. "Don't have to. I figure unless you're dumber than a bag of hammers, that's pretty well understood."

"And you don't seem dumb to me," Myles said.

"I…" I trailed off with a sigh and decided on honesty. "I don't know what's gonna happen with Em. All I know is I *really* like her a whole fucking lot. She's cool, smart, funny, and a hell of an athlete."

"And it probably doesn't hurt that my niece ain't exactly hard on the eyes," one of the triplets said.

"She ain't your niece, dumbshit," Another triplet said.

"Oh? Then what is she, Mr. Expert on Family Relations or whatever the fuck?"

The second triplet—Rem?—flipped his brother off. "First cousin once removed, ya fat, brainless cock-waffle."

The first triplet returned the bird and then slapped his midsection—hard, flat, not quite a six-pack anymore but with visible definition. "Fat, my hairy ass. *You're* fat."

"Oh, real clever comeback, dick-knob."

"Fuck you, assclown."

I'd lost track of who was speaking at this point.

"Shut the fuck up, both of you," the third triplet cut in. "Fifty fuckin' years old and still bickering like goddamn toddlers."

"Fuck you, Ram," the other two said in perfect unison.

I spluttered a laugh and covered my mouth with my fist when they glanced at me. "Sorry, sorry."

"Serious question," Bast said, cutting through the humor despite the calm quiet of his voice. "How much has Sunni told you about herself?"

I shrugged. "A bit. I know you and Dru unofficially adopted her. She told me she didn't come from anything good. That's about it."

He nodded. "Well, her story is hers to tell, not mine. What I will say is that Emerson is my daughter in every way there is but legal. I'd take a bullet for her, and I'd put a man in the ground for her, same as I would my kids or any of my nieces and nephews."

I nodded. "I believe it. She's lucky as hell to have a family like you all."

Zane spoke up. "What my brother isn't saying is that I can and have put men in the ground. A lot of 'em." He tapped his arm, the tattoo. "Saw you notice this. You know what it means, yeah?"

"I do." I nodded. "I care about her. I don't know what the future holds, so the only promise I can make is that I won't play with her feelings."

Crow spoke up, then. "She's got a tender heart under all that fire. She keeps it hidden. Even we who know her and love her don't always see how deep her feelings go."

I used the corner of the blanket to wipe sweat off my upper lip. "I've gotten glimpses of that."

"None of our kids have ever had a serious relationship," Bast said. "She'd be the first, which is weird. Our kids have all brought dates around, but it's never been anything serious. For Emmy to bring you to a full family holiday party is a real shock."

"And you're worried about her," I said, filling in the unspoken. "I respect that. She's told me about the Badd Family Love Charm, or at least *of* it. All I can promise you is that I am not playing with her. I've been in two relationships in my life, and I'm the farthest thing from a player you'll ever meet."

Brock spoke for the first time. "She likes you,

Hayden. I've watched her with you. She may not be aware of it, or at least isn't admitting it to herself yet, but she has feelings for you. Don't fuck around with that. If you aren't there, be real about it, okay? No one here is threatening you. For one thing, that girl wouldn't need help fucking up your life if you hurt her."

I laughed. "No shit. If nothing else, she and Delia would go Thelma and Louise on my ass."

"Got that right," all three triplets said together.

"Look, guys. You think I'd bring my mother here if I was just looking for a…for something casual? I know you don't know me, but I do not and have not ever done casual."

"Emerson's dating history is…" Zane started.

"Her place to tell me," I interrupted. "And she has, sort of. I know she's not done relationships before. I know enough of psychology to know there's probably a reason for that, but I think we all respect her privacy enough to let her be the one to get into that."

"I think we've gotten the measure of the man," Crow said. "He's got good answers."

"I only have one question," I said. "What am I supposed to wear now?"

NINE

Emerson

DELIA AND I WERE IN THE KITCHEN, SIDE BY SIDE AT THE counter next to the range; I was slicing freshly baked French baguettes while Delia arranged them into a massive wooden bowl lined with a cloth napkin.

"You did something with him," Delia hissed in my ear. "Just admit it. I can see it on your face."

"I neither confirm nor deny the allegations," I said, grabbing another baguette and slicing.

"Which is tantamount to admitting *something* happened. You tell me *everything*, Sunni. Why is this any different?"

"Because it's just different, that's why." I glanced over my shoulder, hoping to see him enter the door.

"I hope he's okay. That water is cold as hell this time of year."

Mama Dru patted my hip as she took the full bowl from Delia and replaced it with a second, empty bowl, covering the bread bowl with another napkin to trap the heat in. "He'll be fine. They keep a heated blanket nearby, not to mention the life preserver, and then they go right into the sauna. I'd be more worried about the conversation than the water."

I sighed. "Yeah, I am. But Hayden is no pushover."

"He most certainly is not," Kaye said. "He's always been a bit reserved, but he will stand up and speak out when he needs to."

Kaye was helping as well, on her insistence, chopping up vegetables for the salad.

Delia bumped my hips with hers. "Spill it, sister. Something happened. You know I'll get it out of you one way or the other."

I let out a long sigh, thinking. I did know that my sister would not quit badgering me about this until I gave her something, but I didn't want to betray Hayden's trust by telling her anything he'd be uncomfortable with.

"Dee, I…" I stopped slicing bread for a second and looked at her. "It's different with Hayden. A lot different. I have no problem giving you all the spicy details when it's just a rando hookup. Hayden is not that." I leaned close, whispering. "And that's scaring the actual fuck out of me."

Delia snagged the last slice of baguette, peeled the warm, steaming middle away from the crust, and rolled it into a ball before tossing it into her mouth. "Wait. Hold up. You're telling me you have *feelings* for the boy?"

"He's not a boy; he's twenty-six and a man."

She laughed. "Well ex*cuuuuse* me."

I snickered. "There may or may not have been a rather lengthy and, shall we say… *revealing*…FaceTime last night, or this morning, or whatever."

Delia suppressed a squeal, shaking my arm. "*And?* Is he packing a surprise salami? Guys like that often are."

"Delia!" I scolded. "Surprise salami? Really?"

"You objectify your boytoys all the time, Emerson, so don't give me that fake bullshit."

"Yeah, sure, but Hayden is *not* a boytoy."

She shrugged. "Fair enough. But still…is he? Packing a secret surprise?"

I focused—or pretended to—on cleaning up the crumbs. "Let's just say that I was quite shocked at what was revealed."

Delia buried her face in my shoulder to stifle a laugh. "I knew it! You saucy minx! Getting freaky on the Facetime with Mr. Sexy Nerd."

I had to bite my lip. "It was *so* fucking hot, Dee." I fanned my face.

She whispered directly into my ear. "You want to

play hide the surprise salami with Mr. Sexy Nerd in the worst way, don't you?"

I covered my face with my hands. "It's all I can think about," I admitted.

Her arm went around my shoulders. "I can run interference while you guys can sneak off somewhere?"

I shook my head. "Thanks, but no. That's not gonna work. Something tells me we're gonna need time and privacy. If he was anyone else, sure, I'd be down for a quickie. But with Hayden? No. He's not a quickie sort of guy."

"What kind of a guy is he, then?" she asked, pouring us both a glass of red wine.

I accepted the goblet and sipped before answering. "That's why he's not quickie sort of guy—because I don't know. The FaceTime was…" I sighed, resting my cheek against the cool glass of the goblet. "Amazing. It wasn't, like, weird or kinky. We just…well, you can probably figure it out. We watched each other. But it was the hottest thing I've ever done, Dee. Period. Ever. With anyone."

She stared at me for a long time. "This really is different for you, isn't it? You're not just playing coy."

I shook my head. "No, it really is. And I'm fucking terrified."

Delia sighed a laugh. "You? *You*—Emerson Day— are scared of a *man*?"

"Not *of* him, you dummy."

"Of your feelings *for* him, then, if you simply must be pedantic."

I put my index finger in my mouth and then dipped it into her wine. "Laugh it up, baby-cakes. You're the Love Charm's next victim."

"You don't know that." She dipped her finger in her wine and swiped it down my forehead between my eyes, leaving a dripping trail.

I wiped it away with my palm. "That's how it goes, according to the family lore, and you know it. You're next. Just you watch."

She crossed her index fingers to ward off evil. "You take that back, you daft bitch. I have plans, and they do *not* involve falling in love."

"You just said you wanted a boyfriend for Christmas," I said.

Delia glared at me. "Yeah, a *boyfriend*. I want an endless amount of hot sex, fun dates, and no long-term commitment. I have plans. I have an empire to inherit and expand, and falling in love is one hundred and fifty percent *not* part of that plan."

I laughed. "Well, you just screwed yourself, sweet-ie-kins. You're *definitely* falling in love now."

"Fuck you! Take that back."

"I will not. I'm not in charge of the Love Charm. No one is. I'm just calling it like I see it."

"Well un-call it!" She seemed truly desperate.

"Not how it works, hooker-biscuit."

She tipped her head back and sighed. "I do *not* want to fall in love. I *do not*."

I frowned at her. "Whoa, hold on. This is serious, and it's news to me. What's your deal?"

She shook her head. "Nothing. Nevermind."

"Delia Dru Badd. You made me spill. Your turn."

She shook her head again. "Mmm-mm. Nope."

"Delia. I am every bit as stubborn as you." I leaned close and rested my head on her shoulder. "Now spill. Tell sissy why you're scared of love. Your whole family is one giant testimony to the enduring power of true love, and you're scared of it?"

She sniffed. "Yeah, see? That's exactly why! What if I get it wrong? What if I never fall in love? I've never felt even a twinkling of love for anyone I've ever dated. Like, a mild affection at best."

"You were gaga over Jerrod McMurray and don't try to tell me otherwise," I said.

She blew a raspberry. "I was sixteen, he was eighteen, and he was the hottest guy in the school. It was a crush."

"You slept with him, Delia."

"And it was terrible! He wasn't gentle when he took my virginity, lasted for about a minute, max, and then bragged about it to the whole school."

"Yeah, and you turned the whole school against him for it."

"To protect my reputation and keep Daddy from murdering him and dumping his body in the fucking

Passage!" she protested. "And you know if Daddy found out, every single male member of my family would have shown up at his door with torches and pitchforks. You know how much pressure that is? I'm the oldest Badd girl. All eyes are on me, and who I end up with, and how."

I sighed. "Yeah, I see your point, there. But that's no reason to avoid falling in love."

"You just said you're terrified!" Delia all but yelled, and then dropped her voice. "Sorry. But you can't tell me you're terrified and then turn around and tell me not to be."

"Dee-Dee. Babe. Yes, I'm terrified. But I'm still gonna go for it. What's the worst that can happen? I get my heart broken. I have you, and Mama Dru, and Big Daddy Bast, and everyone else. It would suck, but I'd survive it. And so would you—*if* the worst happened. Which it may not. Again, look at your family."

Delia tipped her head back and groaned. "*Please*, for the love of all that's holy, *please stop* calling my *father* Big Daddy Bast. *Please*. It's gross."

I laughed, shaking my head. "Never."

At that moment, the back door slid open further, and the men trooped in, flushed and laughing, with Hayden in the middle of them, carrying an armload of wet clothes and wrapped in a blanket, wearing someone else's slides. His hair was damp, but his face was red and his eyes were merry. Whatever they said to him, it must have gone well.

I beelined for him. "So. You took the plunge. How was it?"

He laughed. "Fucking freezing. But I feel seriously alive."

"HAYDEN   REGINALD   MCCAFFREY— LANGUAGE!" his mother yelled, not looking up from her cutting board.

"Sorry, Mom." He rolled his eyes and shook his head.

I bit my lip. "Your middle name is *Reginald*?"

He groaned. "*Mom*! See what you did? Now every-one knows my horrible, embarrassing middle name. Thanks for that."

His mom stopped chopping and looked at him. "Hayden, it's not embarrassing, it's a family name going back several generations. I have never under-stood why you're so embarrassed by it."

He just shook his head. "I know you don't, but I am. It's a generational thing, I think." He looked around the room. "Where's Dunc? I need the clothes I left in his room."

I saw an opportunity and seized it. "He's deep into a foosball game with Liam, Lennox, and Nolan. You're not getting him away for a while—once those four start that, it's on like Donkey Kong. They're fanatics. Come on, I'll help you find your stuff."

He followed me away from the main living area and down the hallway. I paused at Dunc's door, looked over my shoulder at Hayden, and then grabbed his hands and pulled him in after me, shutting the door behind him.

He caught up against the door, the blanket clutched closed. His deep, warm, expressive green eyes looked down at me. "Well hello there." An Obi-Wan Kenobi reference—I approved.

I felt tingly all over, heart pounding, pussy soaked merely from being this close to him, knowing he was naked under that blanket. "Hi."

I put my hands on his and gently pried them apart, opening the blanket, baring his body.

"Em..."

In person, he was even more gorgeous. Shredded, lean, and hard. His abs popped, flexing as he breathed. As I watched, his cock hardened, uncurling, and then pointing straight out, and then standing upright against his belly.

"Em, your whole family is out there. And my mom."

I rested my head against his chest. "I know."

"I fucking want you, Em. In the worst way. But I..."

I touched his lips. "I know, Hayden. I just...I had to see you. I had to get you alone, just for a second."

He looked down at me with a haunted, hungry, tortured expression. And then he dropped the blanket entirely. His big, strong hands cupped my face with exquisite gentility. He leaned down, and my lips parted in anticipation.

He kissed me.

Holy god, did he kiss me.

One second, our lips were touching, breaths tangled, and then the next we were devouring each other, all teeth and tongues and lips and breath. His cock was a hard, thick ridge between us, wedged between our bodies.

I palmed his cheek with one hand, loving the rough scratch of his stubble and his soft skin. As his tongue warred with mine, I slid my other hand over his bare hip, his waist. Cupped his bare ass, first palming the taut, hard bubble and then digging my fingers into the muscle.

I had to…I couldn't be this close and not get even a single touch…

I grasped his hot, throbbing cock in my fist, moaning into his mouth as the hard length and silky soft skin filled my hand.

Hayden groaned, a low, ragged huff, and his fingers found the gap between my shirt and jeans, stealing under the waistband to grip my bare ass.

God, I've never wanted anything as much as I wanted Hayden inside me right then. I felt crazed with desire, mad with need.

I broke the kiss, sliding my fist down his length. "Fuck, Hayden. I need you."

"Em, Jesus. The way you touch me…"

I quickened my touch, stroking him faster, keeping my grip loose and light. "Yeah? Like this?"

His fingers dug into my ass, clawing hard and then loosening to withdraw and slide up my back, under my shirt.

"Em," he whispered. "You have to stop. We can't do this here."

"I don't know if I *can* stop," I admitted, pulling away from him to watch my hand sliding the impressive length of his lovely cock.

"Em—shit, shit, shit. It feels *so* fucking good. But your family—"

"I barely slept the rest of the night thinking of this," I whispered, watching as his knees started to dip in time with my strokes. "I daydreamed about touching you all damn day. I'm so fucking horny I feel like I'm going crazy. I *need* you, Hayden. I don't give a fuck about anything else."

"You're all I think about, all the time," he murmured. "Your incredible tits. Your perfect ass. Kissing you till you can't breathe. Making you scream my name."

"Then touch me," I whispered. "Please."

North or South? Which way would he go?

Most men go north, given the choice. I mean, I *do* have pretty epic tits. A big C during the season when I'm leaner and a plump D in the off-season when I'm not as worried about my body fat percentage. Firm, high, tight—I wouldn't say they're my best feature, but several guys have made that claim. Those guys never got a second go because that's shallow as fuck.

Hayden surprised me by flipping loose the button of my jeans and tugging down the zipper. Shoved my jeans and underwear down around my thighs. He cupped my sex.

"Okay?" he whispered, holding my eyes.

"Don't make me beg, Hayden, Jesus. *Yes*—please, touch me."

His fingers, the first three, fit themselves over my slit and his middle finger entered me, oh-so-gently sliding inside me. I whimpered, knees softening. One slow delve into my inner depths, and then he withdrew his finger and smeared my juices over my clit, drawing a shrill gasp from me.

I caressed his cock, twisted my hand around the top, and then rubbed my thumb over the tip, teased the tip with a soft scrape of my fingernail, making him jerk, hissing.

"Holy shit, Em."

He delved into my channel again and swirled more essence over my clit, and then began circling. He tried different speeds, different pressures, different patterns and directions of touch until he found the combination that had me biting his shoulder to muffle my keening— quick, light touches with the pads of his two fingers in swift circles, barely making contact. He had me buckling at the knees within seconds since I was already so worked up.

"Hayden, ohmygod—Hayden!" I bit his earlobe and then let out a shrill whimper. "How do you know my body so perfectly? You're gonna make me come, Hayden. Fuck, fuck. *Fuck!*"

"Come for me, Em. Most beautiful thing in the whole fucking world, you coming for me."

I lost it, then, gripping his cock with a sudden squeeze, sinking my teeth into the tendon along the top of his shoulder as I began to come apart. My knees gave out, and he held me up, one hand cradling my ass to hold me up and the other flying at my core, circling and swiping. I screamed into his flesh and muscle, grinding against his fingers, stars bursting behind my eyes.

Heat blasted through me, seized my core and behind my navel and rocketed through my every nerve and synapse until I was on fire all over, shaking helplessly as he worked me through my climax and down the other side.

When I came back to myself, I pulled away, realizing I'd left a hell of a hickey on his shoulder.

"Oops," I muttered, giggling as I kissed the love bite. "Left a bit of a mark."

When he didn't laugh with me, I looked at him— he was panting, tensed all over, eyes squeezed shut.

"Hayden?"

He swallowed hard. "Just—need…a—a minute."

Oh, fuck. He was about to come. I'd stopped stroking him and was just holding on—and squeezing pretty hard, at that—as I came.

"Oh no you don't," I whispered. "You think I'm gonna leave you hanging?"

"Em, you don't have to…" He shook his head. "I'll be fine."

I took his hands in mine, placed them on my face, and then turned my face into his palm and kissed. "You'll be even better in about thirty seconds."

"Em…"

I sank to my knees, keeping my eyes on his. Smiled up at him. "My turn."

"Em, you don't have to—"

"But I *want* to."

He tucked my hair behind my ears. "Emerson…" he squeezed his eyes shut as I gathered his cock in both hands, pulling it away from his body. "Holy *shit*."

I licked the precum away, and his breath caught. I wrapped my lips around the plump head of his cock and tasted pre-cum beading on my tongue—tangy, almost sweet, a little smoky. Fuck, he tasted good.

I slid one hand down to the root of him and cupped his taut, heavy balls with the other, bobbing gently as far down as his glans.

His fingers tightened on my shoulders—I let go of him long enough to show him what I wanted: his hands in my hair. He gripped a double handful of my curls and held on, tugging gently as I took him in my hands again.

Bobbed down farther and then back up. Cupped my hand around the back of his length and licked up the underside in one long swipe of my tongue, taking him into my mouth and going down on him to the back of my throat, all in a single movement.

"Fucking hell, Em," he growled. "What are you doing to me? Jesus. Fuck…Emerson…fuck, *fuck*."

I felt him pulsing against my lips and knew he was close. I put my hands on his and showed him the pressure I wanted him to apply; he did it exactly as I wanted, pushing me down on him just a little bit, encouraging without forcing. I tasted precum on my tongue, and his knees dipped.

I moaned around him, clawing my hands into his ass and pulling him toward me, bobbing down his length faster now, more aggressively.

"Oh, fuck, fuck, fuck—*Emerson*. Fuck. Oh god, oh god—I'm…I can't—"

Faster. Pulling him to me, encouraging him to move. He was thrusting now, hands pushing me down, showing me how he wanted it.

"Em!" he cried out, teeth clenched. "I'm coming, oh fuck, I'm gonna come!"

He tried to pull away, but I held on to his ass and pulled him closer, taking his thick hard throbbing cock to the back of my throat as far as I could without gagging and then bobbed there.

He keened in a rough guttural voice between gritted molars, fists clenched hard in my hair, thrusting helplessly into my mouth and throat.

And then he came.

A flood of come filled my mouth and I swallowed compulsively, gulping it down. I backed away and pumped his root with my fist and bobbed sloppily on his cock, up near the top, and he gasped, another pulse flooding my mouth with the sweet tang of his come. More and more. I swallowed it all and milked him for more, stroking him slowly as his orgasm faded. His knees buckled and he hissed through his teeth and then growled.

"Fuck, Emerson. Jesus, I…oh *fuck*."

I tasted another bead on his tip and licked it away, pumping his still-hard shaft, drawing more out of him, which I licked away as well.

Softening now, I let his cock flop free of my mouth, giving the drooping tip one last little kiss.

He stared down at me for a moment, pure, unadulterated awe suffusing his features. "Emerson…my god." He buckled, stiffened his legs, and then he collapsed to his knees in front of me.

I laughed, caressing his face. "Hi there."

He seemed stunned. "Emerson, I…"

I laughed again, leaning in, kissing the corner of his mouth. "You act like you've never had a blowjob before."

His cheeks flushed. "I, um…haven't."

I frowned, pulling back. "What?"

"No one's ever done that to me before."

"How?" I shook my head, not believing him. "You

had two relationships. Neither of them ever gave you even *one* blowjob?"

A shake of his head. "No. Nikki, my first girl-friend, was a virgin too, same as me. So that was mainly just…us figuring things out. That wasn't something she figured out, and I didn't know any better." He shifted off of his knees and reached for me, pulling me onto his lap—my pants were still half-down, but I just left them, settling onto his lap, feeling his now-soft organ against my ass. It was wet and sticky, but I didn't care.

"And then Darcy," he said.

"Fucking Darcy. She didn't, either, I'm guessing?"

He shook his head. "No. I'm not sure how much you want to hear, though."

"Anything you want to tell me."

He shrugged. "Okay. So, sex with Darcy was… Compared to Nikki, it was great. I don't mean to say anything bad about Nikki. She was just shy, and awkward. So was I, but we were both still figuring it out. Darcy, initially, blew my mind. But she could only come if I was…" he hesitated. "If I went down on her, or with a toy. Made it tricky sometimes. She wouldn't…well, anyway. That doesn't matter. She told me once that she hated giving oral. I cared about her and wasn't about to make a big deal about it, so…yeah."

I growled, resting my cheek against his bare hot chest. "That's bullshit. She hated giving it, but the only way she could get off it was by receiving it? That's not fair at all."

He shrugged. "That did occur to me, but like I said, I cared about her. What was I going to do, make her? Break up with her because she wouldn't?"

I laughed. "Yeah."

He chuckled. "I'm not like that. I didn't mind." he swallowed hard. "I, uh, like…doing that. A lot. Giving oral, I mean."

I pulled away and palmed his face, tipping him down to look at me. "Well, Hayden McCaffrey, so do I." I thumbed his lip. "A fucking lot. And I have to say, I'm really, *really* happy I got to be the one to give you your first blowjob. Speaking of, what'd you think?"

He stares down at me, dumbfounded. "What… what did I *think*?"

I giggled. "Yeah, hotshot, what'd you think? Give it to me straight."

"My legs literally gave out, Emerson. I think that sorta says it all."

I felt something stirring beneath me. "I suppose it does, at that. You seemed stunned."

"I was." He hesitated. "Tell you a secret?"

"Always."

"That's been one of my ongoing…fantasies, I suppose you could call it." He was speaking slowly, hesitantly. "It's pretty hard to talk about your secret fantasies out loud. But, yeah. And Em, you…that was… my fantasies couldn't touch the reality of how you made me feel. So…thank you. For giving me that. For making my fantasy come true in the most amazing, mind-blowing way."

"Hayden, you gave me a hell of an orgasm, too, you know." I looked up at him, smiling. "And I can't wait to get some real time alone, in a bed, both of us naked together. You're incredible, I hope you know that. Your exes are the biggest fools on the planet." The stirring has become a definite and unmistakable hardening, thickening. I wiggled my ass. "We'd better get back out there. As much as I'd love to stay here and blow your mind a second time, we're gonna get some shit as it is."

He froze. "I…I literally just finished telling your dad how I respect you and care about you. Then I disappear with you during a family party?"

I laughed, rubbing his chest. "Breathe, Hayden. I meant we're going to get teased. I'm an adult, you're an adult, and no one will be mad at you because we took a few minutes to spend time together alone. What we did is our business, but they're gonna guess, and they're gonna tease us about it. It'll be out of love and amusement and nothing else, I promise. The best way to handle it, if you'd like my advice, is to give shit right back. When my family gives you shit, give it back twice as hard. They'll love the hell out of you for it if you do."

He sighed. "That's never been my style, but I'll try. Now, you'd better get up and let me get dressed, or I'll be in here even longer trying to kill my hard-on."

I stood up, somewhat awkwardly since my jeans

and underwear were tangled around my knees. Hayden's eyes fixed on my pussy, his gaze darkening with desire. He rolled forward to his knees in front of me, hands settling on my hips and then sliding around to cradle my ass. My breath caught as he leaned close to me, his breath hot on my flesh.

"Em...you're so fucking beautiful." His eyes flitted up to mine, seeking my permission. "I have to taste you."

"Hayden..." I whispered, feathering my fingers through his soft, cool, damp hair. "You really think I'd stop you?"

His nose brushed my skin just above my pudendum, and his breath huffed hot over my flesh. My skin pebbled and the fine hairs stood up all over my body, and my breath caught in my throat. He pulled my jeans and underwear down around my ankles. Trailed a single fingertip down my slit. I shivered, gasped. His thumbs gently tugged my hood open and his tongue slid upward along my slit, flitting against my clit. I gasped again, a sharp, shrill intake of breath as arousal seared through me like a bolt of lightning.

"Hayden...oh fuck." I gathered his hair in my hands and gripped hard. "Please."

He moaned, a long, low rumble in his chest as if tasting a favorite meal after a long starvation. His lips fused to my flesh and he suckled my clit into his mouth, and my knees dipped. His large, strong hands clasped at my ass, holding me to himself, and he began slowly devouring me. His tongue lashed and swiped, and he suckled and licked. When my knees began dipping and my hips flexing, he stuck with the pattern that brought me there—hyper-attuned to my every breath, my every movement, learning my responses and reacting with exquisite precision. I reached the cusp, whimpering, holding onto the back of his head for dear life, crushing him to me…

Only for him to switch it up, delicately swirling his tongue over my clit, barely touching it, teasing and tickling, and then two fingers slid inside me, filling me, curling and slicking in and out. I held onto him and gave myself over to it, to sensation, trusting him to know my body and give me what I needed, what I wanted.

And somehow, he did know my body.

Or maybe he just paid attention—my knees began flexing and my hips thrusting helplessly, and he sped his touch, fingers plunging faster, tongue swirling and thrashing with ever-increasing intensity.

I felt my climax rising again, potent and wild. I gritted my teeth and threw my head back and keened and whimpered and gasped, thrusting into his touch until I was fucking his face and fingers.

I felt close to breaking and instinctively held back, a little scared of how intense it was, this close to orgasm. I've never squirted before, and this didn't seem like the best place or time for it, and I was afraid if I let go totally, I would.

Hayden seemed to sense my hesitation, that I was holding back. He renewed his assault, his fingers finding a place high inside me that made me cry out, made my knees nearly give out totally, and his lips fused to my sex. His other hand slid up my belly, covered my breast and squeezed for a moment, then tugged down the cup of my bra and palmed the heavy, aching weight of my breast. His thumb brushed side to side against my erect nipple, sending a new thread of thrills through me, eradicating my resistance. My panting and gasping became desperate, and my hips gyrated against him. Nearly unable to keep my feet, I bit down on a scream as Hayden pinched my nipple between his finger and thumb, gently at first and then with increasing pressure, timing each pinch to the flex of my hips, ratcheting the heat billowing through me to new levels.

I shattered all at once.

My legs gave out, and Hayden caught me, helping me down to my knees and then laying me out on my back, and then he was prostrate above me, face buried between my thighs, and he was devouring my pussy with feral desperation, fingers fucking me and pinching my nipple until I was screaming through clenched teeth, spine arching up and heels scrabbling at the carpet.

I came and came and came with such frenzied intensity that I broke into tears, weeping helplessly as wave after wave of crushing orgasmic madness took over, rolling through me like a tsunami. I clung to his head and rode his face, my lungs empty of breath, unable to scream, to breathe, to even whimper, mouth open in a silent cry.

The waves broke and I caught my breath, and still Hayden didn't stop, pushing me to the edge yet again, to a climax so wild I felt like I was breaking apart on some metaphysical level, shattering somewhere deep in my very soul.

Tears leaked out and trickled hot into my ears.

When I finally managed to pull in a breath, I had to beg him to stop. "Hayden, Hayden—enough. I can't—I can't take anymore. Please, fuck, fuck, fuck! Stop! Oh god, you have to stop."

He did, immediately. He reared back to sit on his feet, his mouth shining with my essence, his expression awed and self-satisfied.

I covered my face with my hands, struggling to compose myself, feeling like I was on the edge of breaking down totally, sobbing helplessly for reasons I was entirely too chicken to examine at that moment.

When the urge to have a breakdown passed—a little bit, at least—I wiped at my face and sucked in a shuddering breath. "Jesus crickets, Hayden."

I was jellied. Boneless. Utterly unable to move more than my hands.

I tucked my boob back into my bra and tugged my shirt down. Hayden moved to help, gently lifting me with one hand under my ass, the other tugging my panties back up, finger running around the waistband to settle them in place. He tugged my jeans up, next. Zippered them. Buttoned them. Scooped me up in his arms and stood up with me, effortlessly, as if I weighed nothing.

I stared into his eyes. "That was the single most intense sexual experience of my entire life, I'll have you know."

He frowned. "For real?"

"Absolutely. Without a doubt."

A smile blossomed on his face. "Watching you come is…" he shook his head. "It's a fucking privilege, Emerson."

I wiped at his mouth. "I think you've got that backwards." I patted his arm. "Okay. Put me down, please. You have to get dressed and wash your face."

He set me on my feet, dragging his wrist across his mouth. "There's just one more thing I have to do first."

"What's that?" I asked, desperately trying to ignore the hard-on he was rocking.

"This."

He kissed me again, and I tasted myself on him, as I knew he must taste himself on me. This time, the kiss was slow and sweet and gentle, and somehow all the hotter for it. I lost myself in the kiss, plastering myself against him, feeling him hard between us, clinging to his neck to stop myself from letting this devolve any further.

I broke away with a gasp. "You are a dangerous

man, Hayden McCaffrey. If we're not careful, I'm gonna get addicted to you."

"Would that be so bad?" he murmured.

"No. But we can't do what I want to do here and now." I stepped back out of reach and pointed at his erection. "It goes against everything I believe in to leave you hanging like that."

He turned away, speaking over his shoulder. "Go. I'll be fine. I'll be out in a minute."

"Hayden…" I took a half step toward him.

He stepped back. "Em, I'm *fine*, I promise. Go, or we'll just start it all back up again and they'll have to send a search party for us."

I turned away, hand on the doorknob. "You rock my world. I hope you understand that."

"Took the words out of my mouth, beautiful. Now go, please, before I run out of self-control."

I fled, legs still shaky, mind reeling, heart flailing.

What had I gotten myself into?

I wasn't sure what would happen, emotionally, but one thing was for certain: he was going to give me the best sex of my life.

Shit, he already had, and all we'd done was mess around.

Trouble, trouble, trouble.

And I wasn't about to stop.

TEN

Hayden

WHEN SHE WAS GONE, I SLUMPED, PANTING. IT HAD taken every last shred of willpower I possessed to keep my hands to myself, to let her escape the room, to not rip her clothes off and make love to her on the floor of Duncan's room.

I tasted her on my lips, savoring the essence of her.

God, she came so beautifully, so freely. I'd felt her holding back, and I knew she'd partially succeeded; I was determined to break through whatever barrier she had up, physically and emotionally.

Standing naked in that room, I knew one thing to be true: I was falling for Emerson Day.

Hard.

It wasn't just the physical, either. I mean, sure,

when she sank to her knees and put her mouth on me, the thought that went through my head, which I'd bitten my tongue to keep from saying, was, "Holy fuck, I think I love you." I wasn't about to utter those words in such a flippant manner. But it was also true. I was falling in love with her.

With her spirit, her attitude, her honesty, her love for her family. I was falling in love with the way she made me feel—her physical touch communicated a whole world of emotions. She *liked* me. She appreciated me. She was attracted to me. She made me feel strong, sexy, and confident. She made me feel wanted. The way she'd hauled me in here like she couldn't wait another second to get me alone? It rocked me to my core.

I located my clothes, folded in a neat stack on a sea chest at the foot of the bed. I dressed quickly, forcing my thoughts away from Emerson. I focused on statistics, lines of code, and batches of analytics. I listed all the presidents in order from Washington to the present day. State capitals. Recited pi to fourteen digits.

By the time I had my clothes on, my hard-on was gone. I popped into Duncan's en suite bathroom and washed my hands and face, scrubbed my hands through my hair, and fussed with it for a second.

I was delaying.

Scared of the reactions waiting for me out there.

My *mother* was out there.

I scraped my hands down my face, groaning. I had no idea what I'd say. To anyone.

Sorry for messing around with your daughter in your son's room?

Summoning my courage, I left the bedroom and headed for the kitchen. The volume rose considerably with every step until it was nearly deafening as I entered the kitchen.

A cheer rose as I entered, stopping me in my tracks. Everyone was focused on me.

"Um?" I looked around, baffled. "Hi…everyone?"

Emerson was sandwiched between Duncan and Xavier. She was blushing, hiding behind a big glass of red wine, her eyes on mine gleaming with secrets and amusement and embarrassment.

Baxter swaggered toward me, shoving a glass of amber liquid into my hands, along with a giant cigar. "You survived the Christmas Dunking, Hayden. How do you feel?"

I'd been half worried the whole thing was about Emerson and I vanishing together for…I wasn't even sure how long. "It was…invigorating."

A tall Badd cousin with blond hair, brown eyes, and a broad-shouldered build laughed. "I bet it was invigorating." Jax? I wanted to say he was Jax, Zane's and Mara's oldest.

"If my room smells funny, we're gonna have words, my friend," Duncan said.

Emerson slapped his chest. "Duncan, I swear, if

you don't shut the *fuck* up right now, I'm gonna kick your ass."

Mom paused in the middle of sipping what was probably the same glass of wine. Her eyes went to mine. Mama Livvie leaned close and whispered something to her; Mom bit her lip to keep from laughing and took a sip, hiding a smile behind the glass.

My gaze roamed the room, landing, hesitantly, on Bast. He was looking at me, too, his expression neutral. I felt like I had a sign on my chest announcing what Emerson and I had just done. I didn't regret it, didn't feel guilty, more just...I wasn't sure. It was a complicated feeling.

Bast pushed off the couch he'd been leaning against. "Yo!" he shouted, catching everyone's attention. "A toast." he held up his glass, which contained an inch of whiskey. "To our family and to new friends. Hayden and Kaye, it's been fuckin' amazing getting to know the two of you. I'd like to thank you for being here with us today and extend an open invitation whenever you find yourself in this neck of the woods. Merry Christmas, everyone!"

Everyone lifted their glasses, clinking with those nearest them, and then took a drink.

"On that note, I think the food is done. Ya'll know the drill—Ladies first, starting with Kaye." Bast put a huge hand on Mom's back and nudged her toward the stove and the giant stockpot full of stew.

The women formed a line behind her, Mama

Livvie, and then the other aunts, and then the cousins, each one being served by Dru, who was helped by a young woman around Emerson's age. She had light brown skin, curly black hair, and bright blue eyes. I wanted to say her name was Anya or Arya or something, but I wasn't sure.

Despite the number of people, the line moved fast. In addition to the stew, there was salad, fresh bread, and enough of everything for everyone to have seconds, even thirds.

Baxter gave me a playful shove toward the stove as the last of the youngest girl cousins went through the line. "You're gonna get some shit," he murmured. "Hope you know that."

I took a sip of the whiskey, coughing as it burned going down. I had the cigar in the same hand, unsure what to do with it or how I was going to juggle the glass, the cigar, and the food. "Um. Yeah. I…yeah."

He laughed and smacked me on the back—it felt like being whacked by a cinder block. "She warned you, huh?"

"Um, something like that."

"Bast is gonna fuck with you. You gotta push back." He grinned at me. "I gotta say, it does take some serious cajones to disappear with the host's daughter."

I coughed, choking on another burning sip. "I…"

Baxter guffawed. "Aw man, you're like a deer in the headlights, kid. Bast is gonna eat you alive if you don't figure out something to say."

"Like what?"

"I don't fuckin' know. But stammering and apologizing ain't it, man." He clapped a hand on my shoulder and squeezed, grinding the bones together. "Look, buddy. He ain't mad. Sunni is a big girl. She don't do nothin' she don't want to. Bast knows that. We all do. We're an open family. No secrets. Nothing is off the table. We're all a bunch of loud, vulgar, inappropriate motherfuckers, women included. All of us have snuck away and gotten frisky at a party at one point or another."

"Yeah, but not, as you pointed out, with the host's daughter."

He laughed. "True, true. But if you own it and keep cool about it, it'll all be good. Just don't show any fear."

"Easy for you to say. You guys are all scary as hell." I reached the stove. "Hi, Mrs. Badd."

She frowned at me, eyebrows bunching together. "Who the hell is Mrs. Badd?" She arched an eyebrow. "Because I know you're not talking to me."

I grinned. "Sorry, Dru."

She winked at me. "Better." She scooped several ladlefuls of stew into a waiting bowl and handed it to me but didn't let go right away, leaning close to whisper. "You've put a smile on Emerson's face, Hayden. Whatever you're doing, keep it up. I approve, and so does my husband, although he's gonna make you work for it."

"I'm beginning to really care about your daughter, ma'am. She's amazing. And she's made it very clear that you guys are largely responsible for that."

She sniffed, eyes smearing with unshed tears. "She would say that, wouldn't she? All we did was give her the love she deserves."

"Yeah, that's the special part."

She kissed my cheek, whispering again. "Don't let the boys bully you about taking some time with her, okay? They'll try. Whatever happened or didn't happen is no one's business but yours and Emerson's. That's the line you need to hold, okay? Hold that line, and you'll earn their respect."

I let out a huge sigh. "That I can do. Thank you, Dru." Louder, then: "This looks amazing. I can't wait to dig in."

"Hey, new guy! Move the line!" This came from a few places back—a cousin I hadn't been introduced to.

A girl behind him smacked the back of his head. "Don't be a dick, Merrick. You'll get your food. Can't you see the man is talking to Aunt Dru?"

I held up the hand with the glass in it in their direction. "Sorry!"

The girl winked at me. "You're good. My brother is just an impatient buttplug."

The guy, Merrick, turned and glared at her. "If I'm a buttplug, then you're a dildo someone found on the side of the highway."

Baxter, behind me, shouted without looking at

them. "Ella, Merrick, shut the fuck up before I shut you the fuck up. Merrick—don't be an impatient buttplug. Ella, don't call your brother names."

Both of them snapped their mouths shut. I sputtered a half-stopped laugh. "Sorry, I'm not—I shouldn't laugh."

Baxter grabbed four slices of bread from the bowl and shoved one in his mouth. "It's cool, man. I'm funny and you know it."

Zane, who had been in line behind Baxter, came up between us. "And so humble, too." He glanced at me and jerked his head toward the back deck. "Come on. We're sitting outside."

I turned to look over my shoulder, finding Emerson—she was perched on the back of the couch, her legs around Delia's shoulders. She glanced my way at the same time, shooting me a brilliant smile, and then winked and blew me a kiss before returning her attention to the conversation happening around her.

Zane and Baxter both eyed me.

"I didn't know she knew how to wink," Bax muttered. "What world are we living in?"

Zane shook his head. "You're an idiot. Who doesn't know how to wink?"

Baxter stared at his brother. "Who's the idiot? It was a fuckin' joke, you bag of fuckballs. I just meant I've never seen that girl act this way in the fifteen years I've known her. Jesus. Dense much?"

The two huge men escorted me outside—cold

air blew and snow swirled, but the space heaters and the fireplace-table held the worst of it at bay; once I took a seat on the couch by the table, I was comfortable. There was a massive ashtray full of ash and cigar butts as well as a few small whitish-brown butts that I suspected were joint roaches. I put my cigar in the ashtray and set my glass down as Bax took the seat on one side and Zane on the other. Bast swaggered out next, blowing out through his teeth to cool the bite of stew he'd shoved in, wedging himself on the couch on the far side of Zane.

Within a minute, Myles, Xavier, all three triplets, the giant named Ink, the twins Canaan and Corin, and Lucian were all wedged around the table, plates and bowls balanced on knees. There was only desultory conversation as everyone dug into the stew.

"This is the best stew I've ever had," I said, sipping the throat-burning, stomach-warming whiskey.

Bast nodded. "Sure as fuck is. Dru tinkers with the recipe all fall. It's never exactly the same from year to year, but it's always amazing. I think she put beer in it this year."

"I've never seen a stockpot that big before," I said.

He laughed. "We call it her witch's cauldron. She used something like, fuck, I don't know—five or six pounds of beef, at least, plus a metric fuckton of veggies and several gallons of beef stock. It's been simmering since this morning."

"Well, it's great. Mom and I are so thankful to be

here. Seriously." I held his gaze, hoping he saw how genuinely I meant it. "It's been a rough couple months and this is…" I swallowed hard, eyes burning. "Shit. Um. You guys are the coolest people, and I feel very fortunate to have met you all."

The giant, Ink, nodded, gesturing at me with his glass. "Hear, hear. The Badds make hospitality into an art form. We're all better for how you guys have welcomed us in."

"Damn right," Myles said. "We're all misfits and fuckups and orphans, and ya'll bring us in and make us part of the family."

Bast hunched over his bowl, elbows on his knees, fork dangling. "Mom died, Dad died, and the eight of us boys didn't have anyone but each other. We took care of each other. And then Dru and Mara came along what seemed like at the same time and started taking care of us in ways we didn't know we needed."

Zane pointed at his brother with his fork, speaking around a mouthful. "Exactly." He chewed and swallowed. "I credit the women for bringing us cavemen out of the Stone Age and showing us how to be a family."

Lucian spoke for the first time—he was one of the eight brothers, a younger one, with loose shoulder-length brown hair laced with a few strands of gray at the temples, built lean and rangy. "Bast, you've been the patriarch of this family for twenty years. You gotta give yourself some credit."

Xavier cleared his throat. "I believe twenty years is an inaccurate number, Lucian. Bast took care of the seven of us after Mom died and Dad…" he trailed off, shrugging. "Bast has been the patriarch for probably closer to thirty years."

"Way to make me feel old as fuck, Xave." Bast laughed, grinning at his brother. "But thanks. I just…I was tryin' to do what felt right."

"You did," Xavier answered. "And we are all better for it."

Bast seemed uncomfortable with this conversation. I felt him decide to turn the spotlight onto me, and sure enough, his gaze swung to me. "So, Hayden."

I set my now-empty stew bowl on the table and started on my salad. "Sir?"

"Sir," one of the triplets said—he had a bushy beard, and I thought his name was Ramsey. "Bast, this kid called you sir. Think he's scared?"

Bast stacked his empty bowl with mine. "You and Emerson were gone for a while," he said, eying me. "Couldn't find the clothes, huh?"

"I think if you have questions about that, you should talk to Emerson. Respectfully, sir, whatever did or did not happen is between Emerson and myself."

Bast leaned back, slinging a long, brawny arm along the back of the couch. "Good answer, kid." He grabbed a cigar from a wooden box on the table, a cutter and lighter from a bowl beside it, and clipped and lit the stogie. "Dru gives good advice, huh?"

He handed me the cutter and lighter. I'd never had a cigar before, but it seemed pretty straightforward. I got a piece of tobacco in my mouth, but my embarrassment faded when I noticed Bast plucking at his tongue as well.

I got mine puffing. "You don't inhale these, right?"

Bast laughed. "You *can*, but I wouldn't recommend it."

One of the triplets—Rome? He had shorter hair with heavy stubble on his jaw—pulled something from the inside pocket of the well-worn leather jacket he was wearing. It was a glass tube with a pre-rolled joint in it. He removed it, lit it, inhaled, and passed it to his left. "*This* you inhale."

It came to me after a minute, and I took it, hesitating.

Xavier gave me an understanding smile. "It is legal here, Hayden. We all partake on holidays like this. If you are uncomfortable with it, however, merely pass it along. No one will judge you, regardless of whether you choose to join us or not."

I'd never tried it, despite having been offered a few times. For some reason, however, I felt safe with these people, so I took a small hit, immediately devolving into hacking. Bast chuckled and smacked my back. "There you go, kid. Popped your pot cherry, did we?"

"Yeah," I gasped, catching my breath, head already spinning.

"I gotta ask," Bast said, taking a hit of the joint,

passing it, and then peering at the end of the cigar as if it held some hitherto unknown wisdom. "You and your mom are here on vacation. I assume you're going back to Indiana. So my question is, you and Sunni... what's the plan, there?"

I sighed and laughed, taking a puff of the cigar—it dried my mouth out, though, so I took a sip of whiskey. "Give me mind-altering substances and *then* ask," I said, "I see how it is."

He just shrugged, smirking. "It's a tool in the toolbox."

I tried to blow a smoke ring and managed a wobbly blob. "The honest answer is I don't know. We haven't...we aren't there. We met the other day."

"But you said it's not casual," he pressed. "I'm not pressuring you to label things, but I do want to know your intentions."

I set the cigar down, my stomach feeling a little queasy from the smoke. I accepted the joint again, coughing less this time. I felt floaty, loose. I considered Bast's question—What *were* my intentions?

"Sir, I think you need to ask your daughter that. But more to the point, you need to trust her. She's not a kid. She's a grown woman who knows what she wants. I say this with all possible respect, but my intentions don't really matter. Hers do. I like who she is. I enjoy spending time with her. I enjoy spending time with all of you. I can't tell you what the future holds or whether she and I will be in a relationship or not. I don't know. I know I'm intrigued by her, fascinated by her, attracted to her. I know I will respect her wishes. I can work remotely, however, so *if* things were to progress in that direction, I can go anywhere. That said, my mom is alone now. That complicates things."

"This is a lot of pressure to put on the kid," Myles said. "They're just hanging out. Getting to know each other. None of us knew what the fuck was going on less than three days after meeting our women. Lay off the guy a little bit."

Bast stared at Myles. Blew a perfect smoke ring. Then looked at me. "They vanished together for fifteen minutes during a party. I think I'm entitled to put a little pressure on him. To make sure he's not playing games just to get in my daughter's pants."

"Brother, you aren't thinking clearly," Xavier said. "Even if that was his intent, do you really think he would admit to it except under extreme duress? Are you planning to waterboard our guest? You have to trust Emerson. You have to trust that she can see through him if he is, in fact, being duplicitous. I, for one, do not believe that to be the case. And I suspect you do not either. He strikes me as being honest and genuine. He has answered you truthfully and respectfully—with respect for you as well as Emerson. And, as Myles has said, put all of that aside. They've known each other for an amount of time which can be measured in hours. I think this entire conversation could be considered a little bit premature."

Bast hung his head, nodding. "You're right, Xave, Myles." He looked at me. "My bad. I'm sorry. I shouldn't push. It's not my place."

"Please don't apologize, sir. You do it out of love. I know it. She knows it. I knew this conversation was coming, and I may have been shitting my pants a little bit, but I think that's to be expected. She's a strong woman. I wouldn't be worthy of her if I couldn't handle this. And I can." I sipped whiskey, huffing through pursed lips as it scorched down my esophagus.

Bast regarded me steadily. And then he extended his glass to me. "Well said, son."

I clinked. "All I can do is be truthful."

"Amen to that," Myles said. "Now, enough deep shit. Gimme that joint and let's get to the shit-talking."

The evening wore on, and there was no more interrogation. The men sort of monopolized my time, involving me in a round of pool, which I sucked at, and then got dragged to the sledding run, clothed in Duncan's snow gear, hurtling down the run with a scream trapped in my throat. I was tipsy, or perhaps more than that. Every time I turned around, someone was putting a drink in my hand. It was usually followed with a bottle of water, which I always promptly drank half of and then lost.

Emerson was everywhere, sledding with the older

cousins, in a circle with aunts and girl cousins, a joint passing around. Laughing, hanging off Delia, talking shit to everyone, and having the best time in the world.

Mom, too.

She and Olivia were two peas in a pod. I saw them sitting with their heads together, Kleenex clutched in their hands, weeping—through what seemed like osmosis, I had a vague awareness that she'd lost her first husband as well, and I imagined she and Mom were talking about that. Hopefully, Olivia was giving Mom advice.

At some point, the younger kids conked out in the TV room with a Christmas movie going, a roomful of blanket-covered lumps.

Eventually, I caught Mom coming out of the powder room off the kitchen. "Hey, Mom. Saw you talking to Olivia a lot."

Her eyes swam a little, but she sounded lucid and with it when she spoke. "Yes, quite extensively. She's a lovely woman. She lost her first husband suddenly as well. It was wonderful to have someone who knows what I'm going through to commiserate with." She blinked at me. "I'm glad you brought me, Hayden. This has been a wonderful time."

I leaned against the wall, my head spinning. "It has."

"Hayden?"

I glanced at her. "Yeah, Ma?"

"You and Sunni..."

I palmed my face. "I already got the third degree from her family…twice. We're still figuring things out."

She shook her head. "No, I wasn't going to question you. I was going to say that she seems like a lovely, intelligent, wonderful young woman with a good head on her shoulders. She clearly comes from a wonderful family. You could do a heck of a lot worse."

I laughed. "Mom. I know, okay? But like I said, we're figuring things out. It's been two days. We leave, what, tomorrow? The next day?"

"The day after Christmas. So two days."

"I just want you to be happy. And it seems to me like she makes you happy." She yawned. "I'm probably ready to go soon, though."

"Yeah, probably. I admit I have no idea how we're getting there, though. Brock isn't flying us anywhere."

Claire, Brock's wife, a petite blonde with a loud, colorful personality even among this group, slipped past us into the bathroom, yelling through the door. "There's a car service. Dru has a number for you to text and they'll come get you."

I side-hugged Mom. "I'll get that arranged."

"Thanks, Hayden. I'm fading." She stifled another yawn and headed for the living room.

Olivia slid aside to make room for her on a love-seat, murmuring something to her. I found Dru, got the number, and requested the car service.

That's when Emerson found me, finally, and pulled me outside. She fished a huge fluffy blanket out of a chest that doubled as an ottoman and waited for me to sit down. When I did, she settled on my lap and wrapped the blanket around our shoulders and over our laps.

She rested her head on my chest. "Hi."

"Hey there. Good night?"

She nodded. "Very. I love these parties." She looked up at me. "They didn't give you too hard of a time, did they?"

"Nah." I laughed. "Well, I mean, it could have been worse. The second time, out on the deck—"

"Wait, the second time?"

"Yeah. The first was in the sauna after the dunking and then out on the deck a few hours ago. It was okay. They just want to make sure I'm not playing games. Playing a role to get into your pants. That kind of thing."

"What'd you say?"

"That they, well, Bast, mainly, needed to trust you because my intentions don't really matter, as long as they trust you to know what you want and take care of yourself." I let out a sigh, wrapping my arms tighter around her.

"I like that answer. How did he respond?"

"Well, he was concerned about the fact that I'm only here on vacation."

She pulled back and looked at me. "And?"

"I told him the truth—we're still figuring things out. I don't know what this is. Neither do you, I don't think. But I did tell him that if things with you and me progressed to that point, I work remotely so location isn't a huge deal. The only complication is Mom— she's alone, now."

Emerson resumed resting against me. "You'd relocate?"

"Hell yes. As long as I felt like Mom was okay, yeah." I hesitated. "What, um…what are your plans after you graduate?"

She groaned. "I don't fucking know. I want to play pro and for the US women's team. If I don't make that, I don't know. Coach soccer somewhere, maybe?"

"What's your degree in?"

"Sports management."

"Coaching makes sense, then, I guess."

She nodded. "Yeah, but I'm hoping to play a bit longer. I'm sure I can make a professional team, but the US National Women's Team is the real goal."

"You can do it."

She shrugged, sighed. "Thanks. We'll see."

"When can I see you again?"

She giggled. "See me in what sense?"

I snickered. "Yes."

"A bunch of us women are going to Anchorage to go shopping and have a spa day—another yearly tradition. Brock is flying us. Christmas Eve we're spending at Uncle Xavier and Aunt Low's during the day. We do a candlelight church service in the evening, and then the families all sort of do their own thing that night and Christmas morning, and then everyone comes here around lunch." She grunted in frustration. "So, I don't know, unfortunately."

"Our boat leaves the day after Christmas," I said.

There wasn't much to say, then, it seemed.

"You're not allowed to leave," she whispered. "I do not give you permission. Not until you and I get, like, one fucking hour alone and in private."

"Yes ma'am," I said, laughing.

She looked at me. "Who's joking?"

"I promise. We'll find time together."

A long silence. "What are you and your mom doing for actual Christmas day?" she asked.

I shrugged. "Something on the boat, I think? Not sure."

She sighed. "I'm gonna talk to Bast and Dru."

"About?"

"You should be with us. You shouldn't be alone or on some boat with a few thousand strangers."

"It's okay, Em. You deserve time with your family. We don't want to intrude on that."

"If you're invited, it's not intruding. I just can't unilaterally decide that for my whole family."

"You guys have been so welcoming. You've made what would have been a pretty depressing Christmas into something amazing." I inhaled the scent of her hair.

"I'm feeling things, Hayden," she whispered. "Emotions. Big ones. What do we do with that?"

"I am too, and I don't know. Take it one step at a time, I guess."

She wiggled her butt against my crotch. "I think I know the *big* things you're feeling."

I clutched her hard. "Hey, now. Our car's gonna be here any minute. Don't start something we can't finish."

A sigh. "Fine." She laughed. "I just can't help it. I'm a horny bitch and you turn me on."

"I'm not complaining, believe me." I kissed the top of her head. I touched her chin, tilted her face up to mine. "Thank you for inviting us, Emerson. It's meant more to me, and especially my mom, than I can ever express."

"CAR'S HERE!" A male voice boomed.

I groaned. "That's my cue."

Emerson clung to me. "No. You can't."

I stood up with her, laughing. "Fine. I'll just bring you with me. I'll tell boat security that I grew a barnacle."

She slid to her feet. "Fine. But I protest." She gazed up at me with emotions boiling in her eyes. "I'll figure something out and call you, okay?"

"Sounds good."

"Kiss me?"

"Try and stop me," I said, and cupped her head in my hand, touched my lips to hers, and tasted the sweetness of her lips, her tongue, her breath.

I heard a throat clear and broke away to see Mom with her purse and coat. "Sorry to interrupt, kids."

I touched my forehead to Emerson's. "Soon."

"Soon." She lifted up and kissed me again, a quick peck, and then stepped back out of my arms and wrapped the blanket around herself, watching as Mom and I made our exit—which took a minute since we had to say goodbye and hug a good three-quarters of everyone on the way to the door.

Mom was asleep before we left their driveway. I, however, lay awake for hours after we got back to our rooms, trying to figure out what working things out with her would mean and how we could be together despite the logistical complications.

I fell asleep without any answers.

ELEVEN

Emerson

THE HOUSE WAS FINALLY QUIET. IT WAS ALMOST THREE IN the morning, and I was the only one still up. I was exhausted and wanted desperately to sleep, but I couldn't. My buzz had worn off, leaving me with a headache and a sour stomach.

I had Hayden on the brain.

I got the electric kettle out of the cabinet, filled it, and set it to heating while I found my favorite mug. It was oversized and white with stick figures painted on it, two larger and four smaller ones lined up and holding hands. Each person's name was written above their stick figure stand-in: Daddy, Mommy, Delia, Duncan, Dane, and Emerson. Delia made it in art class in fourth grade and represented the sum of her artistic talents.

It also represented the first time I had a physical representation of me belonging to the Badd family in any kind of official capacity.

I waited for the kettle to click off, poured the boiling water over the peppermint tea bag, and took it outside. The fire was off, as were the space heaters, so it was bitterly cold, but I had a thick coat and my Ugg slippers. I wrapped myself in a blanket, kicked my feet up, and rested the mug on my stomach while it steeped.

The clouds had cleared in the last hour or two since everyone left, taking the snow with it, leaving a wash of brilliant, sparkling, scintillating stars. I stared up at them, thinking.

The main question on my mind was a simple one, yet it didn't seem to have a clear-cut answer: Can you fall in love with someone within seventy-two hours of meeting them?

It didn't seem possible. On the face of it, it seemed ludicrous. You can't know the first thing about a person in that short amount of time. In order to love someone, you have to know them—who they are. What they like, what they don't like. What they believe. I've been friends with good, kind, sexy, decent guys at school for months, years, even. Alex Naismith, for example. He was in my program, plays for the men's soccer team, and was in many of my classes. He was a good guy, got good grades, treated people well, kicked ass at soccer. He had a nice dick and used it well. We'd fucked three or four times, and I enjoyed it—I enjoyed him. But it never went anywhere. Aside from physical pleasure, there was just... nothing. I liked him, but I never felt anything for him but affection and friendship. Why? I liked the person who Alex is. He was a genuinely good person who should have been a perfect match for me. But despite all that, we're nothing more than friends.

Yet, within a few days of meeting Hayden, my world got turned upside down. I couldn't stop thinking about him. I craved him. And yes, it was physical. He was hot as fuck. That black hair, messy and wild, those green eyes...and fuck, that body, all hard and lean and shredded, and yeah, that cock of his. But it was more than that. A lot more. It's his bearing, his energy. He made me feel seen and safe. He made me feel powerful and sexy and wanted.

But what do I *know* about him? He went to Purdue, works in cybersecurity, his father just died, he's an only child...and that's about it. I don't know what music he listens to, his politics, his religion, his taste in movies...

Does that matter?

"Can't sleep, huh, kiddo?" Bast's voice startled me so badly that I jerked, spilling tea on my hand.

"Fuck—ow!" I set the mug aside and shook my hand, hissing. "You scared the shit outta me," I said.

"Sorry," he muttered. "Scoot."

I shifted to make room for him, lifting the blanket. He slid under and covered himself. I leaned against him, grabbing my mug and taking a careful sip.

"Thinking deep thoughts?" he asked, taking the mug and stealing a sip.

I sighed. "Yeah, I guess so."

"Talk to me."

"Why are *you* up?" I asked.

He shrugged. "Got up to piss and had a hunch you were up."

"What, you're psychic, now?" I asked, laughing.

"Nah. A father just knows."

I couldn't argue with that. "I'm wrestling with the question every kid ends up asking their parents at some point."

"Where do babies come from?" he teased, that infuriating smirk of his on his face.

I rolled my eyes at him. "No, I'm pretty sure I've got that one covered, thanks."

He sighed. "What is love?"

"Almost—how do you know you're in love? More specifically, can you be in love with someone you just met?" I looked at him, watching him absorb my question.

He cast his gaze to the sky, thinking for a long time. "Emmy, babe, that is a hell of a question. There is no one-size-fits-all answer." He sighed and stole another sip of my tea. "The moment I laid eyes on Dru, I was…smitten, I guess. I can't think of any better word. But was that love? Or just instant attraction or chemistry? I fought it. I fought it hard. But it was…it's not something you can fight, if that's the person your soul has chosen. My soul chose Dru, and hers chose me. I couldn't walk away, and neither could she. The idea of going through life, of going another day, another week, another month, another year without her just didn't compute in my brain. My body craved her. My soul was comforted by her. It just…clicked."

I sighed a laugh. "So it comes down to…you just know?"

His chest bounced beneath me as he chuckled. "Unfortunately. I wish I had a better, clearer answer for you, but I don't." He rubbed my arm and squeezed me to him. "If you want a more concise answer to whether you can fall in love with someone you just met, then I say yes. You fall in love with a person's soul. Who they are. Their body, too. You can't ignore what a person looks like. But in the end, it's who they are matching who you are that makes a relationship work, and that's something I can't define for you. What works, what makes two people click? Matchmakers may say they know, but I think there's an element to it no one will ever be able to really nail down. So just because you don't know all the details of who Hayden is, all about his life, his past, the inner workings of his personality…to me, that all comes over time. Falling in love is a lot simpler than that. Conducting a successful relationship, a strong marriage? That's a whole hell of a lot more fucking complicated. But falling in love? You ask me, yeah, that can happen in an instant."

"That's what I was afraid of." I sipped tea and stared at the stars.

"Afraid? Why are you afraid? What are you afraid of?"

"I don't know," I murmured. "I haven't gotten to that point of self-reflection yet."

"Well, you need to talk more, I'm here. I can listen, I can give advice. I can toss his ass into the Passage. Whatever you need."

"I don't think Passage-tossing will be necessary, but thanks," I said, laughing.

"I don't either. He seems like a good dude."

I twisted to look up at him. "You know, the whole, um, disappearing thing? That was my idea."

A snort. "It doesn't matter. I wasn't and am not mad about it. I just wanted to know how he'd react under pressure. If he'd throw you under the bus or protect you. He showed up for you. He protected you. Stood his ground. I respect him for that."

"No more tests, okay? Please? I need to be able to figure out what this is and what I want and how it would work out on my own. So does he. And it all just feels…so fucking fast. My head is spinning. I just met him and I feel like…like I've always known him. The thought of him leaving and going back to Indiana and me going back to Seattle and us not seeing each other anymore…it scares me. Makes me feel panicky. But what do we do? I have a life, I have plans, and he has a life and he has plans. And those things are a whole fucking continent apart."

"Are we discussing your love life without me?" I heard Mama Dru say as the sliding door opened and closed.

We both turned to watch her come out, wrapped in a thick red fleece robe with an oversized white beanie with a puffy pompom on top of her head tugged down over her ears. She had a mug of tea in her hands, too, and scurried over to us.

"Let me in, let me in—it's cold out here!" she said, squeezing in on Big Daddy Bast's other side.

He flipped open the blanket and tucked Dru in against his other side, then wrapped the blanket around her again, sighing contentedly. "Good?"

She hummed happily as she snuggled in, only one hand holding the mug outside the blanket. "Yep. Now. What's the tea?"

"Peppermint," Bast said.

Dru and I both laughed.

"I mean, what are we talking about, honey," she said, chuckling as she patted his stomach.

"Oh. Emmy's love life," Bast said.

"And whether you can fall in love at first sight, how to know, and why I'm scared of being in love with Hayden," I filled in.

"Ah. So minor things." She blew across the top of her tea, sipped, and hissed. "Ooh shit—still really fucking hot, Jesus. Okay, um…let's see. Question number one: can you fall in love at first sight? Yes. This big hunk here fell in love with me at first sight. I was drunk and heartbroken at the time, so I fought it quite a bit longer than he did. Question number two: you just know. If the thought of being apart from him makes you panic and possibly rethink your entire life, you're in love. And question number three...that's a trickier one. You have daddy issues, I think."

"Excuse me?" Bast said.

"Not you, honey." She rubbed his chest. "Her biological father."

I frowned. "I don't think about him at all. I barely knew him, I'm not mad at him—he's...he's nothing to me. No one. I don't even know if he's still alive, and frankly, my dear, I don't give a damn."

Mama Dru just sighed. "Oh, honey, I wish it were that simple. But the wounds left by our parents in our youth tend to go unnoticed until we're much older. They get buried very, very deeply. I'm fifty years old and I'm still dealing with my mother's death. My father loved me and took care of me as well as he could, but there was still a part of me that felt abandoned by my mother and by Dad, because even though he was present and doing his best, he still threw himself into work to cope, which left me to deal with shit on my own." She gazed up at her husband. "Bast honey, I know you went through something very similar."

He nodded. "And I'm still dealing with it, still seeing places where it's fucking me up. Mom died, and

Dad withdrew into himself, into work, and into the bottom of a bottle. He never hit us or verbally lashed out or anything. He wasn't...well, he wasn't like Uncle Lucas was with Roman, Remington, and Ramsey before he got himself cleaned up and married Liv. Dad just...he was a ghost. And I was left raising my brothers. Running the bar. I had to grow up real fuckin' fast, and to this day, that's why I tend to be more serious and sometimes kinda grouchy. Felt like I had the weight of the world on my shoulders from a very young age, and that kinda thing sticks with you."

"And so you guys think I'm afraid of falling in love because of something to do with my father?" I looked up at Bast. "Because *you're* my dad. In every way that has ever counted, you're my dad. How can I have psychological hangups I'm not even aware of?"

Dru laughed. "Oh, my sweet summer child." She craned forward, blew across the rim of her mug, sipped the tea, then rested the mug on Bast's thigh over the blanket. "Our deepest hang-ups tend to be invisible until we're willing to see them, and it usually takes something huge like falling in love to see them."

I sighed, resting my head back on the couch. "I've got a lot of thinking to do, I guess, huh?"

Bast tilted his head to one side. "I mean, I don't think it's all that complicated, babe. The fucker abandoned you. You're afraid of letting Hayden all the way in because you're afraid he'll abandon you, too."

"Hmmm," I hummed. "I don't know. I mean, I

have, like, almost twenty good men who stayed. From you to Uncle Errol, you've *all* stayed."

"Like I said, honey, it's deeper than that." Dru tried the tea again. "Your father abandoned you at a very young age and did so repeatedly. Yes, you have all of us who've shown you what lasting love looks like. But the instinctive fear of commitment? That's one of those deep wounds that you have to work past. And at some point, honestly, you just have to assess the risks and either jump or don't. Either Hayden is worth the risk and fear and work, or he's not. And only you can decide that."

I thunked my head backward a couple of times, groaning. "Ugh!" I laughed and sat up to sip. "Why can't anything be easy?"

Bast laughed. "Wish I knew, girl, wish I knew. But nothin' ever is, and that's just life. I will say, though, in this, it's worth it."

"It is?" I asked.

Bast twisted to frown down at me. "Well, yeah. Obviously. Falling in love was scary as fuck, but I haven't regretted it a day in my life. It ain't all been easy. We've had our share of knock-down, drag-out fights about all sorts of shit. I had a hard time adjusting to fatherhood, largely because of my hangups about my father. But I wouldn't change a thing."

I sighed and then groaned. "So I just have to jump…or not."

"Pretty much," Dru said.

"Cool," I muttered. "On a related note, how would you guys feel if we had Hayden and Kaye over on Christmas Day? They're alone. It'll just be them on that giant stupid boat with a few thousand strangers, eating cruise ship buffet food and listening to Christmas Muzak or whatever."

Bast laughed. "I don't think it'd be as bad as you're imagining, babe."

Dru blew a raspberry. "Speak for yourself, husband. Christmas Day on a cruise ship, months after losing their father and husband? That does sound exactly that bad." She looked up at Bast, waiting.

He nodded. "If you feel like you want to share Christmas Day with them, Emerson, then we will welcome them without hesitation, you know that."

"I do. I'm not sure I can explain why, I just feel like it's the right thing to do." I closed my eyes and let out a long breath. "You're sure?"

"Absolutely," Bast said, squeezing me. "They're good people. I like them both, and if you're falling for the guy, then it only makes sense to have them over."

"I have a better idea." Dru hesitated. "Not sure how either of you will feel about this. But what if they came over Christmas Eve and stayed? Kaye can have the basement, and you and Hayden are in your room."

Bast said nothing.

"You're okay with us sharing a room?"

She shrugged. "You're adults. I wouldn't let Duncan or Dane have a girlfriend sleep over, but they're still in high school. You're a grown woman and he's a grown man. Bast, honey, what do you think?"

He considered for a moment. "I think Dunc and Dane take the basement, and Kaye takes Dane's room on the end, with Dunc's room in the middle empty. Delia I'm not worried about."

I slid under the blanket, hiding my flushed face. "Good plan." I shoved one hand out of the blanket and gave a thumbs up. "We don't need to discuss it any further."

Dru reached across and poked me. "Discuss what? How you and Hayden are desperate for time alone? At night? In a bed? When the house isn't full of people?"

I pulled the blanket down enough to reveal my eyes, which I used to glare at her. "Yes, that."

Bast yawned. "You know we're gonna tease you, babe. But I'm cool with it. Set it up."

Dru yawned next. "I probably should get gifts for them, then."

"I don't know," I said. "Kaye would probably not like being given a gift when she didn't have one to give. She strikes me as that type of person."

"So tell 'em tomorrow, and make sure they know they're not obligated to give anyone anything." Bast kissed my temple. "I'm about to ready to go back to bed. You should try to sleep, too."

Dru slid off the couch, tugged her robe closed tighter as a gust of wind skirled, and leaned down to kiss the top of my head. "Love you, Sunni-girl. All you can do is take it one day at a time and listen to your heart. You're a smart girl; you'll figure it out."

"Thanks, guys," I said. "I'll be in in a minute."

They headed in, and a few minutes later, so did I. It took a while, but I did eventually fall asleep. My dreams were of Hayden, and they were *not* PG-13.

TWELVE

Hayden

I DIDN'T SEE EMERSON THE NEXT DAY AND BARELY HAD TIME to text her. She was busy at her Uncle Xavier's house for the day, and Mom and I spent the day together exploring Ketchikan. We bought each other gifts and went to comical lengths to keep them a surprise. I decided I needed to get Emerson something and decided on a necklace with a gold sunburst pendant inlaid with a large iridescent opal in the middle. Mom got Olivia an interior design coffee table book. We went in together to get Bast and Dru a book of historical photographs of Ketchikan.

Mom seemed…sad, I suppose. More so as we neared Christmas Eve. Understandable. I felt it my-self. I kept finding myself checking my phone for a text or a call from Dad; I couldn't imagine how it must feel for Mom, who'd been with him her whole life.

Christmas had always been Mom's favorite holiday. She loved to decorate the house until Dad teased her about it. She'd spend the entire week leading up to Christmas baking cookies and pies, and every time I'd come over, the house would smell amazing. Dad would be chopping wood or watching football, or they'd be snuggled up together on the couch watching black and white Christmas movies on TCM, getting a little tipsy and acting like love-sick teenagers.

We'd watch *National Lampoon's Christmas Vacation* on Christmas Eve and quote the whole thing to each other—mainly Dad and me, driving Mom nuts. *Shitter's full!*

We'd order Chinese and Dad would read the Christmas story from the Bible. No matter how old I got, I cherished those traditions, even if they sometimes seemed a little cheesy. Now, I'd give anything to have one more holiday with Dad.

This was on my mind as I walked Mom to her room.

"Thinking about Dad?" I said as we reached our doors that evening, after dinner onboard the ship.

She nodded, fiddling with the rope handle of the gift bags. "Missing him. Remembering our first Christmas together."

"That's one I haven't heard," I said, leaning against the wall between our doors.

She smiled, eyes glistening. "We were *so* broke, Hayden. We'd just gotten married and had moved in together a few months prior. Your father was still in school, and I was waitressing to put him through it. I got him a digital wristwatch, a refillable pen, and a tie. He got me…oh my, let's see…oh! I remember! How could I forget? It was so bad I could only laugh. He got me a purse. It was so sweet. He was so excited for me to open it. But it was something my grandmother would have liked, maybe. It was enormous and just absolutely hideous."

I laughed. "Dad was not great at gifts."

She shook her head, wiping at her eyes, sniffing and laughing. "No, he most certainly was not."

"What'd you do?" I asked.

She swallowed hard. "What could I do? He was so proud, thinking he'd gotten me something I would love. I couldn't crush him by telling him I'd rather have gotten a blender. I pretended to love it. I should have gotten an Oscar for that." She laughed, ending in a sigh. "A few years later, we were moving, and he found it stuffed in the back of the coat closet. I'd told him I'd misplaced it, acted all heartbroken."

"Mom! You *lied* to Dad?" I was faint with shock.

She just snickered. "Oh, honey, yes. He realized what had happened the moment he pulled it out. He looked right at me and said, 'You hate this, don't you?' And all I could do was admit that I did. He looked at it and started laughing. 'It is ugly as hell, isn't it?' he said."

She shook her head. "After that, I made sure to give him a wishlist sometime around Thanksgiving. That way, he'd know what I wanted and liked. It took the pressure off. He didn't always go off the list, though. Sometimes that worked out, sometimes it didn't."

"Was that the worst gift he ever gave you?" I asked.

"Oh, goodness, no. Not even close. One year, you were…oh, three? Four? He gave me an antique lamp. To be fair, it was a beautiful lamp, and I did like it. But I'd made it clear, I'd thought, what I wanted, and what I was expecting—a pair of earrings. Why he thought I'd like a lamp we didn't need instead of the earrings I specifically showed him and told him I wanted, I'll never know. Men are mysterious that way." She laughed. "I was annoyed, and he didn't get any Christmas—" she cut herself off abruptly. "Anyway. But I got over it, and he bought me the earrings and gave them to me New Year's Eve."

"Remember when he gave me that GI Joe for my birthday?" I said, laughing. "I was turning thirteen. I was like, Dad, this is what I asked for six years ago."

Mom covered her face. "I tried to tell him. He insisted thirteen-year-olds still played with GI Joe."

"The Walkman I actually wanted was from you, then, I assume?"

She nodded. "Of course." She closed her eyes and leaned her head on the door. "I miss him so much, Hayden. Especially now. I miss the way he used to take cookies right off the baking sheet fresh out of the oven and then huff and puff when they burned his mouth. I miss…my god, I miss everything. I miss his stupid gifts. I miss watching *Miracle on 34th Street* with him. It's just not the same."

I moved in and pulled her into my arms. "No, it's not."

She sniffled, pulling away after a moment. "Today was fun, though. This trip has been fun. You've really gone out of your way to distract me and cheer me up, Hayden, and I want you to know that I see it, and I'm grateful." She patted my cheek. "I love you, Son."

I kissed her on the head. "Love you, too, Ma."

"So. What shall we do tomorrow?" She asked.

"I don't know. I was thinking about all the traditions we used to do and how much I miss them. I just…I guess I don't know where to go from here." My eyes burned, and Mom wiped at my eyes.

"Don't you dare, Hayden. If you start, I'll start, and if I start, I'll never stop."

I fought like hell to regain composure. "I know. I know."

She rested her hand on my cheek. "Let's sleep on it and decide together tomorrow, okay?"

"Sounds good."

When I got into my room, though, I couldn't keep it in anymore. I just…lost it. Ugly crying. Snot, sobs, the works. All the grief I'd been shoving aside to be there for Mom all came out at once.

And, of course, my phone burbled—a FaceTime. I

answered it instinctively because the thought of talking to Em soothed me. I kept the camera facing away as I tried to put myself back together.

"Hayden? Why am I looking at the ceiling?" She was outside, wearing a white puffy coat and a purple hat that clashed gloriously with her hair; chatter and laughter in the background sounded merry, and I heard a few people singing "Jingle Bells" off-key while someone else cackled.

"I, uh—" I cleared my throat and sniffed hard. "Hold on."

"Hayden?" She heard it—of course she did. Why did I think I could hide it? "What's wrong?"

To be honest, it took a hell of a lot of courage to show her my face on the camera, knowing I was all blotchy and red-eyed and snotty.

"I'm good. I'm good. Just…ah—um. Let me call you back, okay?"

"Don't you dare hang up on me, buster." There were jostling sounds, and then the noise faded. "There. Now. Talk to me, honey. What's going on? Why are you crying?"

"Mom and I were talking about Dad. And I just…" I shook my head, feeling it all trying to come back up. "About Christmas. I just miss him, you know? It sucks. I'm trying to be happy and in the spirit for her, but it's hard. I miss him. But he was her husband for *fifty years*. I can't imagine how hard it must be for her."

"Hey, it's not a competition. He was your father.

Of course you're gonna have a hard time. It's your first Christmas without him." She sighed. "I wish I was there to hug you."

I groaned, wiping at my face. "Me too." I cleared my throat and tipped my head back, taking a few deep breaths. "So. How's the party?"

"Oh, it's fun. It's always fun. Xavier rarely cuts loose, but tonight he's actually a little drunk. Aunt Low got him to recite *The Iliad* in the original Greek, and he turned it into a one-man play…in ancient Greek."

I scoffed. "For real?"

She nodded, laughing. "He's a savant with an eidetic memory. He can quote entire plays by Shakespeare. *Beowulf* in Old English or whatever. His pet project right now, apparently, is a three-dimensional model of the constellations as seen from Ketchikan from the first record of humans in North America to the present."

I gaped at the phone. "What? Why?"

She just laughed. "It's Uncle X. Who the hell knows? He likes an academic challenge."

"Inventing some of the most important technology of the twenty-first century isn't challenge enough?"

"Apparently not." Someone in the background shouted her name. "Hold on one sec," she murmured to me and then paused the screen; a few seconds later she was back. "Sorry. So, um, do you and Kaye have any definite plans?"

I shrugged and shook my head. "No, not really. We were gonna figure that out over breakfast. Why?"

"Because I talked to Mama Dru and Big Daddy Bast—"

I guffawed. "Wait, hold up—Big Daddy Bast?"

She clapped her hand over her mouth. "Crap. You *cannot* call him that."

"No shit!"

"Delia *hates* it when I call him that."

"Can I ask you a personal question? You don't have to answer."

"Sure."

"Why don't you call him Dad?"

She dropped her eyes. "I don't know. He told me I could a long time ago, but I…" she trailed off, looking away at nothing. "That's probably a deep conversation for another time. Something to do with daddy issues stemming from my actual biological father."

"I don't mean to pry, Em. It's none of my business."

She shook her head, smiling. "Not at all. I don't mind talking about it, just not now. The reason I'm calling, other than just to talk to you because I missed you today, was to invite you and Kaye to stay with us tomorrow night and do Christmas Day with us. Please don't feel like you have to get anyone anything. We want you to spend it with us…if you wanted."

"Em, we can't crash your family Christmas. That's…"

She swallowed hard. "Hayden, I *want* you to. So do my parents." She smiled faintly as if she had a secret. "We may not be *your* family, but we're family. And you guys deserve to spend Christmas with people who know you and care about you. I get it if you guys would rather spend it together."

I didn't answer for a moment. "Are you absolutely sure, Emerson?"

"It's not pity. It *is* compassion, I suppose. But not pity, if that's what you're worried about." She bit her lip, smiling at me. "It's also selfish on my part. I want to see you. I want to be with you. And, um...you'd be with me. Um. In my bed. Dunc and Dane can stay in the basement and your mom can take Dane's room on the end. The room in the middle will be empty."

I realized what she was saying. "Em..."

"Please say yes? I can't bear the thought of you two in some little cabin, no tree, no stockings, no singing carols..." she shrugged, trailing off. "Being alone with you tomorrow night would just be a really major bonus. I want to spend Christmas with you. I don't know... what you and I are or what's going to happen. I don't expect you to know. There are no expectations."

She was nervous, perhaps even scared.

It was a no-brainer. I hadn't been looking forward to a weird, awkward Christmas on the cruise ship myself, as lovely and thoughtful as it seemed it would be. Spending it with Emerson and her amazing family just seemed like the best thing I could ask for.

I knew Mom would agree.

"If you're sure we won't be imposing or anything, then we would love to accept your invitation, Emerson."

"Oh my, so formal, Mr. McCaffrey."

"Indeed, Ms. Day."

"And again, don't get us anything—we're just happy to have you guys come."

I laughed. "Too late. What do you think we spent today doing?"

She sighed and rolled her eyes. "You're ridiculous. Did you get stuff for your other family?"

"Don't have any other family. It's just Mom and me. My parents were both only children. Mom's folks both died before I was born. Dad's dad died when he was like seven, and his mom when I was twelve, I think. If either of them has any extended family beyond that, I have never met any of them. So, no extended family."

"Jeez. So my family is crazy to you, huh?"

I laughed. "Um, yeah. But in a good way. It must be amazing having so many people around you for the holidays."

"Oh, it is. It can be exhausting, especially with so many parties for like three or four weeks straight, but it's fun, and there's so much joy and so many traditions." She grinned. "Speaking of which, just so you're aware, we have a fun Christmas Eve tradition. Everyone gets matching PJs and a book, and we have a low-key, no-cook dinner, and then we watch *Die Hard*."

"*Die Hard*?" I asked, laughing. "I've heard of people who watch that on Christmas, but I've never met anyone who does."

"Well, now you have. It's the best Christmas movie ever. We actually all group-watch it, like the whole clan, everyone in their own houses—it's a whole big watch party thing. We have quote-offs which usually turn into a drinking game. Just so you and Kaye are aware."

"Thanks for the heads-up," I said. "That should be fun."

Someone yelled her name again. "YEAH, ONE MINUTE!" she yelled. "I'm gonna have to go. We're playing Cards Against Humanity. We're also going to a candlelight service tomorrow night, by the way. You don't need to be, like, super dressed up or anything, but most of us do dress nice."

"Mom will appreciate that," I said. "She's...well, not religious, although she grew up religious. She's spiritual. Dad wasn't, though, so we stayed home, and he read the Christmas story in the Bible every year. I think Mom would've liked to go to a service, but I think that was a thing they fought about and that was the compromise."

"Hayden, about you being interrogated—" Emerson started.

"Em, it's fine. I'm glad they did—it means they care. You really don't need to worry."

She rolled her eyes. "I just...You don't...whatever's

going on with us is between us. They know that. They just—"

"Emerson, for real. It didn't bother me. I was a little nervous, especially after, um…you know. But I like your dad. I like your family. I'll answer any questions they have."

She gave me a look that I couldn't quite decipher. "I know my family can be kinda intimidating. My uncles especially."

I just laughed. "Kinda? If someone had told me about them, I wouldn't have believed them. Your family is patently absurd. And I mean that in the best possible way."

"We kinda are, aren't we?" Someone shouted her name yet again.

"Go," I said. "I'll call you in the morning?"

She blew me a kiss. "Can't wait. Merry Christmas! Love you, bye!" Her eyes flew wide and she clapped a hand over her mouth; the screen went black as she hung up.

All I could do was splutter a laugh of disbelief. I immediately texted her.

> ME: Don't freak, Em. It's cool. Way I look at it, either you slipped because you're around your family, in which case, all good, no worries. OR…you really meant it and it just slipped out, in which case, I wish you'd given me a chance to say it back.

My phone binged a few minutes later.

> EMERSON: It slipped out. I'm not sure if it's the first or second, TBH. I'm not sure which is better, either. But thanks for that, regardless.

> ME: No pressure either way. Whether it was an accident or a Freudian slip, it's fine. We can just pretend it didn't happen if that's easier.

> EMERSON: I've never said that to anyone. I barely say it to my family. I don't want to have said it to someone I really do feel it for by accident. It's a big f'ing deal to me.

> ME: I understand that completely. I've never said it either, and I feel the same way.

> EMERSON: So we agree it was an accident and never happened.

> ME: LOL. Agreed. Pick a gnarly card pairing for me. I love that game.

> EMERSON: I will. Can't wait to see you tomorrow.

I hearted the message so she'd know I saw it but didn't feel the need to continue the conversation when she was busy with her family.

I turned on a documentary and spaced out, thinking.

Did she love me? Did I love her? I wasn't sure what love was, other than what I'd seen in my parents: dedication, affection, mutual respect, consideration, compassion, and generosity. They hugged each other, kissed, and held hands right up to the day he died. They argued, not a lot, but they did, yet even in a fight with raised voices, there was never name-calling or insulting or aggression, and they were always careful to make sure I saw them having made up the next day. I saw them love each other every day my whole life.

But what did that mean for me? What did I think about love? What did love mean for me? What did love look like for me?

Something like what Mom and Dad had. I wanted affection, respect, attraction, laughter. I saw all that with Emerson. I saw our relationship developing into something meaningful and long-term. There were a lot of details to work out, major ones with no easy solutions. But before that...I just wanted to see what it could be.

Was I in love with her? That was less easy to nail down. I cared about her deeply, and in a very short time, she'd come to occupy a huge place in my heart. I wanted to know more about her. I wanted to be with her every moment. I wanted to belong with her.

I suppose that sounded a lot like love, didn't it?

I turned off the TV and tried to sleep, but all I could think about was Emerson. Being in bed with her. Sex, yes, of course—after what we'd already shared, it was nearly all I could think about. But there was just as much thinking about just holding her, being with her.

I wasn't sure where things would go or how they'd work out—or even if they would—but I was damn sure I wanted to try.

THIRTEEN

Emerson

IEXAMINED MY REFLECTION IN THE MIRROR FOR WHAT MUST
have been the tenth time. I'd gone too heavy on the
mascara and eyeshadow. I'd gone for a smokey eye,
but I'd taken a wrong left turn at Albuquerque and
had ended up at raccoon. I growled at my reflection.

Delia just laughed. "You are in a *state*, sister."

I glared at her. "I'm nervous."

"Why? It's Christmas Eve with the family. No big
deal." She had teased her hair up and out, gone for a
bright red lip, and very little on her eyes. "You look
fantastic. He's gonna melt."

I had a holly green clingy wrap dress on, the hem
ending just above my knees. Three-inch black heels,
a black faux-fur cape, and a cheap knock-off YSL bag

completed my look. I was waffling between feeling like I'd gone too far and hoping it was enough to take his breath away.

"He's gonna melt, I'm gonna freeze." I let out a breath. "Should I redo my eyes? I feel like I look like a raccoon. Smokey eye gone way wrong. I should redo them."

I grabbed a makeup wipe, but Delia snagged my wrist. "Nope, nope, nope. You look amazing. Stop freaking out. You're overthinking this, Sun-Sun."

"Overthinking it? He's coming to Christmas Eve church. That and Easter are the only days we go to church, and his mother is, and I quote, spiritual. I don't know what I'm doing. I accidentally said I love you."

Delia dropped her lip liner. "Shut the fuck up. You did not!"

"I did. It was embarrassing. It was totally an accident. I was just like, Merry Christmas, love you, bye. It just slipped out. I'm not even sure if I'm even in love with him."

Delia spluttered into her hand, eyes wide. "Oh... my...*god*! What'd he say?"

"I panicked and hung up. But he texted me like five seconds later and told me not to worry. We agreed it was an accident and never happened, but not before I admitted I've never told anyone I love them. I barely tell *you guys* I love you. If I do end up with him, I don't want the first time I tell him I love him to be a stupid fucking accident."

"It was an accident. It slipped out. I was on the phone with a distributor a couple months ago and said 'Okay, love you, bye.' It doesn't mean anything." She shrugged. "I didn't go with that distributor, but not for that reason. Or not totally, at least."

"Delia. I said I love you to a guy I met not even a week ago."

She nodded while shrugging. "I get it. But he didn't freak out, right?"

"Well…no."

"*You're* freaking out."

"Yes." I teased my curls a bit, fluffing and rearranging. "He also said that if I had said to him as, like, a Freudian slip, he wished I'd have given him a chance to say it back."

Delia fumbled her blush brush, caught it, and set it down. "The fuck you say."

"Facts."

"That's…huge. Emerson, that's *huge*. He didn't just not freak out, he was ready to hit you back with it."

"Thus why I'm freaking out! I don't know what's going on! I'm not sure what I'm feeling or how anything would work even if we did decide we wanted to be together. It's all so much so fast, and I feel so much pressure now that I've brought him around everyone."

I tipped my head back and blinked tears away as I fought for breath.

Delia grabbed my arms and shook me. "Whoa,

hey, breathe, babe. You're good. It's okay. There's no pressure. We all just want you to be happy."

I flapped my hands at my face and blew out through pursed lips.

Delia snagged a Kleenex, folded it, and dabbed it beneath my eyes. "Just one request, though."

I took the Kleenex from her and took over the dabbing. "What's that?"

"Remember that my room is on the other side of yours. So, you know, when you and Hayden have hot monkey sex tonight, try not to scream *too* loud."

I burst into laughter. "I make no promises. He's *very* good with his mouth."

"Didn't need to know that," she muttered.

"You were the one begging for details just the other day," I pointed out.

"Well, maybe I've changed my mind, possibly due to crippling jealousy that you get hot monkey Christmas sex. Hot Christmas monkey sex? I'm not sure which is right."

"Let's go with neither, and you never use the phrase 'hot monkey sex' ever again."

"But you're so cute when you blush." She pinched my cheek. "And every time I mention him or sex, you blush."

"Do not," I lied.

"Oh my god, you *so* do. Which is hysterical. You've told me some seriously salacious details about your sexcapades with your boytoys like you were discussing the brunch menu. Yet if I so much as reference Hayden McCaffrey's apparently giant magical dong, you turn fifty shades of red."

"Bullshit," I lied, as my cheeks flamed fifty shades of red.

"I notice you're not arguing the giant magical status of Hayden's dong."

"Because it *is* giant and magical," I said.

"How giant are we talking about?" she asked, leaning forward and dropping her voice to a whisper.

"He has a Goldilocks cock," I said, also whispering. "Not too big, not too small—*juuuust* right."

"Have I mentioned my crippling jealousy of your Goldilocks Christmas cock?" Delia said, still muttering as she put the finishing touches on her makeup.

"You probably should be," I said.

She put her makeup away and then leaned on the counter, staring at me in the reflection. "All jokes aside, no matter what happens, I'm glad you're getting this time with him. If nothing else, I think it's about time you broke out of your casual sex relationship avoidance pattern."

I turned to look at her. "Delia Badd, that is a hundred percent the pot calling the kettle black. You do the exact same thing."

She blew a sarcastic raspberry. "Okay, sure. I do not. I do the exact opposite."

"Okay, fine, but it's the same thing when you boil it all down. I have casual hookups with random dudes to avoid my fear of relationships and intimacy. You're a serial monogamist who consistently chooses men who don't even *remotely* stand a chance of going the distance with you because you are, for some reason, just as terrified of commitment and vulnerability as I am. Opposite approaches to the same problem."

She blinked at me. "We're not talking about me, though. You're the one with a hot guy who loves his mom, has a good job, a giant magical dong, and is showing every sign of being in love with you. I, meanwhile, have a dusty vagina and a cold, shut-down heart with absolutely zero romantic prospects. I'll never leave Ketchikan, and I've dated every decent, eligible male who lives here full-time, as well as at least two of the not-as-eligible ones."

I arched an eyebrow at her. "Excuse me?"

She rolled her eyes. "Not knowingly, but still. I dated this guy, Marco, back in the spring. He's mid-thirties, sexy as hell, and wasn't wearing a ring. Nor did he have a pale spot where one would be—I looked. I always look. So, yeah, we started hanging out, and that turned into hooking up, and good lord, the man gave seriously good dick. And then he left his phone unlocked and open to his messages while he went to the bathroom. And his wife texted him. Her contact name is, I kid you not, The Ol' Ball and Chain." She scooped her phone out of her purse and pulled up a screenshot verifying what she was saying. "He acted like it was no big deal. Oh, yeah, we have an open relationship. And I was like, does *she* know that? And then, over the summer, this guy I was seeing straight up lied to me about being divorced. He *did* tell me he was married but that the divorce had just been finalized. Come to find out, no, they hadn't even actually filed yet, and she was hoping for a reconciliation. How did I find this out, you ask? I'll tell you. I *met her*. While I was *with him*. We were getting coffee before we got down to business, and she showed up. Saw us together. Freaked out, understandably, made a whole big scene about how he was such a liar and a cheater and blah blah blah, she couldn't believe she thought they could reconcile and I could have him."

"What'd you do?"

"I threw my iced coffee in his face." She shrugged. "And then there was Garrison, who it turns out had been cheating on me the whole time we were seeing each other. I broke up with him like three months ago or whenever we had that talk before regionals. I haven't been with anyone since. Thus the dusty vagina."

"That sucks, babe, I'm sorry. Some men are such pigs."

She huffed. "Unfortunately for my cynicism, Hayden proves that it really is just *some* men and not *all* men like I'd like to believe."

I tilted my head, trying to figure that out. "Wait—huh? You *want* to be cynical? Or you don't? I'm not following."

She laughed. "Honestly, I don't even know

anymore. I *am* bitter and cynical, and it's just easier sometimes, but deep down, I do want to believe there's at least *one more* good guy out there who wouldn't mind putting up with my bullshit."

It was my turn to grab her shoulders. "Dee, any man who gets to spend even five minutes in your presence is a lucky, lucky man. And the man who finally proves himself to be worthy of the incredible woman that you are will be the luckiest man alive."

She smiled, shaking her head. "Thanks. I suppose I can allow myself to hope that you're right."

"I'm always right."

"Except when you're wrong."

A knock sounded on the door to Delia's bathroom, where we were getting ready. "Girls? Time to go." Dru said, peeking in. "Wow—I feel underdressed now."

Delia was wearing a red dress that was almost identical to mine in every way except color, complete with matching shoes, bag, and faux-fur cape.

It was a little over the top since everyone else tended to go for dressy-casual, usually jeans or slacks and a nice button-down for the men and slacks and a blouse or a nice dress for the women. Dru, for example, was wearing black slacks with a cranberry blouse, the sleeves pointed and voluminous, the neckline plunging, and a pair of spike-heeled black boots.

"Are we too slutty for church?" I asked.

Dru snorted and shook her head. "I don't think so, no. You're definitely going to get Hayden's attention, though. Not that you need the help. That boy is gaga for you." She smacked Delia's ass. "Who are you dressing up for?"

Delia just shrugged. "No one. Just in solidarity with Em, so she wasn't the only one dolled up."

Dru sighed. "Oh."

Delia laughed. "Mom, do *not* start."

"You have to get back on the horse, Dee. You can't let a few assholes sour you on all men."

Delia huffed. "I said *don't* start. And it wasn't just them. It was all the ones before *and then* them. I'm not getting back on the horse, Mom. The horse can come find me when it's ready to not buck me off."

Dru frowned. "I'm not sure I'm following the metaphor, dear."

I laughed. "Our girl is not great with metaphors." I kissed her cheek, partly to test my new smudge-proof lipstick. "Or logic."

Delia flipped us both off. "*You* have a husband of twenty-some years," she said to her mom, and then turned to me. "And *you* met one of the last unicorns—a good man with a great dick and an amazing personality *and* a job who *also* doesn't seem to be married, engaged, divorced, or with a secret child he refuses to acknowledge or pay for."

All things men she's dated have done. I suppose her cynicism was somewhat warranted.

Dru cupped cheeks in both hands. "Delia, my lovely, head-strong, wild-hearted daughter, I have absolutely *zero* doubt that when you least expect it, a man will come along who'll sweep you off your feet and show you a whole new world." She let go of Delia's face and took my hand in one of hers and Delia's in the other. "Look, girls, in my experience, it's worth waiting for the right one. I didn't discover that until I was literally in the church about to marry a lying, cheating asshole with a comically sub-par dick that he had absolutely no clue what to do with."

"MOM!" Delia shouted. "T-M-I!"

Dru just cackled and stuck up an index finger, wiggling it. "Like this. It was just silly. And then I met your father, and—"

"NOT ONE MORE WORD, MOTHER!" Delia screeched, going shrill and ear-piercing. "I swear to god, not one more word. I'm glad Dad satisfies you, but I do *not* need to know anything about it."

Dru just laughed and pulled us both out of the bathroom. "You're so easily riled, you ridiculous goose." She pushed Delia out ahead of her and smacked her butt again.

"MOM! Hands off the ass. You want to smack someone's ass, smack Dad's. I'm sure he likes it. AND I DON'T NEED TO KNOW!"

"Oh, he does." Dru cackled as we reached the kitchen, where Bast was picking at the leftovers from the cheese and meat tray. She hauled off and smacked Bast's butt so hard the crack echoed in the kitchen.

He didn't so much as flinch, finished chewing and

swallowing, and then turned a playfully baleful, threatening stare at Dru.

"Oh…shit," Dru breathed. "That…*may* have been a miscalculation."

Bast lunged and Dru bolted, but with the spike heels and tight slacks, she couldn't get away fast enough and Bast snagged her around the waist, bent her over his thigh, and spanked her until she started kicking and screaming.

Duncan and Dane emerged from the hallway at that moment, stopped as one, and stared. "Are we going to church or a BDSM club?" Dane asked.

"Or the church of BDSM?" Duncan added.

I couldn't help but notice that while Dru was kicking and screaming, she wasn't actually trying to get away. And when Bast finally set her on her feet, her gaze, as it met his, was visibly excited. He smoothed his hand over her ass and then kissed her mouth before turning to put the tray back in the fridge.

"All right, gang, let's roll out." He shot me a glance. "Sunni, are Hayden and Kaye meeting us there?"

I nodded, slinging my purse onto my shoulder and shrugging my cape tighter around my shoulders. "Yes. I told them it started at eight and to get there at a quarter to at the latest, so we could get seats together."

We loaded into Bast's and Dru's Suburban and headed to the church. When we got there, Kaye and Hayden were just getting dropped off by a ride-share. Kaye was wearing the dress she'd worn to the party, and Hayden was in a pair of black slacks, a white button-down with a red-and-green striped tie under a black V-neck pullover sweater. His hair was slicked back, and he was wearing his glasses.

I, being the shortest, always got the back seat whenever we all rode together. Delia scooted awkwardly out of the SUV ahead of me, tugging her hem down with a wiggle of her hips. Hayden nudged his mother toward the church entrance and jogged across the parking lot just in time to offer me his hand.

"Thanks," I said, smiling at him. "Hard to get out of a car in a tight skirt. There's just no dignified way to do it." I shimmied across the bench, grabbed his offered hand, and wiggled until I could get a foot on the running board. "At least, not without flashing everyone."

He grinned. "I wouldn't mind." He reached in, grabbed me under the arms, and lifted me out without so much as a grunt of effort, and set me on my feet. "You look...fu—um, freaking amazing. Probably shouldn't curse at church, huh?"

I did the hem-down hips-wiggle and didn't miss the way his eyes hungrily tracked the movement. "You look handsome. I love the tie."

He threaded our fingers together. "Thanks. I made a last-second trip to the mall."

I winced. "Oof. How was that?"

He laughed. "It was...very mall-y. But I got a whole outfit, so I didn't show up in jeans and a hoodie."

"It would have been fine, Hayden," I said.

He shook his head. "You don't know Mom. She got Dad to go to church on Easter a couple times, and I had to dress up in a full suit. To her, you just don't go to church in jeans." He looked at me, his eyes lingering on my chest before he yanked them away with a shake of his head. "Plus, I wouldn't feel right showing up like that when you guys invited me to church with you."

"Are you okay with it? Church, I mean?"

"Yeah, totally. I don't have anything against God or church, I just…" a sigh, a roll of one shoulder. "I guess I'm what you might call undecided. I don't know what I believe, so I don't go regularly, but I have no issue with church on Easter and Christmas."

"I'm the same, I guess. If God is real, then I have questions because—well, it's not the time or place for that conversation. But I also feel like if there is a God then he definitely made up for giving me shitty parents by putting Delia and the Badds into my life. I'm just not sure where that leaves me in terms of faith, you know?"

He squeezed my hand. "I get it, Em. And you know what? We don't have to figure that out tonight."

I blew out a long, slow breath. "You're right." I smiled at him. "I'm glad you're here."

"Me too."

"Come on, kids!" Dru said from the doorway. "Seats are filling up fast." She leaned into Hayden, who side-hugged her. "Hi, you! We're so happy you and Kaye could join us."

He bent as she pulled him down and kissed both cheeks. "We're happy to be here—Mom especially. She's vibrating with excitement."

We followed Dru into the sanctuary—it was a decent-sized church, the sanctuary holding maybe five hundred people. Candles lined the stage, dancing and flickering, with holiday-themed flower arrangements a safe distance away from the candles. More candles were spaced along the sides and back wall, and garland wreathed the back of the pews. An acoustic four-piece played "Hark the Herald" as the pews filled and people shuffled inward to make room.

Our family took up almost four full rows—apparently, Uncles Xavier, Roman, and Errol had shown up early to claim the rows so we'd all have room to sit together.

I was on the outside aisle with Hayden beside me, his mother next to him, Olivia next, and then Lucas. We exchanged murmured greetings as the band trailed off and the pastor took his place center-stage.

It was a beautiful service. The message was short and heartfelt, with a moving *a capella* performance of "Mary Did You Know" by Canaan and Aerie—there was no introduction of them or mention of their many accolades as professional musicians. We all stood and sang the traditional carols and hymns; I was somewhat shocked to discover Hayden possessed a beautiful baritone voice.

Kaye was tearful all the way through but seemed to be happy rather than sad.

We mingled in the foyer for a while, eating cookies and hot chocolate or coffee and watching the youngsters scamper and play until their parents shushed them.

Kaye found me, a napkin in one hand bearing a peanut butter cookie with a chocolate kiss in the middle. "I just wanted to tell you how thankful I am that you invited us. You don't know what it means to me to attend a Christmas Eve service."

I went in for a hug, and she pulled me close, clinging tightly. "It's been wonderful getting to know you, Kaye." I dropped my voice to a murmur. "Your son is amazing. It's obvious how much he loves you, and it's truly inspiring to see."

Her eyes shimmered. "I am obviously biased, but I think he's pretty great myself."

We both looked at Hayden, who was playfully chasing a gaggle of young kids around.

"He seems good with kids," I said, smiling as he pretended to tiptoe cartoonlike behind big bad Uncle Baxter, who picked up on the gag and spun at the last second with a Shrek-like roar that caught the attention of the whole foyer.

Aunt Eva facepalmed herself, flushed with embarrassment.

Kaye chuckled. "And no one is more surprised

than me, dear. He's not exactly had a lot of experience with children. Maybe it's his naturally playful spirit."

"Naturally playful?" I asked. "I've not seen that."

She just laughed again. "Oh, honey, you will. He's a kid at heart in a lot of ways. Just try to get him away from his computer game friends." She looked at me with a worried expression. "I don't mean he's one of those people who does nothing but play games. It's just one of the ways he decompresses. He works awfully hard."

"I know what you meant," I said. "My cousin Jax spends every available free moment playing video games. I know how it works."

Gradually, the various Badd families made the round of goodbyes, and everyone went to their respective homes. Kaye and Hayden crammed into our car with us—Duncan gave her one of the front captain's chairs, and Hayden insisted Dane take the other, leaving Dunc, Hayden, and me to wedge ourselves into the back.

Fortunately, it was a short ride home.

"All right, ya'll," Bast said as we gathered in the kitchen. "Real quick, here. In this family—meaning us as well as the larger clan as a whole—Christmas is mainly about togetherness. It's about celebrating what we've built—a family who cares about each other, supports each other, and is there for each other, no matter what. We welcome people in. We do the right thing. We have fun." He focused on Kaye and Hayden. "I know I speak for all of us when I say that we're fortunate to have met you two. No matter what happens, you guys are welcome here." To the kids, then. "Delia, Duncan, Dane, and Emerson. I'm proud of you. I love you." To Dru. "Babe, I—"

Dru lifted on her toes and shut him up with a kiss. "I know. Me too."

Bast laughed. "Exactly." He clapped his hands. "I suck at speeches, so that's enough of that. Let's eat!"

Dru always made a big pot of chili for Christmas Eve that simmered all day. Now, she shut off the burner and set out the various fixings, and we all dished ourselves, took our seats at the table, and dug in.

The men all went back for seconds and thirds. Toward the end, when it was clear the meal was winding down, Kaye pushed her bowl away and cleared her throat. "Dru, Bast, I just…I have to express my gratitude to you both for opening your home and your lives to my son and me. Without your hospitality, this would have probably been the worst Christmas of my life. But then Hayden met this wonderful, lovely young woman," and here she smiled at me with such love and warmth my stomach flipped, "and then, somehow, we got pulled into your lives, and we are the better for it. So, from the bottom of my heart, thank you. *Thank you* for bringing joy to my heart when I thought…well, never mind what I thought."

Dru and Bast linked hands, and Dru addressed Kaye. "It all started sort of by accident, or perhaps unintentionally is a better word. Bast and his brothers brought me in and made me feel welcome. They gave me a family when I needed one the most—I'd just left my fiancé, and it had been just me and my dad for a very long time. And then…I met Bast. When Zane met Mara, I was over the moon. I had a sister, something I always dreamed of. And then, within a few years, I had seven sisters. And then ten, and then fifteen, plus a quasi-mother-in-law."

"Well, it's truly remarkable." Kaye grabbed her son's hand. "We would love to give back even a little bit, if we could, by cleaning up after this delicious meal."

Dru frowned, shook her head. "Absolutely not. Guests don't—" She cut off, glancing at Bast; they had a silent conversation, and Dru sighed. "Kaye, it goes against my hostess's heart, but if it is important to you, then I'll allow it."

Kaye laughed. "It is important to me, and it would mean a lot. I do understand your position, however. I would feel the same way if the situation was reversed."

We all cleared our places and Kaye and Hayden made quick work of loading the dishwasher—they worked together in such effortless harmony that it was clear they'd spent a lot of time together exactly like that. Dru, Delia, and I dealt with the leftovers while Bast and the boys brought in wood and built a fire. Once the kitchen was clean, we all gathered in the living room, where the Christmas Eve presents were under the tree.

Kaye, tucking her legs beneath her on the love-seat next to Delia, looked around. "What's going on?"

Bast handed out the packages, each wrapped in sparkly white-and-silver wrapping paper. "Christmas Eve tradition. PJs, a book, and chocolate."

"Dad, you ruined the surprise," Dane fake-whined.

Bast rolled his eyes as he placed a package on Kaye's lap as well as handing one to Hayden. "You didn't think we'd leave you guys out, did you?"

"I had to guess at your size," Dru said, "so hopefully I was at least close."

"If you shopped in the kids' section, you're probably on the money," Hayden teased.

"Oh, hush you." She stuck her tongue out at him.

Everyone opened their presents—buffalo plaid fleece bottoms and a long-sleeve white waffle print top, a bar of chocolate, and a book picked by Dru. Kaye's was a book on grief and grieving.

Dru grimaced nervously as Kaye read the description on the back without expression. "I, god, I hope I didn't overstep, Kaye. I have no idea what your reading tastes are, and that's a book Olivia recommended to me after my dad died. It really helped, honestly."

Kaye sniffed. "You're so thoughtful—my goodness." She gave Dru a watery smile. "Thank you, my dear. Truly."

Duncan and Dane were already almost done with their chocolate.

Bast clapped his hands. "Okay, PJs on! We meet in the TV room for *Die Hard* in ten minutes." He pointed at me and then Hayden. "Hear me? *Ten minutes.*"

"Dude, really?" I said, rolling my eyes.

He shrugged. "Just covering my bases. It's not Christmas till Hans Gruber falls from Nakatomi Plaza."

Hayden and I went to my room. Once inside, I shut the door and immediately attacked him. I jumped at him, and he caught me, hands under my ass, mouth on mine, my legs wrapping around his waist, hiking the skirt of my dress up around my hips.

We broke after a minute, and Hayden rested his forehead against mine. "Em, Jesus."

"Sorry. I just had to kiss you."

"Don't apologize. I just…I want you so fucking bad it hurts. You in that fucking dress?"

Wiggling the hem back down as I slid out of his hold and backed up a few steps, I twirled in a circle. "You like?"

"I love."

I ignored his choice of words. "I wore it for you."

He stared at me hungrily. "I had to fight an erection the whole evening, so thanks for that."

I giggled. "Good. My work is done, then."

He took a step toward me, hands reaching. He stopped, fingers curling into a fist. "If I touch you, I won't stop."

I bit my lip. "I know the feeling."

"We can't start, Em. Much as I want to, we can't. Not yet."

I rubbed my face. "I know." I let out a breath. "Okay, so we just change. Nothing else."

"Then one of us needs to change in the bathroom because if I have to watch you peel out of that dress…" he shook his head. "I won't be able to keep my hands to myself."

I smirked. "Then it probably wouldn't help you to know I'm commando? No underwear, no bra."

He groaned. "No. Not helping."

I laughed. "Fine. Just unzip me, and then I'll hide myself from you."

He snorted. "I'm weak-willed where you're concerned, Em."

I went over to him and turned around. "Good. That's how I want it."

His fingers slid down my back as he lowered the zipper; I shivered when his lips touched my back between my shoulder blades and then my nape.

"Hayden…no fair," I whispered. "You're lighting a match in a room full of dynamite."

He pressed himself up against me from behind, hands on my shoulders. "How am I supposed to resist you, Em?" He pushed the dress down so it dropped to pool around my feet, leaving me naked and shivering—but not from the chill in the air.

From his gaze that I felt on my bare skin like a

physical touch. From the desire radiating off of him in a palpable wave.

"Hayden," I whispered again.

He rested his forehead on my shoulder, his hands sliding down my waist to rest on my naked hips. "Fuck, Em. You're so goddamn irresistible."

I shuddered, leaning my head back against his chest. "You're killing me, Hayden."

My nipples ached and my core pulsed. I felt him, a hard ridge pressing against my backside. His hands slid around to my stomach, hesitating. Then, with a ragged groan, he cupped my breasts, thumbing my erect nipples.

I whimpered and then ripped myself away from him, pacing forward and raking my hands through my hair. "Hayden, we *can't*."

He spun away, fisting his hair. "Fuck. I'm sorry. I just...I can't help myself."

"I want you to touch me more than I want my next breath." I snagged my PJs from the bed where I'd tossed them, stepped into the bottoms and shrugged into the top in record time. "There. Better?"

He glanced at me, eyes hot. "Marginally better."

I laughed. "It's Christmas jammies, Hayden. Not much sexy about that."

"I beg to differ. You could wear a paper sack and make it sexy."

I went to him and lifted to kiss his chin, just beneath his lower lip. "I'm going out there now, because if I watch *you* change, the same thing will happen, just the other way. And then we'll get in trouble. Bast takes his yearly *Die Hard* viewing very seriously."

He cupped my jaw, bent to kiss me—it was soft and sweet and quick. "Good idea. Go, I'll be right out."

I fled the room. Delia was waiting at her door. "You look flustered."

I flipped her off. "Shut up."

She just laughed. "Secret salami surprise?"

"No. Shut up. We just changed." I pinched her nipple—she'd removed her bra, so she had some serious headlights going; Delia had very prominent nipples.

She batted my hand away. "Then why are you flushed and flustered?"

"Because all we did was change!"

Delia's laughter followed me into the kitchen.

FOURTEEN

Hayden

MOM MADE IT TO THE SCENE WHERE JOHN IS TALKING to Hans on the rooftop, not realizing at first who he's talking to. Dru zonked out not long after that, and Delia and Em made it almost to the end.

Bast wished us all a merry Christmas before carrying Dru to bed. Duncan woke Delia with a tenderness that honestly surprised me—the boys were jokesters and pranksters who didn't seem to have a serious bone in their bodies, but it was obvious from the way Duncan shook Delia awake and the way Dane half-carried her to her room that they felt a great deal of affection for their sister. They both vanished into the basement, leaving me alone with a sleeping Emerson.

I scooped her up and carried her to her room, set her in bed, and climbed in beside her.

She stirred, peering at me blearily. "Hayden?"

I curled an arm beneath her, and she settled onto my chest, messy bun tickling my cheek, hand on my stomach. "I'm here. Sleep, honey."

She hummed sleepily, sighed deeply, and then sank against me. Her leg twitched against mine. She snorted softly.

A deep sense of contentment settled inside me, an all-pervading happiness. I didn't care that she'd fallen asleep when I'd been anticipating finally getting to have sex with her—that barely even registered, and I sure as hell wasn't disappointed. I had her in my arms. She felt safe enough to sleep on my chest. What else could I ask for?

It didn't take long for me to start fading, and then sleep pulled me under.

I woke to the dim gray light of pre-dawn, my internal alarm clock waking me at five despite having not gone to bed until after midnight. Emerson was on her side facing me, one thigh thrown over mine, one hand low on my belly, and the other curled under her chin.

God, she was beautiful.

I stared at her, drinking in her features, the angles and curves of her chin and cheeks, the plump, kissable bow of her lips, the thick black eyelashes brushing her cheeks. Her delicate chin, small ears. Her graceful neck, elegant throat. Her kinky, curly, bright red ring-lets in a bursting halo on the pillow.

As I stared at her, her eyelids fluttered and her green eyes, a few shades lighter than my own, met mine. "Hi there, gorgeous. It's early."

She smiled, a sleepy, happy curve of her lips. "Hi there, hotshot. Sleep well?"

I nodded and scooped her closer, back onto my chest. "Best I've slept in a long time."

She snuggled closer, breasts pressing against my chest, chin on my chest, eyes on me. "I'm sorry I fell asleep."

"I'm not. Falling asleep holding you? What else could I possibly want out of life?" I tucked a ringlet behind her ear.

"Oh, I don't know...sex?"

I shook my head. "That'll happen. I'm not worried about it. The only thing I felt last night as I fell asleep with you right here like this was happy and grateful."

"I really have to pee," she whispered, eyes wide and adorable.

I laughed. "Well then go, ya goofball."

She slid out of bed and scurried into the bath-room; she didn't close the door all the way and I heard the sound of her peeing. It felt intimate in a way that I liked. Weird, maybe, but true.

It also touched off my bladder, and I went next. When I was done, I washed my hands, dried them, and went back into the bedroom.

Emerson had the covers pulled up to her chin. Her eyes were hot and excited, sparking with green fire. "Hi."

I stood beside the bed, stomach doing flips. "Hi."

"A recent survey of everyone in the room has shown that you, Hayden Reginald McCaffrey, are wearing entirely too many clothes." She covered her mouth and nose with the blanket after saying this, her eyes betraying her bright, eager smile.

"Everyone in the room, huh?"

"Yup. Me, myself, and I."

I grabbed the hem of my shirt. "Well, you can add my vote to the poll because I happen to agree."

"Will you heed the will of the people?"

I peeled out of my shirt and tossed it aside. "That answer your question?"

The blanket lifted as she shrugged. "A little. The people demand further action."

I stepped out of my fleece pajama pants, standing in just my black boxer briefs. "Are the people satisfied now?"

"Not quite. We demand total transparency from our chosen candidate."

"Candidate?"

"Just go with it," she stage-whispered. "I don't know shit about politics, but this is fun."

I kept my eyes on hers as I pulled the elastic waistband away from my belly and my burgeoning erection, and then slid the underwear down. The naked hunger in her eyes set my cock to throbbing.

Nude for her now, I remained standing beside the bed. "Acceptable?"

"Almost."

I frowned, laughing. "Now what? I can't get any more naked."

"Now you're too far away."

"Oh. Well then, allow me to rectify that." I pulled away the corner of the blanket on my side of the bed. "But now the people feel *you*, Emerson I-don't-know-your-middle-name Day, are wearing too many clothes."

"My middle name is Grace." Her eyes twinkled, glittered. "And...*am* I, though?"

I slid close to her, reaching for her. My hand met bare skin. I slid the blanket away, slowly baring her throat, and then her chest, and then her breasts, and then her stomach, and then her sex with its closely shorn red fuzz trimmed into a neat, narrow line.

"Oh." I sucked in a deep breath, held it as I drank in her lush, intoxicating curves. "*Jesus*, Emerson. You're so fucking perfect."

She exhaled softly through her nose, shaking her head. "No, you are."

I just laughed. "Can I kiss you, now, please?"

"You'd better, and you'd damn well better not stop this time."

I slid my hand over her belly, marveling at the softness of her skin. Angling closer so I was almost on top

of her, I caressed her breast as I brought my mouth
down to hers. She moaned as I gave her my tongue, and
she took it eagerly, tangling hers against mine, mouth
open to mine, our breaths mingling. I groaned as her
soft hot mouth welcomed my tongue. Fucking hell,
I could come just from the way she kissed me. My
cock throbbed painfully, nudging against her thigh. I
cupped one breast and then the other one, playing with
her taut, hard, sensitive nipples until she whimpered
against my teeth.

I trailed my fingertips down her body, tracing the
delicate line of her seam. Dragged my finger up, and
then down. Her thighs parted, and I delved my finger
inside her pussy, groaning as heat and wetness coated
my finger. She thrust against my hand as I smeared her
essence against her clit, mouth open against mine as
the kiss stuttered and failed, her moan huffing against
my teeth.

"Oh god, Hayden. I love the way you touch me."
She fisted a handful of hair, head tilting back and pressing into the pillow as her hips lifted.

"I love touching you." I dragged my lips down
her chest and sucked her nipple into my mouth. "I
love your skin. I love everything about your fucking
incredible body."

She shoved her hands into my hair, smoothing it
back as I kissed her other breast, going back and forth
from one to the other, kissing and licking and nibbling
her delicious little nipples.

"Hayden, I want you. I need you." She gripped my hair and tugged so I had to look up at her. "Please."

I kissed between her breasts and then pulled against her hold to kiss her diaphragm. And then her belly, and then below her navel.

"Hayden, I don't need that," she protested.

"Maybe not, but I do," I said.

I settled between her thighs, draping their soft weight on my shoulders. Her fingers dimpled against my scalp, her eyes seeking mine, searching me.

I locked eyes with her, pressed my mouth to her pussy, tasting her essence. I ran my tongue up her lips, and then again, and then a third time, and then flitted my tongue-tip against her clit, causing her to jerk, gasping.

"Hayden!" She whispered, breathless, tangling her fingers in my hair again. "Oh, *god*."

I took my time, working her slowly and unhurriedly to the cusp of climax with just my tongue, and then I slid a finger inside her and then a second. I brought her to the edge again, got her bucking and keening through gritted teeth...only to keep her from reaching climax.

She growled in frustration. "Hayden, fuck! Don't tease me, dammit!"

"But it's so much fun," I said, teasing her with little flicks of my tongue to her clit, making her twitch and whimper.

"I need to come, Hayden. Please."

I reached up and grasped her breast with one hand, plunging the fingers of the other into her sex. "Then come for me, Emerson. And don't hold back."

"I—I'm not!" she protested.

"You are."

"You scare me." Her eyes, fraught with wild need, searched me. "You make me feel things so intense that it terrifies me." Cheeks flaming as red as her hair, she spoke in a whisper so quiet I had to strain to hear her. "I'm scared of...of coming so hard I...make a mess."

"Funny thing about messes," I said, "is they can be cleaned up."

"What if I squirt and it's gross?" she whispered.

"If you came so hard you squirted, it wouldn't be gross, it would be fucking hot as hell." I kissed her hipbone, her thigh. "Don't hold back, Em. I've got you."

"Hayden, I..."

"You can trust me, Em. I've *got* you."

She continued to search me until she seemed to find what she was looking for. "I do trust you."

"Then stop holding back. Give me everything, Em. I want everything you have. Everything you are."

"I don't like not being in control," she breathed. "It's hard to let that go."

"You *are* in control, Em. I'll never do anything you don't want or aren't comfortable with."

She stroked my hair, brushed my cheekbone with her thumb. "I know. I just mean that letting go like you want me to...it's hard."

I nuzzled her pussy, kissed just above the keyhole opening around her clit, and then just beneath her navel. "Then we don't worry about it. All I want is to make you feel better than you ever have in your life."

She licked her lips, eyes shimmering. "Hayden—god, you're sweet." She slid her fingers into my hair and pressed me downward. "Make me let go, Hayden. Show me how."

I grinned, sliding off the foot of the bed. Grabbing her ankles, I drew her toward me, eliciting a freshet of breathy giggles from her that made my heart leap with a wild burst of possessive need and frantic love.

Dropping to my knees, I pulled her hips toward me and she hooked her thighs over my shoulders. I cradled her ass in my hands and supported her lower half. I fused my mouth over her slit and huffed a hot breath against her.

She whined in her throat, reaching down to hold my head. "Hayden…"

I teased her clit with my tongue, making her buck in my hands. "You want it?"

She thrust against my mouth. "I fucking need it. Make me come, Hayden."

I sucked her clit into my mouth and devoured her until her hips began to flex and buck on their own, and this time I didn't stop. I brought her to the edge and pushed her right over it.

She knotted her fingers in my hair and crushed me against herself, grinding her sex against my mouth.

Grasping my hair with one hand, she yanked a pillow with the other and pressed it against her face, screaming into it as her climax ripped through her.

As Emerson bucked and thrust and screamed, I shifted her forward and slid my two middle fingers inside her tight, clamping channel. Soaked and slippery, her inner walls rippled around my fingers as I plunged them into her and withdrew, plunged in, curled toward myself, and then set a hard, rough rhythm. She met me thrust for thrust, screaming into the pillow until her lungs ran out of air, and then she threw her head back and gasped for air, a shrill, desperate whimper in her throat.

"Hayden, oh fuck, fuck, fuck!" She gasped, ass lifted off the bed as her spine arched.

I continued plundering her dripping, clenching pussy, continued devouring her clit.

I felt another wave of orgasm seize her, and now she curled forward, almost sitting up, only to jackknife backward, heels digging into the mattress and driving her hips up, screaming through gritted teeth.

She abruptly and roughly shoved me away from herself, pulling me upward and guiding my face to her breasts. One hand clutched the back of my head, and the other clawed down my back.

Thrusting madly and helplessly against my driving fingers, she cried out in a staccato series of whimpering, breathy grunts. Once more, she curled forward, and I felt her walls clamp down around my fingers with crushing force—

Hot wetness soaked my fingers and knuckles, and Emerson slammed the pillow over her face and screamed into it, shaking and shuddering and twitching and screaming, fingers clawing down my back, thrusting against my hand, wetness pulsing out of her.

The wracking intensity of her orgasm finally released her, and she sank back down to the mattress, threw the pillow aside, and looked down at me.

She looked shell-shocked. Stunned. Awed. Her eyes were wet with tears, and she was panting, each gasp a shuddering sob. "Ohmygod. Ohmygod. Oh…my…*god*."

She seized my wrist with an iron grip and pulled my hand away. I knelt at the foot of the bed, one of her feet in my hands, watching her fight to recover. Her eyes never left me, and I couldn't decipher the myriad emotions I saw flashing across her lovely face.

She extended a hand to me. "Come here."

I took her hand and let her pull me, crawling up the bed to kneel over her, straddling her prone, naked perfection. "Hi."

She wiped at my mouth with her palm. "Hi."

Reaching down between us, Emerson clasped my semi-rigid cock in her soft, small hand. With a few strokes, I was fully erect again. She caressed my length, never taking her eyes off mine.

"I need you," she whispered.

"I need you, too," I whispered back.

She glanced to the side, at her nightstand, and then slid open the drawer, withdrawing an unopened box of condoms. "I got these the other day," she murmured. "Just in case."

She opened the box, pulled free a string, and ripped one packet off. Tossed the rest and the box together back into the drawer. Tearing the packet open, she tossed the wrapper aside and fiddled with the condom, figuring out which way it unrolled. Holding my eyes, she grasped my cock at the base with one hand and fit the condom to my tip with the other, and then stroked my length hand over hand until the latex sheathed my organ.

I hung my head, groaning at her touch. "Fuck, Em."

She pushed at my shoulder, and I fell to my back. Sliding a thigh across my torso, she settled astride me, sitting high on my belly. For a moment, she just sat there, hair wild and bright, breasts high and firm and round and proud, nipples hard and begging. Her hands braced on my chest, and then she caressed my chest and my stomach, flicking my nipples. Leaning forward, she lifted an inch or two and rubbed her sex along my hard, aching length.

I slid my hands up her thighs to grip her hips, desperate to feel her take me into her.

"Em, fuck—please," I whispered, lifting and thrusting as she teased my cock, sliding her slick slit up and down my shaft, smearing her dripping juices all over me.

"Payback's a bitch, huh?" she asked, hands planted on my stomach.

Her tits swayed with every movement, bouncing against her chest. I cradled them, caressed them. "Fucking love your tits, Emerson."

She just grinned, rubbing herself against me all the faster until I was flexing and thrusting.

"Please, Em," I whispered. "I fucking need you."

"You need me?" She braced one hand on my chest and leaned forward, lifting her ass off my stomach.

"Yes," I breathed. "I'll beg. I'll plead. I just…I need to be inside you. Fucking need it."

She reached down between her thighs and grasped my cock. Lifted me away from my stomach. Angled me, touching the crown to her slit. I threw my head back into the pillow, groaning. "Fuck, Em."

Another moment of hesitation, her eyes locked on mine, and then she slowly sank down. I growled, the sound morphing into a gasp as my mouth dropped open. She took me slowly, centimeter by centimeter, her mouth falling open too, eyes going wide.

Deeper, deeper, until I bottomed out inside her. Wrapped up in her tight hot wet pussy, I couldn't breathe, couldn't move, couldn't react in any way except to grip her hips where her thighs bent to meet her waist with such force I was sure I'd leave fingerprints in her fair flesh.

"Oh, fuck—Hayden!" She gasped as her ass settled onto my hips.

I caught my breath with a ragged gasp. "Emerson. You feel…" I clenched as the need to release rippled through me.

"Home," she breathed, finishing for me. "You feel like home."

"Yes," I said, "like home."

She fell forward, arms going around my neck. "Take me, Hayden. Make love to me. Please."

I drove into her, pushing deeper, even as I was already seated as deep as I could go. She moaned, burying her face in my throat.

"Again," she demanded.

I thrust into her again, and she growled, spine arching inward as I ground deeper into her.

I felt her rippling around me, felt my climax building. "Em, holy shit, you feel so fucking amazing." I dragged clawed fingers down her spine and grabbed her ass. "I never want it to end."

She pressed her mouth to my chest, shaking her head. "Me either."

"But you feel so fucking good, Em." I fought it back, and knew I'd lose the fight—soon. "But I…you feel too good."

She raised her head, eyes finding mine. "Don't hold back, Hayden."

I pulled her upward and then crushed her down, thrusting into her at the same time. "I can't wait much longer, Em. I'm sorry—I'm sorry, I can't—" I gasped, feeling it build and build, becoming a wild, frantic need that I couldn't hold back.

Her arm slid beneath my neck and her hand cradled the back of my head, and she drew her legs up so she was sitting on her shins. Her lips pressed to my ear. "Fuck me, Hayden. Give me everything you've got, baby. I want it all—right *now*."

She punctuated this with a sinuous roll of her hips. I'd been inside her for a few minutes at most, and I was lost, gone. Done. I crushed her hips in my hands and shoved her down onto myself hard, thrusting up, growling, groaning, gasping. Emerson set the pace, rolling her hips with that slow, sinuous, beautiful torture, mouth against my heart, breathing hard, panting, whimpering. Every sound she made was one of pure ecstasy, shooting straight down into my balls, making them pulse and clench.

I cradled her ass in my hands, palms pulling the thick, soft, beautiful globes apart so I could drive deeper—with every thrust, Emerson whimpered in my ear, breathless and wild.

"Em, oh god, Em. Oh fuck." I was still holding on, still trying to hold out, to make this heaven on earth last as long as possible.

"Hayden," she gasped. "You're gonna make me come again." She clung to my neck with one hand, the other palming my face, thumb on my lips. "Come with me, baby. Please. Please, Hayden."

I gave up. Gave in. Let go of the last of my control and let Emerson Day completely take ownership of me. I felt her start to come, felt her pussy squeeze hard around me in wave after wave of hot, clamping pressure, and she cried out, burying her gasping, keening, breathless screams in my shoulder, lips quivering against me. She abandoned the slow, deliberate, sinuous rolling of her hips and slammed down on me, harder and faster with each thrust.

I had no choice but to match her, to join her. I gripped her hips and pushed her down, pulled her up, meeting her downward thrusts with upward drives, grunting rabidly through gritted teeth.

"Yes!" She sobbed, openly weeping now. "Hayden, yes, yes, yes! Oh fuck yes!"

She shuddered all over, and her pussy clamped down so hard it almost hurt, and that was my undoing.

"Emerson! Oh—holy fuck, Em!" I lost all control, then, however much I had left, that is.

She was shaking and shuddering and crying out in a nonstop series of sobbing gasps which began to match the pace of my helpless, mad fucking thrusts. I lost all ability to be gentle, to moderate my power— all I could do was take her, give her what she'd begged for: everything.

And yet, the further into wild desperation I flew, the more eagerly, willingly, and passionately she met me there. She drove against my mad thrusting and fucked me back just as hard.

I came with a ragged groan that turned into a shout—she clapped a hand over my mouth and then pressed her lips to mine, not kissing but devouring my groans, my moans. Heat pounded through me, tension releasing like a tidal wave. I saw stars, and then my vision narrowed and I lost all bodily function, dizzy and gasping. Emerson kept her mouth against mine, panting as she slid down my cock again and again, even as I subsided from the peak of my orgasm. More and more—she drew it out of me, making me shudder and whimper as she continued to ride me through the last throes of aftershock.

Eventually, my cock began to soften, and she went still.

She clung to me, kept me inside her, arms around my neck, face buried in the side of my neck, her soft hot quick panting breaths huffing against my skin.

For a long time, we stayed like that. I caressed her everywhere my hands could reach, petting her hair, smoothing my hands down her arms and back, her butt, her thighs.

"My god, Hayden," she whispered after a time I couldn't measure—it could have been ten minutes, it could have been an hour.

"I know. Same."

She shook her head, then met my gaze. Hers was wet. "No, I don't think you do."

"So tell me, honey."

She swallowed. "Okay. But…will you hold me?

Like last night? I've never felt so…safe. So…" a shake of her head as words escaped her. "Being in your arms like that, I feel like I can finally breathe for the first time in my life."

"Let me take care of this real quick," I said.

She rolled off me, hissing as I slid out of her. I moved to my feet, but my legs gave out and I collapsed back to the bed.

I laughed. "My legs don't work."

Laying naked on her back on top of the blanket, she smiled. "Good. I like knowing I can do that to you." She wiped at her face with both hands. "I have to pee again, but I don't think I can stand up yet."

I fought to my feet, steadied myself, and then went into the bathroom. I wrapped up and discarded the condom and then found a washcloth on an open-face shelf above the toilet; I wetted it with warm water and cleaned myself, rinsed it out a few times, and then brought it to Emerson. I washed her, as well, gently and carefully. When I was done, I tossed the washcloth in the sink and got back in bed.

Emerson immediately slid over to me, curled up almost entirely on top of me, thigh over crotch, hand on my belly, cheek on my chest.

We lay in easy, happy silence for a while.

"Hayden?"

"Mmmm?"

"Merry Christmas. I think I love you."

FIFTEEN

Emerson

MY HEART SLAMMED IN MY CHEST A MILE A MINUTE, FEAR rocking my stomach, creating a racket of doubts in my gut.

He didn't say anything for a long while, and I swallowed my fear, waiting.

He touched my chin, and I forced myself to look at him. "Merry Christmas, Emerson." He kissed my mouth, soft and slow and sweet. "I love you, too."

"Is it crazy?" I asked, on the verge of panicking.

"Maybe, yeah. But if so, then I'm crazy." He brushed a thumb over my cheekbone, over my eyebrow, my lips. "That was the most intense experience of my life, Em."

I squeezed my eyes shut, unable to hold his gaze.

"I've…" I shook my head. "I'm at a loss for words. I didn't know it could be like that."

"Me either."

"Em, baby, you're shaking." He tilted my face toward his again. "Talk to me, please. What's up?"

"Scared," I whispered.

"Of what?"

"Loving you." I choked on my whisper. "I'm terrified of not being enough…for you—for you to…stay. To love me back."

"Jesus, Emerson, of course I—"

I touched his mouth. "Please, just let me say this. I didn't understand it until I talked to Dru and Bast, but… my mom never really loved me. She either couldn't or didn't, I don't know. Gambling always won. And my dad—my *father*, I mean—he…he was never around. Never wanted me. Never stayed." I felt tears leak out. "I know I have Bast, and Delia, and Dru, but—"

"They can't erase the wounds left by your biological parents in your youngest formative years," he filled in.

"Exactly." I sighed. "You're very smart, you know that?"

He rolled me to my back, wedging me between his body and the bed. One hand framed the side of my face, the other tenderly cupped my breast, affectionately strumming my nipple.

"There's nothing I can say that will take that away right now. You're allowed to be afraid. But hopefully you'll give me a chance to prove to you that I'm not going anywhere."

"Except back to Indiana."

He nuzzled closer. "Hey, hold on, now. I mean, yeah, my life is there…for now. But it doesn't have to be."

I risked a hopeful look at him, even as guilt ripped through me. "I can't ask you to uproot yourself from the only place that's ever been home, Hayden."

He nipped my lower lip, kissed the corner of my mouth. "What if I was getting restless there? What if…" he swallowed hard. "What if it feels impossible to go back there, now that Dad is…now that Dad's gone?"

"What about your mom?"

He sighed. "That one I don't have an answer for right now, unfortunately. But I can promise you this: I'm here. I'm in love with you. We can find the way forward together."

"You're in love with me?" I whispered, eyes still leaking stupid tears I couldn't seem to stop.

"Yeah, Em, I'm in love with you."

"Even though it's too soon and we're both certifiably nuts?"

"Yup."

"I have to finish school," I said.

"I know."

"I want to play professional soccer. I could get drafted by a team anywhere in the country, if not the world."

"I know."

"That would mean living who knows where."

"I can work from anywhere. And I've always wanted to see the world outside of West Lafayette, Indiana."

"I'm in love with you, too. I don't think I am—I *know* I am."

He kissed me. "I know."

The kiss was the spark.

Within a matter of moments, the tender kiss became frenzied and hungry. I pulled him more fully over me, reaching between us to grasp his erection. I stroked him, feeling him grow harder in my hands with each slow caress of his rigid length.

He groaned as I pumped him into a frenzy. "Em—wait, wait. Slow down—I want to be inside you. I'm about to come, and I'm not sure how long I can hold it back."

I slowed my strokes, watching his handsome face go through a wash of emotions. His jaw tightened and his abs tensed, and he growled, trying not to thrust, desperately holding back.

"I like that you can't hold back."

He shook his head. "I want to last longer for you."

I pulled his face down to mine and kissed him deeply, thrusting my tongue into his mouth and biting his lower lip. I twisted my fist around the head of his cock, playing with his balls with the other.

"I love it, Hayden. I *love* knowing I make you lose

control. I love knowing I turn you on so bad you can't stop yourself from coming." I rubbed the weeping tip of his beautiful, hard, glistening cock with my thumb. "I love knowing I do that to you. I don't *want* you to last longer. I want you to fuck me so hard I can't breathe. I want you to fuck me every chance you get. I want you to fuck me and I want you to come right away. I want you to come so hard you see Jesus, Mary, and all the saints. I want you to make love to me. I want you to never, *ever* hold back."

He sank backward, pulling out of my hold, grabbed my wrist, and surged forward, pinning both of my hands over my head. He looked at me with a ferocious love, a fierce need. Despite his unrelenting grip on my wrists, he dipped his face to mine and his mouth covered mine and I tasted his breath and his stubble scratched my face and his tongue found mine. My eyes closed as he kissed me, and I fought his hold, wanting to touch him, to caress him, anywhere, every-where—I wanted to make him come, to feel him let loose and show me the power I had over him, the plea-sure I gave him. He effortlessly kept my hands pinned overhead, and somehow, that only made the arousal smashing through me pulse all the hotter. I moaned into his mouth and continued to wrestle for control of my hands.

The kiss deepened, turned wild and ravenous, our mouths clashing and warring, tongues tangling and teasing. My pussy throbbed, dripped. I bucked upward and hooked my legs around his waist and locked my feet at the small of his back. Pressed my sex against his, feeling his long thick hard cock sliding bare against my pussy.

Without breaking the kiss, still trying to free my hands from his grip and loving every second of the struggle, I tipped my hips, catching the slick, weeping tip of his cock against my pussy. He moaned long and low in his chest, pushing his hips toward mine, easing the head of him inside me. I whimpered into his mouth, into the kiss. I almost got one of my hands free, but he repositioned his grip at the last second and my whimper turned to a feline snarl of aroused frustration. He crushed my hands deeper into the pillow over my head, gave me more of his weight.

I paused for breath, lips motionless against his as I gasped oxygen into my starved lungs. And then I slammed my mouth back against his, sucking his tongue into my mouth and groaning in pure delight as he responded in kind—never in my life has merely kissing been so arousing, so erotic, so thrilling.

But I needed more.

I felt him not quite inside me, his plump cock-head splitting my nether lips apart, teasing, torturing. Hayden darted his tongue into my mouth, and I pushed my hips against his, pulling him to me with the power in my lower half.

There was no discussion, no hesitation. On either of our parts.

He slid into me, bare.

Helplessly, I inhaled a shrill gasp of wondering, awed, overcome ecstasy as he filled me to bursting with his naked cock. I felt every inch of him, every ridge, every vein. He bottomed out inside me, our hips meeting, bellies touching. My tits flattened between our bodies, nipples aching and throbbing. My core pulsed, my belly was tight, my lungs empty, my mind whirling.

He groaned raggedly, dropping his head to the crook of my neck. His iron grip on my wrists went slack and he pressed his palms to mine, threading our fingers together, and now, instead of fighting his grip, I clutched his hands for dear life, overcome by the feel of him bare within me, so intimate, so vulnerable.

With another rough, shaky moan, Hayden drew his hips back, drawing a hoarse whimper from me as his cock slid slick and hot between my lips, and then gently, lovingly, tenderly drove himself back into me.

I cried out as he filled me to aching, searing fullness, shaking all over.

Another slow, gentle thrust, and we both groaned together. I freed my hands from his and clawed desperately at his shoulders, a ripping, smashing climax building inside me. I dragged my fingernails down his back, and he, with a rough snarl, pulled back and slammed into me, this thrust ungentle and wild. He drove a fist into the bed beside my ear and gripped my breast with bruising power, slamming hard into me again.

I sank my teeth into the thick, hot, dense muscle

standing out along the ridge of his shoulder, muffling my cry; smoothing my palms down his back, soothing where I was sure I'd left marks, I palmed the taut bubble of his ass, and then dug my fingers into the muscle and pulled him to me, driving my hips into his thrusts. Loud wet squelches met our thrusts, and flesh smacked together with slaps, his groaning becoming grunts, animal and primal.

I tilted my hips, and now his cock slid against my clit as he pounded into me, and that was my ultimate undoing.

Orgasm shattered me all at once, my fingers spasming into the hard muscle of his ass and my teeth locked in his shoulder and I screamed against his flesh, clinging to him, and my scream became a sob as heat sliced through me from my core to my toes.

Hayden's thrusting faltered and he groaned a raw, ragged sound, and I felt his cock pulse inside me.

And that's when a terrible realization hit me. "Hayden—Hayden, *don't*—you can't come inside me," I whispered, frantic and panicked, pushing at his hip. "Pull out, baby—you have to pull out!"

With a rough, panting groan, he yanked out of me. He froze, shuddering. I clutched his hard, wet, throbbing cock in both hands and stroked his pulsing length. He pushed up, palming my breasts, head hanging, face a rictus of pre-orgasmic tension. I kept my legs locked around his waist, pumping his cock, twisting my fists in opposite directions with each slick stroke.

Hayden gripped my tits and fucked my hands, eyes closed, jaw tight.

"Look at me," I whispered. "Hayden, look at me."

His eyes flew open, and he gasped a teeth-clenched groan, and he came. Hot ropes of come sluiced out of him, laying in a thick white stripe on my belly. I sped my strokes, and he shook all over, falling forward, hands catching his weight, and he came again, and now his come splashed on my diaphragm and between my breasts, and he thrust harder into my plunging fists. Laying beneath him, feet hooked behind his butt, I stroked him through another grunting spasm, hot come pooling on my tits, chest, and belly.

At long last, Hayden's orgasm faded, subsiding until a string of come dripped onto my stomach, connecting us as his cock slowly softened.

Panting, he sank to sit on his feet. I lay with my feet drawn up to my ass, knees bent.

I reached for his hand. "Hayden, I'm sorry."

He blinked at me, frowning. "*You're* sorry? For what?"

"Making you pull out like that."

He shook his head. "We got carried away. I should have known better. I'm the one who's sorry."

"I just…" I scrubbed my face. "This is embarrassing, but I forgot that I'm not on birth control right now."

"And I just assumed you were. Or, actually, I didn't even assume—I wasn't thinking. I got lost in the moment, lost in how fucking amazing it felt to be bare inside you."

"I did, too."

"I just...I know better. I shouldn't have put you at risk like that."

"Hey, hey, hey," I squeezed his hand. "No, look at me, listen to me, Hayden: I made the choice, too. It felt *so* fucking incredible, having you bare inside me. I've never...I've never had unprotected sex before. I wasn't thinking, I wasn't prepared for how it would feel and I got carried away. You couldn't know I'm not on birth control—of *course* you'd assume I was."

He shook his head. "I just...I *shouldn't* have assumed. I should have thought. I should never have let it get to that point."

"Stop, please. Nothing happened, okay? You pulled out." I rubbed his thighs. "It felt amazing. Better than amazing. I loved every fucking second of it, and I *do not* regret it. I want to do it again. So don't go hogging all the blame, here, okay?"

He held my eyes, hesitated, and then nodded. "Okay." He rolled off the bed. "Let me clean you up."

He vanished into the bathroom, and I heard the faucet running, and then he returned, cock hanging heavy between his thighs, every muscle rippling and carved from marble, hair messy—fucking gorgeous.

"You're so fucking sexy, Hayden," I said as he knelt on the bed beside me.

He grinned, blushing. "You don't know what it

feels like to hear that—to really feel that from you. You really know how to stroke my ego."

"I'm not stroking your ego, Hayden," I said, grabbing his hand as he wiped his seed off my skin. "Hey, listen. I'm not. I'm telling you the truth. You're sexy as fuck, and I feel like the luckiest woman in the world for getting to be with you."

He held my gaze. "Thank you, Emerson." He folded the washcloth and wiped away another puddle of his come. "Jeez, I really made a mess, didn't I?"

I laughed. "Yeah, you did. And it was honestly hot as fuck."

He arched an eyebrow at me. "It was? For you, I mean."

"Yeah, honey, it was. It's new for me, but it was hot. I'd absolutely do it again. Watching you come, watching it happen, feeling it, taking your come on me? Yeah, it was hot as fuck."

"Pulling out is risky, though," he said.

"Yeah, it is." I took the washcloth from him and finished cleaning a few places he'd missed, and then handed it back. "Toss that and come back to me."

He threw it into the bathroom sink with a wet plop audible from where I was and then returned to the bed.

I opened my arms. "Come here, baby."

He moved over me, and I pulled him down to me, cradling his head on my breasts and locking my legs around him again.

He pulled in a long breath, held it, and let it out slowly. "I like this. A lot."

"Me too." I stroked his hair, his back, his arms, everywhere I could reach. "About six months ago, I met a guy. He was no one special, just some dude studying in the library. I know this is probably uncomfortable to hear, but you deserve the truth."

"You had a life before me, Emerson. I understand that. I'm okay with it. It's part of who you are, and I'm very quickly coming to love the woman that you are. I'm not threatened by or jealous of your past. I may not love thinking about you with someone else, but it's reality. I was with other people before you. All that matters is that we're together now."

I scratched his back, caressed his ear, his hair. "I appreciate you saying that, Hayden. You just...you deserve the truth. I'm not apologizing or ashamed."

"It kinda sounds like you are, a little bit."

I sighed. "Maybe a little."

"Don't be."

"I'll try. The point is, I hooked up with that guy. It was shockingly shitty. And it wasn't him. He was a decent dude. He didn't do anything wrong. It was just..." I twirled his hair around my finger. "It was just shitty. I won't go into details, but it was...I dunno...boring? Forgettable. I went home feeling awful about myself. Like, what am I doing? Why am I doing this? It hadn't been fun or enjoyable for a long time. So why do I keep doing it? These hookups with guys I don't know and don't care about, don't want to know or care about…I was over it, all at once, suddenly."

I shifted my thighs tighter and higher around his waist, clinging to him, caressing him, wanting to offset what I was saying with reassurance that I was here for him, and with him.

"Em, you don't have to—"

"I do," I interrupted. "For me, if not you."

"Okay."

"After that, I just kinda…stopped going out. Stopped trying to meet people. Guys, I mean. It helped that school got busy, soccer season kicked off, and then mid-terms…Weeks went by, and then months, and I wasn't missing the hookups. So, I stayed focused on school and soccer. I hung out with my teammates instead of guys. And then, two months ago, my birth control ran out. I wasn't having sex, and I realized I wasn't interested in having sex with random guys anymore, and there sure wasn't anyone I was interested in romantically, as in emotionally, so…why bother renewing it? I felt okay without it. Better, even, in some ways. My periods got heavier, but not too bad, and my emotions and moods…well, I guess I just felt like I didn't need it or want it."

"I get it. I mean, I don't get it—I'm a guy. But I can understand what you mean." He sighed again, happily nuzzling his face against my chest.

I smiled down at him, toying with his hair and massaging his scalp. "My point in telling you this is that I totally forgot I wasn't on birth control until you were about to come. I just…it hit me all at once, right then, and I panicked."

"It took me by surprise, for sure, but like I said, I was so lost in the moment and how good it felt that I wasn't even thinking about the consequences, whether or not you were on birth control, any of it."

"We both did, Hayden. Stop trying to hog all the blame. And there's nothing to feel about. You pulled out well before you came. Nothing happened. Okay? I just need you to understand why I had to make you plan out like that."

He lifted, shifting forward, levering over me. Gazed down at me, eyes bright and bold and clear. "I understand, Em."

I scratched his back with gentle fingers and then palmed his ass, squeezing and petting it possessively, merely for the sake of enjoying his body. "First chance I get, I'm going on birth control. Now that I've had you bare, I'm not sure how I'll go back."

"I had the same thought. But I also can't put your future and your plans at risk, Emerson. I won't." He leaned down to kiss my chin, my cheek, my forehead, and finally my lips.

I patted his butt. "We should get ready. We like to do Christmas early around here."

"So do we." He rolled off me, slid off the bed on my side, and then bent to scoop me up in his arms.

I snaked my arms around his neck. "Why, Mr. McCaffrey, where are you taking me?"

"I feel a responsibility to conserve water by showering together," he said, carrying me into the bathroom.

"Oh, goody," I whispered, nibbling on his earlobe. "I wasn't done with you anyway. Now we get to play in the shower."

Once we were done in the shower—which was a long one that involved several more loud orgasms on my part and Hayden painting my tits and stomach with his come—we dried off and put our Christmas PJs on.

Opening my door, I heard quiet chatter from the kitchen.

Hayden hesitated. "Do you think anyone heard us? I'm not sure how quiet we were."

I laughed. "No point worrying about it now. Worst case scenario, we get teased a little bit."

He spun in place, wrapped me in his arms, and hugged me tight. "I love you, Emerson Grace Day. I hope you feel that down to your bones."

"I do." I exhaled shakily. "I feel it so clearly. And I hope you feel how much I love you. As has been previously agreed upon, I know we're crazy, talking about love after barely a week, but I know what I feel."

"Me too."

I stepped out of his arms. "I'm giving Bast and Dru kind of an unexpected and probably very emotional gift today. It could get intense. Just F-Y-I." I threaded my fingers in his. "I did get you something. Nothing big, but I think you'll like it."

He squeezed my hand. "I got you something, too."

I shook my head. "No matter what it is, this already has been the best Christmas of my life, just because I got to meet you."

He didn't have a chance to respond because we entered the kitchen at that moment, and judging by the suppressed laughter on everyone's faces, we hadn't been subtle.

SIXTEEN

Hayden

ALL EYES TURNED TO US. MOM STUDIOUSLY FOCUSED ON her coffee. Duncan and Dane were visibly suppressing laughter. Dru and Bast were trying to act normal, but they too were clearly trying not to laugh. Delia had her back to the kitchen, stirring creamer into her coffee…but her shoulders were shaking.

Emerson ran her gaze around the kitchen. "All right, get it out of your system, the lot of you." She fixed her stare on her brothers. "Come on, you two. Hit us with the jokes."

Dru cleared her throat. "No one is going to make jokes, my love. You and Hayden were not exactly…discreet. We can all acknowledge that without resorting to crass and juvenile humor." She pinned her son with a hard look. "Right, boys?"

"Mmm-hmm. Yup, got it, Mom." Duncan avoided his mother's stare.

"*Moi?* Crass and juvenile?" Dane said, clapping a hand to his chest, faking outrage. "Why, I never."

"I'm not gonna feel safe until someone makes a joke," Emerson said.

"Sounds like someone had a very merry fucking Christmas," Delia said, turning around, mug held against her chest. "Ohhhhh Christmas dick, ohhhh Christmas dick, how lovely is your Christmas dick," she sang. "Ho ho ho, sounds like you've been a very *Badd* girl, Emerson." She paused to take a sip. "You want more? I got more. I can keep going."

Emerson pursed her lips in what seemed like an attempt to keep from laughing. "Nope. That's good. Thanks, Dee. I feel much better now."

"I live but to serve," Delia said. "And from what I heard...*three times*...so does Hayden." She winked at me. "Didn't think you were getting out of this unscathed, did you, buddy?"

"Delia." Bast's voice was quiet but firm. "That's enough."

Delia blew a kiss at us. "Just helping out."

"This is excellent coffee, Dru," Mom said, a little too loudly. "What brand is it?"

For some reason, Mom's attempt to force normality into the situation forced a snort out of me—it was just so…perfectly timed. My snort turned into a choked laugh, and then when Mom glanced at me, confused, I utterly lost it. Emerson stared at me for a moment, and then she was laughing too, and within seconds, everyone was.

"What's so funny?" Mom demanded. "It was an honest question."

I went to her and hugged her from behind. "I know, Mom. That's why it was funny. It's okay to acknowledge the situation, you know."

She sniffed imperiously. "That's just not my style, Hayden Reginald. I didn't hear a thing." She took a sip of coffee. Eyed me, a strange expression on her face. "Incidentally, Hayden, your father was blessed with an extraordinarily short refractory period as well. I remember the three-times-in-one-morning years." A pause. "Quite fondly, too."

I stared at her, stunned. "*MOM!*"

The whole room lost it again.

She just shrugged, looking at me with big innocent eyes. "What? When in Rome, right?"

I covered my face. "I need coffee. Or a hot spoon with which to dig my brain out of my ears."

"Oh hush, you," Mom snapped. "We all had to listen to you two going at it like horny rabbits. You can darned well take a few jokes." She pointed at me. "What I said wasn't a joke, mind you. In his prime, your father could take me around the world three or four times in a morning."

"Jesus crickets, Mom," I groaned. "*Please* stop. I'm begging you to stop."

"Not what you were saying a few minutes ago," Delia quipped. "Sounded more like 'yes, yes, yes, yes' to me."

Dru snorted, clapping a hand over her mouth. "Delia!"

Bast cleared his throat. "Are we done?"

"I dunno," Duncan said. "I think that's up to Hayden and Emerson. You need a minute? One more round before we open presents?"

Emerson looked up at me. "I'm sorry for my family, Hayden."

I just grinned. "Funny, I'm not."

She leaned against me, and I wrapped my arms around her waist. "Okay, we can move on now," she said.

Delia set two mugs of coffee on the counter in front of us. "Here. Caffeinate yourselves. There's a pile of presents with my name on it over there. Literally."

"Wait." I sniffed the air. "Why do I smell cinnamon rolls?"

Dru nudged Delia away from the oven with a hip. "Because…" she tugged on oven mitts and pulled out two trays lined with rows of cinnamon rolls dripping with frosting. "I made cinnamon rolls. Christmas Day tradition."

"You all have some amazing traditions," Mom said as Dru slid a roll from the tray onto a plate and set it in front of her. "I haven't had one of these in years. It looks delicious, Dru, thank you."

"Oh, it's store-bought. I just popped 'em in the oven." Dru served me one and then herself. "The rest of ya'll can get your own."

There was a comical rush for the rolls, then, as Delia, Emerson, Duncan, and Dane all tried to get one at the same time, a process that featured a lot of playful pushing, pulling, wrestling, cursing, and laughing.

Bast waited until the chaos had settled before grabbing one for himself. "We raised a bunch of wolves, Dru."

"No kidding," she answered, around a bite. "I blame you."

"You married me," he said, shrugging. "And kept letting me put kids in you."

"I *let* you put kids in me?" She smirked at him. "I seem to remember it differently. You wanted to wait the whole six weeks after Dunc was born. I'm the one who jumped your bones before a month had gone by."

"It's a miracle we don't have six, like Rome and Kit-Kat," Bast said.

"Not really. You getting snipped may have had something to do with it."

"Why are we talking about this?" Dane asked. "Because I don't need to know this."

"Your father has very potent baby gravy," Dru said, popping a bite into her mouth. "Something to remember. Always use a condom, boys. Babies are forever."

Both boys groaned, covering their faces.

"CAN WE STOP TALKING ABOUT SEX?" Duncan shouted. "My virgin ears are burning."

"Virgin ears?" Dane said, cackling. "If you're a virgin, then I'm the pope. You and Kendall weren't exactly leaving room for the Holy Spirit in the back of Kendall's Yukon after prom."

"Dane," Duncan growled. "I'm gonna kill you."

Bast just laughed. "You think we don't know? If you thought you were bein' sneaky about it, son, you've got another thing coming."

"The condoms randomly appearing in your suit coat pocket didn't give you a clue that we knew?" Dru said.

Duncan was blushing furiously. "I thought that was Dane trying to be funny."

"If I was trying to be funny about you popping your cherry with Kendall, putting condoms in your suit coat wouldn't be my move. A twelve-inch black dildo, maybe."

"Dane Andrew Badd," Dru snapped. "*Cherry popping* is a vulgar and offensive phrase."

"Sorry, Ma," Dane mumbled.

"I must admit, this is the strangest conversation I've ever had, let alone on Christmas Day," Mom murmured into her mug.

Dru just laughed. "Oh, Kaye, hang around this crew long enough, you'll soon find out that this is actually pretty tame."

"Oh…oh my." Kaye shook her head. "Maybe you all need to go to church more, in that case."

"MOM!" I shot her a horrified look.

Bast just snickered. "Good one, Kaye."

Mom shot me a snooty look back. "See? I can be funny."

I palmed my forehead, shaking my head with a sigh. "So I'm discovering."

As if upon some unspoken cue, everyone migrated to the living room. Dru and Bast took the loveseat nearest the tree, Delia took one corner of the couch, Emerson and I took the other, and the boys took the middle, with Mom in between Delia and the boys.

"Okay, Kaye and Hayden, we usually do this is one at a time from youngest to oldest. We don't go in for all-at-once chaos like those heathens in Bax and Eva's house."

Dru smacked his shoulder. "Don't be a dick, honey. They have their way, we have ours."

"Their way means a pile of wrapping paper taller than me. Everyone yelling and shouting at once. I think Liam and Lennox actually got into a fistfight one year."

"Yeah, but that was over a girl," Duncan said, "not the presents."

"Oh." Bast shuffled through the pile of gifts, found one, and tossed it to Dane. "For you, the baby of the family."

"Oh boy!" Dane said with over-the-top enthusiasm. "I hope it's My Little Pony!"

"Still too soon," Delia sniped. "I was crushed that year."

Dru threw her head back and groaned. "My *god*, not this again! They were *sold out*! I went to every store within a *hundred miles* and spent *three days* trolling every toy-selling website on the internet. I *tried*, okay? I'm sorry! Do you need therapy?"

"Yeah, but not for that." Delia blew her mom a kiss. "You made up for it anyway."

One by one, the Badd kids opened their gifts: gift cards to favorite stores, a new wireless mic-headphone gaming headset, an expensive, imported lotion only available from one store in Paris...

When the kids had all gone, Dru and Bast exchanged theirs with each other. Next, Dru fished through the pile and came up with a gift bag which she handed to Mom.

"Oh, goodness," Mom exclaimed. "You didn't!"

"Of course we did," Dru said. "And it's not like I didn't see the gifts *you* brought."

Mom gestured at the bags we'd brought. "Well, go on! We can open them together."

Mom got a cashmere sweater, lilac, V-neck, thin and delicate and beautiful. She'd gotten Dru a jar of hand cream she claimed had done wonders for her hands. Dru immediately put it on, oohing and ahhing over the scent and how her skin just drank it up. Dru and Bast flipped through the photo book, remarking on how different everything looked.

Around it went again, this time the kids all giving each other gifts, and of course Dru and Bast hadn't stopped at just one, so it went around again. Emerson got a smart wool scarf, a coffee mug with her college logo on one side and the date of her soccer team's nationals win on the other, and a Coach wallet clutch.

When it seemed like pretty much everyone had gone, I gave Emerson the small gift bag containing my present to her.

She shot me a soft smile and then tugged the tissue paper free. Within was a small white box containing the necklace. She lifted the box free, opened it, and her eyes went wide.

"Hayden!" she gasped, looking at me with wonder. "It's incredible."

"It reminded me of you—your nickname, Sunni."

She rested the pendant on her palm, staring at it. It was almost as big as her palm, the rays long and pointy and serpentine, the central opal bigger than my thumb and gleaming iridescent in the early morning sun shining through the bay windows.

"Put it on me?" She breathed, handing it to me and turning her back to me.

I slid her profusion of curls aside and rested the pendant on her chest as I hooked the ends together at her neck.

She looked down at it, eyes shimmering. "It's gorgeous, Hayden. Thank you so much. I love it. I'll never take it off." She leaned in and kissed me. "I hope you didn't spend a fortune on it."

"Oh, don't worry about that," Mom said. "Hayden is very good with money. He rarely spends anything and makes a ton."

"Mom," I muttered. "Come *on*."

"What? It's true!" She rolled her eyes. "It's good to see you being generous again. I was worried that greedy, ungrateful bitch had ruined you. It seems Miss Emerson, here, is pretty much the opposite."

I gaped at my mother. "Seriously? Language!"

Mom gaped back at me. "Oh, what, you can drop F-bombs all day long, but I call that awful, selfish, greedy girl the B-word *one time* and you're calling me out?"

Emerson cackled. "He told me about her, Kaye, and I agree with you. She was a seriously ungrateful bitch, by all accounts."

Mom sniffed at me. "See? She agrees."

"So do I! That's not the point."

Emerson knelt at the tree and retrieved a small package, which she handed to me. I tore the wrapping open, revealing a small wooden box. Opening it, my heart stopped.

Within was a plain brass key on a cushion of red velvet. It was on a keyring with a small handmade leather heart.

I looked at her for an explanation.

She bit her lip. "Um, the cutesy explanation is that it's the key to my heart."

Everyone awwwed except Dane, who faked a retch, earning him a no-look middle finger from Emerson. "The other, more practical explanation is that's the key to my apartment in Seattle. I live with four other girls from my team, so it's loud and wildly estrogenic, but...um, yeah."

"For real?" I lifted the key out, running my thumb over the teeth. "The key to your apartment?"

"I want you to visit me." She dropped her eyes. "I know we haven't talked about things, and this isn't the time or place for it, but yeah, it's the key to my apartment."

I pulled her close. "I'll do more than just visit, Em," I whispered.

"I was worried it was too soon," she whispered back.

"It's not."

We turned our attention back to Bast and Dru, who seemed to be waiting for something, even though all the presents had been passed out.

"We have one more thing," Dru said. "For Emmy."

Emerson frowned. "For me?" She blinked, chewed on her lower lip. "Okay, well, actually, I have one more thing for the two of you."

Delia seemed about ready to wiggle right out of her seat, her blue eyes shining with secrets and joy.

Emerson eyed her. "You know something."

"I know a lot of things," Delia answered. "Em, I think you should go first."

"Open first or give first?" Emerson asked.

"Give first."

Emerson nodded. "Okay." She let out a breath and went into her room, emerging a moment later with a thin flat rectangle wrapped in red-and-white penguin-themed paper, adorned with a huge golden bow. She stood in front of Dru and Bast, hesitating, running her thumb along a taped seam.

"I, um." She swallowed hard, looked back at me as if for courage, and then at them again with a heavy sigh. "Here. Just open it." She sat on the edge of the couch, knee bouncing, hands wringing.

I took her hand, and she seized mine in a crushing grip.

"Fuck, I'm so nervous," she whispered to me, burying her face in my arm.

She rolled her face on my arm and watched past the edge of my bicep as Bast and Dru tore the paper together. Within was an 8x11 manila envelope tied with red string. Bast opened the flap and pulled out a thin sheaf of paperwork.

He frowned, then leaned across Dru and snagged a pair of reading glasses from a side table. He pointed at his boys without looking. "Not a word about the readers, you two."

They both held up their hands without a word.

"What..." he murmured. "What is this?"

Dru was already weeping. "It's name change paperwork, honey."

Bast shook his head. "I…yeah, so I see." He looked at Emerson. "Is this real?"

She nodded, hands pressed together, fingers steepled in front of her mouth and nose. "It's long overdue."

"Will someone please explain?" Dane asked after a moment of silence.

Emerson looked at him with surprising tenderness. "I changed my last name."

He looked at me, then at her. "You guys got married already?"

Emerson laughed, snorting. "No! God, no. I changed my last name to Badd. I am officially and forever Emerson Grace Badd."

"What if you get married?" he pressed.

She shrugged. "I'm not changing it. I may hyphenate, but I've been a Badd since I was six years old. It's long past time I became one officially."

"What about your mother?" Dru asked, her voice a whisper.

Emerson shook her head. "She didn't even know me the last time I was here. Early onset dementia. She's been showing signs of it for years, but recently, she's gotten way worse." She shrugged. "She hasn't been my mother…well, ever. You have."

Dru pulled her hand inside her sleeve and dabbed at her eyes. "On that note…Bast, honey?"

Bast reached down the side of the couch, producing a similar package that had been stuffed between the side of the couch and the tree. He looked shaken, emotional. Swallowing hard, he handed the package to Emerson. "Here, babe. Best to just open it and talk after."

Emerson held the package for a moment, eyes welling. "No." As if she knew what was inside without looking.

"Open it, honey," Dru whispered.

Beside me, Duncan and Dane were quiet, serious, even a little teary-eyed. Delia was barely holding back tears of her own.

Emerson ran a finger under a taped-down flap of wrapping paper and slid the manila envelope out, a match to the one she'd given them. This, too, contained a sheaf of papers, official court documents.

Emerson just shook her head. Looked up at them. Tried to speak but couldn't.

Bast produced a pen from somewhere. "All you gotta do is sign, honey."

Emerson flipped through the adoption paperwork and signed in the necessary spots. She set the pen aside and held the papers, gazing down at them as tears slid down her cheeks.

"Like you said, it's long past due," Bast said, his voice thick. "You've been a member of this family since you were six years old, Emerson. Now it's official." He held up the name-change documents. "In every way there is."

Emerson wept, leaning against me, staring at the papers as if she couldn't believe it.

"Go hug them," I whispered.

She set the papers on my lap and rushed across the room, throwing herself at Bast and Dru.

They pulled her onto the loveseat with them, both of them wrapping their arms around her.

When her crying subsided several moments later, she sank to sit on the floor in front of them, wiping at her eyes.

"Mom...Dad." She breathed. "You've been my parents my whole life. You're the only parents I've ever known. I was always so scared it would just...go away somehow. I couldn't bring myself to call you Mom and Dad."

Dru grabbed her hand. "We know, Emmy. We've always known. We never wanted to take away from your connection to your past. It never mattered to us whether it was official—you're our daughter."

"But then Delia let it slip after your summer break that you wished it was official," Bast said. "So we decided to make it official."

Emerson looked at Delia. "Snitch," she whispered, crawling over to her, where the two women embraced, both crying. "I love you."

Delia laughed, sniffling. "Love you too, sister."

"What are we, chopped liver?" Duncan asked.

"You knew too?" Emerson asked.

"It was a group decision," Bast said. "There obviously wasn't any question, but we felt it was only fair that they get a say."

Emerson slid between the two boys and hugged them both. Then she went back to Dru and Bast. "I'm so thankful to you. More than I can ever say. You took me in and showed me love. You gave me a family. A whole life I'd never have gotten otherwise." She hugged Dru first. "I love you, Mom." Bast, then. "I love you, Dad."

Bast tipped his head back, sniffing hard and groaning like a bear. "Shit." he pulled Emerson against his chest. "My girl. Love you so fuckin' much, Sunni-girl. Been waiting for you to call me Dad since that day on the dock sixteen years ago."

"I think this must be the merriest Christmas I've seen in a long, long time," Mom said, dabbing at her eyes. "God is good indeed."

Dru looked at her. "It's a wonder that you can say that after your loss."

Mom shrugged. "I had fifty amazing, wonderful years with my husband. I mourn him. I will always mourn him. But I know my husband. He would want me to live my life. To move on as best I can. I'm still figuring out what it will look like, of course, and it will certainly take some time. But I...I can hear him, almost." She dropped her voice into a startlingly good impression of Dad. "'You'd better not be moping around, Kaye McCaffrey. I may be gone, but you're not.'"

I choked. "That's exactly what Dad would say."

"Of course it is." Mom reached over to me and squeezed my hand. "I miss him, Hayden. I miss him so bad, sometimes I think it'll kill me. But it doesn't, and it won't. And I will not be paralyzed by grief. It's not what your father would have wanted. And so, I carry on. And I find the joy in the places where it can be found." She gestured around the room. "I've found an absolute ocean of joy in meeting you all. In watching this huge, crazy, hysterical, and *wildly* inappropriate family love each other. You've brought so, *so* much joy to this old, tired, grieving heart, all of you." She turned a look on Emerson next. "And you, my dear. Seeing how you care for my Hayden? That brings me more joy and hope than I can even express. I know, I know—it's new, and you're still figuring it out. I won't put any undue pressure on you. I'm just glad I made Hayden go out by himself that day."

She took Mom's hand and kissed the back of it. "Me too, Kaye. Me too."

SEVENTEEN

Emerson

OH MY GOD, THE CHAOS.

By noon, the entire Badd Clan was at our house. Kids from grade school up to high school seniors rampaged and gallivanted about the house, sledded down the refreshed sled run, threw snowballs, drank hot chocolate by the gallon, shared new toys and exclaimed over new gadgets and huddled together watching YouTube and TikTok and whatever else. Adults milled and drank and ate, teased, laughed, chased squealing children, yelled at teenagers, retrieved wayward bottles of booze that had mysteriously ended up near those teenagers…

It was glorious mayhem.

I got pulled in a dozen different directions by a

dozen different cousins. Jax wanted a beer pong re-match, Liam, Lena, Lennox, and Lucas—varsity soccer players at their high school—wanted me to give them juggling pointers, Delia wanted to abscond with a bottle of tequila and talk about sex and Hayden and sex with Hayden even though she's definitely *not* jealous...

What I didn't get was five minutes alone with Hayden. His time was monopolized even more than mine—everyone wanted to impress him, hang out with him, include him in whatever shenanigans were in the offing. We saw each other in passing a few times, but most of the day we barely saw each other.

By evening, Kaye was thoroughly drunk and being tended to by a watchful Mama Livvie. She was a hysterical drunk, it turned out.

By midnight, Kaye had long since been helped to bed, the youngest kids were piled on the floor of the TV room with blankets and throw pillows while The Grinch played quietly on the TV, most of the adults were in varying stages of inebriation, and I was absolutely shitfaced and unsuccessfully looking for Hayden.

The shitfacedness wasn't helping. I kept getting assaulted by walls, and gravity kept playing silly buggers with my balance.

I heard his voice coming from the basement, so I headed that way. Only, when I reached the top of the stairs, I couldn't figure out which set of stairs I was supposed to go down. I didn't remember Bast and Dru—Dad and Mom, rather—having four sets of

basement stairs, but the evidence in front of me suggested otherwise.

Unable to decide which set of stairs was real, I
found myself forced into a role I generally loathed:
damsel in distress.

"HAYDEN!" I yelled, weaving on my feet well
away from the stairs themselves, fearful of the unpre-
dictable gravity monster trying to hurl me down the
stairs and thus put an end to my soccer career, if not
my life.

"HAYDEN!"

"Yo, Hayden, I think Em's yelling for you," I heard
Dane say.

A moment later, I saw a rotating cake display of
Haydens peering up at me from the bottom of the
stairs.

"Em?"

I waved. "Hello."

He grinned. "Hi, babe. You good?"

I shook my head, which ended up with my head
wobbling on my neck and pulling me off balance. "I
wanna go down there."

He trotted up the steps, magically deciphering the
mystery of which set to use. "I take it you need help?"

"Yup. 'M a little nee-nib-ree-aded. Shit. Nee...in...
bree...ated." I tried to slap myself in the forehead and
missed, almost falling over in the process. "Oops."

Hayden chuckled. "I have a better idea than going
downstairs."

I stuck my tongue out and blew a raspberry, or tried to—I only succeeded in drooling on myself. "You're down there. I wanna go down there where you are."

He laughed even harder. "Well, I *was* down there, but now I'm up here."

I peered at the stairs. "You are?" And then at him. "Oh. Hi. You're cute. I think I'll keep you."

He brushed his thumb over my lips and chin. "And you, my love, are extraordinarily intoxicated."

"Yup! Once a year. Christmas day. Thasssit." I blinked at the four of him. "Are you extraordinallilly Intox...Ixton... whatever you said?"

"No, I'm good."

"Why not?"

A shrug. "I don't like being drunk."

I felt a hot bowling ball form in my throat. "Not sure I do either, anymore." I swallowed hard. "It snuck up on me." A horrible thought occurred to me. "Are you mad that I'm drunk?"

He scooped me up in his arms, and my head lolled heavily against his chest. "Not even slightly. You're allowed to cut loose once in a while."

"I gotta take care of myself. At school. My grades, soccer...gotta do good. If I lose my scholarship, I might end up like..." I frowned at Hayden's rotating face. "I dunno wha'ta call her. The lady who had me. My womb donor? I don't wanna hate her, Hayden. But I kinda do. Y'know? Like, my stupid sperm donor, I don't hate him. He was never there. He came, he went, he was consistently inconsistent. Hey, I said that right, I think."

"You did," he said, weaving through the kitchen.

Someone kissed my forehead. I opened my eyes to see Mom looking down at me. "Hi, Mama."

Her eyes turned hazy with tears. "Hi, honey."

"I got shitfaced."

"So I see."

"Hayden is taking me somewhere." I looked up at him. "Are we going to bed?"

"We sure are."

I patted his chest, and felt a nose, somehow. Weird that he has a nose on his chest. "Oh goody. I like bed with you. You have a big penis and it's very yummy."

Mom spewed something red between her fingers; she ripped a piece of paper towel from the roll and cleaned herself up. "*Okay*, I think you really need to go to bed now."

Hayden just laughed.

I looked at Mom. "I love you."

"Love you more, sweet girl." She kissed my forehead again. "You'll keep an eye on her?" She asked me.

"An eye on who?" I asked.

Mom just snorted. "Not you, baby. I was talking to Hayden."

"Oh."

"Of course," Hayden said.

"I have to pee," I said. "But I lost the way to the bathroom."

"I got you covered, honey."

The Hayden boat carried me through the kitchen, down the hallway, and to my bedroom. I found myself on my feet in the bathroom, Hayden tugging my PJ bottoms down. I tried to help and only ended up tripping.

"Just let me, okay?" He slid the bottoms off. "Have a seat." He helped me sit down on the toilet. "Can you go?"

"Go?" I frowned up at him. "Go where?"

"Pee, babe. You said you had to pee."

"I did?"

He sighed. "Oh boy. Yeah, you did."

I shrugged. "Oh." I went cross-eyed as I summoned my pee, and discovered I did in fact have a lot. I looked at Hayden, who was facing away from me. "I've never peed in front of a dude before."

"First for me, too."

"You think it's weird?"

"Not at all. I'm glad you're comfortable enough with me to do so."

I wiped and went to pull up my pants, but I was sitting down still, and also wasn't wearing pants. "You took away my pants."

"You spilled something on them."

"Oh."

"You want something clean to wear?"

"No. I like no pants. Do you like no pants?"

He laughed. "I don't typically sleep naked."

I stabbed a finger at the ceiling and almost poked my eye out. "Ow, shit." I tried again and managed to miss my face the second time around. "I do. I sleep naked all the time. Alone. I don't sleep with boys." I peered at him. "I slept with you last night."

"We did sleep together."

"It was nice. I like sleeping with you. You're the only boy I've ever slept with."

He looked at me. "Really?"

"Really. Apparently I have Daddy issues. In my stupid brain," I poked myself in the temple. "In my stupid, stupid brain, all men are my sperm donor. Even though Bast, my real dad, never left, and Uncle Zane and Uncle Brock and Uncle Bax and Uncles Canaan and Corin, Uncle Lucian, Uncle Xavier, Uncles Roman and Rem and Ram…they all stayed. But apparently it doesn't fucking matter to my stupid brain, so I fucked a bunch of random dudes because I'm scared of trusting men. Even though I trust all of *those* men."

"It's not stupid, Emerson, It's human psychology."

"But I trust you." I tried to get out of my top and got lost. "Help."

Suddenly, the shirt vanished and I was naked.

"I'm naked," I pointed out, in case he had missed it.

"I'm well aware." He took my hands and helped me up. Squirted hand sanitizer on my hands.

"Nookie time?" I asked, rubbing my hands together.

He guided me out of the bathroom and into bed. "As tempting as you are, no. Not in this state."

I blew a raspberry at him. "I may be drunk, but I can still consent." I clapped his face in my hands. "I consent to anything you want to do to me."

"Em, honey, no."

I frowned at him. He was standing beside the bed on my side, having straightened so his face was out of reach. His zipper, however, was not. I reached for it, found the right one on the first try, and got it down. His lovely penis filled the opening, pushing against his underwear.

"I can suck your cock." I looked up at him, giving him what I felt was my best sultry expression. "I want to suck your cock, Hayden. You want me to suck your cock?"

He pulled out of my reach. "Always. But I wouldn't feel right about it when you're this drunk."

I blew another raspberry at him. "Lame. Your cock wants it. Look at him! He's begging for it."

He stuffed himself back into his pants and zipped himself away, wincing. "He very, very much does want it. But it doesn't feel right. I love you, and I won't take advantage of you."

"But what if I *want* you to take advantage of me?"

"Then I'm a fool for turning down a blowjob. But

I'd rather be a fool than feel like I've taken advantage of someone I care about."

I nodded. "I suppose that's a good answer. Sober Emerson will probably have some feelings about all this. Drunk Emerson is just horny." I flopped to my back.

Hayden tugged the blankets out from underneath me and covered me with them, tucking them under my chin. He shucked his shirt and jeans—apparently he'd changed out of his PJs and into jeans and a T-shirt at some point.

I watched him slide into bed beside me. Pushed the blankets down around my stomach. "Hey. Guess what."

He grinned. "What's that?"

I grabbed my tits and shook them. "I have big boobs. See?"

He laughed. "You sure do. You have the sexiest boobs I've ever seen."

"You should see Delia's," I said. "Hers are even bigger than mine."

"I think I'll stick with yours."

I nodded seriously. "That's a very good idea. You should definitely stick with my boobs." I held them and looked down at them. "Hey, remember when you came on mine? Twice?"

He groaned a laugh. "Yes, Emerson. I remember quite well."

"You made them sticky. I liked it." I looked at him.

"Wanna do it again? You can come on my tits any time you want."

He inhaled, held it, and let it out. "You are *not* making this easy on me, you know that?"

"Making what easy?"

"Being good."

I rolled toward him and faceplanted into the pillow. "Oops, I missed."

He scooped me up and settled me in the crook of his arm. "Better?"

I nodded against his chest. "Your chest makes me sleepy."

"Good. I've got you, Em."

"I know." I looked up at his chin. "You're a good man, Charlie Brown."

He laughed. "I try."

I felt sleep pulling at me. "Can I ask you a serious question?"

"Always."

"How do we know that we really love each other? What if it's just that the sex is the best sex anyone in the world has ever had? What if you realize you only like me for sex?"

He pushed a curl away from my face. "I was in love with you before we had sex."

"You were?"

"Yeah."

"How do you know?"

"Because I'm in love with the person you are,

Emerson. Yes, I'm wildly, helplessly, and utterly at-tracted to your body. You're the hottest, sexiest, most sensual woman I've ever met. Sex with you is abso-lutely mind-boggling. But I would still be in love with you even if sex wasn't an option for whatever reason.."

"So if I was paralyzed and couldn't have sex, you'd still love me?"

"I think most paralyzed people can still have sex, Emerson. In one way or another. But yes."

"Oh." I clicked my fingers against my thumbs as if my hands were crab pincers. "I still have these. I could always just give you handjobs and blowjobs."

"Em?"

"Uh-huh?"

"Ssshhh."

"Hayden?"

"Hmmm?"

"What are your thoughts on handjobs?"

"What?"

"How do you feel about handjobs?"

"I...I'm in favor?"

"But, like, compared to a blowjob."

"Oh." He thought for a moment. "You know, I don't know. I don't know that I've had a handjob. Like, only hands from start to finish. You finishing me off when I pulled out...did that count as a handjob?"

I hummed a noncommittal sound. "Mmm? Yes and no."

"I guess the honest answer is that as a male, any

touching of the penis is the best thing in the world. Hands, mouth, vagina, feet, boobs, however we can get our penis touched is good."

"But a handjob by itself is kinda lame, isn't it?" I paused. "Also, don't say vagina. It's a stupid word."

"Noted," he said. "And lame? No, I wouldn't say it's lame. But if I had to pick between a handjob and a blowjob, I'd probably pick a blowjob.

"Real talk, now, hotshot. Blowjob versus sex."

He sighed. "Em, go to sleep."

"Answers! The people need answers."

"Sex. I'd rather be connected to you. Feel that intimacy with you. A blowjob feels fucking incredible, but it's purely for me. Sure, you may not mind doing it. Maybe some part of you even enjoys it, I don't know. But it's not *for* you, at the end of the day. You do it to make me feel good. The enjoyment *you* get is making *me* feel good. But given the choice, I'll always pick sex."

"I *do* enjoy it. A fucking lot. Making you feel good makes me feel good. It turns me on."

"For real?"

"Oh yeah." I fumbled my hand under the blanket and found his crotch. "I still want to go down on you, Hayden. I know I'm drunk, but I really do."

He snagged my wrist and moved it to his chest. "I'll tell you what—when you're sober, we'll talk about this. If you tell me that you would consent while sober to doing something drunk, then the next time you get wasted, I'll go along with it. But right now, this is the first time I've been with you drunk. I respect you. I love you. And I won't put you, or me, or us in a position where you might feel like I took advantage of you."

I huffed in annoyance. "Fine. Be all *good* or whatever."

He chuckled, making me bounce on his chest. "I will."

"Your dick does not thank you."

"No, it doesn't. My dick thinks my conscience is a dumbass."

I tangled my fingers in his. "I've never met a man who would turn down a blowjob."

"Oh, I don't know about that. I think every male in your family would do the same in this situation."

I realized he was right. "Hmmm. True." I sighed. "I guess I meant the kind of guys I used to hook up with."

A long silence.

"Hayden?"

An amused snort. "Yes, Emerson?"

"A part of me wishes I hadn't slept around so much. I wish I had more of myself to give you. You're such a good person. I spent so long looking for something in all the wrong places. I feel kinda stupid about it now."

He touched my chin. "Look at me, please." I forced my eyes open—the rotating cake display of Haydens had reduced to only two, wobbling in and out of focus.

"Hi. You're hot."

He smiled. "Thanks, but listen. Okay? You listening?"

I nodded. "Yes sir." I saluted and smacked us both. "Sorry."

He mated our hands and slid them under the blankets. "You need to let that go. You shouldn't feel guilty or stupid or anything else. I am amazed at the person you are. I love who you are. You impress me. I'm proud of you. I'm proud to know you. Proud to be with you."

"Mean it?"

"Down to my bones, Em." He kissed my knuckles. "You give me everything. You haven't held anything back, even though you're scared. You're brave. You own your sexuality. I'm not jealous or threatened by your sexual history. In some ways, I benefit from it. I hope we're committed to each other and monogamous—I don't want to share you with anyone, but I have absolutely *zero* negative emotions about your sexual history. I don't like to think about you with someone else, but…"

I sighed. "I normally don't feel this way about it. I never have. Men can do it and they're heroes, rah rah rah, yeah dog, all that shit. Women do it and we're sluts."

"Double standards. It's dumb."

"Exactly. I just…I want you to be proud of me. I guess I crave that attention."

"This is some very deep self-analyzation for one-thirty in the morning on Christmas while drunk."

"Yeah, well." I shrugged. "It's all been there in my brain this whole time. It's just choosing this moment to come out."

"Makes sense. Any other deep thoughts or questions?"

"Yeah, two things."

"Okay. Shoot."

"The key. Is it too much pressure?"

"Not at all." A sigh. "I don't really want to talk about this too much until you're sober, but I was actually thinking a lot today about what I want and where I want to be, and what I kept coming up with is that I just want to be with you."

"Same." I sighed sleepily. "Next question. Me changing my name."

"I think it's beautiful. It's absolutely beautiful, and I feel privileged to have gotten to witness it."

"I won't take anyone else's name." I looked up at him. "I know this is probably absolutely cuckoo for Cocoa Puffs to talk about at all, let alone right now, but…if we get married someday, I won't take your name. Maybe a hyphen, but I will always want my last name to be Badd. It's who I am. It's who I've always been."

He cupped my face. "It's not crazy. And I would never ask you to. I know what it means to you. I see how much it means to you and your family. If we get married, I wouldn't ask you to change your name. If you wanted to hyphenate, that would be your choice."

"We just met. We're in love. And now I'm talking about getting married and taking names. It *is* crazy."

He laughed. "Yeah, a little. But like I said, I'm fine being crazy."

"Last question."

He sighed a laugh. "I can't wait."

"Are you my boyfriend?"

"I sure as fuck hope so."

"Good. Because I'm your girlfriend." I sighed happily. "If I hadn't gotten adopted today, I'd say you were my best present ever. I'm not sure how to rank one above the other."

"You don't. Being adopted is beautiful. And you're the best gift I've ever gotten and will ever get."

I sighed again. "Okay. Sleepytime, now."

I woke up with my head in a vice, sand in my mouth, cotton in my throat, and acid in my stomach. I lay in bed for a while, desperately hoping to be able to fall back asleep where it didn't hurt to exist due to my own choices, but alas, no such luck. Once I'm up, I'm up.

"Fuck." The sound of my own voice, a barely audible croak though it was, sent pounding agony through my skull, so, naturally, I did it again. "Fucking fuck me."

I opened my eyes very slowly and very cautiously, and that hurt. The blinds were shut, so there was only a dim yellow glow seeping in from the edges, and that hurt, too.

I farted, and that, indeed, also hurt.

I closed my eyes again and rolled over onto my stomach, which continued to cause unimaginable agony.

"Ow."

I tried a second time to slip into the sweet embrace of death, where at least it wouldn't hurt; I was denied entry, damn the world.

I cracked an eye open halfway, and that was tolerable. I spied a forest-green Stanley on my nightstand.

"Please have water in you," I whispered, and my voice, even in a whisper, came through a cheese grater with rocks and acid. Did I throw up? I didn't remember throwing up.

I reached for the Stanley and the promise of sweet, sweet water, the nectar of life, and discovered to my nauseated horror that the other side of the bed was, at minimum, six thousand miles away. Which meant I had to drag myself across the vast wasteland of my queen bed, certain I was going to perish from thirst before I reached the promised land; if the thirst didn't kill me, the pounding in my head every time I moved would.

I finally was able to get my hand around the

handle of the Stanley and dragged it toward me. It was heavy and sloshed—so far, so good. It even clinked. If this was ice water, I swore to name my first child after whomever arranged for this life-giving gift. I rested the Stanley on my belly and tipped it toward myself, craning my neck and reaching with my lips for the straw… water colder than the Weddell Sea sloshed onto my chest, provoking a breathless shriek of shock.

Yep, ice water.

Very, very, very cold ice water.

"Fuck," I snarled again.

I struggled mightily against the implacable forces of gravity and managed to sit almost entirely upright. I panted after my labors and then rewarded myself with a sip of water.

"Oh, thank you sweet baby Jesus."

"My name is Hayden, actually."

I screamed, dropped the Stanley and caught it by some miracle, spilling more ice water on my naked stomach, and then farted again.

"I must have had beer last night," I croaked.

"What *didn't* you have?"

"I don't know." I cracked my eye open and located the owner of the voice—Hayden, sitting in the chair in the corner of my room, laptop on his knees, shirtless in blue jeans, the light of the screen bathing him blue. "Beer gives me farts."

He chuckled. "Oh, I know. You've been blowing ass for three hours."

"I would be so embarrassed I want to die for farting in front of you, but I hurt too much." I took another sip of water, sighed, and sipped again. "I feel like someone dragged me backward through a woodchipper and then set me on fire."

He got up, set his laptop down, still open, on the chair, and rounded the foot of the bed. He picked up something on the nightstand and handed it to me. A shot glass full of tequila.

"Fuck you. I thought you loved me," I rasped.

He laughed. "Take it."

"I might throw up."

He bent and picked up a small trash can. "Wouldn't be the first time."

"Is that why my throat hurts?"

"That and the yelling during the card game."

"I don't remember yelling during a card game."

"What *do* you remember?"

I took the shot glass and threw back the contents, hissing as it scraped down my throat and hit my stomach like a bomb. "Ah fuck, that's awful."

He took something else from the nightstand: a pair of aspirin. "Now this."

I swallowed them with a long drink of water. "The last thing I remember is…" I hunted through hazy snatches of memory. "Foosball with the L-gang."

"The L-gang?"

"Yeah, Canaan and Aerie's kids—Liam, Lennox, Lucas, and Lena. They're the L-gang. Delia, Dunc, and

Dane are the D-gang. I'm an honorary member of the D-gang even though my name doesn't start with D." I winced and touched my head. "Talking is hard."

Hayden laughed. "I bet. You really tied one on last night."

I rested my head back against the headboard with a sigh. "I'm sorry."

He sat on the edge of the bed. "For what?"

"Making you babysit me. Getting sloppy. Embarrassing myself."

He pressed a gentle kiss to my cheek. "Nothing to apologize for. There was no babysitting. You didn't embarrass yourself." He tilted his head to one side. "Mostly."

I sipped water. "Meaning?"

"I was carrying you to bed, and we passed your mom. She kissed you on the head and you announced that I have a big penis and it's very yummy—that's pretty much verbatim."

I shook my head carefully. "I mean, it's true, so whatever." My stomach cramped, and I winced until it passed—I wasn't about to cut loose any more cheek-flappers in front of Hayden. "So, other than that, and apparently a lot of gas, what else?"

"Do you remember anything before you fell asleep? Us talking?"

"Nope. What'd I say?"

"Oh, well, a lot of stuff, most of it silly, drunk nonsense. But you talked about having father issues because of your biological dad, and being embarrassed about your sexual history and how you wished you had more of yourself to give me. You tried to, um, go down on me."

"Tried to? Was I too drunk to follow through?"

He shook his head. "No, I wouldn't let you."

I stared at him. "Why?"

He frowned. "You were blasted, Emerson. I'm not about to take advantage of you like that."

I melted a little. "Hayden, honey. You should've let me. I like doing that to you. I'd do it sober, so it's not taking advantage when I'm drunk."

"I just…this is new, you know? I feel like I know you, but I couldn't let that happen in that situation. Drunk consent is not consent." He shrugged. "I don't regret it. I'd make the same decision."

"God, Hayden, can you be any more perfect?" I rested my hand on his knee. "Thank you for taking such good care of me."

"I'm far from perfect, Em. But I am in love with you, and I will always protect you, even if it's from yourself."

"I talked about my daddy issues, huh?"

"Yup."

"It's stupid. I shouldn't *have* daddy issues—Bast has been my father, my daddy, my whole life."

"It's not that simple, Em. The things people go through when they're very young stick with you. Bast is an amazing father. He loves you. But that doesn't change the fact that your biological father abandoned you, and that shit leaves scars."

I moaned. "I'm way too hungover for this shit." I sipped more water. "What else did we talk about?"

"How you won't take my name if we were to get married."

"Oh for fuck's sake. Really?"

He just chuckled. "It's fine."

"A little soon for that talk."

"No, it's not. You changed your name and got adopted on the same day. It's a lot. It's gonna be on your mind."

"Could you stop being so understanding for one second? Like, for real. Do something selfish. I'm starting to worry you're not real because so far, you seem way too good to be true."

He shook his head. "I'm just this guy, you know? I never put the toilet seat down, I leave my clothes on the floor instead of the hamper until I have to do laundry or go naked, and then I live out of the clean laundry basket. I hate reality TV. I hate pop music. I'm not perfect." He reached out and cupped my boob, squeezed it. "There. I did something selfish."

I cackled. "Oooh, a boob-honk. The horror."

"Wait, asymmetry irritates me." He caressed and then honked the other boob. "There. Fixed it."

I shook my head, snorting a laugh. "If that's your idea of selfish…"

"What, you think I'm gonna be like, 'Hey, about

that blowjob you offered me last night' when you're hungover as fuck?"

I shrugged, nodded. "Uhhh, yeah. Most guys would."

"I don't know about that."

"I do."

He shook his head. "To be fair, I don't have a lot of friends, so I don't know."

"You don't?"

"Not really. I have a group of people I've been playing Diablo with for several years, but I only know them online."

"But no I-R-L friends?"

A shrug. "Nah. I'm a homebody, and kind of a loner. I was your stereotypical gamer kid and computer dork growing up. Meaning, a complete loser. I got fit and got contacts, but that didn't change my essential nature. Inside, I'm still the kid who's more comfortable alone in front of a computer than in a group of people."

"You seem perfectly comfortable around all of us," I said.

"I've mastered the art of faking it until I make it. I always have a voice in the back of my head telling me I'm not cool, none of these people actually like me, I'm such a loser, blah blah blah. I just tell that voice to shut the fuck up."

"Does it work?"

"Most of the time."

"Huh." I smiled at him. Threaded my fingers with his. "You're not a loser. You're the best person I know."

"Until we're supposed to go out on a date and I'm still in front of my computer, finishing a raid or a batch of analytics."

I thrust my chest out and shook my bare tits at him. "I'll just do this."

He grinned. "That'll probably work."

"Would you ever choose your computer or your game over sex?"

"Fuck no. I literally daydreamed as a teenager about a woman pretty much exactly like you. The way you want me, the way you touch me, the way you seem to be genuinely attracted to me. You are, very literally and most sincerely, everything I've ever daydreamed and fantasized about. So no, I'll never choose anything over you. And if I ever do, please just shoot me."

"I *am* attracted to you, Hayden." I let out a breath. "Okay. I need to shower. Hopefully that'll help me feel more human."

"Coffee?"

"Shower first."

He leaned in and kissed my cheekbone. "Brush your teeth, too."

"Why do you think I haven't kissed you?" I shook my head. "Hayden, I promise, I only get like that once a year. I don't drink much the rest of the year."

"I've already told you, you don't need to apologize,

explain, or feel bad. I love you, and I like taking care of you." He stood up. "I'll leave you to shower."

I caught his hand before he got away. "Hey. This is sober me telling you this—next time, say yes. Okay?"

He grinned. "I hear you. And I will, now that I know it's what you want."

"I'd make good on it now, but I wouldn't want to put my puke breath on your lovely penis."

He lifted our joined hands and kissed the back of mine. "Get a shower, babe. I'll be out in the kitchen."

I watched him go.

That there is a good man. I'm not letting him go. Would I move to Indiana and give up soccer for him? I damn well might.

I just didn't want to have to make that choice.

What do you do when love and life take you in opposing directions?

EIGHTEEN

Hayden

I LOOKED WITH INTENSE FRUSTRATION AT THE PILE OF FOLDED clothes on the bed and then with manic, irrational anger at the already-full suitcase next to the pile.

"Same amount of clothes, all the souvenirs in a different bag, and yet I somehow have *less* space in my suitcase than when I arrived." I dragged my hand through my hair, which was standing on end already from having raked my hands through it so many times in my fruitless endeavor to pack. "How is it possible?"

I also didn't need to pack yet, because we still had the cruise back to LA.

The ship was scheduled to leave in a few hours and I had no choice but to be on it. I couldn't leave my mom alone. I had a life to go back to in Indiana—even if just to pack it up and….what? Move to Ketchikan? Where Emerson does not, in fact, live? To Seattle, where she'll only live long enough to finish out the end of her college career?

I had no answers.

How could I leave Mom? I am an integral part of her daily life. When Dad *was* working and she needed something, she called me. I lived less than ten minutes from them and worked from home, so I could go over to reach that vase or open the jar lid or get the TV back on the right setting so she could watch her reality TV while folding laundry.

Dad's gone. She'll need me more than ever.

Emerson has her life at least roughly planned out—play professional soccer somewhere, somehow. And with her obvious talent, impressive-as-hell statistics (I did some research), and charismatic on-pitch star power, she was poised to become the next big thing in women's pro soccer.

Which wouldn't happen if she was with me in Buttfuck, Indiana. I'm aware that's not exactly fair to the lovely burgh that is West Lafayette. I exaggerate. But the point stands.

If I love her, the last thing I would do is selfishly derail her dreams, sidelining her immense talent and potential.

I love her. Way more than should be possible, considering how short a time I've known her. Days. Not weeks, not months, not years. Days…which can be measured in literal hours.

"Fuck this," I muttered.

I grabbed handfuls of carefully folded shirts and jammed them into the suitcase, followed them with more handfuls of jeans and khakis and loungewear shorts and underwear and socks, jamming everything in and slamming the suitcase lid closed.

Did it zip?

Not even fucking close.

Sweating, irrational rage pumping through my veins, I leaped into the air and landed a resounding People's Elbow on the suitcase, aggressively hauling at the zipper. I managed to get it halfway around before the zipper pull snapped off.

"*FUCK!*" I yelled, my voice turning into a raspy gargle at the end.

"Hayden Reginald McCaffrey!" Mom's voice appeared inexplicably at my left ear. "Now, now, son. This kind of tantrum isn't like you."

"Sorry, Mom," I muttered, slumping onto the edge of the bed, hunched over, head in my hands.

She rested her hands on my shoulders. "Sit up straight."

"No."

Mom sighed. "Hayden." She squeezed gently. "Sit—up—*straight.*"

With a sigh that was equal parts petulant groan

and sarcastic, head-shaking exhalation, I did as I was told. "There. Happy now that my posture is correct?"

Ignoring my outburst, she inhaled with slow deliberation. "Take a deep breath and hold it."

"I don't need a breathing exercise."

"Don't make me repeat myself, son."

What was she going to do? Paddle me?

Yet, I was psychologically incapable of outright disobedience, which was probably at least partially responsible for my current emotional state. If I was capable of that kind of behavior toward my mother, I would be able to leave Indiana to be with the woman I loved.

Thus, I closed my eyes and drew in a long, slow, deep breath until my lungs protested. I held it for a full ten seconds and then let it out over a space of almost twenty seconds, until I was forcing the last of the air out of my lungs.

"Good. Again." She pushed down on my shoulders as she inhaled through her nose while I did the same. We held it together, and then let out our breath in unison.

A third time.

Finally, Mom let me go and pointed at the chair in the corner of the room, opposite the door I'd forgotten I'd propped open in case Mom needed my help while packing.

"Sit."

"Yes ma'am," I mumbled, sapped of all energy now that my anger had been taken away.

I slumped into the chair, kicked my feet out, and slid down into a petulant, childishly provocative half-laying position, my head craned uncomfortably as I lounged halfway out of the chair.

Mom just snorted at me. "Grow up, Hayden."

"Fuck, fine," I snapped, sitting up.

Mom scooped everything out of my suitcase and onto the bed. Ignoring me, she refolded all of my clothes and neatly arranged them in the suitcase with such precision that Marie Kondo would have been impressed. The lid closed easily and she used the other zipper to shut the maroon, hard-sided suitcase.

She patted it with a smile at me. "There. Nothing a little mommy magic can't fix."

I glared. "Thanks, Mom."

She eyed me for a long, silent moment. With a frown and a sigh, she slid the heavy suitcase to the floor, kicked off her mint-green ballet flats, sat on the bed, swung her legs up, and lounged. Patted the bed beside her. "Come. Sit by Mama and let's talk."

I shot her a droll look. "Really?"

"Yes, really."

"I can talk to you from here."

"Yes, but you'll do it from *here*." She patted the bed again. "Come. Sit."

I stared at her, but her gaze brooked no resistance. "Just say whatever you have to say."

"I will. Once you come—*here*."

"Mom—"

"Behave like a six-year-old, and I'll treat you like one. Now, come sit beside me like a good boy."

Feeling roughly six inches tall, I did as I was told and shuffled with immense teenaged angst to the bed, sitting beside Mom. I threaded my fingers behind my head and stared at the ceiling, hating the burning lump in my throat with every fiber of my being.

"Mom, I—"

"Hush, son, I'm thinking."

I clapped my mouth closed and let her think. She never, ever spoke to me this way, which meant she was deadly serious. When Mom stopped being the sweet, adorable little Kindergarten teacher and out came the core of steel that was usually hidden by her ten-mile-deep layer of sweetness, even Dad knew to shut up and pay attention.

So, in the interest of self-preservation, that's what I did.

She didn't speak for a very long time. When she did, it was in a soft, quiet, almost distant voice. "I miss your father so badly, Hayden. *So* badly. I wake up thinking about him, and I go to sleep thinking about him."

"Mom, I—"

"Shut up and listen to me, Hayden."

My mouth shut so fast my teeth clicked together. She has never once in my entire life told me or anyone else to shut up.

She didn't look at me. She lay on the bed, staring

at the ceiling with her hands folded on her stomach, heels together, toes pointing away in a V.

"Harold was my entire life," she said, eventually. "We met when I was nineteen. You probably aren't aware of this because I don't discuss it very often, but I came from a very broken, dysfunctional, and extremely abusive home, Hayden. My father was a vicious drunk who beat my mother regularly."

"*What*?" I breathed. "Are you for real?"

"Yes." Her voice was faint, coming from a distance of fifty-some years. "My mother was his greatest apologist, too. 'He doesn't mean it. He doesn't understand what he's doing. He loves me, he just doesn't know how to show it. He came from a very bad home.' The excuses were endless, even though he beat her so badly she was in the hospital at least once a month. There was nothing anyone could do because she never said a word about what actually happened. She fell down the stairs. Bumped into a corner. All the classic excuses. When he wasn't beating her to within an inch of her life, occasionally quite literally, he was yelling at her, berating her, demeaning her. And me. I hated my life. I hated my parents. I hated my house, the town I lived in, the state I lived in. So, I buried myself in school and focused on getting into a university as far from them as I could. And I succeeded. The day I graduated high school, I packed my belongings and took a Greyhound bus from Bangor, Maine to West Lafayette, Indiana. I'd gotten special permission to live on campus over the summer while I worked. I got a head start on the reading, waited tables, and learned to enjoy my new-found freedom."

"Mom, I had no idea."

"I know, honey. Like I said, it's not something I've ever told you. I don't like talking about it because it's ancient history and because you were too young, and then when you were old enough, there didn't seem to be a point in bringing it up." She shrugged. "I vowed that when I had a family of my own, I would never, *ever* allow things to be like they were for me growing up. Anyone who exhibited even a hint of violence or aggression, I avoided like the plague. Once I was free from my parents, I discovered I liked people. I found my voice. I discovered a personality beyond conflict avoidance. And then, on the first day of my sopho-more year, I met a handsome young chemistry major named Harold McCaffrey. He was playing chess in the library and wiping out everyone who challenged him."

"Sounds like Dad," I said. "I never even came close to beating him, and I was captain of the chess club."

"He could have played in international tournaments; he was that good. But his real love was chemistry. He just enjoyed chess, and he worried that if he played it professionally, it would stop being fun." She sighed, re-membering. "I knew from the moment I saw him that he was going to be the rest of my life. I never spent a single day apart from him from that day forward. I have never so much as held the hand of another man. We

never talked about dating or going steady, we just…
were. He proposed the day we graduated. He bought
the ring for a hundred and fifty dollars at Sears." She
held up her left hand, sliding off a thin, tarnished gold
band with a shard of cubic zirconium so small it barely
caught the light. "This ring."

"You never upgraded?"

She shook her head, smiling to herself as she looked
at it in the early morning light streaming through my
cabin window. "Of course not. I couldn't care less about
a diamond. He wanted to upgrade it, ohhhh, ten, fifteen years ago? I didn't want a new ring with better
gold and a real diamond. I wanted *this* ring, the one
he put on my finger that day on the quad, still wearing our graduate robes and hats." She slid it back on.

I waited, knowing she was just getting started.

"We wanted kids so bad, Hayden. So bad. But IFV
wasn't really a thing back then, and it's not like we had
the money anyway. I just couldn't conceive. And if I
did, it didn't last more than a few weeks. Eventually,
we just gave up hope. I focused on my kids—my students. I showed them the love I wanted to give to my
child. Harold taught high school chemistry while working on his graduate degree and eventually got a job at
the university. We traveled in the summers. We played
bridge and bowled with friends. We fought about your
father refusing to go to church with me."

"Why did he refuse? I've never understood."

"Oh, well, that's a long story. The short version is

that he grew up in a *very* strict, *very* controlling home. In a very different way, he was as abused as I was. There was no alcoholism or physical abuse, but there was mental, verbal, and emotional abuse. And it was all done in the name of religion. It turned him off to the whole thing. He had no problem with me believing and attending, and even bringing you, after you were born, but he refused to have any part of it. He refused quietly, as was his way, but his resistance to religion, and anything that even smacked of it, was total and unyielding."

"And to you, your faith was what helped you heal from what you went through," I surmised, putting the pieces together.

She looked at me with a smile. "Exactly. It was the one point of contention in our marriage. I am not a religious person. I am, however, a *spiritual* person. My faith is quiet and personal. Mostly. I did everything I could to be loving and patient with him about it, to show him a different way, but…he just couldn't get past his anger toward the whole business of religion, faith, and churches."

"That makes a lot of sense."

Mom fell silent for a while again. She rolled to her side and looked at me. "We come to the reason for me telling you all this."

"You mean it's not just a mother-son bonding moment?" I asked, smirking at her.

"Not exactly, no." She smiled. "Back to my first

statement. Your father was my entire life. From the day I met him, I was never apart from him. The longest we were apart was when your father went to a chemistry symposium of some sort in Palm Beach. He lasted one night, called me in the middle of the night, and had me on a flight before noon the next day. He couldn't bear it, and neither could I."

I shook my head. "One night? Really?"

She smiled. "I think you're probably starting to understand that, aren't you?"

Oh. I was starting to piece together what she was angling at. "Mom—"

"Just listen, Hayden. Nothing I have ever said to you in your whole life is as important as this, okay?"

"Okay, Mom. I'm listening."

"Harold is gone. I am not." She touched my lips as I opened my mouth to…I wasn't sure what I intended to say, honestly. "Hush, son. Hush and listen to your mother. I will never not miss him. I will never remarry. Neither would he, had I had been the one to go first. He was it for me. He was my life, and now he's gone. So…now what? What do I do with myself? How do I go on without the one person who made sense of my existence?" Her eyes watered. "Just listen. Just listen." A wet sigh, as she let the tears trickle down to wet the pillow.

A long silence.

"I am not your responsibility, Hayden." She clapped her hand over my mouth yet again. "Still talking." When

I subsided, she continued. "I'm *not*. I have to learn to stand on my own two feet, now. I have to redefine who I am. I have to rebuild my life. And Hayden, my dear, sweet, wonderful boy, I can't do that if I'm reliant on you."

"Mom—come on, listen to me…you—"

Her eyes blazed. "No! *You* listen to *me*, Hayden McCaffrey. I love you more than life itself. I would do *anything* for you. And I *know* you. You're a mama's boy. But it's time."

"Time?" My voice cracked. I cleared my throat and tried again. "Time for what?"

"For you to launch."

"I have my apartment, a car, a whole life. I *have* launched, Mom. I'm not some thirty-year-old living in your basement with Cheeto dust on my fingers while I play World of WarCrack."

"I know that, my love."

"Then what are you saying?"

"Why are you angry?" She asked, an abrupt redirect. "Why were you taking that anger out on your poor, innocent luggage?"

"I couldn't get it to close," I muttered, knowing how futile the lie was.

"Hayden."

I rolled my back and groaned. "Ma. We're not talking about this."

"We sure as hell are, son." I glanced at her in shock.

"Yes, you and your new friends are rubbing off on me. It seems I curse, now."

"Guess so."

"I'll ask you again, and I expect an honest, forthright answer." She grabbed my hand and squeezed hard. "Why are you angry?"

"I'm not angry. I'm… frustrated. Confused."

"About what?"

"What to do."

"About what?"

I sat up and pivoted to face her. "You *really* want me to say it?"

She remained lying on her back, head turned to the side. "Yes, I do."

"I don't know what to do. My life is in Indiana with you. Hers is in Seattle, and then wherever she ends up after that, playing soccer. I love her, and she loves me, but our lives are in opposite directions."

"That's exactly what I'm talking about, Hayden." She sat up now, mirroring my position. "I'm telling you that it's time for you to go a different direction."

"I don't know what that means, Mom," I said, panic and hope warring in my gut. "What different direction?"

"I really need to spell this out for you?"

"Apparently, that's what we're doing right now, so yeah, I guess you do."

She sighed, looked down at her hands. "I'm retiring effective immediately. I'll stay long enough to see a good temporary replacement installed in my classroom and say goodbye to my students. But I'm selling the house, retiring, and leaving Indiana for good."

I shot to my feet, paced away a few steps, and stared at her, lungs empty, mind reeling. "*What*?! Since—since when?"

"I decided this morning. I've spoken to Shelly, the principal, and Shawn, the superintendent. They've been expecting it and have a temp ready to go and a list of permanent candidates to interview lined up. Roger, my friend Tammy from book club's husband, is a realtor. I told him where the spare key is, and he's going to take photographs and get the house listed this week. He expects it to sell within weeks at most."

"Where—" I halted, cleared my throat, and tried again. "Where will you go?"

She shrugged. "I'm not sure, long-term. Short-term, once I've settled things in Indiana, Olivia's husband, Lucas, is planning a four-week hunting trip to the interior with his son and business partner, Ramsey. While he's gone, she's taking a trip to Mallorca, and she's invited me to go with her."

"Mallorca?"

"It's an island in the Mediterranean."

"I know where Mallorca is," I muttered.

"Olivia and I are a lot alike. I enjoy her company, and it will do me good to get out by myself, away from everything, and pick Olivia's brain about life as a widow and starting over, moving on, all of that." She took my hands. "I don't know where I'll end up after that."

"But…" I shook my head. "You're retiring, selling the house, and leaving Indiana…*permanently*?"

She smiled. "Yes."

"What…what about me?"

She just laughed. "Surely I raised you to be smarter than this, honey."

"What?"

"You're staying here, Hayden."

I boggled at her. "I…"

"You would never leave me. You think I need you." She held up her hand to forestall me. "And you're not wrong. I have relied on you for a very long time. It hasn't been fair to you. You've been trapped in Indiana, Hayden. You never even *considered* another college."

"Because I got Dad's discount on top of my scholarships and grants. It was almost free."

"And when you graduated, you were offered incredible jobs all over the country. All of the top companies in Silicon Valley offered you lucrative positions. Which one did you take? The one that let you stay in Indiana and work remotely." She squeezed my hands. "I have to stand on my own two feet. And you have to go find your own life, which is most definitely *not* in Indiana. It's here, with Emerson. It's wherever and however you and Emerson decide to live your lives together."

To say I was stunned was a colossal understatement. "Mallorca?"

She laughed. "The house has been paid off for almost twenty years, and the market has only made it more valuable. Your father had a remarkably well-funded life insurance policy. I'll have my retirement and social security, as well. All that to say, I won't have to worry about money. So, I'm going to go through our belongings, and I'm going to donate most of it, save a few important things for myself and for you—sentimental objects, mostly. The rest I'll either sell or throw away."

"But—but—that…that house…our home, everything in it…" I stammered, trying to wrap my head around the idea of that house no longer being home, no longer being where Mom and Dad were.

"It was *our* home, Hayden. Harold's and mine. And yours, too, for a while. But really…it was ours." Her smile was soft and sad. "Every room, every inch of every carpet, every corner—all of it is *ours*. I personally painted every room. Your father built the deck himself. We designed the kitchen remodel together."

"Exactly! How could you sell it?"

"How can I *not*? How can I live in that house another moment? Every second I spend there is a reminder that Harold isn't in it. My husband is *gone*. The life I had is over."

"Mom—"

"It *is*, Hayden. I have to accept that. And so do you. I have to start over, and I can't do that in the house I lived in with my husband for fifty-one years. I *have* to sell it. I *have* to leave Indiana." She tipped her head back and sniffled. "I'm not forgetting him, Hayden. How could

I? But he's not in that house. He's my husband, my best friend, and my soulmate. He lives in my heart and my memories. My love for him will never die, never fade. But if I mope around that house and that town, seeing him every time I shop for groceries, every time I park the car in the garage and get nervous about scraping the side again, every time I go up the stairs and expect him to goose my bottom, every time I pass his study, every time I go past the university…I'll not be *living*—I'll be waiting to die so I can be with him."

"*Fuuuuuck*, Mom," I whispered.

She didn't correct me, which said as much as any of her words. "Harold wouldn't want me to live out the rest of my life, however long that may be, waiting to die, haunted by him. I have to do this for myself. And I also have to do it for you because you're so damn stubborn and so damn loyal that you won't choose yourself. You won't choose Emerson—you'll choose me. And as your mother, I simply cannot allow that."

"You're my *mom*."

"And she's going to be your wife and the mother of your children." She leaned forward, face close to mine. "But only if you have the courage to choose that. To leave behind everything you've ever known, strike out on your own, and build for yourself the life you want. You can't do that if you're trapped in West Lafayette, Indiana, chained to my grief."

"I wouldn't be chained to your grief, Mom, good lord. And when did you become so rhetorically gifted?"

"You *would* be. This is me setting you free. I love you. I will miss seeing you every day. I'll still call you an obnoxious amount. But it's time. Long past time. You don't need a mother anymore, anyway, Hayden, you need a girlfriend, and then a fiancé, and then a wife. It's her, and you know it. It's as plain as the nose on your face, my sweet boy. Choose her. Choose yourself."

I shook my head. "Mallorca."

She laughed in exasperation. "Mallorca is just a vacation with a new friend. Stop getting hung up on Mallorca. It's not about Mallorca. I'm not moving there. Good grief. Stop fixating on the wrong thing."

I laughed. "I guess I am, aren't I?"

"You are."

"This is really what you want?"

"What I really want is for your father to be alive. But he's not. Honestly, Hayden, once my initial shock wore off, I started to feel…desperate. Desperate to get out of there, to get away from…everything. And now that the cruise is winding down and I'm faced with the prospect of going back to live there? I just can't. I *cannot*. I *cannot* sleep in that bed alone. I *cannot* wake up alone. Make coffee alone. Go to work alone, and come back, alone, to a silent, empty home that you're not in, that he's not in, that I'm in *alone*. That's no kind of life. Not for me. I can't do it. I was awake all night thinking about this, and I realized I just couldn't go back. The house is being sold, and our fifty years' worth of stuff—whatever I don't get rid of, that is—is going into storage. I'll rent a short-term apartment while I go through the stuff, I suppose. I just simply *cannot* spend another night alone in that house."

"I have a better idea," I said. "I bought my condo furnished. For me to pack up and move out is a matter of a few suitcases and a handful of boxes. I'll put the bulk of my stuff in storage with yours, and you stay in my condo. Once you're done, I'll sell it."

"That's a good plan. I like it."

"You don't want me to help you go through everything?" I asked.

She shook her head. "No. It's part of the grieving process. I have to do it alone. If I need help with heavy lifting, I have plenty of friends from work and my book club with big strong husbands." She patted my hand. "And if you stay to help, it'll only make it harder for you to leave. So what you're going to do is take your suitcase and go back to the Badd's house. You're going to spend the rest of break with her and figure out what the next few months look like for the two of you. You're going to pop back into town to get whatever you need, put the rest in storage, and go. Wherever that is, whatever it looks like, as long as it's with the woman you love."

"It's a terrifying prospect," I whispered.

"It truly is. I've never been alone. I had that first year, my freshman year, and that's it. I'm almost seventy years old and starting over. So yeah, it's *really* frightening. But also…a little exciting."

I laughed. "It feels wrong, somehow, to be excited. But...yeah."

She shook her head. "It's not wrong. It's right. It's what your father would want for us both. We're not going off to enjoy our lives while he's wasting away with some terminal illness, Hayden. He's dead and buried and looking down on us from Heaven, telling us to move on already, dammit."

I laughed, the sound thick with emotion. "You're right."

"I'm your mother. Of course I'm right."

My next laugh was less emotionally charged. "And so humble."

"The other change I'm going to make is a haircut. I was thinking a blue mohawk."

I stared at her. "No."

A laugh. "Not a blue mohawk, then. But I won't be a teacher anymore. I'm getting rid of most of my teacher clothes, and I'm cutting my hair, and I'm gonna start dressing like a sexy granny."

"Mom." I put my hands over my face. "If you show up in leather pants and a bustier, I'll have an aneurysm."

She patted my hands. "I don't know about all that, but we'll just have to see, won't we? I just want you to be prepared for a new me the next time you see me." A sigh, a smile. "Mrs. Mac is no more."

"Mrs. Mac?"

A shrug and a nod. "It's what everyone at school has called me for years. Students, faculty, everyone. I'm not sure some of the younger teachers even know my real name at this point."

I flopped onto my back. "It's a lot to wrap my head around."

"It is."

"Why do I feel there's a whole part of you that's about to come out that no one ever knew existed?"

She hummed a thoughtful noise. "Hmmm. Interesting. I suppose because it's what's happening. I've been this person my whole life—the teacher, the wife, the mother. I love being those things—I *have* loved it. I don't regret a single thing. But now I have to become someone new, and this time, the only person I have to consider is myself. I can't be who you want me to be. I can't be who I was with your father. I can't be the person I am at school with the kids and my colleagues. I have to be a new person only for me. And honestly, I'm looking forward to it. I'll bring my love for Harold with me. I talk to him at night. But I *have* to move on, and I'm going to." A pause. "I'm not okay. But I will be. I'll become the new me one day at a time. And I will do it with the same energy and spirit and joy as I've tried to approach everything else in my life. I'm still me, but I'm just...I'm being forced to evolve, Hayden. And so are you."

"I guess I have some thinking to do."

"No, you have some talking to do—with Emerson." A pause. "Some advice, Son?"

"Please."

"Open your mind. Totally. Rethink everything. Where you go, what you do, what you want to do. Do you love your job? Are you passionate about it? Is it a calling? Or just a job? Is it a career you want to spend the rest of your life pursuing?"

"I…"

"You don't need an answer now, honey. You need to think about it. Talk to Sunni about it. Reflect and really be honest with yourself about who you are, who you want to be, and what you want out of life."

"You're sure it's not crazy for us to be looking at life together when we've only known each other a matter of days?"

"If it is, you're asking the wrong girl. I knew the very moment I saw Harold that he would be my husband. I heard it like a voice from God. 'That man right there is the rest of your life.' I never doubted it. When the heart knows, it knows. And your heart knows. So does hers. I see it and so does everyone else." She rolled into me and kissed my cheek. "But it only matters that you and she know it."

"And we know."

She slid off the bed. "Exactly. Now, get your big butt off that bed and go get the girl."

I threw a pillow at her. "Big butt?"

"Oh shush. You're fitter than those silly models on Instagram that Becky is always showing me."

"What?" I laughed.

"Nothing. Never mind. Just get out of here. Love

awaits, my son." She stood in the doorway and blew me a kiss. "I love you. I'm proud of you. But if you're still here in five minutes, I'm gonna be mad."

"Yes, Mother," I said, laughing.

"I have a hair appointment followed by a mani-pedi, so if you'll excuse me." She wiggled her fingers at me, blew another kiss, walking backward. "See you in a month or two, Hayden."

And then she was gone.

I looked around the cabin, spotted my charger still plugged in by the bed and pocketed it.

I set my suitcase on its rollers, shouldered my duffel, and headed toward the exit, wondering how mothers always knew exactly what you needed to hear when you needed to hear it.

And somehow, it never occurred to me even doubt that someday, Emerson would be exactly the same way.

I was whistling as I all but jogged to shore, hailing a ride-share on the way.

Time to see about a girl.

NINETEEN

Emerson

I SAGGED AGAINST THE GOALPOST, PANTING RAGGEDLY. A few yards away, just beyond the goal area and penalty arc, Frida sat on a ball, guzzling water. Frida was an employee of Uncle Bax's, a personal trainer and former pro footballer who played for Munich-Bayern as well as Germany's national team. She was lured here a few years ago after she hung up her boots and has steadily built a clientele. She was hard as nails, took no shit, and had a knack for pushing you past your limits without totally breaking you. Hiring her was not for the faint of heart.

I hadn't technically hired her, but she acted like I had, and it was exactly what I needed. I'd come here to work out, get some drills in, do some lifting, maybe run some laps. Anything other than sitting at home, eating junk food, and moping around about Hayden.

Their ship left today. Back to LA, and then they'd be on a plane to Indiana. Hayden had promised he was going to meet me in Seattle after the New Year and we'd figure things out.

But…it felt like the end, like the whole thing had been a holiday break romance. Whirlwind, exciting, intoxicating…and fleeting.

Once he was back home, I'd be out of sight and out of mind. He'd have his mother to take care of. Granted, Kaye seemed to be doing remarkably well, all things considered, but I also had a strong gut feeling that she was the kind of person who would put on a brave, happy face for everyone and would only allow herself to truly feel her deepest emotions when she was alone.

I pushed away from the goalpost, rolled the nearby ball toward me with my toe, flicked it into the air, and booted it at Frida. "Come on. Again."

Without moving from her perch on the ball or putting down her water bottle, Frida headed the ball away. "No. You are not only practicing your skills." She stood up, scraped a hand through her short white-blond hair, and sauntered over to me. "You are avoiding. Who is he? Hmm?"

I shook my head. "Doesn't matter anymore. He's gone, or as good as."

"It matters to you. You are heartbroken. You cannot practice away a broken heart."

"Sure I can. Soccer is how I get through everything."

Frida sighed. "This, I understand. When Maria left me, I was like this, heartbroken and angry. I put myself into football. But it wasn't for football. It wasn't for my team. It was to not have to think or to feel."

"Right, and? Why is that a bad thing?" I asked.

"Because to be truly great, you have to play from the heart. I worked harder than ever, played harder than ever. And I was terrible. I cost my team a title."

"That was a bad call by a biased ref, Frida."

"You forget that I was zero for sixteen in shots on goal that game. Three unforced errors. Two turnovers. Several penalties—I forget how many. It was the worst game of my entire career. You know why?"

"Because of your broken heart?"

"Well, *ja*, this too, but really because I was not focused. I was angry and hurting and unwilling to do what I must do to be better."

I sighed. "I appreciate what you're saying, Frida, truly, but I'm not even on a team anymore. I have offers but haven't decided. I want to graduate first." I shook my head. "My point is, I don't have anyone to let down. There are no tournaments, no games. So yeah, I'm focusing on soccer instead of my feelings because I can. Because there's nothing to do. It was clearly a holiday romance that meant more to me than it did him."

That wasn't fair and I knew it, but my heart didn't care about fair.

Hurt seared through me as I thought of how sweetly Hayden had kissed me as he left, promising to call, to come see me, to figure things out between us. And how, despite his sincerity, I just couldn't shake the feeling that when all was said and done, he'd end up staying in Indiana. With his mom. And how could I be mad about that?

I grunted in anger and hurt and confusion, spun on my heel, and kicked a ball as hard as I could. It soared clear to the other side of the pitch and over the back of the net, bouncing off the wall and rolling away.

Frida watched my tantrum with an arched eyebrow. "Tell me."

"What?"

She jogged to a ball over near the corner and passed it to me. "We will work on ball-handling while you tell me everything."

"I don't want to talk about it. I want to forget it."

She shrugged, snagged her bottle, and walked away. "Suit yourself."

"Frida!"

She waved a hand without looking at me. "You cannot escape yourself, Emerson. You could kick a ball to the moon, and still this hurt would be there. You are angry. Do you know *why* you are angry? Who you are angry at?" She finally stopped and turned to look at me. "No. You do not. And so it will be there inside you like a parasite. I know this. It devoured me until there was nothing left."

"It was just a holiday romance. It didn't mean anything."

Frida laughed at this. "You are a terrible liar."

I hung my head, tugged the headband down around my neck and fluffed out my curls, then tossed my hair back and replaced the headband. "You're mean."

"Yes. I am a terrible bitch. Everyone knows this. But I am also right."

I'd been training with Frida in the off-season and during breaks since she was hired by Bax, and in some ways, she knows me as well as anyone, even though we've never spoken to or seen each other anywhere but the pitch or the weight room. So yeah, I knew she was right.

"What do you want me to do, Frida? What am I supposed to say? That I love him? That I want him to... what? Abandon his mother when she just lost her husband of fifty years? That I'm angry at him for choosing her instead of me? You know how selfish and irrational that is?"

"You cannot make a shitty, selfish emotion go away just by ignoring it."

"Fine. So there it is. I said it out loud. And oh, look! It's still there. Speaking it out loud didn't magically make it go away. Who knew?"

Frida rolled her eyes at me. "Admitting you have a problem is the first step in solving it."

"What is this, love-sick anonymous?" I wiped the sweat off my face. "Look, Frida, I appreciate what you're trying to do. It just hurts, and I'm mad and confused and there's not a damn thing to do about it. I love him, but I guess not enough to give up my dreams and go live in Indiana with him. And I certainly can't ask him to abandon his grieving mother not even three months after her husband died. What's the solution? There isn't one. It just sucks. It's not his fault, it's not my fault. It's just…life."

Frida nodded. "Well, there it is, hmm? Now, I have to go, Emerson. I have a date with a Greek performance artist named LaLa."

"There's a Greek performance named LaLa living in Ketchikan, Alaska?"

She laughed. "So it would seem. She speaks very little English, and I speak no Greek at all, but she has giant boobs and a beautiful smile and laughs at my phone's translations of German into Greek, and when she laughs, the sun seems to shine a little brighter."

"Well then, go have fun with your Greek performance artist with the big boobs." I squeezed her hand. "Thanks for working with me. I really did need it."

"Any time. *Auf Viedersehen*, my friend."

"See ya."

After she was gone, I moped around the indoor pitch alone for a while, chasing balls around and half-heartedly practicing footwork drills, but the truth was my heart wasn't in it anymore.

All I could think about was Hayden.

At home, I filled up on leftovers and watched Dunc and Dane yell at each other while playing Injustice. Delia was working, Dru was out with some of the other aunts, and Bast was on the phone with the manager of the Anchorage location—and didn't sound happy with the conversation. Except for the boys' playful hollering, the house was quiet and empty.

Between matches, the boys gathered a bunch of snacks and slices of pie and plopped back down.

Dunc swallowed a massive bite of pumpkin pie and then sniffed the air. "Dude, who smells like burnt onions and dead feet?"

"Fuck you," I muttered.

Dunc leaned toward me and then reared away, gagging. "Em, dearest sister of mine whom I fear and love in equal proportion...I say this with all possible love and respect, but please, go shower."

Dane popped a buckeye into his mouth, speaking around it as he chewed. "You smell awful." It came out *OOH H-MEH AH-HUH.*

I pulled my shirt away, tucked my nose under the neckline, and sniffed. I pulled away with a gag. "Oh, fuck. You're not kidding."

Duncan shoved a buckeye into my mouth, effectively preventing me from speaking. "Shower, woman. Shower. Smelling like a zombie won't fix anything." He shoved me off the couch, requiring me to either stand up or fall down.

I elected to stand up, chewing the treat. "Asshole." *AAA-HOE.*

"You love me and you know it." He picked up a slice of pie with his hands and shoveled half of it into his mouth, chewing until he could enunciate halfway clearly. "Come on, Dane. You gotta pick someone besides Batman this time."

"Why? So you actually stand a chance of winning?"

"It's cheap! You use the same move over and over again. Time it right and there's no defending against it."

"Exactly. It's not cheap, it's winning."

"It's cheap."

"Fine. I won't use the move, and I'll still kick your ass with my Batman."

"He's not *your* Batman."

"You're just salty because you suck with everyone."

I left the boys to their squabbling and headed for my room. I closed my bedroom door but didn't bother locking it—the boys know better than to come in if my door is closed. I stripped out of my sweaty, smelly clothes and twisted on the shower. While the water heated, I brushed my teeth because I realized I couldn't remember the last time I had over break—gross, I know, but what else are holidays for? Holiday carbs and calories don't count, and neither does hygiene. The boys hadn't changed out of their PJs since Christmas Eve, and that was two days ago.

I raked a brush through my hair, yanking out the worst of the snarls.

I took the world's longest shower, washed my hair twice and conditioned it once, lathered up, rinsed off… all while trying like hell not to think about Hayden in this shower with me.

Eventually, I had to get out. I wrapped my hair in a towel and lotioned my freshly shaved legs and everything else. I knew I should use the diffuser on my curls, but I just didn't want to. I'd air dry in bed for a while and doomscroll on my phone instead. Maybe that would give me the motivation to take care of my insanely demanding hair.

I exited the bathroom, tugging my hair free of the turbaned towel and using it to squeeze handfuls of hair. As such, the towel obscured my vision, but I knew the steps from the bathroom to my bed blindfolded.

Seating myself on the edge of my bed, I flipped my hair forward and hung my head upside down, sliding my fingers through the ringlets.

Something to my left caught my eye: a black sock. A black sock that seemed to have a foot inside it. Crossed over it was a second sock. Attached to the socks was a pair of black jeans. Still upside down, I followed the jeans—inside of which appeared to be legs—up to a black-and-gold Purdue hoodie.

My heart pounded like a tribal drum. My mouth went dry. My stomach flipped.

I froze with my hands in my hair, upside down.

Hayden.

Inside the socks, jeans, and hoodie…was Hayden.

Still upside down, I glanced at my clock: 12:47 pm. "Um. Hi?"

He smiled at me, and the smile possessed secrets and was rife with amusement, and love, and desire. "Well hello there." Ah yes, his best Obi-Wan Kenobi impression. It shouldn't make me feel juicy down under, but it did.

"I…your ship…it…it left?"

"It did."

"Why…" I sat up, flipping my hair backward. "Why aren't you on it?"

"Because I'm here."

I tightened the towel around my torso and re-tucked it in place. "So I see. In my room. While I was in the shower."

"I thought about getting in with you."

"Why didn't you?"

"I figured we need to talk first."

"I suppose it would be hard to talk about things if I have your cock in my mouth."

"Our your pussy in mine."

"Right. Such things do make conversations tricky." I stared at him for a long time. "Hayden…what are you doing here?"

"I love you." He shrugged as if that was all the answer I needed.

"You could talk while I suck, and then I talk while you lick?"

He laughed. "Or—hot take, here, I know—but we could talk and *then* get to the licking and sucking."

"Then we need to stop talking about licking and sucking," I said.

"Agreed."

I stood up. "Let me get dressed first."

"Want me to leave?"

I frowned at him. "Why? You think I'm suddenly gonna be shy about you seeing me naked?" He just shrugged, and I tugged the towel off and tossed it into the hamper. "Just stay there where you are and keep your hands to yourself for the next thirty seconds."

He made a big show of sitting on his hands, but there was no escaping the way he very thoroughly eye-fucked every inch of me as I shimmied into a purple thong, stuffed myself into a loose, comfortable black camisole, and then tugged on my favorite pair of heather-gray yoga pants. They were my favorite because they had a pocket in the thigh big enough to hold my phone, and they made my ass look goddamned fantastic.

When I was dressed, I sat on the bed facing Hayden, who was sitting in the chair in the corner—the in-between chair, I call it, where I keep the clothes I've worn that I'm not ready to wash yet but don't want to put back in the drawer.

He slid his hands out from under his thighs and shook them out, sighing. "God, that was difficult."

"What? Keeping your hands to yourself?"

"Yes." He gestured at me with a flick of a finger. "Not that that outfit is helping."

I frowned and laughed, shaking my head. "It's a shitty old cammy and yoga pants. Barely a step up from period week sweats."

"We can agree to disagree on that one, babe."

I ran my fingers through my hair again. "Okay, so…again, what are you doing here? Why aren't you on the boat?"

He pointed at the floor: his suitcase and duffel bag were there, the duffel on top of the suitcase, held in place by the handle. "I'm staying here with you."

I shook my head. "But…your mom."

He let out a long sigh. "Apparently, she's decided to take immediate retirement, sell my childhood home, and….I'm not sure what. She's going to Mallorca with Olivia. And then what? I don't know. She doesn't know, beyond rebuilding herself and her life as a widow."

"I…wow. And you weren't expecting this?"

"Not at all." he sat forward, wiping his face with both hands. "I've been sick over everything, Em. I was going out of my mind this morning. I got into a fight with my suitcase…and lost."

I snickered. "I've been there. Suitcases can be tricksy little fuckers."

"They can." He scraped his hand through his hair,

mussing it up further, making it so sexy my mouth watered and my pussy clenched. "I just didn't know what to do, you know? Like, I fucking love you. I desperately want to be with you. But…how could I leave my mom alone in a time like this?" He shook his head, extending his hands out to the side and then slapping them on his thighs. "I couldn't. I just…couldn't. And neither could I ask you to give up your whole life, your dreams, everything, to…do what? Move to Indiana? Coach peewee soccer when you could be playing at FIFA in a few years?"

"I've been sick about it, too," I admitted. "You're too far away."

He held out his arms, and I took the invitation eagerly, leaving the bed and curling up on his lap. I tucked my feet between his thighs and the side of the chair, leaned into his chest and let him support my back with his arm, settling my head under his chin.

I exhaled, finally feeling at peace in the world once again. "Hayden, I wish I was more selfless. I wish I was the type of woman who could set my dreams aside and just go to Indiana with you and be a stay-at-home mom. I'm just not that person, and I'm sorry."

He didn't answer for a while. "Take that back."

I pulled away and looked into his eyes, a confused frown overtaking my face. "What?"

"Take that back. What you just said—take it back."

I laughed in disbelief. "I…I mean, you can't take

back words, Hayden. And it's true—I wish I was less selfish, less focused on my goals."

He turned me toward him so I was straddling him, facing him. "Emerson Grace, I fucking love you. I love who you are. I love that you're a fierce competitor. I've watched a lot of highlights from your games. I've brushed up on your stats. I'm learning about soccer so I can better understand exactly how fucking talented and hardworking you are. I don't *want* you to be more selfless. I don't *want* you to give up your dreams. If you gave up your goals of making the US Women's National Team and playing professionally, you would be depriving the world of sports of someone who I truly believe will go on to be one of the all-time greats. You have that amount of talent and drive and charisma. You have that work ethic. It's who you are, and I'll be damned and double goddamned if I'll get in the way of that. It's who you are—it's your destiny."

My throat closed up and tears spurted out of my eyes and trickled down my cheeks. My heart swelled in my chest until my stomach flipped in protest. "Hayden," I said, choking on my emotions. "You're being silly."

"The fuck I am," he said, his voice fierce and intense. "I believe in you more than I've ever believed in anything. It would be a tragedy of epic proportions if you gave it all up to be a housewife in suburban Indiana. There's nothing wrong with that life—it's a beautiful thing if it's what both parties want. But it's not what you want. It's not what you're built for."

"I *do* want kids someday," I whispered. "I do want a family. I want to be a mommy. I want to be the mother mine wasn't—the mother Dru *is*. Just not yet."

"God, Em, I hope you didn't think I was in any way implying you're not going to be an amazing mother. I just meant—"

I put my fingers over his lips. "I know what you meant. I was clarifying."

He cupped my face in his hands, caressed my cheekbones with his thumbs. "Why would you give everything up to do nothing in Indiana when I can work from anywhere in the world? I can work anywhere I have a decent internet connection. And honestly, as much as I like where I work, I'm not passionate about it. I enjoy the work, but I don't *love* it." He closed his eyes, drew in a massive breath, held it, and let it out slowly. "What I'm realizing—what Mom forced me to understand literally just now—was that when Dad died, it blew up our lives. His death totally destroyed the status quo of who Mom is and who I am."

My eyes teared up again, this time in grief for him. "Hayden, I don't know if I've ever said this, but I'm so sorry for your loss. I hate those words because they just seem so inadequate, but they're all I have."

He smiled. "Thanks. It really is all there is to say. But my point in saying that is not for sympathy or to sound all poor me. Yes, I'm gutted by Dad's death. So is Mom. But what she told me is that Dad wouldn't want us to stop living. He wouldn't want us to try to force ourselves back into the old patterns of life that we occupied when he was alive. That life is gone. Mom can't live in that house anymore. And I get it—I feel the same way. It's…I dunno. Haunted is the closest thing I can come up with, not that Dad is a ghost with unfinished business, but it's just too much. Too many memories. In the weeks after his death before we left on this cruise, I saw him everywhere. I kept walking into that house expecting to see him in his office grading papers and tests and lab reports. Coming in from grilling on the back deck. Stumbling around in his tighty whiteys in the morning, looking for coffee, like he did when I lived there. She's selling the house because she has to move on, and she can't do that living there. But it's not just the house. It's the whole life we had."

"So…what does that mean for you?" I asked. "For me. For us."

"Mom told me in no uncertain terms that you and I are meant to be together. But her uprooting everything, it's not about you or me or us—it's truly for herself. But she…" he trailed off, started again. 'This is hard to say."

I leaned into him and kissed his cheekbone beneath his eye, his forehead, hands framing his face, gazing into his holly-green eyes. "Just say it, honey. Whatever it is."

"She knew I wouldn't…I wouldn't be able to leave her. Not on my own. No matter how much I love you, I just…I couldn't have…" he swallowed hard, eyes screwing shut. "I just *couldn't*, Em."

"No, of course you couldn't." I brushed the pads of my thumbs over his eyelids. "Look at me, baby, please." His eyes opened. "I wouldn't have asked you to. I would never have expected you to. I wouldn't have *let* you. Not now, not in a time like this. She's your *mom*. You love her. How could I possibly take you away from her when she needs you and be able to look myself in the mirror?"

"She took that choice out of both our hands. But like I said, it really boils down to her doing it because it's what she needs—I see that. I'm grateful for it. That doesn't mean I'm not a little scared—I've never lived anywhere but Indiana. Moving out was hard enough, and I only moved ten minutes away. But it's what I want. Honestly, it's what I need: to be with you. To figure out, together, what our life is going to look like."

"I like the sound of that."

"I know it's zero to a hundred in nothing flat, but all I want is to do life with you. What that looks like, where we go, how we get there…we can figure all that out one step at a time."

"Doing life with you sounds pretty fucking perfect to me," I said.

He dug his fingers into my hair, nails sliding over my scalp, making me shudder with delicious anticipation as he claimed my mouth in a slow, scorching kiss.

His hands raked through my hair, jumped down to cradle my ass. Slid upward, under my camisole, palms searing over my bare back, taking the thin layer of lace and silk with it. I lifted my arms overhead and he peeled it off of me; my heavy, aching breasts lifted with the garment and then bounced free. His hands immediately went to them, and I lost my breath as he thumbed my rigid nipples, making me throw my head back with a gasp. His lips grazed my throat as his hands cupped and kneaded my breasts, and I leaned back and guided his mouth to my nipple. I whimpered between gritted teeth as searing arousal shivered through me.

"Hayden," I whispered. "Take me to bed. Please. I need you to make love to me."

He rose to his feet and my legs locked around his waist. He kissed my throat and then my jaw beside my ear and then claimed my mouth, driving his tongue into my mouth. I groaned as his tongue dominated mine and then shrieked a shocked laugh as he threw me onto the bed. I hadn't even bounced once before he pounced, grabbing my yoga pants at the waistband and hauling them down, taking my thong with them and stripping them inside out, tossing them aside. He hovered over me, kissed one breast, the other. Kissed my diaphragm, my belly. My navel. My hipbone. The tender silken no man's land between hipbone and labia. And then his mouth was on my pussy, and there was no lead-up, no build-up, no teasing. Just his tongue assaulting my clit with ravenous hunger, eager and quick. I rose to the cusp of climax within seconds, and then he slid a finger inside me, and then a second, and then a third, and then he was plundering my sex with slicking, plunging fingers and suckling my clit and pinching my nipple all at once, and I came with a scream, snagging my pillow and muffling myself as I bucked and thrashed.

After that first, he switched it up. Removed all but one of his fingers and let me gasp and whimper back down the other side of the orgasm, mouthing my clit slowly. He lavished slow, tender love on me, then, kissing me and fingering me with delicacy and affection, gradually ramping me back up to a whimpering, sobbing, weeping climax.

Upon a third, I was wrung out and shattered, hyper-aroused and wild with need for him. I sat up, pushing him away. Wiped his mouth with my hands and then kissed him, ripping his sweatshirt off and hurling it aside, the white T-shirt underneath still tangled up in the hoodie. I shoved him to his back and yanked at his fly, his zipper. Ripped his jeans off inside out and then drew his underwear off, revealing his beautiful cock. It was hard and thick and weeping pre-cum, begging for me. All I wanted was to take him barely inside me, but I knew better. I'd gotten birth control and had taken the first pill, but we had to wait at least a week before we went bare again.

I grabbed a condom from the drawer, ripped it open, and rolled it onto him, biting my lip with arousal at the way his eyes rolled back in his head as I slid the latex onto him with a hand-over-hand caress.

Swinging a leg over his hips, I straddled him, grasped his cock and sank on him, taking him all at once in a single slow slide. He threw his head back and groaned loudly—I giggled and clapped a hand over his mouth. I tangled my fingers with his, palms to palms, and braced against his hands for balance as I sat tall astride him. Lifted, slicking him almost all the way out of me, and rolled my hips in a wide circle—and slammed down, ass meeting his thighs with a resounding clap. I whimpered past clenched teeth as he drove deep, pushing against our joined hands and slid back up. Slammed down again. And again. Faster and faster. My tits jounced with a rough ache at each clap of our meeting bodies, and his eyes devoured each bounce and shift and sway.

He groaned raggedly with his head pressed back into the pillow as I slapped down onto him yet again, feeling my orgasm pulse hot and chaotic and intense in my belly. Once more—I leaned forward and let him support my weight with our joined hands, drew my sex up along his throbbing cock, feathered a few short hip-rolling thrusts, and then sank one more time…

I came apart with a breathless cry, and Hayden caught me as I fell forward onto him, pushing back and down hard and fast and wild into his thrusts, crying openly, weeping raggedly through my climax. I pressed my open, quivering mouth to his chest, gasping shrill and staccato as wave after wave of ecstasy smashed me into shuddering, collapsing shards of myself.

And then he came.

I felt him pulse thick inside me, felt the heat of his release fill the condom inside me, and he clutched my ass and held me in place as he fucked into me through his orgasm.

"Oh fuck I love you," he gasped. "Em, I love you. I love you. I love you so fucking much."

Still shattering around him as he came inside me, all I could do was find his mouth and kiss him as we came together. "I love you, Hayden. Oh god, my love, don't stop. Don't ever stop."

He didn't.

He loved me through our united climaxes until we were both helpless and boneless, and he cradled me in his arms as I lay prone on his body, not wanting to move, to lose him inside me, to lose his arms and his heat and his strength, not even to reposition.

I fell asleep like that and only woke up a couple hours later to find that he'd cleaned up and returned to spoon me. I felt him wedged semi-solid between my ass cheeks, his hand loosely cupping my breast, breath on my shoulder.

He woke up slowly, breathing a sleepy, grumbling groan. Squeezed my boob, and then, seeming to wake up enough to be cognizant of our positions, he loosed his hold to a gentle caress.

He hardened against me. I moaned with aroused anticipation as I felt his cock grow longer and harder, slowly spreading me apart. When he was fully erect, I reached between my thighs and fitted his tip to my opening, and he slid in easily. I was soaked, slippery and slick, and he plunged deep, hips tapping against my ass. He kissed my shoulder blade as he thrust, and then my nape.

I rolled to my left, and he went with me; I put my knees beneath me and stretched my torso out long, flattening my chest against the bed, tipping my ass high.

"Ah fuck, Em," he growled, taking rough possession of my wide-spread ass with his hands. "So fucking perfect."

I drove back into him as he fucked me, then. It didn't take long for him to lose control, grunting, slamming deep.

"Come on my ass," I moaned, fingering myself, face pressed into the pillow. "Come on me, Hayden. Come all over me."

He fucked me from behind once, twice, a third time, hard and rough and beautiful. And then I felt him yank free of me and felt his hand grindingly wildly on his cock. He came with a teeth-clenched growl, and I felt him unleash on me, hot come painting my ass cheeks and the small of my back and my spine, again and again and again, until he finally sank to sit on his feet, panting. I collapsed forward, shaking with the aftershocks of my orgasm.

I let myself stay boneless as he slid off the bed and came back with a wet, hot washcloth and wiped me clean, and then himself.

After discarding the washcloth, he lay on his back and pulled me into the nook, which was very quickly becoming my favorite place in the whole world.

"We can't keep doing that," he whispered. "You feel too fucking good. I won't be able to pull out one of these times."

I groaned a laugh. "I know, I know. I just couldn't help myself. You feel too fucking good, bare inside me." I cupped his cock and balls in my hand, just to hold him, to feel him. "The good news is, I started birth control. We should be good to go in a week or so. We'll just have to be more careful until then."

We lounged in silence, basking in the afterglow… until he started to twitch and respond under my hand.

"Better let go unless you're ready for round three," he mumbled.

"You have somewhere else to be?" I asked.

"No."

I clutched him, caressed him. "Then hush up and let me have my wicked way with you."

"Do you think sex will continue to get better every time like it has?" he asked. "Because every time I think it can't get any more fucking incredible with you, it does."

I pushed the blanket and sheet away and slid my face along his chest and then over the rippling field of his rock-hard abs on my way to the promised land. "I don't know, but I pray it does, and I plan to spend the rest of our lives finding out."

EPILOGUE

Hunter

"I HAVE THE REPORTS YOU REQUESTED, MR. HAWKINS." The girl stood in the doorway of my office, quaking in her Louboutins. Her voice was barely above a whisper.

What was her name? Ella? Elin? Something like that. She was the new assistant to my secretary, Harriet Bowman. Harriet was the one human other than my father who wasn't scared of me, intimidated by me, or attracted to me. Or all of the above at once; that, honestly, was most common. Tall, broad-shouldered, striking rather than attractive, Harriet was sixty years old, a grandmother, a Marine Corps veteran who retired with honors after a long career as an attaché to a three-star general and had spent most of her career in the Pentagon. She was known, both affectionately and with abject terror—depending on who you asked—as Harriet the Hatchet.

I loved her. I would murder anyone who crossed her, but I wouldn't need to because Harriet would eviscerate them before I could blink.

Harriet did not fuck around. She didn't hire losers, sycophants, desk bunnies, or simpering doe-eyed lapdogs.

This girl seemed like all of the above rolled into one. Yes, she was conventionally attractive, with long slender legs, small, firm button tits propped up to look bigger by expensive lingerie, heels that pushed her taut little spin-class ass up to the stratosphere, and wavy bottle-blond hair she probably got blown out twice a week while scrolling on her giant iPhone with her inch-and-a-half long french manicured nails.

I've fucked pretty much every version of this girl that has ever existed in this city, and I've had my fill of them.

I'd have to have a word with Harriet.

First, however, I needed to get through this hopefully brief conversation with Elin, Ella, Eloise, whatever her fucking name was—hopefully without saying something cruel or ending up with her under the desk getting her aggressively scarlet lipstick on my dick.

I closed the lid on my laptop and leaned back in my chair. "Bring them."

She clicked across the acreage of my office, a stack

of reports clutched to her chest. The closer she got, the more she quaked. Also, the closer she got, the more caked-on was her makeup. Underneath it, she was probably a very pretty girl. And I'm sure Harriet had her reasons for hiring her, but good lord.

She stopped at the back left corner of my desk and extended the stack of reports toward me. "Here you are, sir."

"Thank you…" I searched my prodigious memory for her actual name. I came up empty and took a shot in the dark. "Elin."

"Uhhh…it's…umm, my name is Elara, sir." *Eh-LAH-ruh.*

"Elara?" My eyebrows knit in confusion.

"Yes, sir."

"I see." I had the E-L down, at least. I tapped a clear spot on my desk. "Put them here, please."

She set them down and stepped away, visibly shaking, looking close to tears. I slid the blue-blocking frames off my face and tossed them onto my desk, eying her as I leaned way back in my chair, assessing her.

This girl was petrified. Scared shitless. Had I met her and bitten her head off already but forgot?

"What's wrong?" I asked, genuinely trying to sound concerned.

I mean, I was. I needed her to perform. I had an empire to run. I didn't have time to massage the fragile ego of a petrified desk bunny.

She lifted her thin shoulders a quarter of an inch. "N-nothing, s-sir."

I rolled my eyes and huffed. "Don't bullshit me, sweetheart. I eat the world's best liars for breakfast. Truth, now. What—is—wrong?" I flicked a finger at her. "You're shaking in your shoes and look like you're about to start bawling. Did I say something mean? If I did, I'm sorry."

She gasped, shaking her head, eyes flying wide. "Oh! No—no sir. No. It's…it's nothing."

I stared at her for a moment. Despite her obvious turmoil, she was holding steady. Maybe there was something in there I could work with.

I jutted my chin at the chair. "Sit."

She hesitantly clicked over the chair and slid her hands under her butt to smooth her knee-length black pencil skirt as she sat. "Sir?"

I opened my bottom right drawer, pulled out my bottle of 18-year Macallan, a single tumbler, and poured a finger. Set it in front of her. "Shoot it."

"I…what? I'm working, sir."

"So'm I. Drink."

"I don't think I could, sir. It wouldn't be right."

"I'm your boss. I own this whole building and employ everyone in it. I'm telling you to." I pulled out a second tumbler and poured a measure. "Would you feel better if I joined you?"

She shrugged. "If you insist, sir."

"I do."

She reached a shaky hand and took the glass in slender fingers, brought it to her lips, sipped carefully, and then shot it. She coughed delicately, covering her lips with the back of her glass-holding hand. "Wow."

I shot mine and put the bottle away, stacked the glasses, and set them aside. I watched her eyes swim a little.

"Now. Truth. You're scared of something. Or someone. Explain."

She looked at me for a long moment, chest rising and falling faster and faster. "I…I lied on my resume, sir. I'm not qualified for this job." Her eyes watered. "I just…I need it so bad. Please don't fire me. I can learn. I just—I can't fail. Not again. My parents would never forgive me."

I held up a hand as I opened my laptop. I shot Harriet a text asking for the resume in question, received it in the thread as a text file, opened it, and scanned it.

"Let's see…" I read out loud a few of the line items. "Brigham Young University, top of your class. You're Mormon?"

"I was, sir. Not anymore."

"Alright. Summa Cum Laud. MBA in Business Management. Interned at Goldman Sachs, Ernst and Young…excellent recommendations across the board from people I know personally." I half-closed the lid and looked at her. "Where's the lie? I can verify all of this in a matter of minutes."

She screwed up her face—an "I'm not gonna cry" expression that made me panicky and nauseous. "My father works at Goldman Sachs, and my maternal uncle is a partner at Ernst and Young. I got those internships through pure nepotism."

"I see." I snagged my phone and found the contact I wanted, dialed and put it on speaker with a shushing gesture at Elara.

It rang four times. "Hawk. What's up, bro?" Jonathan Givens, a rising star at Ernst and Young and a long-time friend, business rival, and squash partner.

"Need to verify a recommendation."

He snorted. "You're doing the dog work yourself... why?"

"Humor me, Givey."

"Fine. Name?"

"Joseph-comma-Elara—E-L-A-R-A."

"Joseph...Elara. Oh, shit. Her. Yeah, I remember her. Mile-long legs and big brown doe eyes."

I arched an eyebrow at her, and she flushed. "Focus, Givey. My time is more valuable than yours."

"Fuck you, Hawk." He hummed as he read. "Well, I never interacted with her myself. To be honest, she was on a higher floor than me at the time. Her uncle is the newest partner, so everyone expected her to be the usual nepo-hire, but all her reviews are stellar. Top marks across the board."

"That's what I needed to know. Thanks, bud."

"She's not your usual type," he said. "In the office or...elsewhere."

"Yep, got it," I said, "just double checking."

"You gonna be at the club later?"

"To kick your ass on the squash court? Yeah, I'll see you there. Later, Givey."

"Later, Hawk."

I hung up the phone and tossed it onto my desk. "I'll shoot you straight, Ms. Joseph. I don't hire based on anything but results. Harriet knows that. She knows I don't tolerate bullshit."

"Sir, I—"

"Not done." Her teeth clicked closed and I kept going. "Furthermore, I freely admit there was a period when I first took over from my father where I went through PAs faster than a whore goes through condoms. And that, I admit, is because I hired them for their looks and their willingness to be more than just PAs." A pause. "Meaning, I banged them all. Repeatedly."

Her eyes widened and she blushed. "Sir, I..."

"Hold on. Almost done." I sat back. "I no longer do things that way. I no longer have sex with my PAs or anyone else I employ. I hired Harriet because she terrifies me. She protects me from myself. She knows better than to hire someone who will distract me. Therefore, if Harriet pulled the trigger on you, then she had her reasons. If you think she wasn't aware that your internships were the result of nepotism, then you're either delusional or not as smart as she must have assumed."

I sat forward, elbows on the desk, fingers braided together. "Ms. Joseph, I shall give you some free and unasked-for advice. If you're going to lie about your resume, then own the lie and never let anyone know you lied. Run with it. Shaking in your shoes, scared everyone can see that you're a big fat faker? You may as well just hit your knees and start sucking, honey, because that's the only way up the ladder for a faker."

She swallowed, tears in her eyes. "I understand, sir."

"Do you?" I slid my blue-blockers on. "Are you a faker?"

"N-no," she whispered

"What was that? I didn't catch it."

Louder, then. Confidently. "No sir. I am *not* a faker. I can do the work. I have no interest or intention in climbing the ladder…" She flushed scarlet. "The other way."

"You picked a savage, brutal, barbaric, male-centric industry, Elara. Toughen up. Never let 'em see you sweat."

"Yes sir, thank you, sir." She started to rise.

"Hold on." I pushed the reports toward her. "Summarize."

She took the stack. "Sir?"

"Give me your thoughts on what's in there."

"Um. I just printed and collated."

"And read them—scanned them, at least. And formed opinions. I'd like to hear yours."

She frowned, blinking thoughtfully as her brain turned on. "Well…" She flipped through them—they were collections of write-ups, reports, industry articles, and stats on my newest project: restaurants. She scanned the top one. "This one is no good. Huge overhead, bloated menu, gimmicky atmospheric premise, high turnover."

She handed it to me, and I scanned it, set it aside. "Agreed. Next."

"This one has promise. Slow start, numbers-wise, but they've stayed focused on a small, core menu of well-reviewed favorites. But they're a single location, a mom-and-pop shop. With enough investment, it could grow legs, but as of now, I would pass."

I scanned it and tossed it on the reject pile. "Again, agreed. Next."

And so we went, report by report, discarding all but three until we got to the last report.

She took a while reading this one. "Um? This one is…different, sir. All the others are local to the five boroughs. This one is in Alaska. Uh, let's see. They have four locations. The original is in Ketchikan, Badd's Bar and Grille—along with Badd Kitty and Badd Night. Badd as in a name—B-A-D-D. Single owner, middling numbers for the first twenty years or so. They turned a consistent profit but never really improved on that margin until…twenty-some years ago."

I frowned, curious. "They've been in business for forty years?"

"Yes sir. They didn't expand until the sons took over from the father. Father died suddenly, it looks like, left the bar to his eight sons in his will."

"*Eight*? Jesus. Ever hear of birth control?"

Elara glanced at me, disapproval fleeting across her expression, quickly hidden. "They've become a huge tourist draw in the Ketchikan area. They coordinate with the cruises—it looks like one of the eight brothers does flightseeing excursions. Another brother—wait…" She frowned, looked closer. "Sorry, sir, a cousin, not a brother—he owns an outdoor exploration company with *his* father, the uncle of the eight brothers. They do day hikes and overnight camping hikes, as well as longer-term hunts into the interior upon request."

"I might need a chart of the relations, good lord." I rolled my hand. "The business, Elara. Thoughts?"

She tipped her head side to side. "They've seen year-over-year increases in revenue over the last five years, which follows a trend of increased activity on social media. Looks like they hired someone to shake things up, and it worked. Their newest location is in Anchorage. It's doing well but not great. They're a family-run business. The owners tend bar and cook the food, do security, everything. The brothers and cousins are all…" She blushed. "Rather good-looking, sir, and they feature quite regularly on their social media. It's part of their draw. They do a lot of bridal shower business, I bet." She set the report down and gazed into the space, thinking; I waited. "It's risky, sir. They're a family business. My guess is they're proud of that and thus are unlikely to sell. Or at least not in a traditional sense. But they know what they're doing. They run a tight ship, from what I can see—I don't have a detailed breakdown of their numbers here, just a surface-level look. My opinion on this one is it could really do well, but you'd have to get creative. They won't just sell outright and turn over the keys to the kingdom to some faceless mogul in Manhattan. But if you're willing to play ball a little... differently, you could do something very interesting."

"I see."

She was still thinking, so I let her think. "If you want a more traditional approach where you just offer them a bag of money and do what you want," she sorted through the keep pile and picked one, "this is your pick. But if you want a challenge and an opportunity to do something a little different, you go with this Alaska one."

I took the two reports and browsed through them, diving into the numbers. Decision time. I stood up and faced my floor-to-ceiling windows with their spectacular view of Manhattan, Central Park in the distance. Horns honked below. A flock of pigeons fluttered past.

Elara waited in silence.

I looked once more at the Alaska option folder in my hand, the cover sheet with a color photo of the exterior of the original Badd's Bar and Grille. How long had it been since I'd had a real challenge? Since I did anything besides give orders and watch my minions do the dog work, as Givey calls it?

A long time. Too long.

Time to get my hands dirty.

"There's one word you used that sold me, Elara." I turned and looked at her, where she sat with her knees together and angled to one side, back straight as a ruler.

"What word was that, sir?"

"Challenge." I tossed the New York option on the discard pile and handed her the Alaska folder. "Get me a closer look at the numbers on this one, and then get me a flight to Anchorage. I'll need a car and driver—wait, cancel that—just a car. A truck or SUV, preferably, nothing flashy. A rental property outside town—rent it or buy it, I don't care. Use your best judgment, as long as it's quality—built to last. I like lodge style, hate modernism. What else?" I paced, thinking. "Robert McIlhenny is my proxy while I'm gone, but I'll be online and will be available by phone, text, or email if needed. I'd like to leave ASAP, so have Harriet massage my calendar. Anything that can be a Zoom, switch it to that. If it can be an email, even better." I looked at her, finally. "Got all that?"

"Yes sir. But—sir, I…I was supposed to be working on the reports for the Navetta account."

"Navetta account?" I closed one eye and stared with the other at the ceiling, recalling. "Oh, right. Mark Navetta, CEO of Prime Meridian Medical. We're investing in their infrared sanitization system."

"Yes sir. You wanted to see the latest numbers."

I waved a hand. "That can wait, they've put up solid advancements in the last few months. I'm not worried. I was thinking of increasing our investment just to get them to market faster."

"I've started going through the reports, sir. They're very close to market from what I can tell, albeit that is not a field I know much about."

I nodded. "Very good. Then skip the reports for now and just keep an eye on them yourself."

She blinked at me. "Sir, I...I'm Mrs. Bowman's P-A. I have a whole pile of assignments. I'm not sure I can get all that done as well as what you're asking me to do. I'm willing to try, but..."

"HARRIET!" I yelled.

My door opened, and the woman herself appeared—tall and thin with silver hair, she wore a sleek black power suit with a white button-down, sensible flats, and had her hair in a severe bun. "You bellowed, sir?"

"I'm stealing Ms. Joseph from you."

Harriet regarded me without expression for a moment. "For what purpose? And for how long?"

I shrugged. "For as long as I need her and for the purpose of doing business shit."

Harriet's lips quirked. "Hunter, may I remind you—"

"You may not, Harriet. It's not like that. She and I have discussed that. Ms. Joseph has a keen mind for business, and I think she's wasted compiling reports."

"You and she have discussed…"

"My former predilection for banging my assistants."

Elara spluttered in surprised laughter; Harriet allowed a small smile. "You did?"

"We did." I held up the Alaska folder. "I have a project. I'm leaving for Alaska as soon as you can clear my schedule to do so. Elara can fill you in on the details." I looked from Elara to Harriet. "Next time, don't overhire. She's way overqualified for an assistant. Grab someone from the temp pool if you need a grunt to print and staple bullshit. If you need a permanent assistant, hire someone. But I've officially stolen Ms. Joseph from you."

Harriet nodded. "Noted, sir."

"Excellent. Now, you two coordinate on the assignments I gave you, Ms. Joseph."

"Can I get a back-of-the-napkin pitch on this new project that's taking our owner and CEO to Alaska?" Harriet asked. "So I can properly field the inevitable questions."

"Oh. Right." I thought about it. "We're expanding into the restaurant business—you know this, we've invested in three places so far. This new one is…a personal project. I'm bored, Harriet. All I do lately is read shit, sign shit, run numbers on shit, and give orders about shit. I want to *do* shit. This company can run itself without me for a while. Call it a working vacation. I'm going to be courting a giant family of Alaskans who very likely won't want to sell and who, by the looks of them, might very well throw me into the water by way of rejecting my proposal."

"Sounds hazardous, sir." Harriet produced her phone. "Should I add security to your plans?"

"Nah. I'm good. I'm going incognito, Harriet."

She sniffed—her version of a laugh. "Sir. Incognito? You've been on the cover of *TIME* magazine."

"I'll wear a hat and sunglasses. It works for Ryan Reynolds."

"No, sir, it does not." She sighed, shook her head. "But as you wish. Elara, come. We have logistics to work out, it seems."

Elara rose and glided to the door but stopped. "Mr. Hawkins, sir?"

I looked up from the Alaskan option. "Yes, Ms. Joseph?"

"What...what just happened?"

I grinned at her; she looked a little faint when I did so. Good to know I haven't lost my touch. "You just got promoted."

She gulped. "Oh. I...I see. Thank you, sir."

"I am where I am because I have an eye for people. I don't give a shit about experience or credentials or which school you went to. I care about results. I care about your passion for what you do. I once promoted a man from the mailroom to the boardroom because I talked to him and saw the potential in him. That's what I do best, Ms. Joseph—see potential in things and maximize it."

"I will do everything I can to live up to the potential you see in me, sir."

"I have no doubt you will." I sat down at my desk and returned to the mind-numbing work of spreadsheets and expense reports.

My hindbrain, the part that wasn't needed for the work at hand, was ruminating on Alaska. I've been to a lot of places—Paris, Rome, London, Antarctica, Berlin, Auckland, Shanghai, Moscow, Oslo... but never Alaska.

I wondered what the women in Alaska were like. I imagined a herd of tall, curvy blondes in red flannel and skintight jeans chasing me across a tundra...or whatever was in Alaska.

Maybe I'd see a moose—that would be cool. I've heard they're much bigger than you think.

Eventually, I finished my work. I worked out, played squash with Givey, and went home, stopping at my favorite Chinese place for carryout. As I ate my General Tso's, I researched Alaska. Swiped through several years' worth of IG posts from the official Badd's Bar account; whoever was running the account was a goddamn genius. Their content was fucking stellar. Most of the posts were from the original Badd's Bar and Grille or a place called Badd Kitty. The posts featured live music, tasty-looking, simple, high-quality food, booze, pretty women and hot men—as a culturally verified hot man myself, I can recognize my own kind—all with cutesy captions with relevant emojis and hashtags.

I'm no social media expert, but I know a quality marketing account when I see one. And this one? Top notch.

I went to sleep rolling through ideas for expansion that wouldn't mean ruining the home-cooking, family-party vibe that seemed to be the bread-and-butter of the Badd's Bar brand. I had a million ideas; the only question was whether the family would bite or if they'd throw me to grizzlies and go back to splitting firewood and wrestling wolves or whatever backwoods bullshit Alaskan hot guy badasses like these Badd brothers got up to.

ALSO BY JASINDA WILDER

If you enjoyed this book, you can help others enjoy it as well by recommending it to friends and family, or by mentioning it in reading and discussion groups and online forums. You can also review it on the site from which you purchased it. But, whether you recommend it to anyone else or not, thank you *so much* for taking the time to read my book! Your support means the world to me!

My other titles:

Forbidden Fruit

Wild Ride: Biker Billionaire

Delilah's Diary

Big Girls Do It:

Big Girls Do It
Married
On Christmas
Pregnant
Rock Stars Do It
Big Love Abroad

The Falling Series:
Falling Into You
Falling Into Us
Falling Under
Falling Away
Falling for Colton
The Ever Trilogy:
Forever & Always
After Forever
Saving Forever

From the world of *Wounded:*
Wounded
Captured

From the world of *Stripped:*
Stripped
Trashed

From the world of *Alpha:*
Alpha
Beta
Omega
Harris: Alpha One Security Book 1
Thresh: Alpha One Security Book 2

Puck: Alpha One Security Book 4
Lear: Alpha One Security Book 5
Anselm: Alpha One Security Book 6
Sigma
Gamma

The Houri Legends:
Jack and Djinn
Djinn and Tonic

The Madame X Series:
Madame X
Exposed
Exiled

The Black Room (With Jade London)

The One Series
The Long Way Home
Where the Heart Is
There's No Place Like Home

Badd Brothers:
Badd Motherf*cker
Badd Ass
Badd to the Bone
Good Girl Gone Badd
Badd Luck
Badd Mojo
Big Badd Wolf
Badd Boy
Badd Kitty
Badd Business
Badd Medicine
Badd Daddy

Goode Girls:
For a Goode Time Call…
Not So Goode
Goode To Be Bad
A Real Goode Time
Goode Vibrations
Dad Bod Contracting:
Hammered
Drilled
Nailed
Screwed

Fifty States of Love:
Pregnant in Pennsylvania
Cowboy in Colorado
Married in Michigan
Christmas in Connecticut

Billionaire Baby Club:
Lizzy Goes Brains Over Braun
Autumn Rolls a Seven
Laurel's Bright Idea

Club Sin:
Rev
Kane
Chance
Silas
Saxon

Blood Heir
Blood Heir
Blood Bonds
Blood Reign

Standalone titles:
Yours
The Cabin
The Parent Trap
Wish Upon A Star
Big Hose

Non-Fiction titles:
You Can Do It
You Can Do It: Strength
You Can Do It: Fasting

Jack Wilder Titles:
The Missionary

JJ Wilder Titles:
Ark

Only one way to find out. To be informed of new
releases, special offers,
and other Jasinda news, sign up for
Jasinda's email newsletter.